Dragon's Vein

Matthew Johnson

Dragon's Vein

Published by Untold Stories

Riverside California

This is a work of fiction. Names, characters, businesses, places, events and incidents are either the products of the author's imagination or used in a fictitious manner. Any resemblance to actual persons, living or dead, or actual events is purely coincidental.

ISBN: 979-8-9873724-1-8
ISBN-13: 979-8-9873724-1-8-1

DEDICATION

To all the hard-working artists. May your dreams come true.

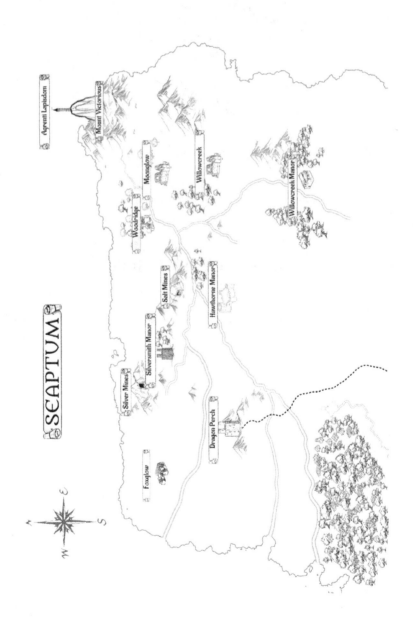

ACKNOWLEDGMENTS

I would like to thank all those who put in time and effort to make this project come to fruition. First off, to my editor Evelyn Jimenez for scouring through my mess of words and straightening out the story. Sophia Chin for the beautiful chapter headings. Farah Evers for the amazing cover. Michael Baker for designing the map. Everyone in my MFA program UCR Palm Desert for helping me see how to critically shape my book. Last of all, my lovely wife Wendi who is my creative counterpart.

Part I

Innocence

CHAPTER ONE: PUNISHMENT

She lurks in shadows as you sleep
Seeking souls that she shall keep
Before you wake you may mistake
Hands of love 'round your throat creep
Down, down, down, she drags your soul
Where forever never find sleep no more
—Children's Rhyme

"Don't touch that!"

Tiny bristles beckoned Joanne's fingers to stroke them, promising it would be like running silk bed sheets through her closed fist. Like stroking the sun's rays bursting from the clouds. Like catching water. Only this flower was more fire than water. Long, bright orange petals, each with a dark red stripe down the center, enflamed her imagination. She could grasp

1

fire without it searing her flesh.

Touch me, they whispered. *You'll like it.*

"Don't! Touch!" Her tutor's sharp reproach silenced the seductive voice. Joanne snatched her hand away, imagining the flower would suddenly grow teeth and snap off her fingers.

"Why?" Joanne pushed a strand of golden-brown hair from her face and glanced over at Teresa reaching for her, wax tablet and stylus tossed aside into a cluster of blue bells. Brown eyes wide as porcelain saucers, her tutor grabbed hold of Joanne's slender right shoulder and shoved her. Joanne rocked backwards. The fringe of her white dress pulled up around her knees, and she nearly tumbled heels-over-head. She sat up, eyes wet, heart beating quickly, half-expecting the flame flower to leap at her.

"I'm so sorry," Teresa said, her voice flat. She crouched on her haunches in front of the flower and leaned forward. Joanne lifted a foot, ready to give her tutor a hard kick, planting her face first into the fire flower, the very danger she had warned Joanne against touching.

Then Joanne might learn what was so dangerous by observing the effects on her tutor's face. A sensible thought cured the urge to lash out, a sense of self-preservation: killing Teresa would cause greater trouble with her father, and would not be worth the satisfaction of her foot smacking the round target.

When she sleeps tonight. Joanne set her foot down. *I will cut the curls from her hair.*

Teresa clicked her tongue and sat upright on her knees.

"Just as I expected," she said, and waved Joanne to come closer.

Joanne reluctantly clambered to her feet, wiped bits of grass from her backside, and noticed a green stain on the hem. She would be blamed for it, not Teresa. She would get a tongue lashing for being improper and wallowing in the mud like a piglet. She would lose her sweets for the night. *But Teresa will pay more dearly. An ear missing, maybe. Or a finger for touching me with those grubby, greasy—*

"Dragon's vein," Teresa said. "Very poisonous."

"Poisonous," Joanne repeated.

"Yes, poisonous." She pointed at the petal Joanne had nearly touched. "The bristles here attach to the skin and don't rub or wash off. Then when you eat, you ingest an enzyme they secrete and it enters your belly. Slowly it passes through your blood and melts away your innards like ingesting fire, only flames you cannot douse with water, though you may drink a well-full."

"Sounds painful," Joanne said and took a step back.

"I imagine so. I wonder what it's doing down here in Nemus." She glanced over her shoulder at Joanne. "It's native to Seaptum. This is an invasive species that will spread like fire sparked on dry tinder."

"What does invasive mean?"

"Intruding where it's not wanted," Teresa said, leaning back on her haunches. "A pretty thing, isn't it? Though very dangerous to play with. I will tell the Ground's Master—"

A shadow cast over them.

"Learning some botany?" A deep, commanding voice asked. Joanne jumped and spun around to face her father, Lord Desmond. He smiled, the mirth reaching the corners of his mouth and dying there. His dark brown eyes pinned her in her place as neatly as a hawk's gaze freezes the mouse. She nodded, words a lump in her throat.

"What have you discovered so far?"

Joanne licked her lips, mouth dry and full of cotton.

"The pretty ones are the most deadly." As soon as the words left her lips, she cringed at how stupid they sounded.

A spark shone in Lord Desmond's eye.

"Clever girl."

Joanne fought the need to shuffle her feet. Compliments were rare and often disguised some other intention. He turned his gaze on Teresa, and Joanne let out the breath she held back, her tight back relaxing. Until he spoke. "Give me a moment to speak with my daughter."

"Aye, my lord." Teresa curtsied, head bowed, and then hurried away deeper into the flower garden. Joanne wished she could follow. Would even forgive her tutor her faults, if only she could escape her father's company. The times she was left alone with him hadn't been pleasant, resulting in mostly behavioral reprimands. Not the physical kind, but the heart-wrenching words of disappointment cutting close to the wick.

Does he know I planned on cutting Teresa's curls? It was a silly idea, though at the moment, her father looming over her, staring into her eyes as though he could read all her desires for good and ill, the idea he could read her mind wasn't such a fantasy.

Lord Desmond lowered himself down to a knee in front of her, something he hadn't done since she was a child and broke a flower vase. He maintained eye contact, the weight of it pinning her in place, and she stiffened, waiting for him to strike her. Heavy hands pressed on her shoulders, and she thought maybe he was going to pull her into an embrace. *Don't move. Be still and you will be fine. This will pass and the shadow will move along.*

"You are growing up so quickly," he said, stating it as a matter-of-fact. "I would say you are far superior to all the flowers in the garden in how pretty you have become. Nevertheless, beauty is not only to be admired. You, like these flowers, have a role to play."

Joanne nodded, her tongue caught up in the roof of her mouth. She didn't understand the purpose of flowers any more than her own.

"They use their beauty to attract bees. To pollenate them so more flowers can grow, and in turn the bees create the honey you enjoy in your tea." Lord Desmond paused, allowing the information to sink in.

Bees have little stingers. Joanne began to fidget and dug jagged nails into her palm to stop. Her father hated fidgeting. *Some flowers will burn you inside out.*

"What is my purpose?" she asked.

The spark shone in his eye again. *Did I please him?* She was not used to seeing him happy. Especially since her eldest brother, Henrick, died in battle a season ago. Her father had been in a dark, foul mood, raining down insults and punishments as freely as the whip's thorned-fob stripped the skin off her backside. *What have I done to deserve his pleasant attention?*

A deep, rattling came from Lord Desmond's throat. It sounded like the beginning of a coughing fit. Then she recognized it, like some exotic bird's song she hadn't heard in a long while. He was laughing.

"Sweet child, where did you get such wit?" He drew her in, giving her a wooden embrace. His rigid body held her a moment and then he put her at arm's length again. It was so brief she could have imagined it. The light had gone from his eyes and his smile faltered, jaw set in the familiar unyielding position. "One day you will marry a prince."

"Yes, father," she said, giving the expected response. "Thank you."

Lord Desmond nodded, patted her shoulders, and straightened up. He seemed to consider her a moment, but she noticed his eye staring at an object over her shoulder. They narrowed and he pushed her to the side.

"Dragon's Vein," Lord Desmond said. He removed a cloth handkerchief from the front pocket of his vest, bent over and plucked the flower by its stem, careful not to allow it near his skin. "I should like a whole garden full of these."

"Why?" the question slipped out before she could bite the question back.

He gave a half-grin, holding the flower up to the sun.

"Much like you said, 'the pretty ones are the most deadly.'" He walked away, shadow slipping off Joanne and leaving her squinting at the sun.

Joanne hummed a lullaby as she worked the knife through coarse hair. She sliced back and forth, carefully not to yank too hard and wake Teresa. Later Joanne would place the stolen locks in a wooden box and hide it under her bed. She smiled at the idea of Teresa waking, going through her morning routine of washing and dressing lost in thoughts of flower names and identifying birds, dreaming about flouncing past the kitchen so the cook could eye her up—her tutor didn't think anyone was aware, but Joanne knew and this bit of knowledge would be something she might leverage at a later time. Well, Teresa would pick up the brush and run it through her hair. The bristles would come up shorter than she remembered. At first confusion. Fingers searching the same spot for the curls she adored so much, petting them day after day, only to discover the missing patch. And the she would scream. Scream in frustration at what was lost. Teresa wouldn't directly accuse her, but there would be angry glances, perhaps wet, red eyes and pouting lips as she spoke in short, haughty phrases. Joanne would smile, as pretty as a flower, knowing she had ruined her tutor's peace.

Don't ever push me again!

The knife slipped clear and a fist full of hair dropped into Joanne's lap. She tucked it away in the fold of her night gown. One cut should be enough, but—

Joanne's mother didn't yell at her about the grass stain. She didn't say a single word. Her mother rarely spoke unless it was to lecture Joanne on proper etiquette. Silence was enough to rebuke. A quick look and then an upward turn of her nose. Joanne felt it worse than a leather strap across her bare backside. For supper, which Joanne ate alone, she was served watery green parsley soup, hard heel of bread, and weak tea. All a reminder that if she played like a common peasant, she would eat like one.

Another pass of the blade. Another chunk of hair. Payment for the stained dress and poor meal. Joanne slid her hand over her tutor's hair and gripped a handful. She brought the knife up.

Teresa gasped, eyes opening in the dark.

Joanne panicked. Her blade slipped, slicing soft flesh. In the moonlight, a gush of dark-colored blood streamed out onto the white, down-stuffed pillow. Teresa's eyes widened. Pain and fear filled the pupils now pinpricks of light.

"What—" Teresa tried to ask. Joanne cut her off with another swipe across the throat, diagonal and severing the windpipe, or trachea as Teresa once taught her its proper name.

Teresa's hands shot to the gushing wound. Her lips gasped, opening and closing like a drowning fish. Red streams ●trickled out at the corners, painting pink lips a dark red. She arched up, bloody hand reaching for Joanne. Joanne backed away, knife dripping scarlet drops onto the carpet. She watched Teresa try to comprehend what was happening. Her struggle against death. Does everyone struggle the same? Joanne wondered, captivated by her tutor's eyes. How the light slowly dulled in the pupils. How her waving hand dropped to the bed and her stiff body sank in on itself. Blood squeezed out from under the slender hand that once held a wax tablet, first gushing, bubbling from the wound as her hand fell away, and then became a dribble.

Joanne listened, heart pumping, body numb. The last sigh passed bloody lips. She waited, expecting a cry from the guards, a shout of murder. Rough hands to grip her shoulder and drag her to her father's room. There... there... she would rather cut her wrists and bleed out than face those cold, steel eyes that would make the knife seem dull compared to the jagged, bone cutting gaze.

She waited, breath caught in the back of her throat until she was suffocating. Suffocating on the death she had created. Then she let out a slow gasp. When no cry came and no hands grabbed her, she gradually backed out of her tutor's room. The knife gripped by her pale fingers, she walked down the hall to another room in the servants' block. The door handle turned easily. She entered, quiet on her toes and floated past the snoring man.

His snores stopped and she froze, catching her image in a small mirror. Moonlight shone from the window, revealing a spectral figure covered in red. A revenging spirit rising up from the grave, red hands holding a bloody knife.

The man turned on his side, mumbled some words and breathed heavily.

One heart beat passed. Two. Three. Four heart beats. He didn't turn on his side accusing her of the foul deed. He slept on, innocent of the night's crime. She slipped the knife under a bundle of clothes. Then she left the room, softly closing the door.

Back in her room, she stripped from her night gown and dipped it in cold water. She scrubbed her hands until they turned pink and then dumped the water out her window. Still naked, she climbed back into bed and pulled the covers over her head. She closed her eyes, the image of her tutor gasping and reaching for her floated behind her lids, forcing them back open. She remained that way until dawn stole through her window when she tumbled into a faint stupor, haunted by breezy gasps strangled into gurgles. Then the edges frayed, turned dark and viscous.

A voice called her name.

Joanne.

Thin, dark wings flapped, thrusting decay and rot over her. She was outside, standing on a dark lane between twisted black trees. It wasn't any place she had recognized. Not any place she would find herself in the middle of the night. Mother! She wouldn't be here alone in the brightest day light. Especially not with something stalking her. Something that smelled like it crawled from the grave. Fear took control and she ran away from the smell and noise. Overhead, wings punished the air, tracking her. Seeing but unseen. Should it catch her, Joanne was certain the thing would eat her, the way she once witnessed a hawk plunge down on a sparrow, squashing its wings and tearing into its belly with sharp talons. Blindly, she ran, because running was the only thing she could do in this place. Running and crying for her life.

Through blurry tears she saw a form take shape at the end of the lane. A small hovel, the kind peasants might live in. Next to it was large a stack of wood, taller than her, an axe embedded in a stump. She wiggled through a gap between the stacks of wood, bottom pressed against a cold, stone wall. The sound of her heart pounded in the tight enclosure. She stared out, straining to hear any sound. A moment passed and then another. She could see nothing. Hear nothing.

A powerful stench filled the space. She coughed, trying to keep if from filling her nose and throat.

Come out. Come out. Scared little mouse. A sing-song voice, cloying sweet both tempting and yet dripping venomous threats. Leaving the hole meant facing the creature waiting for her, but staying…. She coughed louder, gaging on the stench. Decay and rot burned in her lungs. She was drowning and decided to drag her body from the logs before they became a carrion marker.

Ah, there you are. Dark wings folded together, collapsing into a shadow-cloaked figure. *Child, I know what you did. The blood has just dried under your fingernails.*

Are you going to punish me? Joanne asked. She stared at the red ichor crusting under her nails and rubbed them on her nightgown. Deep red blotches stained the material, stiff and calloused on her finger tips. She remembered stripping off the nightgown, but here it clung to her like thief's brand.

The shadow figure laughed, deep and cruel.

Why would I punish you? She deserved it for laying hands on you without permission.

What do you want? Joanne pressed herself against logs, reaching back to find a loose one to use as a bludgeon. The wood pieces seemed glued together.

Do you know who I am, child?

Joanne jumped and nodded. Her hands swung out in front of her, balling up in her nightgown.

Then you know what I want. Cold air prickled Joanne's skin. *There will come a time, little mouse, when you will need me. Desperately need me. Let the desperation fill you. I will come. I will help you.*

What do you get in return?

The shadow figured didn't respond, but drew closer. Darkness enveloping her like a cold, wet blanket.

What do I do? Her heart raced. She wanted to run, both to and away from the shadow. Let it embrace her so she didn't have to face the morning. Face the guilt and shame of her actions.

Patience, my dear one. A long, dark finger reached from the shadow and stroked her cheek. A shiver ran down her neck, her spine, and tingled in her belly. It held her, pinned like a mouse under the cat's paw, hoping for a quick release.

Then it was gone.

The shadow left her trembling by the wood pile. Cold retreated, replaced by a warm, tacky wetness that ran down her head, dripping into her lap. She looked up and saw Teresa laying over the wood pile, throat gashed, skin flapping. Blood rushed in a fountain over Joanne's face. She opened her mouth to scream, but the sound was lost. Caught in blood-soaked cotton stuffed into her mouth. The tangy sweet blood choked her. She reached inside her mouth and drew out a flower, orange petals with a strip of red. The bristles pierced her fingers.

You can't scream. The pale face of her tutor leaned into her own. Red, stringy drool hung from her lips. *You can't make a sound. I couldn't when you slit my throat. Leaving me to drown in my own blood! Murdering brat!* Drops pattered on Joanne's face, frozen in horror as her tutor leaned in closer. Throat flapping like an extra mouth, gaping and drizzling blood all over her face. *You. Killed. Me.* The corpse punctuated each word with more splatter. *You killed me. YOU KILLED—*

Her door slammed open. Joanne sat up in bed, sweaty hair clinging to her forehead. The cover slipped down to her naval and she gripped the mattress, digging her nails into it. Two armed men fumbled into the room.

"She's safe." One guard cried out. He had a sword drawn and sheathed it before turning away from her. She caught the blush on his clean shaved cheeks before he looked away.

"Please, get dressed," the guard said.

Joanne realized she was nude and climbed out of bed. Heaped on the floor, where she dropped it last night, was the bloody night gown. She kicked it under the bed and went to her wardrobe. She took out a plain blue dress and pulled it over her head.

"What's going on?" she asked, hoping they would attribute her shaky voice to being startled awake.

"There's been a… death," the other guard replied. He was shorter, dressed in the same grey house guard uniform. The house crest, thorn-wrapped dagger, pinned their cloak on the right shoulder.

"Who?" She didn't mean to ask, but the word was out before she could stop it.

The guards remained silent.

"Who?" She repeated with more force.

"Your tutor, milady," the guard said. "I'm truly sorry for—"

"Who killed her?"

"We don't know. The Keep is being searched as we speak," the taller guard said, "My duty is to secure your safety. Are you… decent?"

"Yes." Bare feet prodded cold, stone floor. Again, she shivered. *Get a hold of yourself.* She tossed her disheveled hair over her shoulder—no time to properly brush it— and walked past the guards. They caught up and flanked her. Mother knew they wouldn't allow her to walk the halls alone. Not with a killer loose in the castle. Joanne looked down at her hands and noticed a dry speck of blood under one nail. She balled it into a fist to hide the nail. If she missed that detail, what other damning evidence might show?

It's not like I woke up covered in dry blood. Then she would begin the day in chains rather than pattering down the hallway to the big double doors leading into her father's private chamber. Two more men guarded it, swords drawn to ward further attack. Joanne grinned. If they only knew the truth, would they let her get so close to her father? The doors closed behind her. Tall windows at the back of the chamber let in bright light. Her grin faltered. Lord Desmond sat in his chair, fingers steepled together under his chin as he glared at her.

He knows! She stiffened, sucking in her bottom lip.

Lord Desmond turned to her mother, who paced behind him, placing a hand on her slender arm.

"I told you she was fine," he said.

"Blessed Mother." Amaria Desmond pressed her fist to her forehead. She glanced at Joanne, a look of almost endearing concern flashed briefly, and then, was gone. Amaria sat in a chair and closed her eyes. She tugged a small vial out of her robe. A clear liquid swirled inside it. She popped the stopper and swallowed the entire contents. "I pray for a quick end to this misery."

"Report," Lord Desmond said to the guards.

Joanne moved out of her father's sight, to the back of the room where both her brothers Thomas and Alfred, kept out of the way. Thomas leaned against a bookshelf, watching the soldiers move in and out of the room while Alfred pressed against the windowpane to glimpse the activity outside on the Keep's South wall.

"Did you hear?" Thomas asked Joanne, a smug grin on his face. He was dressed in his grey doublet, a rapier swung from his hip. His dark brown hair was sweaty, clinging to his forehead. He smelled like he'd just wrestled a bear, but that's how he'd always smelled, damp fur and shit, coming off the practice field. It explained his rapier on his belt, since Father would forbid him joining the hunt. Thomas had other ways to inflict misery. "Your tutor is dead."

"I know." Joanne turned her head away so she didn't have to smell him anymore.

"Who told you?" He folded his arms, nose wrinkling, and lip curled. She felt a small delight in his disappointment. Thomas always reveled in bearing grave news. He was the first to tell her of Henrick's death, abandoning her to cry the rest of the day in her room. She would never forgive him for that moment.

"My escorts."

"They should be whipped for revealing such horrible information without proper leave." He began to stalk toward their father.

Joanne grabbed his arm. "I made them." He looked down at her fingers pressed into his sweaty shirt. It was a mistake touching him, but she didn't want anyone else to suffer because of her actions.

"Even so," Thomas said, crunching her fingers in his vice-like grip. She pressed her lips together to keep from crying out. He gave a final squeeze so she could feel the bones grind and tossed her hand off like flicking away a spider. "Some people need to be reminded of their place."

"How long are they going to hold us in here?" Alfred asked. His black hair was also a mess and he was naked from the waist up, wearing only his small clothes. He gave a big yawn, revealing yellowed teeth. "I got to piss."

Joanne felt a tingle in her bladder. She was surprised she hadn't soaked her bed from the dream of the... she couldn't remember what the dream was about, though it raised goose flesh along her arms and neck.

"Until they deem it safe," Thomas said, returning to his bored posture against the bookcase.

"How long do you think?"

"There's a vase in the corner, just don't let Father catch you urinating in the gift from Master Lelwing," Thomas said. "Else he'll make you a eunuch."

"You would like that," Alfred said. "Though you'd still have smaller fruits than either Joey or me." He poked Joanne in the side and she shoved his hand away.

"My horse has more common decency than you two boys," Joanne said. "How'd they find out she's dead? I have a lesson with her in a few bells before midday. *Had*."

"The cook sent a boy to give her the usual honey and whey breakfast." Thomas nudged Alfred. Alfred smiled and nodded, although Joanne could tell he didn't understand the joke. "The boy returned without a tray, legs soaked in goat's milk. The cook alerted the guard and I followed them from the practice yard to her room. A bloody mess. Someone split her throat like butchering a ewe. She was covered in blood. Dried by the time we arrived. When the cook picked her up, she peeled off the sheet—"

"Enough," Joanne said, her stomach turning, ready to toss up what remained of last night's green soup.

"You wanted to know," Thomas laughed. Alfred chuckled, though a bit more uneasily. "Just think, little sister. You could've been the one to find her."

Never would have gone back to that room. Teresa's eyes, wide and accusing, staring at her in a death gaze. Joanne shivered. She went to the corner and put her back to it, wondering how long it would take them to find the bloody knife. And if they would connect the murder to her.

Her own bladder began to pinch and burn while Alfred complained of having to urinate, and eat. "Oh, got to piss first then get a slice of bacon," he said. Before Thomas could comment, a pair of soldiers entered the room. One carried a wrapped object as long as his forearm.

"Report, milord," the guard said.

Lord Desmond waved for him to continue.

"All rooms all clear and the night watch reported nothing suspicious on or around the grounds," the guard said. "However, a search of the rooms yielded this." He set the wrapped object on the table and unwound it. Lying in the white cloth was the knife, edge discolored by dried blood.

"Where'd you find it?" Lord Desmond asked.

"Marret Mathers room, sir."

"The cook?" Thomas whispered in disbelief. "Why would he murder her?" Joanne shrugged.

"It was hidden in a bundle of clothes," the soldier continued. "There were spots of blood all around his floor and in the hallway leading to his room."

Lord Desmond frowned, the scar on his jawline drawing thin. It didn't sound right to Joanne either, and she was the one who placed the knife under the clothes.

"Arrest him," her father said, "and take him below."

"Already done, sir."

"Very good." He folded the knife back into the cloth, seemed to consider it. Then snatched it up and placed it in the desk drawer. "You're all dismissed."

"Thank the Mother," Alfred said and ran out.

"Doesn't surprise me one bit," Thomas said and sniffed. "Sorry sot took too much interest in her. Father, perhaps have the Master Surgeon see if she was violated before her throat was slit."

"Very wise, Thomas. Go and instruct him yourself," Lord Desmond said.

"Right away, father." Thomas bowed and left.

Joanne was the last to leave. Head down so as to avoid eye contact, she walked past his desk.

"Joanne."

She froze, hands cupping her elbows.

"Yes, father?"

"It seems your studies have been unceremoniously cut off." His tone lacked humor, though there seemed to be some understanding. Again, he had almost read her thoughts, or maybe she wore guilt on her face, bright and crimson. "I will not hire another tutor. Instead, your mother will find you someone more suitable to a different kind of education."

"By your will, father." She waited for him to say more.

Lord Desmond looked at her hands and made a thoughtful grunt.

"Hopefully she doesn't end up like your last one."

"I pray Donn show her mercy," Joanne said, giving the respectful response when speaking of the recently deceased.

"Mercy," Lord Desmond said and turned his attention to a yellow parchment. "Someone should have."

Joanne winced. The last comment was like a blow across her back and she waited for more. Lord Desmond waved her away as though she was a fly buzzing around his head. She fled to the garderobe, barely moving her dress out of the way before the urine flowed. Sitting on the cold, hard stone, bottom hanging over a dark hole, she grabbed the side of her head. All she wanted now was to take back the knife swipe. She would give anything... except, it was done. What was done couldn't be undone.

Especially when it involved death. The only task she had was to clean up the remains of her connection to the murder. She stood up, adjusted her dress and went to her bedroom.

The door remained open as she had left it. The bed covers were tossed back and it didn't appear anyone had entered since her flight. *Now to remove the last piece of damning evidence.* Very careless of her to have left her bloody night gown lying about for anyone to find. Not that she had much choice. Couldn't very well ask the armed guards to be so kind and burn the gown for her. Dark Mistress watched over her that the guards didn't see it.

Joanne went to the bed and knelt, searching for where she had kicked the bloody gown. She remembered it sliding across the wooden floorboards and disappearing into the dark under the bed. Her breath caught. It wasn't there.

Maybe I kicked it further in. She slid on her belly and felt around the hardwood floor. Dust and cobwebs stuck to her fingers. She climbed all the way under so her feet stuck out. It was dark and the wood cold. Her arms thrashed about, searching. Realization sank in her stomach like a hard piece of bread. It was gone! Someone took it! Or, maybe one of the guards had seen it and came back during the search. They'll be coming for—

Something grabbed her foot and she yelled, hitting her head on the wooden slates holding up her mattress on the frame. She kicked and heard a grunt. Foot freed, she spun on her belly like a fish flopping on sand. A pair of sandaled feet were visible beyond the bed's frame.

"Who's out there?" She recalled her dream of hiding in a wood pile. "What do you want?"

"Milady, it's me." A familiar voice.

"Selene?" Joanne wiggled closer to the opening

"I'm sorry for touching you." A scared voice on the verge of tears. "I saw feet and I didn't know who was under there."

First thing you do is grab them, silly girl. What if it had been the murderer? Joanne suppressed a laugh and crawled out from under the bed. Selene, a dark-haired girl, a year younger than Joanne, backed away. Her brown eyes were shimmering and wide. She dropped her head in deference when she saw Joanne.

"Help me up." Joanne offered her a hand.

Selene hesitated, then took it. Joanne got to her feet and brushed off thin, gray dust webs.

"You didn't see anyone else in here?" Joanne asked.

"No, milady."

Joanne's eyes narrowed. The younger girl trembled and her face grew pale. She picked at the fringes of her simple brown shift.

"Is there something you aren't telling me, Selene?" Joanne lowered her voice, the way she heard her father do when one of her brothers tried to lie.

"No," Selene said, not making eye contact. "I came here to help you dress."

"As you can see, I'm not naked."

"Yes, milady."

"Where is my night gown?"

Selene flinched and her shoulders sagged.

"What did you do with it?" Joanne grabbed the girl's shoulders, ready to shake the information from her. Part of her knew that Selene would have to disappear. She couldn't leave another carved-up body for servants to find. At least not without drawing suspicion, and possibly the ire of her father. Nevertheless, she couldn't have her chamber maid telling rumors about the blood-stained nightgown either. "Where is it? What did you do with it?"

"I threw it in the kitchen's fire," Selene finally said. Tears ran down her cheek and she began to sniffle. "I was cleaning up for you."

Fires? Cleaning up? Oh, Dark Mistress could it be...the mark of my sins burned away?

She was free and clear.

Joanne wrapped her arms around Selene, squeezing her. Her maid stiffened and then relaxed, allowing herself to be hugged.

Probably relieved I didn't stab her in the back.

"Thank you," Joanne said, whispering into Selene's ear. She kissed the girl's cheek. "I won't forget this."

Thank you, Dark Mistress, for not making me kill her!

Yet!

CHAPTER TWO:
CONFESSION

The noose burns the hand which yields it.
— *Executioner's proverb*

Joanne sat by the open window, thumbing the pages of *Historia Nemus*. A warm breeze blew a strand of hair across her eyes and she swatted it away. "The Lady Amaria summons you," Selene said, standing in the doorway. Her hands crossed in front of her and eyes on her feet, occasionally glancing up from her deference. Selene waited patiently, body stiff and possibly fighting the urge to fidget. Joanne knew Selene feared reparations for irritating both Amaria and Joanne, though each carried different consequences.

Selene still must fear me more, knowing what I did. Joanne smiled and turned a page. Burning the bloody evidence made her complicit as well.

Three days had passed since Teresa, her tutor, was discovered. The young chamber maid avoided Joanne in that duration when she didn't have to complete her duties like setting out her mistress's clothes, filling and emptying the water basin, brushing her hair. For her part, Joanne had stayed in her room, pouring over all the books, notebooks, sketches that Teresa had kept. Books Joanne secreted away before they cleared her tutor's room— she made certain to avoid the accusing red stains on the stone at the edge of the stripped bed. Later that night, she examined her contraband. Their subjects varied from botany, animal taxonomy, mathematics, fables, and treatises on Nemus relations with Seaptum, and other nations Joanne never heard of, some that no longer existed. Nations and their people dead, like her brother Henrick.

She traced her finger over an ink sketch of Mount Noctis. There Henrick fought bravely, holding the pass against Seaptum invaders. Henrick who had played games with her, taught her various card tricks, castles and kings, and how to hold a sword. To an eleven-year-old, it seemed Henrick would be around forever.

Then he wasn't.

"Milady—"

Joanne held her finger up in a "hold-your-peace" gesture. Seaptum, Nemus' northern bordering kingdom wanted to reclaim the entire continent, returning it under one rule the way it had been before the split. That was the simple answer Joanne was told when at eleven she had asked why people were fighting. The three separate sections, Seaptum, Nemus, and Meritum which occupied the south past the Desert of Lost Souls, used to be one under some king whose name she couldn't recall. The history was boring to her then. Why anyone required so much land was beyond her. She set the book down, wishing Teresa was here to answer her questions about politics. It was her own fault the tutor joined Henrick in Nahrangi, the place of rest. Or perhaps she still waited Donn's judgement in Gehenna.

Joanne doubted she would see either again, since she was certain Arula was her destination. Eternal damnation and torment alongside other murderers.

Lips pinched together, Selene fidgeted with her skirts.

"Fine." Joanne shut the book and placed it on the neat stack. "Let's go see what mother wants from me."

Selene followed a few steps behind Joanne, keeping hold of her thoughts. Joanne tried to get the nature of the summons from the chamber maid, but when Joanne asked her a question, Selene found her sandals to be of great interest. A very good chance the girl didn't know anything. Her mother wasn't much of a talker. "Fetch my daughter" would be quite a lot of words for Lady Amaria to speak, regarding Joanne. It hadn't always been that way, but things change when one gets older, Joanne noted, and when death snatches away the beloved, eldest child.

At Lady Amaria's chamber doors, Selene came forward and opened them. Joanne moved past without sparing her so much as a glance. The door clicked behind her. Joanne was alone with her mother, though alone was not the proper term. Not when the room was strangely filled with other guests. A red embroidered carpet, gold etched borders shaped in vines covered the hard stone floor. Lady Amaria sat in a cushioned chair next to the cold hearth, a silver chalice clutched in her right hand. Across from the chair was a settee, its back turned to Joanne. A flat-topped, black hennin poked over the settee's back, black gossamer veil draping behind it. Joanne tried her best not to laugh at such a silly and antiquated hat.

Only old and musty women wear those things.

"Come in child," Lady Amaria said. "Don't stand there gawking about. It's not very proper."

The hennin slowly turned, revealing a round, pasty face. Dark blue eyes looked her over and rouged lips formed a tight smile. The tiny chin and high cheekbones made her head look like a squash, the hennin forming the flattened tip.

"Forgive her ill-manners, she has been without proper adult guidance since the incident," Lady Amaria said.

Of course, Lady Amaria, her mother, had left her to her own devices without once asking after how her child felt about the murder of her tutor. That would require her mother to treat her with some sort of dignity, rather than an object to be avoided. None of these things could be expressed to Lady Amaria. It was above the duty of the High Lord's wife to care for her offspring.

Joanne dipped a small curtsy. A little late by decorum standards, but enough to display her knowledge that she knew she was being rude. Standing in display was enough to foul her mood and she bit the inside of her cheek to prevent giving a rather curt response which would have doubled down on her rudeness. Especially since she wanted to say she had seen a turnip with more coloring and less wrinkles. *Probably more personality, too.*

"This here is Lady Bodaline," Lady Amaria said, glaring at Joanne in the way she might convey her thoughts demanding her daughter change her disposition. *Hard bread and watery soup for supper if I don't comply.* Joanne tried a smile, but it faded at the next words out of her mother's mouth. "She's your new maid-in-waiting. You'll learn the proper actions of a woman, that do not include filling your head with useless knowledge from books."

Lady Bodaline stood up and closed the gap to Joanne. Her hair was black, a touch of grey creeping at the temples spoke of her age. Her strides were graceful as though she floated rather than walked across the carpet. Her large bosom pressed against the modest, black dress, a white lace-collar covering her neck. Lady Bodaline matched her in height, or perhaps was shorter, the silly hat made it hard for Joanne to judge. Her new maid-in-waiting gave a low curtsy, palms up and held it until Joanne acknowledge her to rise.

"Mother bless me, but you are prettier than what Lady Amaria described," Lady Bodaline said, smiling to reveal tiny, white teeth. "I swear to do my best to demonstrate all I know—"

"What about Selene?" Joanne asked, looking past the older woman to her mother.

Lady Bodaline's smile faltered.

"You no longer need her," Lady Amaria said, gripping the stem of the goblet, though Joanne saw her thin fingers twitch, tapping out her mother's impatience. "Lady Bodaline has brought her two granddaughters to dress, groom, or otherwise smooth out your rough edges. Oh, don't look cross, child. Selene will assist the new cook in the kitchens. I've indulged your whims enough."

"My granddaughters are such lovely young ladies—"

"I don't give a rat's pink ass about your granddaughters," Joanne said. "I want Selene."

She knows too much to let her out of my sight.

Lady Bodaline squeaked and Lady Amaria set down her goblet. She rose from the chair, eyes locked on Joanne. Fury blazed enough to light the room. Joanne didn't flinch. She didn't look away and give any sort of deference. She wouldn't, couldn't give up Selene. When her mother's arm cocked, Joanne knew she wouldn't strike her, not in front of all these subordinate women. Then a hard palm smacked her across the cheek and Joanne's head snapped sideways. Heat rose on her skin and she knew there would be a bright, red mark in the shape of a hand. Hate trembled through Joanne, from her lips to her shaking knees. Her mother had never struck her.

"You will speak well or you will hold your tongue." Lady Amaria rubbed her wrist.

Tears shimmered in Joanne's eyes and she willed them back. Through pinched lips, her jaw aching as she spoke, she answered, "Yes, ma'am."

"Apologize."

Joanne turned to Lady Bodaline whose face puckered, lips moving but no words forming. She reminded Joanne of a rabbit twitching its nose.

"Forgive me, milady, for my rudeness." She tried to keep the fury and hurt from her voice. "It won't happen again."

"You are forgiven," Lady Bodaline said. Her cheeks remained red and she seemed stiff, the cheer now chilled. "Losing someone close to you tends to make one very excitable. "

Joanne covered her snort, making it into a strange whimper.

"It gets easier with time." Lady Bodaline reached out to touch Joanne, but she flinched back, leaving the woman to cross her hands demurely in front of her. "I will show you how to control those nerves so you are… less excitable."

"Lady Bodaline and her granddaughters will move into the rooms down the hall from you on the morrow," Lady Amaria said. "You will show them complete respect. No more of your little outbursts. Otherwise, your father will hear of it. He can tame that wild tongue of yours."

My father will do more than tame me. This slap will seem like a tickle.

"May I go?" Joanne asked.

"Anything you need to hear or see more of from the child?" Lady Amaria asked.

"I've seen, and heard enough," Lady Bodaline said.

"Very well," Lady Amaria turned her back on Joanne and went to her chair. "You'll have a real time of it taming this one. I almost pity you."

"Pity." Lady Bodaline smiled, reminding Joanne of a jackal grinning at a crow in the fable, right before the crow's head got stuck in a jar and the jackal ate it. "No need to pity me, milady. I raised all four of my daughters to adulthood. Each of them was as wildly spirited as the next. Now they are quiet little dormice, happily married and settled. Children are like wild horses. You just need to know how to break them in order for them to be sociable."

I bet none of your daughters killed a person. Joanne tried a smile, found it hurt her cheek and dropped it. Instead, she gave a low curtsey.

"I look forward to our training sessions," she said and headed for the door.

"As do I, child," Lady Bodaline said to Joanne's back. "As do I."

"Selene." Joanne entered the kitchens, fists balled up and ready to hit something, or someone. The younger girl was hunched over a steaming basin of water, shoulders working up and down while she scrubbed a pot. Her eyes widened and she dropped the pot into the tub.

"What happened?" Selene put a hand to her own cheek, the hurt Joanne felt mirrored in her maid's eyes.

"What happened? What happened!" Joanne stopped pacing. She searched for something sharp, but no knives were in view. This was good, because there was no one around to stab except Selene and she wanted to hurt her, to strangle her, to do something to release her pain. No, she couldn't, wouldn't, she wanted to possess the girl, not harm her the way her mother harmed Joanne by trying to take her away. "I'll tell you what happened. The Lady Amaria is replacing you."

"Mother, no!" Selene gasped. "Where will I go?"

"Nowhere," Joanne said. She took a breath, collecting her wild thoughts that turned to claws wanting to strike out at anyone. "You'll be here in the kitchens, but you won't be allowed to dress me or bring me food anymore. So incredibly unfair. The bitch!"

"It's not very nice to speak that way about your mother," Selene said, looking around the kitchen.

"What? Are you going to run and tell her?" The claws came, ready to tear Selene apart. Although they were of similar height, Joanne stood larger—a cat looming over a scared dormouse. Joanne slapped the younger girl's arm and Selene squeaked.

"N...no. I would never say anything." Selene slunk away, becoming even smaller.

Selene's the perfect little girl. Someone my mother would want, but Donn can eat her heart, I'll never be one. I swear it by the Shadow.

Joanne grabbed Selene by the hair and held her face over the hot water.

"You tell anyone anything… and I'll drown you."

"I swear by the Mother and Father," Selene said, her voice shaky, fingers gripping the basin's metal edge. "May they tear out my tongue and feed it to the crows."

Joanne released her and they both collapsed onto the floor. The sat very still, though Joanne's chest heaved from the anger, from nearly drowning the one person who has ever done anything selfless for her. Laughter crawled up her throat like bile and Joanne couldn't stop it. Not even when the tears stung her eyes. She stared at Selene. Her maid's confused expression caused her to laugh harder until her belly hurt and she leaned forward. The laughter subsided into wet, hiccoughs.

"I'm sorry, Selene." She hiccoughed and covered her mouth. Laughter threatened to begin again. She pinched her lips, bringing on a fresh spout of tears that she wiped away with the heel of her hand. "I didn't mean… I know you… I feel like I'm losing everything."

"You still have me." The sincerity was so raw, Joanne flushed.

"I don't mean to treat you so terribly." She tried to find words, to beg for forgiveness. The disappointment her father would have in her, for subjugating herself to a servant, chained the plea inside, though allowing something else to escape. A warm tingling in her underbelly and a strange flutter in her stomach. Selene watched her, innocent eyes bright, expectant.

Joanne leaned over and kissed Selene's small mouth. Chapped lips pressed against her soft ones and she tasted the bitter lye soap used to clean the pots. The younger girl tensed, her soft body ready to recoil at the slightest hint of violence, though the violence had melted out of Joanne leaving this one desire. Selene felt it and she relaxed, allowing their mouths to press harder into each other. The kiss lasted only a few heartbeats, but it seemed to go on much longer. Then they parted, staring into each other's eyes.

"You will always have me," Joanne said, her chest rising and falling in rapid breaths.

"Here you are!" Thomas barked, boots clomping on the stone floor.

Joanne's head jerked in his direction. Fear crept up on her and she gripped it in grease slick fingers.

"What game are you playing at?" Thomas laughed. He wore a grey uniform with the rose and dagger on the breast. "Pigs in mud? Suckling away on the teat?" He made a disgusting sucking noise, lips pressed together and face screwed up to look like a pig.

"What do you want?" Anger scorched through her words.

"Nothing," he said.

"Why are you bothering me?"

"Because father wants to see you," Thomas glanced at Selene and grinned. Joanne wanted to punch the smug, knowing grin back into his teeth. "For Mother's sake, don't tell him you are playing in the kitchens. It would break his heart to hear you wasting the precious tutoring you received, dallying with those beneath us. She is a pretty bauble, but remember, she is only a bauble. Once broken, you'll find no more interest in her."

You must love the sound of your own voice. Joanne glared at him, rather than give him satisfaction of acknowledging her annoyance.

"You don't want to keep Father waiting," Thomas said and nodded at Selene. "He might have her pretty little head."

He turned on his heels, measured steps marching away.

"Not a word to anyone," Joanne said, but she smiled. Couldn't hold it back.

Selene shook her head.

Joanne resisted another kiss.

Thomas was right about one thing, and it irked her beyond all end. Lord Desmond would not approve of the company she kept.

"Crime and punishment." Lord Desmond leaned over the side of his chair, saffron and cinnamon cloves on his breath. He drank them in a tea to help digestion—Teresa had explained their medicinal purposes to her in what seemed another life. Standing in the Keep's lower room, very near the dank cells housing prisoners, skin prickled t the cold seeping into her ski, the torch light guttering in some unknown breeze, was enough to give Joanne indigestion. "A civilized nation needs to govern the baser people, to prevent them from giving in to their animalistic desires. Otherwise, we would do nothing more than eat, rut, and kill."

Joanne nodded, again, guilt flaring up. She squashed it the way she would a wriggling bug.

"Since it is we, the governing lord of the land, who set the rules, we also must be prepared to mete out punishment in accordance to the rules.

Especially when the trespass is done in our own house," Lord Desmond said. "No greater depravity than befouling one's home, or those who watch over it."

The office door opened and two soldiers led Marret Mathers inside the room. Manacles chained his feet and hands, forcing them to half-carry the former cook, one bare foot dragging on the stone. A bloody rag wrapped around his right toes hissed with each struggling step. Mathers' head bobbed as he was carted between the soldiers with less care than a sack of potatoes. Joanne stared at his ruined face. Both eyes were bruised, swelled shut. His nose was crooked and dried blood caked his upper lip. His jaw hung more to the left than a normal person's. He looked like someone took a meat pulverizer to his face. He was shirtless as well. Several raw, puckered cuts zigged from his chest to the waist of ragged pantaloons. Bile crept up into Joanne's throat, but she swallowed the bitterness down.

"Wha...what happened to him?" She bit her lip to keep more words from escaping.

"Confessions are messy," Lord Desmond said. "When our hearts lay on Donn's silver platter, we want the god of judgment to taste sweet honesty and not bitter deceit. So, we assist the accused in understanding the truth. It's much better for them in the life beyond and helps us judge accordingly."

"Except we cannot taste the evil in a man's heart," she said. *Or woman's heart*, the accusatory thought stung her, caused her flesh to crawl. She shoved it away. "How can we tell if a man is innocent?"

"No one is ever innocent." Lord Desmond held her gaze a moment, and she felt her heart on a platter, ready to be consumed. Then he broke it and rose from his chair. "Bring the accused forward."

The guards stopped and one waved a rag of pungent salts and vinegar under the cook's nose. How he could smell in all that ruin baffled Joanne. Mathers gasped and coughed; a red string of spittle drooled down his chin.

"Have you anything you wish to say, Master Mathers."

Marret raised his head slowly as though he were lifting a lodestone drawn to his manacles. One, puffy-eye opened. Red veined and weeping, it lolled in the socket before focusing on her father. Clarity entered in and rather than fear, as Joanne expected, anger sharpened the look.

Lips crusted in dried blood peeled apart, revealing a few empty holes where teeth once occupied. "I...I," Marret began. A thick tongue wormed out and licked his split lips. "I did no wrong."

"You stand accused of murdering a young woman in her bed," Lord Desmond said. "Violating her and cutting her throat, leaving her to bleed out like a pig before the roast. You see no wrong in this?"

"My lord." Marret winced at the description. "That is a great wrong, but not done by me."

"The knife, Master Mathers, was hidden in your quarters, Teresa's blood dried on its sharp edge and, after examination of the body, your seed spilled in her womb. You were seen loitering around her quarters on various nights, presumably working up the courage to rape her as she slept."

"No, my lord!" Marret writhed in his chains, trying to approach the dais steps. One soldier kicked him in the back of the knee and Marret folded forward. He grunted, weeping on his knees, looking up at Lord Desmond and then Joanne. There was hurt and fear in his one good eye. "It weren't like that. Not like that at all."

"What was it like?"

"I love her. Qetesh knows she loved me, too." Marret's chin dropped to his chest. "Mother blessed truth. We lay together that night, but it was mutual, not ra… I didn't force her to do anything. She invited me to her quarters. She found a new flower and wanted me to crush its petals, to season the soups. Said it would, 'Spice it up, some. Add heat to our bellies.' I never saw it before, don't trust nothing I never heard of, let alone feed it to my lord and protect—" He coughed on the last word. "But I promised to test it out first. Next thing I knew, she had my pants down and…"

Joanne didn't pay attention to the rest of Marret's story. Her mind was on the flower he'd mentioned would "add heat to the bellies." *Dragon's Vein?* She doubted that it was the same flower. Teresa said it was deadly to consume. Teresa wouldn't poison her family. The tutor had been with them since Joanne could remember. It must've been another flower.

"Sounds more like an obsessive fantasy," Lord Desmond said. "You confess to speaking with the victim on the night in question. You admit to fornication, that it was your seed drying in her cold womb. Now tell us how you held her down and proceeded to slice her throat."

"The last part never happened." Marret was getting angry. He tried to stand up, but the guards shoved him back down.

"It happened, Master Mathers. We have the corpse and the knife." Lord Desmond's mouth tightened, the scar across his cheek standing more prominent. "Donn will soon know the measure of your heart. Ease your suffering here on this plane by confessing." Lord Desmond removed a small knife from his belt. He held it before Marret Mather's eye, slowly dipping the point and pressing it to Marret's right nostril. "Tell me a different story. One where you crept into Teresa's bed, lay your stinking bulk over her small, fragile form."

"No." The word came out as a hoarse whisper.

Lord Desmond flicked his wrist and the flesh parted neatly in half, red droplets speckling across her father's white sleeve. Marret's head jerked back and he cried out. Lord Desmond placed the blade in the left nostril.

"Was her cunt tight on your prick? Did you come right away, or after she tried to scream. Her warning cries cut off by cold steel. Warm blood spurting out over your hands."

Another wrist flick and more flesh tore. Marret's nose looked like a strange red moth had landed on his face, flaps of skin fluttering under swollen eyes. Joanne belched, doubling over. She closed her eyes, telling herself not to vomit. Chains clacked and the links went taut. Marret groaned, unable to bring his hands up to comfort his abused nose.

"You killed her. You may not have intended it, but it happened."

"Ohhhh!" The strangled pain-filled response sounded like one a wounded animal would make.

Lord Desmond grabbed Marret's right ear.

"Either you aren't hearing me or you still don't want to tell me what I want to hear." He sawed the knife back and forth. Marret's ragged, hoarse screams bubbled up and he tried to pull his head away. The soldiers held him, blood staining their gray uniforms. Lord Desmond dropped the severed ear in the cook's lap and began working on the other side.

A foul smell filled the cold room. Joanne wrinkled her nose in disgust. Marret defecated on himself, brown staining the bottom of his soiled pantaloons. *The coward.* She almost believed her father's version of her tutor's death. Had to believe it. Otherwise, that would be her under her father's knife, begging for him to stop.

"The suffering could all end," Lord Desmond said. "A few words, then the pain of this world will be a distant memory. Do you want it to end?"

"Ye… yessh." Marret panted.

"Say it."

"I… I kill her."

26

"Louder."

"I. Kill. Her." Tears mingled with blood running over his cheeks, dripping off his chin.

Lord Desmond wiped his knife on the Cook's blood-stained pantaloons. He patted the man on the head, and nodded. "Take him back to his cell." The guards lifted Marret Mather under an arm, carrying his limp body, ruined face dripping a red spatter-trail.

"The gallows moon rises this evening." Her father took out a white kerchief, twisting it through his bloody finger and staining the cloth red. Specks of blood dappled his grim face. He looked a ghastly figure, one she was certain to visit her nightmares. He went to the window, back to her. "We hang him the next morrow. I suggest you wear black."

"Yes, father." Joanne hesitated, but the words came anyway. "What if he spoke the truth? That he didn't truly kill Teresa?"

Lord Desmond turned and his eyebrows raised.

"Then Donn will judge him fairly."

CHAPTER THREE: HANGING

Justice is one man's revenge on another.
—Magistrate's Curse

"A lady must never wear black." Lady Bodaline frowned at the dress laying out on the bed. Her chirping, haughty voice set fire to Joanne's nerves and she used her entire will-power not to punch the woman in her throat. Lady Bodaline's granddaughters would take offense at her assaulting their grandmother and report Joanne's behavior to her mother. Beaty and Susie moved about Joanne's chamber, preparing outfits, boots, and jewelry to match. Beaty was eldest, at sixteen years old, and Susie a year older than Joanne at fourteen. Both girls were pretty, pale complexioned, had bright blue eyes, and pink lips. Beaty wore a modest light blue cap while Susie's was sea green, covering their dark hair.

Joanne had placed the dress out and was ready to slip it on when Lady Bodaline bustled in and began chastising her.

"Black is for mourning her husband or family member." Lady Bodaline clucked, examining the dresses her granddaughters held up. Emerald and sapphire. Gaudy colors meant for courtiers to gawk at and smile their approval. Too bright for an execution. Lady Bodaline nodded at Beaty's choice: the sapphire one like she was rising from the sea. "Last I saw, you are still a maid and your family is alive."

A lady must never defy my father. Or if she does, then she must be ready for pain. The memory of Lord Desmond slicing off the cook's ears and nose shivered through her.

"My eldest brother is dead," Joanne said, putting as much bite into the words as she could muster. Being defiant was made all the more difficult standing in only her undergarments.

"Oh, yes. I remember the Lady—"

"Please stop," Joanne said. Lady Bodaline blinked. "I know you don't care about me beyond what stature you and your granddaughters claw out among the rest of the merecats in court. Don't speak to me as though you know me or my family. You work for my father. My father told me to wear black. Do I need to tell him who dressed me?"

"Why didn't you just say so," Lady Bodaline said, though her tone was too sweet, condescending. Again, Joanne wished she could pluck out her tongue. "We wouldn't want to disappoint your father the least bit. Beaty, be so kind as to put those away."

"Yes, grandmother." Beaty nodded and carried the sapphire gown back to the wardrobe and hung it up.

Lady Bodaline held the black gown up. It was made of silk and Joanne wore it once to her brother's funeral at the insistence of her mother, although Henrick's body was left in the wilderness, unable to be recovered, like some common peasant to be feasted on by wild animals. Lady Bodaline clucked her tongue and shook her head.

"Susie, bring yours here."

"Are you color blind?" Joanne backed away. "That's green, not black. My father said—"

"All well and good you wish to follow your father's demands, but I was brought in to guide you into becoming a woman. Part of being a woman is understanding men have no taste when it concerns a woman's dress. In fact, they are more interested in what is concealed beneath the gown, than its color or grace as she flows in it," Lady Bodaline droned on. "We are the

29

light in the darkness of their hearts and so must apparel ourselves accordingly, else we become nothing more than an ink blotch, annoying and messy. Besides, Lord Desmond has more than enough problems to concern his mind than the color of his daughter's gown."

"Finding me a new lady-in-waiting," Joanne grumbled.

"Arms up!" Lady Bodaline ignored her last statement.

Joanne kept her arms folded.

"Either you allow us to dress you, or you shall go out as you are."

"The black gown." Joanne glared, tightening her arms under her chest like chains, hands gripping her sides.

"What hour was the… the execution taking place?" Her lips pursed together and she motioned to the window where the sunlight brightened. Joanne glared at it and then Lady Bodaline. She knew full well the execution was taking place on the parade grounds at first light. "The morning ages quickly and you may disappoint your father more by not showing up."

Joanne tightened her grip, pinching her thighs until her fingers ached, and scowled at Lady Bodaline. The soldiers would march the doomed cook to the parade grounds where a scaffold was assembled for the occasion. Her father would oversee it from his balcony, knuckles white and twisting the railing while he pondered how his daughter could disobey him. She could see the scar draw in tight as his jaw set on some harsh punishment for her. More than cold soup or a missed meal. He wouldn't hold up the entire event because his daughter was absent, no, she would suffer for it later.

All over the color of a dress.

Joanne thrust her arms up.

Lady Bodaline smiled.

Petty victory for petty people, a quote her father often said, *holds as much satisfaction as stepping on an ant. Crush one and more will come. Pour boiling water over their hill and they all drown.*

"See, that wasn't so bad." Lady Bodaline stepped back and scrutinized Joanne. "A simple braid and you are ready to present yourself. Oh, how you clean up nicely. Very nice."

Let's see how you clean up after my father hears how you defied him and he puts you out on your fat bottom.

Joanne ran from her room. Bumbled better fit the description of her flight. Her feet felt clumsy in the high-arched shoes, the billowy skirt of this gods-awful dress was better fit to sail a small boat than for running. She held the hem, trying not to step on it and fall face first into the stone wall.

"Wait!" Beaty yelled from behind.

Oh, what now?

Beaty followed after her, sternly approaching like she had a stick shoved up her backside.

"You mustn't run," Beaty said. "Walk briskly as though carried on breeze, but never run."

"Not even if chased by a dragon?"

"With your stubby legs, running would prove just as useless."

Instead of throwing an angry retort at her, Joanne did something unexpected. She laughed. "My father is the dragon. If I don't reach my appointment on time, then I am as good as roasted meat," Joanne said and began walking briskly.

"An awful meal you'd make." Beaty kept pace with her longer legs. "Not enough fat on your bones. You'll sizzle away to nothing but gristle and sticks. Why does he want you as witness to the execution, anyway? Did the cook forget to season your porridge?" Her voice lowered, taking on a mischievous tone. "Or maybe he touched you in places a man likes to touch women."

"He murdered my tutor." The lie came easily. "Didn't your grandmother tell you?"

"No, she didn't. My apologies for being so flippant." To her credit, Beaty sounded sincere unlike her grandmother Lady Bodaline. "She only tells us what we need to know in order to fulfill our duty. She's not one to engage in gossip."

"What did she tell you about me?"

"A strong-willed girl with a head swelled full of ideas and self-importance."

"Of course, I'm important. I am the only daughter of the Lord of Nemus." Joanne stuck her chin out, peering down her nose. She almost tripped and settled her eyes on the floor. "Besides, I am to marry a prince one day."

"A perfect match," Beaty said.

"How so?"

"You both can talk about how important the other is while lords and ladies preen about, heads bobbing like hungry birds snatching crumbs from the tiles."

"You're jealous?"

"I would never envy your position," Beaty said. "We were all born to suffer, but some suffer more than others."

Cook Mathers lost his love and soon his life. He suffered more than anyone, more than mother and father losing their first-born son. At least Henrick died a hero. But Mathers was a simple man, until I took it all away.

"How will I suffer more than a scullery maid?"

"The scullery maid needs to worry about clean pots and linens. She keeps her head down, does her duty efficiently, then she will find a man, marry, birth more children to bring her joy in old age," Beaty said, sounding full of wisdom and dusty quotes. "A Princess has to bear the burden of the entire realm. There are certain expectations placed on her like providing a male heir."

"From the books I've read, that is a duty done on her back," Joanne said. "The other is back-breaking work. If the scullery maid displeases the lord, or lady, she could be turned out. She will freeze in the snows, or starve, or worse. Give me fine clothes, a warm fire, full belly, and books to read, and I'll gladly lie on my back for as long as my prince likes."

"Wise words, little princess."

Joanne heard the biting humor in her tone, but let it go. Beaty knew nothing. She was the granddaughter of some wealthy peasant, or something along those lines, what did she know of royalty?

They reached Lord Desmond's chambers and Joanne stood at the door. She listened, but there was silence. *Oh no, did I miss it?* A cold breeze blew from under the door. Joanne shivered, skin prickling at the thought of being too late. One execution was over and hers was about to begin. She swallowed hard, looked back at Beaty. Beaty said nothing, hands folded neatly in front of her, while her eyebrows raised as if to ask— "what's keeping you?"

Joanne smoothed the front on her dress, silky material running like water beneath her finger tips. She steeled her heart for what came next and pulled open the door. The temperature was colder in the chamber. White drapes blew inward like smoke tendrils from the balcony window, revealing three figures standing outside in the cold. Their backs were to Joanne. She hesitated. They hadn't notice her. *I could still retreat to a corner of the Keep, hide like a little mouse from the cat.* She sensed Beaty behind her. Eyes scrutinizing her every move, possibly to report back to Lady Bodaline, who in turn would tell Lady Amaria and her father would know of her cowardice. Those eyes acted better than a knife pressed against her back. She stepped through the drapes, walking through the shroud to the gray morning light.

Lord Desmond leaned against the railing, two soldiers standing at guard on either side. They glanced at Joanne but made no movement as she and Beaty approached. Three stories below the balcony, wooden gallows were constructed on the parade grounds. More soldiers gathered beside and in front of it. The entire household guard, soldiers, servants, everyone except for her mother and Lady Bodaline and Susie filled the grounds, silent as ghostly figures. The gallows were empty, a rope swaying back and forth above the wooden platform.

Not too late! She released her breath, realizing she was holding it.

"I remember telling you to wear black," Lord Desmond said. His gazed turned from the parade grounds to Joanne. A lump filled her throat. "Did you forget my words?"

"N..no, father."

"What's this?"

"I tried to tell Lady Bodaline—"

"Not hard enough," Lord Desmond said, sharp steel in his voice. "She serves you. If you are unable to command those who are designated to serve, then you become the servant. You." He nodded to Beaty who curtsied and stepped beside Joanne. "What's your name?"

"Beaty, milord." She curtsied again, keeping her eyes low and hands out to the side.

"Strip that ridiculous gown off of her." He turned away, back to surveying the parade grounds. "This isn't some ball. No suitors to sweep you off to brittle music. Here there is only death. We see the guilty off to Donn in the proper garb, or none at all."

Joanne flushed, though she didn't argue. She knew she failed a test of sorts. Beaty smiled sympathetically and turned Joanne around. She unlatched the back hooks keeping the gown closed. The cold breeze nibbled her neck and she trembled. The gown slipped over her head, leaving her in her white small clothes, exposing her arms and legs to the weather. Joanne cupped her elbows.

"It's cold." A whine entered her quivering voice.

"Yes. Yes, it is," Lord Desmond said, returning his attention to the parade grounds.

Beaty left the balcony, taking away the offending green gown. The guards had common decency not to stare, though she caught one sneering and nodding his head.

"Does something amuse you?" she snapped, glaring at the man.

The sneer remained, but the soldier turned to face the parade grounds. Movement below caught the attention of all the witnesses. Their heads turned to follow a line of soldiers march from under the balcony in two rows. Silent as wraiths, they escorted a man, nude from the waist up, shoulders hunched. Red slashes crisscrossed across his back, gaping like open mouths. Joanne approached the banister and watched over the edge as they passed. Cold breeze blew strands of hair across her face. She brushed them aside, listening to the chains clatter with every step Cook Mathers took. He looked thin, a sack of flesh slung over his bones like a wash woman's heavy burden.

Did they provide him a last meal? What would he desire? Could he even eat knowing this morrow would be his last?

Joanne kept silent and watched the procession stop at the foot of the gallows. Two black hooded men came down and took the cook under the arms, leading him to the center of the platform, beneath the swaying rope. They turned him around. Joanne sucked in her breath. Marret's nose hung in shreds, both eyes swollen and purple. The hooded men took out iron keys and proceeded to unlock the chains. Marret Mather's head turned, surveying the crowd and stopped, looking up the balcony. Looking at her. Joanne stiffened. She wanted to hide behind her father, but gripped the banister instead.

Does he suspect? Did father tell him?

Then his head sagged and she felt an odd relief.

A magistrate wearing black robes came forward. He unrolled a parchment, vellum shaking in the wind. He raised it up and announced in a clear, high-pitched voice.

"To the charge of murder, rape, and conspiracy to murder, Marret Mathers, you have been found guilty. Under the eyes of Mother and Father and the children of the gods, and by the laws of Nemus, the penalty for your crimes is hanging until dead." He lowered the parchment and addressed Mathers directly. "Do you have any last words?"

Mathers lifted his head again. His shoulders tensed and neck strained as he opened his mouth. Then closed it. Opened again, lips trembling as the words came, quiet at first and then echoing across the parade ground.

"I… I nevah… hurt her!" He looked up, directly at Joanne. "I nevah hurt her!"

"Much too late to recant," the Magistrate said. "May Donn weigh you justly."

"I nevah hurt—"

A hood was placed over his head, cutting off his pleas. They tied his hands behind his back and knotted his ankles together. Next, a rope was lowered over the hood. The Executioners tugged the knot to ensure it was secure. Then Magistrate and Executioners turned to the balcony.

What are they waiting for?

"Give them the signal," Lord Desmond said. "Raise your palm, fingers splayed."

Joanne raised a trembling hand.

"Close your fist."

Fingers tightened, nails digging into her palm.

As though she had pulled the lever herself, the floor opened beneath Marret Mathers and he dropped, the rope catching under his chin. His legs kicked and his body spasmed. It went on for several heartbeats, the pound of her heart thudding in her ears. Joanne realized she still held her fist up and lowered it slowly. Marret Mathers jerked a couple more times before going still.

"What lesson was learned?" Lord Desmond asked.

The pretty ones are the most deadly.

"Condemned men lie," she said.

"Yes, they will say anything to preserve their life for a few more breaths." Lord Desmond turned his stone gaze on her. "What about those who condemn the man?"

Joanne's heart picked up the heavy thud again. Her chest hurt under his scrutiny. He was playing games with her. The truth must read on her face like words of the sentence on the Magistrate's parchment. While everyone else at the execution wore black, she stood in her white small clothes, exposed to it all. Might as well be red. Red as the blood on her hands, under her nails, rising to her cheeks.

"She who condemns the man, must carry out the sentence."

Lord Desmond nodded.

"Always wear black to an execution." He leaned in like he was about to kiss her cheek. Instead, he whispered in her ear. "White is for the innocent."

She walked the halls of the Keep, alone and in her small clothes. Most of the servants would be returning inside from the execution to pick up where their lives left off. Joanne had a moment to sulk. A moment to think about her father's disappointment, and whether he knew the truth. If so, why did he let an innocent man die for her? Was he protecting her? Teach her a less—

Her chamber door was open and she heard someone shuffling around. She slipped off her shoes and ran on her toes, making little sound on the stone tiles. At her door, she peered around the frame. A girl, Susie, picked through the stack of books on Joanne's writing desk. She lifted three and turned as though about to exit.

"Leave those alone!" Joanne charged into her room. Susie froze, books clutched to her chest. "Put them back!"

"I was just looking at them," Susie said. "I didn't mean—"

Joanne tore the books from Susie's hands and placed them back on the shelf.

"Do you know what they do to thieves?"

Susie shook her head, blue eyes widening.

"They chop off her fingers." She made a cutting motion. "I would make you wear yours around your neck so you'll always be reminded when the urge to steal creeps up on you."

"I wasn't taking them for me." Susie pouted. She reminded Joanne of

Lady Bodaline. The same plain, doughy face giving her an appearance of stupidity, even if she were the smartest person in the room.

Touching my possessions without permission proves she's not very bright.

"Doesn't matter." Joanne grabbed Susie's hand, squeezing her fingers together. "You serve me, not the other way around. If I wanted you to wear a dead rat on your head, you would ask me how to wrap the tail. Do you understand?"

Susie nodded, trying to pull her hand away from Joanne's grip. The knuckles grated and Joanne grinned at the sound. Susie gave a small whimper.

"I'm sorry," she said. "Please let me go."

The whiney voice made her squeeze all the harder. It wouldn't take much more pressure to snap the bones like twigs. The pleasure at the pain in the stupid blue eyes that had dared try to defy her. She needed to suffer. Needed to hurt.

"What are you doing?" Beaty asked.

Joanne released Susie's hand. Susie stole it back and pressed the fingers to her chest, giving her sister a grateful look.

"She was stealing my books."

"No, she wasn't."

"I caught her with them in her hands."

"Yes, it's because grandmother wanted them removed from your room."

"Why?"

"Grandmother says, 'A lady should be witty for her husband, but never a bore. Too much reading makes one somber, a rainy cloud rather than a cheerful sun.'"

"Where'd she gain so much wisdom?'

"From her mother, more than likely." Beaty held out her hands. "I suggest you keep only two books and give us the rest to take to her. Otherwise, she'll strip your room bare searching for them."

"What if I don't want to give them up? She has no right to take my things."

"Only the right given by your mother. Besides, she'll say it's time to put away childish things and commit to becoming a lady."

Joanne selected two books.

"Fine, she can have the rest, but do not touch another thing in my room without asking for my permission."

"As my lady commands." Beaty curtsied and gathered up the rest of Teresa's books. Susie followed her, giving a fearful glance back. Joanne glared at her and Susie scurried along. The two books she kept were *Historia Nemus* and the sketchbook— all that remained of her former tutor, whose body was interred in potters' ground by the Church of Paturnus. She had not lived long enough to marry and have children. In a way, the sketchbook was her legacy, and Joanne swore to protect it. It was the least she could do as atonement for taking the unfortunate woman's life.

No matter the prince I marry, he'll never be cleverer than me.

Joanne wrapped the books in old stocking and slid them along the headboard of her bed against the wall. They would be easy for her to access, but wouldn't be seen when they changed her bedsheets. Then she slipped on a comfortable dress and made her way to the kitchens.

Selene was stirring a pot of dirty clothes over the great fire in the kitchen. Again, the strong odor of lye filled the hot room. Sweat beaded on Joanne's lip as she watched Selene. The way her brown smock stuck to her back, the slender shape of her shoulders moving as she worked the wooden stir around, lifting up linen to check on it and then lowering it back inside. The young servant girl didn't notice her, humming a low tune in time of her rotation.

"I met my love in the copse stand
Fingers entwined, her hand warm in mine
We walked the trees, eating sweet berries
Listening to the bees and dreamt of honey
And whey and of our wedding day."

"Who do you intend to marry?" Joanne asked, laughing as Selene gasped and spun, holding the wooden stir like a sword.

"You scared me half-to-death," Selene said and lowered the stir.

"Half-dead, half-alive," Joanne said. "Breathing in that nasty stuff will make you more dead than alive."

"I don't even smell it anymore."

I hope it hasn't started rotting your pretty head. Joanne moved into the kitchen. Selene was alone. The other maids and servants were off, probably mourning Mathers, and would return shortly to make the midday meal.

"Well?" Joanne asked.

"Well what?"

"You never answered my question." Joanne narrowed her eyes. "Who do you intend to marry?"

"Oh, no one," Selene responded and her brow furrowed as she thought through the next part. "I mean, it's not about my intentions. Not that I have any intentions at the moment… no, it will be as the Mother wills."

"Not Qetesh?"

Selene blushed. The red on her cheeks brought out a pretty glow and Joanne wanted to touch them, pinch them softly. And brush her lips against them.

"I don't know anything more about love than I do the countryside beyond the Keep." She turned back to stirring the pot. "I don't reckon I ever shall."

A silence fell between them, filled by the bubbling water.

"I can't stand them," Joanne said.

"Who?"

"Lady Bodaline and her granddaughters. Do you know what they did?"

"No."

"They embarrassed me in front of my father and now took my books."

"I'm sorry."

"It's not your fault. Never apologize for someone else."

"They sound like wretched creatures."

"Yes. Yes, they are."

"Are you going to—" Selene left the thought unfinished, snapping her mouth closed.

"Get rid of them?" Joanne finished the thought for her.

Selene nodded.

"No, I can't. How would it look if my new lady-in-waiting turned up dead in very much the same way as my tutor? There aren't any more cooks to blame. Father suspects me as it is, so I can't. I must be on my best behavior until I can find another way to dispose of them."

"Couldn't you dismiss them?"

"Mother won't allow it." Joanne gave a long sigh. "I guess I must endure them, for now."

"We all have our burdens to bear."

Some have it easier than others.

"Why did you come down here?" Selene asked.

"To see you."

"Why?"

"Because you are the only decent human being in the entire Keep. Everyone else is pretentious, hiding behind their smiles and deeds, all the while waiting to rise up to a new station in life, or hold onto the power no matter who it harms." Joanne touched Selene's shoulder and traced her fingers up the slender neck and to the warm cheek, damp with sweat. She stepped in closer and Selene retreated a step, too close to the fire. "I'm just as bad as any of them. That's why I come. To be reminded of the good things in life. Does it bother you?"

Selene blushed.

"It does bother you." Anger rose up in her. "Fine! Be that way. I won't come see you again." As she reached the kitchen door, she turned back. "You can choke on that lye for all I care."

Joanne returned to her room and threw herself onto the bed. She buried her face into her pillow and cried. Cried until sleep took her. In a dark dream, the Mistress of Shadows came. This time, Joanne didn't hide, not that she could if she wanted to, but sat by the wood pile and listened. The Mistress of Shadow's words reminded her how terrible life was for the powerless. They brought Joanne comfort. In the late afternoon when she woke, she knew she had captured the eye of a goddess. Anything could be hers. Anything.

CHAPTER FOUR:
A PROPOSAL

To slay a monster, one must become a monster.
—Lord Desmond, moments before executing King Reuban

The seasons moved along, achingly slow. Moments of tedium broken by the endless prattle of Lady Bodaline instructing Joanne the "proper" ways to dress for various dinner parties, meeting with dignitaries, for balls and an endless list of events, all which never happened. She was scolded for choosing the wrong spoon to eat her soup, for slurping— gods how could you not slurp soup!— and for using her fingers instead of a knife to spread jam on her bread. She was rarely allowed to venture outdoors, unless it was to exercise in the gardens— which meant walking and not running around. Either Susie or Beaty always accompanied her. Even at night she was never alone; Lady Bodaline's granddaughters took turns sleeping in bed alongside Joanne. They even followed her to the garderobe. Joanne couldn't speak to Selene even if she had wanted to. She wrote her a long note, apologizing for her behavior, but crumpled it up and tossed it in the fire, realizing the scullery maid couldn't read. Others could, and they might punish Joanne by hurting Selene.

They tried teaching Joanne how to knit and stitch, play the lute and drink tea while listening to conversations. Joanne lacked the patience, tangling the yarn up, pricking her fingers and once tossed the lute against the wall where it shattered, playing a final, somber note. Joanne wished she had a book, but they stayed hidden, collecting dust behind her headboard.

Several mornings she'd watch her brothers practice with swords in the yard. She noticed how Thomas used brute strength to defeat his opponent while Alfred developed clever deception, luring his attacker in before striking a vicious blow. She dreamed of being outside, wielding a wooden sword rather than being chastised for the crooked cross-stitch.

She had rare interactions with either Lady Amaria or Lord Desmond. When her first blood came on the Yule night during a cold snow storm, Beaty, not Lady Amaria, had to explain to Joanne that she wasn't dying.

"Mother's blood," Beaty explained, helping Joanne wash the blood from her legs. "This will happen every full moon, so you have to be prepared."

"*Every* full moon?" Blood flowing from her underbelly every full-moon sounded like a punishment. Blood weeping for the blood of Teresa.

"Unless you are pregnant, then you get bloated for nine months."

"What about my brothers?"

"The only blood they'll have is when they slice their fingers on a blade."

Mother, why'd you make me a woman? Boys have all the fun.

Her chest ached. Her belly ached. Often together, but worse apart.

Yule gave way to Planters. Along with the Sowers Rains, came Joanne's fourteenth name day.

Joanne woke before first light, Beaty snoring quietly beside her. She preferred having Beaty sleep beside her over Susie, because Susie thrashed in her sleep, making squeaking noises like a mouse being chased by a cat. Joanne lifted the cover and slid out. She tip-toed across the room and opened the door. A small object wrapped in cheese cloth was on the floor outside her door. She picked it up and unwrapped the cloth. A soft spice cake soaked in honey was inside.

Selene? She looked up and down the corridor. It was empty. Had to be Selene. No one else would bother taking such care to bring her her favorite cake. It had been a tradition for the last four name days. Cook Mathers would make her the cake and Joanne would wake to Selene holding the small present on a plate. The spice cake felt heavier than a rock. She had betrayed both, and yet, here was the gift.

Maybe I am forgiven.

The dead cannot forgive. Her stomach soured and she wrapped the cake back into the cheese cloth. When she got the chance, she would sneak to the kitchens and thank Selene. The gaggle of hens continuously pecking at her could roost for now. It was her name day; she deserved a moment of peace. She went back to throw on some cloths and begin her escape. Beaty sat up, stretched and yawned.

"What's that?" Beaty asked.

"Spice cake," Joanne said. "It's my name day tradition."

"Already?" Beaty said. "Mother bless you and Father keep you safe for another. Oh, I have nearly forgotten! A much grander gift arrives this morrow for you."

"What is it?"

"I cannot say," Beaty said. "It would ruin the surprise."

"I'm not sure I like the idea of a surprise."

"Doesn't matter, I'm still not telling you."

Maybe it's a horse. I have a stable full of them, though I am not allowed to ride. She split the spice cake in half and offered it to Beaty. Together they ate. "I hope it's a dragon."

"Be careful what you wish for."

Lady Bodaline bustled into the room, Susie not far behind.

"Rise and shine, ladies." The older woman clapped her hands together three times.

"You're right," Joanne said to Beaty. "I already have a dragon."

Both girls burst into laughter.

"When you two are finished giggling like a gaggle of geese, we have a young lady to prepare for her name day presentation."

Lady Bodaline gave her a choice of dresses: a blue gown the color of a Sower's sky, pleated bodice covering her shoulders and a modest neckline, or a cream-colored silk one, smooth as honey-laced milk. *White is for the innocent*, her father's words echoed in her head. She chose the blue gown.

They braided her hair and painted her nails. She never understood why they painted her nails, because she wore matching gloves covering her fingers, hands, and forearms. White stockings constricted her legs and blue slippers were placed on her feet. It all seemed excessive for her name day presentation. Especially since her previous thirteen, or the ones she could remember, were spent in a simple dress as she gathered flowers in the gardens or lazed about, sipping sweetened hibiscus teas, eating spiced cake and playing with her dolls.

No one explained the reason for such detailed preparations. They added a gold chain and a sprinkle of rosewater, which made Joanne sneeze. Lady Bodaline smiled, an almost genuine affection making her seem younger, her face more cherub and less doughy. Joanne didn't trust her any less.

"When do we breakfast?" her stomach grumbled.

"After, my dear." Lady Bodaline said, sickly sweet voice poured over pride. She reached out and pinched Joanne's cheeks, hard between thumb and forefinger. Joanne winced and knocked the older woman's hands away. Lady Bodaline grinned. "For a bit more color. Yule made you so pale, ghastly. Now you look more alive."

Last person who touched me no longer is alive! She hadn't thought about her tutor, or had nightmares, for a very long time. Not since Cook Mather's hanging. Although, she did fantasize about the ways her lady-in-waiting could die, mostly in moments of boredom.

A servant knocked on the door. Joanne turned, hoping to see Selene. She was disappointed. A comely girl, much older than Selene, and much wider, cast her eyes around the room. She wore the house livery, showing the dagger and thorny rose above her right breast, marking her as a personal servant, most likely attached to Lady Amaria. A smile flashed on the servant's face and her eyes widened a moment before she recovered her neutral demeanor. The woman's expressions and reaction were all the reflection Joanne needed to view her beauty. She stood straighter, like one of those preening birds in Teresa's books.

"Is milady ready?" the servant asked.

"Yes, yes, we will be right down." Lady Bodaline scrutinized Joanne and bobbed her head like a duck snatching a fish. "A picture of near-perfection, Qetesh bless me."

Qetesh? Invoking the goddess of love seemed strange. Before she could consider it further, Joanne was swept out of her room and to the staircase. Lady Bodaline led the procession while her granddaughters took up the rear.

The servant met them at the bottom of the stairs and took them to the East Annex. Chatter echoed down the hall. *A name day party this early in the morning?* It would explain the care given to her dress and lack of breakfast. She hoped there would be a table full of food. Spice cake and other sweets. Maybe Selene would be serving, then she might get in a word or two without her entourage overhearing. A simple thanks. Or perhaps a kiss on the cheek. Maybe an apology for the way she ignored her.

"I'm sorry," Joanne mumbled.

"My apologies, but did you say something?" Lady Bodaline asked.

"No," Joanne said.

"Remember, a lady doesn't mutter her words," her high-pitched sonorous voice cut through the din. "She speaks clearly when the circumstances demand, or she remains quiet, smiles and listens."

"Yes, lady Bodaline, she listens to the prattle of self-important people." Joanne grinned.

"If that's what it takes." Lady Bodaline sniffed and marched through the Grand Hall.

People filled the Hall, splitting it in half. Those dressed in dark blue to the left and bright reds to the right. At the center was a table full of food. Sweet meats, honey mead, wine and spiced cake caught her attention. Her stomach rumbled and she headed for the platter of sweet meats. Lady Bodaline blocked her path.

"Eat *after* the guests have been introduced," she said, low enough for Joanne to hear.

Frowning, Joanne peered around the room. The din of chatter had ceased. A dozen faces turned in her direction. Lady Amaria flashed a satisfied smile, while Thomas and Alfred looked bored. On the opposite side of the table were people she had never seen before. They were all pale, as though they just blew in from a snow storm. At the forefront was a striking young man, blonde hair neatly cut and oiled back, strong chin and sharp nose. He wore a red uniform, well-cut to display his strong figure and a golden sun emblem on each shoulder. Beside him were more men in plainer uniform.

Behind them a boy sneezed. His face was pox marked, deep pits puckered in angry red and pink on his pale forehead, nude chin and cheeks. His cloths hung off his stooped, thin torso, like he stole them from a scarecrow.

A high-pitched squeak escaped his throat every time he exhaled. Thin black hair covered his flaky scalp, white flakes covering the slopped, red shoulders. Blue, rheumy eyes watered as he stared at Joanne as though she was a morsel to eat.

A fool to accompany a prince's retinue?

Joanne's belly churned and she turned back to the cool gaze of her mother.

Her father's words returned to her. *"One day you will marry a prince."*

Lord Desmond wasn't a part of the crowd.

"Joanne, come here, my dear," Lady Amaria said, a forced smile on her lips to match the false endearment in her voice.

Joanne went to her mother and nearly flinched when she placed her hands on her shoulder, holding her out like a present. She even had the pretty packaging, lacking only the bow. Her mother's touch was light, as though she would dirty her fingers with any harder a grip.

"Lords of the Northern Kingdom, I present to you our youngest, and only daughter, Joanne Desmond." Lady Amaria sounded eager. A nervous, cold feeling sunk in Joanne's belly. Why were there representatives of Seaptum in the Keep? These savage northerners, killers of Henrick! She would rather spit on them, than share so much as a crumb. She felt her lips curl into a sneer, but fought them back, twitching into what she hoped was a smile. Lady Amaria continued to speak, every word sending shivers down Joanne's spine and shards of ice into her gut. "This morn marks her fourteenth name day. Her maiden's blood has flowed and she has reached womanhood. She is ready to be wedded and to produce a multitude of heirs."

One day you'll marry a prince.

Did her father sell her off at so young an age?

"We are grateful for this meeting," the taller youth with sun emblems on his shoulders spoke. "I am Gallium, Prince of Seaptum, second son of King Dryd, guardian of the realm belonging to the Mother and Father. This here is Fraum, eldest son of King Dryd of Seaptum. Heir to the—"

Fraum let out a big sneeze, rocking his head forward, nearly cracking it against the table edge, and bobbing back up. Loud, wet sniffles followed by wiping gleaming snot onto his red sleeves.

"Heir to the Silver Throne," Gallium finished, giving a tight smile.

I think I am going to throw up. Joanne tried to step back, but her mother held her out. A human sacrifice. *Mother, if you ever loved me, let me be betrothed to Gallium, not this pink-headed rag of snot.*

"Don't tell me you started without me," Lord Desmond said, entering the Hall. "My apologies for my late arrival."

"You have come in time for introductions," Lady Amaria said, and gave a soft laugh.

"I am acquainted with our guests."

"My father sends his greetings, and his regrets for not accompanying us to this wonderful land," Gallium bowed his head. "He sends these gifts and this treatise bearing his royal seal in exchange for good faith agreement between our lands. May we find peace and live as the gods intended."

"Peace as the gods intended," they all spoke, touching their lips and their foreheads. Everyone except for Fraum. He was busy holding back another sneeze, nose wrinkled like a pig about to wallow in mud.

"We keep our good faith," Lord Desmond took Joanne's hand in his own warm one, "by offering our daughter's hand in marriage one year from this date, on her fifteenth name day."

Joanne's legs became melted wax, ready to spread across the floor, and she had an urgent need to pee. She allowed her father to lead her to Gallium, heart pounding now in her ears. Her face flushed warm. The white glove was removed from her right hand and Joanne reached out to Gallium—the striking young man moved to the side—and her hand touched Fraum's pale lumpy flesh. Her fingers curled back in revulsion. His squeaking breath grew louder and he made a sharp gasp, a strangled clicking noise in his throat. His hand was cold, wet and sticky. Her gorge rose up, but she swallowed the hot, bitter vomit.

"I accept," Fraum said in a nasally voice.

Unable to contain her horror, Joanne broke free of Fraum's grip and ran for the door. Lady Bodaline tried to step in her path, but Joanne shoved her, a harsh gasp coming from the lady-in-waiting's gut. She leapt up the stairs two at a time, ignoring the clamor behind her. Bedroom door slammed and she tossed herself onto the bed, slurpy tears soaking her pillow.

"You decline this match?" Lord Desmond stood in her doorway. His voice was low. She knew that tone. Although he sounded in control, reasonable, it was a warning, a flash of lightening before the thunderous downpour.

"I can't marry him, father," she said and sat up, swiping away her tears. "He's a monster."

"What the gods take away in physical nature they make up for in other ways." He entered the room and stood before her bed. "They have a great wealth, greater than you'll ever find in Nemus. Their military strength is unprecedented. You'll be queen and rule over it all, uniting Nemus and Seaptum for countless generations."

I don't care if I am queen of everything above and below. Not if it meant being married to that hideous deformity.

"Please, Father, no."

His hand was swift. Joanne's head rocked back and she toppled across her bed.

"I'll mark you so you're ugly, too." Lord Desmond took out his belt knife and pinned his prostate daughter on the mattress. The sting of his words and hand burned upon her cheek. Watching the blade's tip hover over her eye, Joanne's bladder loosened. A flick of the wrist and the sharp edge would slice her flesh cheek to jaw as simple as tearing a petal from a rose. She had seen him do it to Cook Mather's nose. "Then you will be the right match for him. A pair of godsforsaken beasts rutting together to produce more vile creatures."

Joanne shut her eyes, whimpering.

"*Please, Father, no,*" he mocked and leaned in over her face so she could see the scar he suffered leading men in a charge against the Wise Council— a war which sealed his control over the land. Spittle hung from his lips. "Insolent bitch! After all I have done for you. To secure your future, to save—"

He broke off, punching the bed beside Joanne's head. The force of his anger made her squeak.

"I'm sorry, please stop," Joanne said, trying to pull her pinned arms away from her sides. Her father's thighs held them tight. The knife point that had eased away, came close again.

"Remember the garden? Remember the flowers and the bees?"

"Yes," Joanne said, although her mind drew blank on it.

"You have one purpose. One singular purpose."

His weight on her chest made it difficult for her to breath.

"I will do it." Joanne gasped. "I swear to marry F—Fraum. I will do my duty, like the bees and the flowers."

The blade disappeared and the bed creaked as Lord Desmond's weight released her. He straightened his blue uniform. She noticed for the first time how he was dressed as though ready to lead men into battle, minus his armor. Joanne let out a strangled breath, tears rolling down the sides of head and dribbling into her ears.

"You will come down and apologize for your behavior. Nerves over the engagement. Upset stomach. You passed out and hit your face on the wall." Lord Desmond explained each part very slowly. "Repeat it."

"I will apologize for my nerves, nervous over the engagement. My stomach hurt and I had to hurry away. I passed out and hit my face on the wall." She pressed her hand to the mark, wincing at the sharp pain. She sniffed back more tears and climbed from bed.

"Good." Lord Desmond turned his back on her. "Try not to muck it up."

Her tear-blurred eyes tracked him. Beaty curtsied as Lord Desmond stalked past.

"You made quit the impression," she said. Holding out a kerchief, she dabbed at Joanne's eyes. The tenderness of it made her want to cry again. "My grandmother made an excuse. Saying you were feeling ill."

"Was the prince upset?" Joanne imagined Fraum was furious, probably throwing a huge fit and tossing plates of food about. That's what she would have done in his stead.

"Your prince charming snorted so loud I thought he had defecated all over himself. Turns out the snort is his way of laughing without choking on his own breath," Beaty said. "I don't envy your position, milady."

"We have a full year before the wedding," Joanne said. "Maybe he might choke to death on his snot."

"Maybe," Beaty said, linking her arm through Joanne's. "Gods only know what will happen."

Gods are cruel, truly cruel. They are probably laughing, if they notice me at all.

In the Grand Hall Joanne recited her lines exactly as her father proclaimed. Prince Fraum patted her hand, upper lips gleaming and he wheezed, red nostrils flaring. She did her best not to steal her hand away from his clammy touch. She sat beside him, shoulders rounded so she wouldn't accidentally touch him. He grinned, bits of cake stuck between yellowed teeth.

Joanne picked at her plate, appetite lost, perhaps permanently.

"This must come as such a surprise," Prince Gallium said, almost sympathetic.

"Surprises are expected on one's name day," Joanne said and glanced at Beaty seated beside Lady Bodaline. She smiled demurely, as though at a private joke. *She knew. She knew I was to be engaged to a monster.*

"I assure you, milady, there will be a few more. Pleasant ones." Prince Gallium smiled to show his jest, though his meaning, whether intended or not, was clear to Joanne. Fraum shifted uncomfortably, making a gurgling noise in the back of his throat at his brother's comment. The moment passed as Prince Gallium raised his cup. Others followed suit. A dozen cups held in her direction like executioner arrows. "Health to my soon to be sister. May you have many more name days and they find you in great joy and wealth. Mother bless you and Father keep you safe."

"Well said," Lord Desmond replied. They collectively drank. "We have rooms prepared. You and your brother, Fraum, shall stay here at the Keep for the remainder of your visit."

"Which must be brief," Prince Gallium said.

Not brief enough. Joanne lifted her cup and drank off the bitter mead. She offered it up again for it to be refilled. She nearly spilled it upon seeing Selene holding the pitcher ready to pour. The young serving girl kept a blank face, though her cheeks blushed. She looked older, prettier than last Joanne saw her.

"Thank you," Joanne said. *Qetesh knows how much I miss your face.*

Selene nodded and returned to her station on the back wall.

"We spend the night and leave at first light," Prince Gallium said. "I am sure this gives our newly betrothed time to pack."

Joanne spit a mouthful of mead back into her cup.

"What?"

"You are to return with Prince Fraum and myself to your new home."

"So soon," Lady Amaria said.

"I am afraid so, milady," Prince Gallium said. "Your daughter's safety is our upmost concern. The Sowers rains will fall and I don't want to be caught out in the floods."

"Isn't the wedding next Sower?" Joanne asked. "Why am I to go now?"

"Because I want it so." Fraum wheezed. "To be better acquainted before we wed."

Joanne looked to her father for help.

"A wise decision," Lord Desmond said. He refused to acknowledge Joanne. *Shouldn't surprise you after he threatened to slice up your face and make you as hideous as your betrothed.* She wanted to hate him for the reaction, for ignoring her even now, but all she felt was a lump in her throat as she held back tears.

"Am I to go alone?"

"You will want for nothing," Prince Gallium said.

Except for friends. She could count those on one hand, and still have fingers left over. Better to have a few people she could trust, then none at all. Alone in the land of her enemy… it would be like dying of thirst in a sea of water. With one crusty, scum coated flask to provide succor.

"She may bring a lady-in-waiting," Fraum said. His voice cracked and he smiled. Leaning into her, his shoulder brushing against hers, he whispered. "A name day present for you."

"Two." Joanne blurted, nearly jumping from her seat.

Prince Gallium narrowed his eyes at her.

Fraum shrugged his thin shoulders.

"As you wish."

"I would be most honored—" Lady Bodaline said.

"Beaty." Joanne cut her off, then looked behind her. The servants were all watching her, except for one. "Selene."

The young serving girl startled, spilling mead onto her smock.

"Done," Fraum said.

"They must be ready by first light," Prince Gallium said, sounding annoyed. "Or they get left behind."

"Why me?" Selene asked. "Don't they have enough young girls to wash the dishes and dust the linens?"

"I'm sure they do," Joanne said. "You won't be in the galley."

Selene tilted her head.

"Where will I be?"

"In my chamber." Joanne scanned her room for the things she couldn't bear to leave behind. There were a few items. She ruffled behind the bed's headboard and brought out the books she had saved. "You will protect me from that creature they force on me for a husband."

"I don't know how to fight or hold a sword."

"Not yet." She placed the books in her chest on top of some clothes and moved to her wardrobe to make certain she didn't miss anything. *A sword won't be what you need in this situation. You have all I desire.*

"Who will train me?" Selene whined. She had a knapsack containing all her valuables, which wasn't much. Joanne wondered why the younger girl would bother to bring anything beyond a few outfits since she would be adorned in dresses more elaborate than any she had ever seen. "It isn't right for a lady to fight with a sword."

"In Seaptum, all the women fight with swords."

"All?" Selene narrowed her eyes.

"Fine, some do," Joanne handed Selene some small clothes to pack in a wooden chest. "They have a story of a great woman warrior. Gethalda was her name and she was not much older than Beaty. The men were away fighting or hunting, leaving those too ill, or old to travel. A great bear, starving from the cold and smelling the food roasting over the fires came into the village. He killed a woman in her home, stole her child and would have escaped with the boy in his teeth. Gethalda took up her sword and chased the bear down before it disappeared into the trees. Claws and teeth were no match for Gethalda's sword skills."

"She killed the bear?"

"Yes, but the bear had her head in its great mouth. As she ran the sword through its heart, her head was crushed."

"What about the boy?"

"Froze to death before anyone was brave enough to venture out looking for him."

"That's not a very happy story."

"I never said it was."

"So, we will be fighting bears?"

"Where we are going, I think is larger than a village."

"I have never left the Keep's grounds."

"Me, either." Joanne stared out the window. "Foster's Manor is basically the same and this place. Anyway, this should prove quite the adventure."

CHAPTER FIVE:
DISCOVERIES

Not all journeys end in discovery.
The most important one leads to the self.
—Philosophia en Vitae

Morning light came too soon. Joanne rolled over. Selene's warm body pressed against hers—neither Susie nor Beaty came to help her undress and prepare for bed. Lady Bodaline was probably upset that Joanne didn't choose her or her youngest grandchild. Not that Joanne could trust Beaty, but she got along with her best of the three. She was satisfied with her choice for ladies-in-waiting. Selene stared up at the ceiling.

"What are you thinking about?" Joanne asked softly.

"I don't understand anything," Selene said.

"Of course not," Joanne said. "You were brought up to dress and care for me, then to wash dishes. What else could you learn during that time?"

"Unlike Beaty."

Was there a hint of jealousy?

"She was born into wealth. You weren't." Joanne leaned on her elbows, trying to catch the younger girl's eyes. Selene kept them on the ceiling like there was something more interesting up there, besides a cobweb and spiders. "I don't know why you are carrying on like this? Don't you want to go?"

"As you pointed out, I don't know much else besides dressing you and scrubbing pots." A tear slipped down her cheek. "I think you're mocking me, or chose me to spite others."

When Joanne picked Selene over Lady Bodaline, the baffled look on the older woman's face was satisfying. Her own mother refused to say a single word to her the rest of the evening, while her father brooded. Only Alfred dared speak to her, giving her a small ring, big enough to fit her little finger, a green stone set in the silver metal. "To remember your favorite brother," he said, and kissed her cheek before gallivanting off to admire the Seaptum horses in the stalls. They were much larger than horses found in Nemus, possessing a thicker coat and mane to keep them warm in the snows. All information she'd found in her former tutor's book.

"I chose you," Joanne said, caressing the younger girl's smooth skin, tracing the back of her fingers down the jawline. "Because I trust you. That's more than enough reason, more than I'll speak on. You have two choices. Remain here, scrubbing pots, marrying some stable boy, bear lots of children, who will in turn serve my family."

She turned Selene's head. *Such beautiful eyes. Frightened, yet full of desire.*

"Or you may come with me and become my lady-in-waiting. Perhaps one day marry a noble man and order around your own castle of servants."

"I want to go," Selene whispered.

"You won't regret your choice." Joanne brushed Selene's warm lips with her own. Pressing a light kiss and then proceeded to tickle the girl. Poking her ribs, stroking her neck, and finger tips running over hard nipples of budded breasts. Selene giggled and squirmed away.

The bedroom door opened.

"If you don't want to be left behind—" Beaty said, voice trailing off. She stood in the doorway, arms crossed and frowned. "This is no time for games. Are you even packed and ready to leave?"

"Yes." Joanne threw a pillow and it struck Beaty in her disapproving face. A strand of hair puffed up and both girls giggled again in the bed. "If you are going to frown and pout the entire time, maybe you should be left behind."

"Then you'd have to take my grandmother," Beaty said, throwing the pillow back at her. "Should I tell her to gather her things?"

"You'll do no such thing!" Joanne threw off the bed covers and stood with her arms up. After a few moments of Beaty and Selene staring at her, she huffed. "Well, are you going to dress me or not?"

Donning a simple blue dress and boots, Joanne made her way down the stairs trailed by Beaty and Selene. Lady Bodaline gave a demure nod of her head when Joanne passed. *Any colder and I would need a fur coat.* A grin lifted her wrinkled jowls at her granddaughter's approach. Joanne expected more weeping, or at least a tearful embrace from the old woman, but to her credit, she didn't flinch beyond the smile and Beaty kept her place. Joanne smiled. Beaty now belonged to her until she no longer wanted her.

Next in line were her brothers, Thomas and Alfred. Thomas ignored her, leering at Selene who shrank away. If she hadn't chosen the scullery maid as one of her own, she was certain Thomas would get a bastard or two on her. Removing his pleasure made the decision even sweeter. *He'll just find another poor girl to rut on.* She couldn't save them all. Not without gelding her brother.

Alfred wrapped his arms around her, nearly knocking her over.

"I'm going to miss you, Joey," he said and kissed both of her cheeks. Motioning to her wheezing betrothed, he added: "If Lord Snot-Pus gives you any trouble, let me know and I will ride up there and kick him in the sack."

"Thank you," Joanne said. "I will be fine." *I'm going to be a queen. No one would hurt a queen.*

Alfred squeezed her hand and stepped back in line. Thomas elbowed him in the ribs and mouthed some degrading comment to him while he rubbed his side.

Near the end of the line, Lady Amaria and Lord Desmond waited. Lady Amaria lifted her arms like she would embrace her daughter. She settled for a pat on her shoulders, looking over her head. She sniffed. "Yes," was her only comment, responding to a question only she knew, but it confirmed so much for Joanne. She would never see her mother again.

And that was fine.

Her father's gaze made her want to shake. No matter how many layers of clothes she wore, everything was bare, open and raw for him to sift through with those piercing eyes. All her desires, fears, and wrongdoings. He knew. Chiseled in his stone features. She expected an accusation of murder and conspiracy, to be dragged away and chained in a dark place, her screams unheard as she wasted away. A ghost to haunt the depths. Whispers of the princess that once was, a queen never to be.

Instead, he knelt. Gripping her arms in his large hands, fingers light, at eye level, her equal in this measure. His stone-gray eyes softened and he seemed almost mortal.

"Joanne, you have my blessing and all of Nemus at your disposal." She teared up at the declaration. "When next we meet you will be a princess, then a queen. Be harsh, yet fair. Strong and compassionate, but never let compassion make you weak. You are and always will be a Desmond. Unify the lands. Remember your garden and tend each flower well."

"Yes, father." A wall had broken inside her and she threw her arms around his neck. For another instance, she felt his warm embrace. He kissed her forehead and stood over her, no longer the frightening mountain looming above, ready to crush her, but a fortification she would leave behind. "Gods bless you and safe travels."

"Is milady ready to go?" Prince Gallium asked.

Joanne nodded, words stuck in her throat.

He offered her an arm and then escorted her from the Keep. Servants of both Houses were loading carts lined up in the main yard. She looked around and didn't see her husband-to-be. Then she heard a sneeze. It came from the doorway of a large, black carriage. There were no insignias to mark it as anything different from any other common carriage she had seen at rare festival held at the Keep. No gold inlays, the horses appeared to be average gray geldings, and the driver wore an indistinct uniform. It was the only carriage in the entire retinue of open carts and wagons, but other than that, it could be any one wealthy enough to own a carriage.

"Best we be inconspicuous when travelling rather unfriendly territories," Prince Gallium said, noticing her scrutinize the carriage. With the door opened, she could hear his brother's moist breathing. *How did he not drown in his own snot?* Black curtains hung over the windows and the inside looked very dark, like he was in a different world where it was still night.

"He doesn't like the sun," Prince Gallium said and smiled. "Or I should say, the sun doesn't care much for him."

"A good thing he is from the north," Joanne said.

"Yes, otherwise he would have died from overexposure long ago," he said. Joanne heard a bit of sadness, though Prince Gallium gave her an earnest look.

And leave you Crowned Prince.

"That would be tragic, for you to lose a brother," Joanne said. "I lost my eldest brother in the war,"

"A great loss."

"He died fighting your men." She studied his face, but he didn't betray any thought or feeling this time.

"The war has ended." Prince Gallium held her hand. It was warm, strong, and assuring. He brought it up and kissed her fingers. "Beauty has tamed the beast."

We shall see. She smiled and let her hand linger in his. The moment passed swiftly. Prince Gallium helped her climb the three steps up to the interior. She ducked her head under the eave. A strong odor, bitter and yet, sickly sweet struck her. Joanne coughed, covering her mouth to hide her disgust. Prince Fraum huddled in the dark corner, blankets wrapped around his frail form. He wheezed and sniffled. Runny red eyes stared at her in an unreadable expression that could either be disgust or desire. Joanne's legs stiffened. Panic nibbled at her courage. She forced herself to move, to climb in and sit on the plush cushions. Being alone, breathing the sickly-sweet stench for gods-knew-how-long it took to arrive at their destination, the wheezing, choking, and sticky, rheumy-eyed glances, seemed more daunting than her bravery could muster.

"May I have my ladies accompany us?" she asked.

"One," Prince Fraum said. Spittle ran down his chin and he grinned, revealing yellowed teeth. "I wouldn't want you believing I am always indulgent."

"You are very kind." She fought her gullet to keep the remnants of her meager breakfast down. She wanted to call for Selene, but thought better of it. Beaty would display better decorum in this situation.

"Please send for Lady Beaty," Joanne said to the man at the door. Prince Gallium remained close-by giving instructions to plain-clothed, yet armed men.

"I will see to her arrival myself," Prince Gallium said, breaking off the conversation. He bowed to her and gave his brother a nod.

Prince Fraum continued to look at her and she shifted uncomfortably. His eyes narrowed, slipping into slits and for a moment she thought he might have fallen asleep. His chest rose and fell, a funny squeaking noise sounded every time he exhaled. She began to relax and settled into the cushion, teeth grating against the squeaks. She wasn't sure how long the trip north would take. Those rheumy eyes on her and wet, squelching noises would drive her mad. Even accompanied by Selene or Beaty. She would have to ask to ride in a cart just to escape.

Escape.

For how long?

She was to be married to him and all his glory.

"You find my brother pleasing to look at?"

Joanne jumped, heart pounding. His eyes were back on her. Red and sticky. She took a breath, thought about lying and decided against it.

"Yes."

Prince Fraum wheezed and coughed, holding up a stained handkerchief to his mouth. A string of spittle connected it to his chapped lips. "What about me?" Wet eyes seemed to stare into her, the way her father's had.

"Y-yes," she said, cursing the hesitation.

His hand shot out from the blanket and gripped her arm. Fingers pinched her flesh, stronger than she'd image he could be in such a sickly state. He yanked her arm and she squeaked in fear more than pain.

"Don't. Ever. Lie to me." He wheezed louder between each word, punching them with a strong shake. Her teeth clicked and she bit the tip of her tongue. Blood filled her mouth. He dragged her closer, so her face was close to his own. "Do you understand?"

Footfalls approached and her heart pounded. Prince Gallium might be able to save her from this monster once he saw how he tried to pull her arm off like a boy plucking wings from a fly. If he treated her this way before they left her father's Keep, how would he be when in his own land? She could scream. Call it all off.

The war has ended. A reminder of her purpose. A token in the treatise. The prize, the martyr of peace. Her placement among the flowers and bees. Joanne stiffened her chin and nodded.

"Good." Prince Fraum released her. "Remember."

"We will be leaving shortly," Prince Gallium said, glancing at Fraum's hand on her arm. Joanne blushed, her skin prickling and she felt hot and cold, her heart pumping in fear and something else that she couldn't identify. "I am glad to see you two getting on so well."

"Thank you, Prince Gallium." Joanne held Prince Fraum's gaze, fearful of what the sick Prince might do if she looked away. Maybe bite her like a rabid dog, which he pretty much did already. Her arm hurt where his fingers had pinched her. Then Fraum smiled, almost friendly, gave her a gentle pat, and retracted his hand.

"Good morrow, both of you." The carriage door shut and Joanne looked away from her betrothed. Across from her Beaty sat, hands demurely in her lap. She showed no sign of reacting to the carriage's stench. A look of concern remained unspoken, but clear on her face. Joanne gave a smile to signal all was well. Easier to lie without words.

"Would you be so kind as to pull the drapes closed," Prince Fraum said. The threat had left his voice and he sounded almost apologetic. "The sun makes me ill."

Joanne watched him, waiting for him to snarl or smack Beaty for moving too slowly. Instead, Fraum settled into his blankets, rheumy eyes narrowing on Joanne. She felt his coldness and wondered how he could ever love. How could she ever love him?

Beaty secured the black curtains, cutting off all but a little light. Soon the carriage began to rock sided-to-side, jerking forward. Joanne's fingers twitched to brush aside a curtain, to take one last look at her home. She tightened them until nails dug into her palms. No need to upset the Crowned Prince any more than he already was. Closing her eyes, she allowed herself to drift, listening to the monotonous squeak of the carriage wheels and wheezing from her betrothed's nose.

The fresh smell of cut wood impinged by pungent damp rot drew her attention to the wood pile. It seemed familiar, like she had been here before, although she had never left the Keep or Foster's Manor. A dark red stain marred the central part of the wood stack and darkened the soil. Her bare toes sank into the loamy ground and she backed away from the stain. Light dimmed and a shadow moved over her. A mist appeared, a dark hole in the air. She heard a crow cry in the distance, the only sound outside her own breathing.

Who are you? She asked, reaching back for a chunk of wood to defend herself. The move felt familiar, almost rehearsed, like she had asked the same question, reached for the same chunk of wood hundreds of times before. Blessed Mother and Father, she couldn't remember why or when.

You know who I am, child. The mist took shape. A woman wearing a dark cloak and black trousers appeared, arms folded and head leaning forward to hide her face in the cloak. Lightning flashed in the distance and Joanne heard waves, as though they were close to the sea. A bell tolled. *You need me.*

I don't. Joanne said. *Not yet.*

You need me. The hood slid over raven black hair. Her face was obscured in shadow. *He will kill you, otherwise.*

She didn't need to ask who the *he* was.

There will be war. One your father will lose, has lost. The shadow swept aside her retort. *I feel your need, child. That disgusting sack of pus placed his hands on you. Dared to treat you like a doll to be his play thing. You have killed for less.*

Less, hissed a voice from under the wood pile. A gray hand, dirt-streaked and covered in blood reached out, grasping her ankle. Joanne squealed and hopped out of reach. Cruel laughter followed scraping dirt. Teresa's red stained teeth grinned up at her. *Don't forget me. Don't forget what you've done.*

Or me. Dropping from a tree branch, rope tied around his neck, Cook Mathers' vertebra made a popping sound. Hooked fingers reached up for the rope and slid it over his head. He dropped to the ground, ankle twisting to the side. He lurched toward her. A rotting stench preceded Mathers and Joanne coughed, covering her nose and mouth in the crook of her arm. Cook Mathers grinned, a worm crawled between broken teeth. *You cooked my goose real good.*

What's one more? The shadow melted away from the woman's face. Pale, yet beautiful. Dark eyes stared at Joanne, hunger filled and Joanne shivered. *Doesn't he deserve it? Don't they all deserve to die for your dear brother Henrick?*

Yes, Joanne said. *Everyone* deserves *to die. There are no innocents.*

He is right beside you. Kill him and blame your servant. She offered a black gloved hand. *Let me help you.*

The sweet, lulling voice, dripped honey. Joanne imagined her hands around Prince Fraum's throat. His head smashed against the carriage door, nails tearing into his flesh as Beaty watched horrified, never knowing she would take the fall. Joanne would be returned to her home in the Keep, or maybe be forced to marry Prince Gallium instead. Prince Gallium, he would be next in line to the Seaptum throne. King Gallium and Queen Joanne.

I will be queen anyway, Joanne said. *Why take the risk?*

Clever girl, the shadow said. *Don't out-think yourself, or you may end up like your friends here.*

Teresa and Cook Mathers laughed, holding hands. Teresa gripped a bloody knife while Mathers dangled a rope.

We will be waiting for you, Teresa said.

Joanne jolted awake. It was dark and she felt lost between the dream and wherever here was. Across from her Beaty sat, watching her with indifference, her hands gripping the bench to keep from falling into Joanne's lap. Fraum moaned and stirred, shivering despite his blanket. Joanne reached over to adjust the blanket to cover his exposed shoulder, and faltered. Dark bruises covered her arm where he had grabbed her. She tried to cover it but, Beaty noticed the marks and frowned. Her eyes shot to Fraum and back to Joanne's arm. Joanne tucked it under her left one. She shrugged. It happened and there wasn't anything she could do about it. She learned a lesson, a harsh one. To always tell Prince Fraum the truth no matter how much it might hurt him, or her.

Beaty continued frowning, but didn't respond. Joanne was certain she would hear about it later.

The carriage door opened, sending a spear of light stabbing into her eyes. She blinked and held up a hand to block the painful jabs. A soft clunk marked a stool placed on the ground to aide in her exit. Beaty exited first, taking the hand of a dark uniformed servant. Joanne followed next, breathing in the fresh air, legs aching from being squashed in the carriage. The sun was at an angle marking the time just past midday. A small pavilion had been erected off to the side of the road, the grass covered in blue blankets. Pillows were set up around a small table, not much higher than Joanne's knees, at the center of the pavilion. Servants bustled around, placing cups and plates on the table.

Selene stood to the side, observing the proceedings, hands twisting together. *She's used to doing the serving and not watching others serve. I will have to keep her busy until she eases into her new role. So much easier to mindlessly act, than make choices that impact hundreds, thousands!* Joanne stretched her lower back and neck. The seats in the carriage cushioned, but too long sitting hurt all the same as if she slept on a wooden plank.

"Over here, Selene," Beaty called. "Milady needs our help."

Selene smiled with obvious relief at having a purpose.

"The scullery maid garb is out of place in your new position. Not that it was ever in fashion." Beaty clicked her tongue, taking in the simple brown smock Selene wore. "Don't you have something more appropriate to wear, girl?"

Selene blushed and shook her head.

"First thing I advise is getting her a proper gown befitting a lady-in-waiting," Beaty said.

"The second?" Joanne asked.

Beaty waited for a servant to pass out of hearing and lowered her voice. "Don't ever be in the company of either Princes without one of us present."

Prince Gallium smiled and waved her over to a cushion.

"Especially that one," Beaty said. "He is the most dangerous."

The pretty ones are the most dangerous.

"I will keep your words in my mind." Joanne made her way to a set of cushions, sensing Beaty and Selene following like shadows. It was their duty to watch after her while Joanne knew she had to present herself as congenial, even if she wanted to vomit and run away. Her father would never forgive her if she damaged this alliance—or worse as he had promised. Smile and talk pretty, though she seethed like a thorn in the sole of her foot. She sank into a cushion beside Prince Gallium. "Won't Fraum be joining us?"

"He'll not leave his carriage until well after the sun sets," Prince Gallium said, pouring a dark amber liquid into a cup and handing it to her. She smelled it—*honey mead*—and took a sip. "You'll hear whispers that he is a ghoul, but ignore them. He merely feasts on the blood of rodents."

She nearly choked on the mead, spilling some over the side of the cup and onto her travelling gown.

"It was a jest." Prince Gallium laughed.

"Look at what you gone and done." She scolded, setting the cup down. "I'll never hear the end of it from those two."

"They are only children." Prince Gallium waved away her concern. "Wasn't the scrawny one a laundress? She'll know how remove the stains once we get you out of the dress."

"Speak plainly," Joanne said, though her heartbeat quickened. "We are to be brother and sister in marriage."

"Forgive my quick tongue," Prince Gallium said. "It sometimes speaks before the words have been fully thought out. My father says it will be the end of me. That I'll insult someone much too large for me to handle, someone perhaps like yourself, and I'll end up with my neck in a noose."

"If you only knew, my Prince," Joanne said. "A tall tree fitting for such a tall-tale." She mimicked being lynched, then stopped. The horror of the dream returned— Cook Mather's vertebra popping as he hung and the worm squirming through his teeth.

"Eat up, my Princess," Prince Gallium said. "We don't break again until sunset."

"I have suddenly lost my appetite." Joanne drank the cup of mead, her head feeling lighter, light enough to float from her shoulders.

Prince Gallium frowned. "Was it something I said?"

"The gallows humor, please excuse me." She rocked forward, hitting a knee on the small table, nearly knocking everything over if it weren't for Gallium holding it steady. "I apologize." She stammered and stumbled off.

Beaty came instantly to her side.

"You are being too blunt," she said. "You need to know when to use a needle in place of a knife."

"Both poke holes and draw blood," Joanne said. She eyed the carriage, desiring nothing more than to lie down. Fraum was lurking inside. She could almost hear his wheezing rattling about like some cat choking on a hair ball. She settled on a spot of shade behind the carriage.

"The needle can stitch things up," Beaty said. "I suggest you practice on your mouth. Be silent and observe."

"What do you think?" Joanne asked Selene. The young girl nearly toppled over in surprise. "If you are going to be one of my ladies, then I require your advice as well. Speak up and be heard."

Selene glanced at Beaty. The older girl remained expressionless.

"They don't feel right," Selene said, hastily adding, "to me."

A pause as Joanne waited for Selene to share more, then she let out a sigh.

"You both win," Joanne said and slouched in the grass. "I will play the coy little mystery girl."

"There will be a time and place for you to speak up," Beaty said, touching Joanne's arm. Joanne winced and pulled away. "Especially when one is injured. You must never tolerate a man to hit you, or you will always suffer at his hands."

A servant brought a basket over to Joanne. It was full of apples with skin so golden they could have been plucked from the sun.

"From the Prince." He placed it at her feet, bowed, then left.

"Would you like to taste it to make sure it's not poisoned?" Joanne asked, holding up a golden apple. Beaty rolled her eyes and Joanne bit into it. The crisp crunch against her teeth, she chewed, letting the sweetness fill her mouth. "First thing I am going to do when I become a princess is send father enough of these trees to fill the entire lands of Nemus with this sweet, golden fruit."

"I think he'd prefer a different sort of gold," Beaty said.

All the gold and steel I can pry from the cold lands.

They broke camp and Joanne rejoined her betrothed in the carriage. It badly needed airing, smelling of sour sweat, urine, and some darker stink. Fraum slunked away from the light, cringing in his corner.

"Get in, get in," he said, slurping back some snot. "Sun's too bright, I don't know how you can stand it."

"Like all flowers, I require a bit of sunshine to bloom," Joanne said.

Fraum's rheumy eyes stared at her. They held as much warmth as icicles. He gave a smile, one to match his gaze. "I suppose. Take it all in while you can, because where we go, flowers don't bloom but once a year, and then they wither and die on the stems. It is those grown accustomed to the cold and darkness which live the longest and bloom the brightest." He finished by wiping his nose on his sleeve. The fringes of his tunic were getting a little crusty and the blue had streaks of greenish-yellow. Joanne felt her stomach turn, but she stared into those hard blue eyes.

"You'll find, my lord, I'm not the kind to easily wilt. My stem is made stern."

"Yes, I know of your tragedies," Fraum replied. "A brother and a tutor. One to a northern sword and the other a knife in the dark. A pity."

He didn't sound very empathetic. Then again, speaking through phlegm would make even the warmest words seem sickly. Fraum studied her, trying to gauge her reactions. Joanne smiled and nodded. Her true disgust buried beneath a mask. *Smile pretty and you can get away with anything. Even murder.*

"Will milady require warmer clothes?" Beaty asked Joanne, though she knew her maid made a clever address to Fraum.

"The finest seamstress and tailors will be at your ready to provide you with some comforts," Fraum said. "Though the fashion may be more modest than the whorish outfits I've noticed Nemus's ladies find appealing. No exposed shoulders and breasts like a common cow waiting for her udders to be stroked."

I wouldn't want to expose my arms around you, anymore.

"Prudent and sensible," Beaty said. "Preserve modesty at all times is a virtue in a ruler."

"Ruler!" Fraum snorted laughter, a bubble of snot coming from his left nostril. "She will have no power, any more than chip decides the outcome of a card hand, or an ass the burden it bears."

Charming as ever. Joanne forced the smile and willed her eyes not to roll.

"The role of women is clear in regards to maintaining the bloodlines connecting the right to rule, but a woman is an extension of her husband. Her actions are reflective of him and the throne," Beaty said. "Also, equally important is honoring the marriage contract that serves as a bond between two powerful houses in their respective lands."

Mother bless Beaty and her grandmother. Joanne knew if she tried to engage this slimy, little snot bucket who was to be her husband, in this power debate, she might end up punching him in the windpipe and crushing the wheeze from him. She chose well in Beaty. She could almost forgive Beaty's grandmother for being such an intolerable dusty twat.

"This talk of responsibility tires me," Fraum said. "Do either of you know a song that can sooth my aching head?"

Beaty shook her head.

Joanne sighed.

"I only know the lullabies that Selene used to sing to me, but I'm not of the best voice to grace your ears."

Fraum waved for her to continue.

Joanne began the song. It was about Sin and a man she fell in love with who happened to also be a pirate. As she sung, she recalled the forbidden romance between a goddess and a human. How Sin came down in human form, a young girl, to aide a small village who prayed for her intercession in harassment by men from the sea who would steal their children and sell them as slaves. Sin allowed herself to be captured by the pirate captain who was enraptured by Sin's beauty. The goddess plotted to kill him, but instead spared him as he begged for her heart. Caught up in lust and longing, Sin surrendered herself to the Pirate Captain in exchange for his vow never to bother the villagers again. She got pregnant in her human form and had twins whose fate was tied to the cycle of the moon— the first skin changers. Sin's lover broke his promise and turned to slaving again, and as his punishment, Sin occupied him and forced his ship into a devastating storm. She plead with Mother to allow him to Ascend, but she was denied. Her lover's soul was cast into Arula.

At the end of the song, Joanne was in tears at Sin's lament. Fraum, however, snored rather loud. Beaty squeezed her hand.

"Well sung," she said. She was also close to tears.

How could the gods be kind to humans when they were cruel to each other?

Fraum remained asleep until the carriage came to a halt. Joanne peeked out the of the shade and saw the silver moon rise over the tree tops. The western sky was a deep red, like blood spilt across the clouds and lit on fire.

"Beautiful, isn't it?" Fraum asked. "Like the burning of a city."

"How many cities have you watched burn?" Joanne asked.

"One."

Before he elaborated, the carriage door opened and the same footstool was in place. Fraum was allowed to exit first, followed by Joanne and Beaty. There was a soft breeze, warm and soothing after being cooped up inside the box with the foul air. Fraum wore a shawl like a shroud over his thin shoulders. He shuffled along like a man three times his age and one closer to his grave than his mother's womb.

This is what my father wants me to marry? What if he dies before the wedding ceremony?

Prince Gallium stood next to her, close enough that his shoulder brushed hers. Joanne side stepped close to Beaty.

"Forgive me. I didn't mean to startle you," Prince Gallium said, and smiled.

Watch out for that one.

"I'm not startled," Joanne said. "I'm not used to so much attention. Back at Foster's Manor, I was used to having freedom to explore when not under the watch of my tutor. Being cooped up like some bird in a wobbly cage isn't what I'd call the start of a wonderous adventure."

"This is only the first day," Prince Gallum said. "There are two more until we reach the borders of Halvorstrum in Seaptum, and then another two before we reach the gray walls of Argenti Lapisdom, if the weather holds and the roads are not boggy, tough at this time of year they are mostly clear and fields of poppies and moon stones to bring some cheer."

What about Dragon's Vein? She wanted to ask, but didn't think discussion of deadly flowers was a good way to foster trust.

"Sounds very tedious," Joanne said.

"Perhaps I might be able to convince my brother to let his little bird stretch her wings and ride with me for some side excursions," Prince Gallium said.

Fraum looked over his shoulder at them and frowned.

Don't think he'll let me pee in the bushes without some sort of entourage.

"We shall see," Joanne said.

The pavilion tent was erected, pillows set around a table and a chair for Fraum. Bread, nut pastes, mushrooms, and various sweets were served with seasonal vegetables provisioned from Lord Desmond's own stores. Fraum picked at his food, chewing with such disdain that Joanne wondered where her husband-to-be took his pleasure.

"Are you familiar with the *Philosophy of Natura?*" Joanne asked out of boredom.

"Yes," Fraum said. "Though I find it an immature observation of one who has too much time lingering in the grassy fields, staring at clouds, and not enough getting their hands dirty."

"You'll find that my brother is a fairly avid gardener," Prince Gallium said and winked. "He likes to spend his hour a day outside pulling up plants and cursing the Master of the Ground and Gardens for allowing useful plants where his weeds grow."

"They are not weeds," Fraum said. "They are medicinal plants. As you know our healers are incompetent and I must tend my own plants that heal and revive my humors."

"Of course, we wouldn't want you in bleak disposition all the time."

Joanne was used to her brothers being snide and even mean to one another, and sometimes her as well, so she wasn't impressed with their banter. Though, she did note how Fraum deferred to his brother.

"What kind of plants do you grow?"

"Nettles, mostly," Fraum said, dabbing spittle from the corner of his mouth. "I dry the leaves and make a tea to help with my inflamed joints. I was born in the deep winter with certain maladies of the blood and bile that I nearly died. By Mother's blessed hand, I survived, though, I suffer a weakness unbecoming of a ruler, as you may have noted. I need my teas to restore my health and the fool grounds tender destroy my patch of nettles. He's fortunate I am benevolent enough to suffer and not hang him from the elder berry and harvest corpse moss from him."

"Because father won't allow it," Prince Gallium said.

"There are other ways," Fraum said and rose from his chair. "If you excuse me, I must drain my bladder and evacuate my bowels."

He gave a curt bow and shuffled off. Two attendants followed. One held a cup and the other a spoon of sorts.

"My brother likes to have his piss captured in a cup, which he smells and observes the color," Prince Gallium said.

"The spoon?" Joanne asked, though she had an idea.

"Some surprises you'll just have to wait for on your bridal night." Prince Gallium grinned and emptied his mug.

Beaty leaned in and whispered to Joanne. "Might be best if we make ourselves comfortable for the remainder of the ride." Joanne nodded, rose, and curtsied to Prince Gallium.

"My attendants and I will be over in the bushes there," Joanne said.

"Watch out for snakes. They like to hide in pretty bushes before striking with their venom." Prince Gallium laughed and held up his cup for a refill.

Several paces away, Beaty leaned into Joanne. "Again, I cannot emphasize enough. That one is very dangerous! Do not spend an instant alone with him. Else, like a snake, he will wind his scaly self around your legs and slither up your skirts before you know you have been bitten."

"The other will leave a slime trail like a snail," Joanne said.

Selene giggled.

"From what I heard, riding in the coach with all your trunks," Selene said, "is that they plan on stopping at some inn called the Squealing Hog up the north road near the sleepy village of Domicus."

"At least we won't have to spend the night outdoors or worse, locked inside the carriage and listening to the wheezing, snotty snores," Joanne said, peeling down her undergarments and checking the ground for snakes before she squatted. "Do you think my husband-to-be is tasting his droppings?"

"Or having one of the attendants do it," Beaty said. Joanne didn't know how she could keep a calm expression over such absurd traditions. "They didn't seem so keen on following him."

"These northerners are disgusting," Joanne said, standing and adjusting her undergarments. "I guess I will have to demonstrate civility and set up some sort of school where their healers can learn from ours. Then they might not be so bestial in their habits."

When they returned, the meal had been cleared, the pavilion broken down, and the stools stationed by the carriage doors. Fraum was being helped inside while his brother stood by his horse, an air of arrogance in his stance, lauding over the fact that he could ride the saddle while Fraum was packaged away with the women in the carriage. *He's arrogant, self-aggrandizing, and... and...* Warmth spread from her cheeks and sparked desire in her underbelly. Prince Gallium looked over his shoulder at her approach. Joanne quickly averted her eyes, hoping he didn't catch the spark of desire in them, despite Beaty's warnings. Some dangers were difficult to avoid.

"Rest now, the night has yet to begin," Prince Gallum said and winked at her.

Joanne walked past in silence, though she was drawn to him the way all bad choices attracted her. Once sealed in the carriage, she settled against the padded bench, Beaty next to her and closest to the door.

Fraum stared at her, goose flesh rising along her arms the way it would when she knew her father was upset and she was forced to wait in anticipation for the blow—rarely from his hand, but his words bruised her deeply. Fraum sat up, leaning close to Joanne so she could smell the sour mucus on his breath.

"Don't get too comfortable with my brother," Fraum said. "One day I will have to kill him."

The carriage rattled as the horses pulled them back onto the road. Fraum smiled at her, eye cold as stones locked onto hers. Then he slowly returned back into his spot, staring ideally out the window.

Joanne glanced at Beaty to see her reaction, but her young maid had closed her eyes.

I'm to be married to a cold-hearted monster.

Lord Desmond had sold her to someone just like him.

Daddy's girl.

CHAPTER SIX: GAMES

No one wins when the Hang Man comes
Someone swings when the Hang Man comes
A rope and a twirl, tug'a the neck and a swirl
Round n'round you go until your feet have no floor
Then swing to and fro to Don you will go
                                        —*Drinking Song*

The Squealing Hog was as fit a name for the tavern as any Joanne should encounter—not that she had been to a tavern, or any common place where the dirt-poor wallow away their sad, miserable lives. The place smelled of used undergarments, sweaty with a hint of bloody musk, and wood smoke. A minstrel plucked out a sappy tune crossed between a wild cat's mewl and someone puking. Blurry-eyed men clustered around tables, slurping on mugs or lighting up pipes. A harried woman slapped a wooden tray full of frothy mugs at such a table. Joanne caught her eye and noticed that she had one blue and the other was a filmy gray. Crow's feet waddled at their corners. Her graying blonde hair was tied up in a red rag. Her smock was low cut that Joanne wondered how the woman's dugs didn't flop out onto the table.

"We keep to the rooms, tonight," Beaty said, ushering her along. "Don't stare at the folk here, else they might turn feral and snap at you."

Whispered conversations abruptly ended when Joanne and the Prince's men drew near, only to turn into whispering wisps, rustling leaves in the breeze as they passed. Joanne didn't think it was a common occurrence for people from two powerful nations, ones who once warred with each other, to grace the vestibules. Some of these men may have even fought in border skirmishes against Seaptum.

Prince Gallium spoke to a short woman with thick arms. She nodded, eyes moving across their entourage. She held up a hand displaying three fingers. Prince Gallium said something else and the woman shook her head. The three fingers remained up. Joanne knew they were negotiating. Prince Gallium spoke again and the woman nodded, staring directly at Joanne. A small purse was dropped onto the bar and the woman scooped it up, making it disappear down the front of her bodice and between her large bosom.

"Janus smiles on us," Prince Gallium said. "They have three rooms available, one for the ladies, one for you, brother, and the other for me. Some hot food of whatever remains of what they call an evening meal will be brought up. I can't guarantee it will be good, but there will be ale."

"A master negotiation with peasants," Fraum said, clapping three times. "Next you will be dealing for bones with the dogs on the street."

"I'd rather my brother have a warm room than the cold ground for his bed, tonight," Prince Gallium said. "Father forbid that he should grow ill and pass before we reach home with his bride-to-be. We wouldn't want the Princess Joanne to wear black before she puts on the white."

"As you say," Fraum said. "You will make a wonderful outpost magistrate after the wedding."

"You are too kind, brother," Prince Gallium said. "Let's inspect our rooms. I'll see to the rotation of guards posted at our door. Wouldn't want any of these bumpkins getting an idea they could earn some easy coin robbing a few royalty in our sleep."

The wooden stairs were slanted, forcing Joanne to hold onto the rail.

They creaked and squealed with every step. A narrow passageway led past a series of closed doors. Prince Gallium handed Fraum a key and Selene the other one.

"Careful not to touch too much. Don't know what bugs you might pick up," Prince Gallium said and winked.

The room was dark and Selene found an oil lamp that she used a taper to bring a flame from one of the hall lamps to light the one in the room. It smelled musty, like wet straw and sour sweat.

"Selene will see that our trunks are brought up, along with a few extra blankets," Beaty said. "We really don't want to sleep on a bed that may be filled with lice. It'll make for an uncomfortable trip."

"How am I supposed to sleep in such deplorable conditions," Joanne said. "Might as well stay in a stable with the horses."

"Milady will soon learn that these are the conditions in which everyone outside of the Manor and Keep live," Beaty said. "Such luxuries are not afforded to those who scratch a living from the ground and serve the lord of Nemus."

Few are born to rule others and make tough decisions. Joanne kept that opinion to herself. It was something her father often said, but Beaty wouldn't understand since she had also grown up in luxury, a luxury afforded to her by Lord Desmond. "I guess I can endure a night or two sleeping on straw. There is only one bed. I doubt it will hold more than two at most. Where will you and Selene sleep?"

"One on the floor, unless milady prefers that as her choice over the straw bed?"

"No, I will sleep in the bed," Joanne said, plucking at her bodice which seemed to stick under her arms. The carriage was warm and she sweated in every crevice it seemed "Any chance of getting a warm bath?"

"Not unless you want to be up all night waiting on the water and tub to be brought up," Beaty said. "Perhaps that can be arranged at the next stop."

Selene entered the room, leading two younger attendants who each carried a trunk. They set the wooden casements down, bowed to Joanne, and hurried out. *Probably to secure some ale and maybe a warm bed outside of the stable.* That's what Joanne would do if she was a young man free of duty after a long journey. Qetesh! She would do that too, if not for the watchful eye of Beaty.

As promised, Selene dressed the bed in a burgundy quilt and a wool blanket, while Joanne stripped to her small clothes. Beaty placed a white nightgown on her and had her sit in a wobbly wooden chair, running a coarse brush through her hair. She wasn't any gentler than her grandmother, Lady Bodaline, tearing through knotted hair the way the cook would snip the ends off of peas. A quick brushing of her teeth and she was bundled into the quilt, the bedding beneath hard and scratchy. The sounds of music and laughter would be nearly unbearable to allow any sleep.

"Try to sleep," Beaty said, sidling up against Joanne. She was stiff, boney, lacking in the softness Joanne enjoyed in Selene, who was curled up on the floor. "Tomorrow's travel will be a little more tolerable."

Selene was dimming the oil lamp when there came a knock on the door.

"Is the Princess-to-be asleep?"

Prince Gallium.

"She is—" Beaty started.

"—not," Joanne cut Beaty off, and climbed out of the quilt, despite the withering look.

"I was wondering if milady was interested in a hand of cards and perhaps some local gossip?" Prince Gallium asked.

"No," Beaty mouthed.

"Give me a moment," Joanne said, motioning for Selene to help her into a clean dress and a hooded cloak. She slipped on her traveling boots and stood at the door. "I won't be up long, Beaty. Don't be so sour."

"I'll attend my mistress," Selene said—she had donned a brown dress and was finishing buckling the strap on a shoe. "See nothing improper occurs."

Beaty folded her arms, frowning at the both of them.

"Fine," she said. "I'm not the one who has to deal with Prince Fraum's or Lord Desmond's discipline should something improper occur."

Fraum should join us. But he didn't seem the type to enjoy cards or the company of strangers. In fact, she didn't know anything he enjoyed except for sneering at her and threatening his brother. Not a good combination for an enjoyable night.

Prince Gallium waited for them across from his door. Joanne hesitated. *He wasn't talking about cards and gossip in his room, was he?* Seeing Joanne and Selene, he motioned them to follow down the hall and led them to the stairs.

"Observe from up here," Prince Gallium said. "It is much easier to find a table that isn't too crowded, or too isolated."

There seemed to be fewer people since they had arrived, but the inn wasn't close to empty. Several tables were occupied by men pulling on mugs and roaring laughter. Three had women in bright skirts and low cleavage clinging to a few older patrons who were dropping coins on the table and keeping the ale flowing while their hands fondled the cheap lace and painted, pale, fleshy thighs.

"There." Joanne pointed. Four men were playing cards, but two threw down their hand and walked away.

"Good eye, Princess," Prince Gallium said. "Let's take their seats before they change their minds."

"I must warn you, I'm not very good at cards. My mother never taught me and my brothers were more into fighting," Joanne said, following him down the stairs. "Also, I don't have anything of value on me—"

"No worries, Princess," he said, stopping at the bottom of the stairs and taking a hold of her hand. A weight was placed in her palm. He winked. "I have you covered on both accounts."

When he stepped away, she opened her hand to see the small bag of coins. They moved through the crowd and arrived at the table. One man, his face sun-darkened and a patchy beard clung to his cheeks, stood up. He wobbled some, red eyes cast around the room and held his balance by slapping a palm on the table top.

"Stepping away so soon," Prince Gallium said, startling the man and causing him to fall back down into his seat.

"Father's cock, who are you and why do you care where I go or what I do?" the man asked.

His partner, a younger boy, less blurry-eyed, but with a scar traveling from the right side of his lip up his cheek bone, remained silent, though his hands were held under the table. Joanne wasn't sure if he was reaching for a weapon or stroking himself—neither of which she desired to learn.

"My companions and I were looking for a way to liven up the evening with a hand or two of japes wild. You know, to shake off the tedium of travel," Prince Gallium said.

Both men eyed Joanne. Mister Wobbly grinned, revealing brown stained teeth, while his companion kept a stoic face—he could have been thinking about his next drink or contemplating his chances of robbing her blind. Joanne found it hard to read a man who didn't wear his intentions as clearly as the moon shining in the night sky. She disliked him immediately.

"For the right price, we accommodate all visitors to this here establishment," Wobbles said.

"I think you might find this to your satisfaction," Prince Gallium set his coin bag on the table. Wobbles reached for it, but Prince Gallium drew a dagger and stuck it to the table inches from the drunk man's out-stretched fingers. They retreated like a startled cat about to have its tail stepped on. Prince Gallium smiled and retrieved both dagger and coin purse. "There's more, if needed."

Joanne nodded at the meaning behind the Prince's words. If these two tried to cheat or steal from them, they'd lose more than a few coins.

"By all means, take a seat," Wobbles said.

His partner didn't flinch, nor did his eyes leave Joanne. She wanted to hide behind Prince Gallium, but showing weakness would encourage his boldness. *He wouldn't look at me like I was a leg of lamb were he to know my father.* She couldn't very well announce it either, not without spoiling the evening's fun before it had begun.

Prince Gallium pulled out a chair for Joanne before taking his own. He gave Selene a few coins. "Be a good lass and inform our host and hostess that our mugs shouldn't run dry."

Selene curtsied and looked to Joanne. Joanne nodded to show her approval. Though she was nervous, a thrill thrummed beneath the surface. To be this close to common folk, those not serving her or her family, had an inherit danger to it. Prince Gallium seemed at ease, but he had the dagger, and probably frequented taverns. She only had her wits. *Let's see how the cards fall.*

"You familiar with the Queen's Hangman?" Wobbles asked.

Queen's Hangman, an ominous name.

"I have heard of it," Prince Gallium said. "Remind me of the rules again."

"We are each given seven cards and keep them face down in a pile. For every card we draw and place face up in the court, or the center of the table, we drop a coin in the Queen's box. The one who pulls the Queen's Jewel, which is this card here, wins the court and the riches. However, if the Spaded Jape is dropped, the one who placed it must immediately drop in four coins to pay off the Hangman or lose all his, or her, coin."

Wobbles flipped the cards over to demonstrate the play. The Queen had a crudely drawn woman, one breast was bare and she wore a rather lascivious look on her face, and a crown of diamonds floated over her head.

There were three other queens, each as lustful as the next, but only the one with a diamond counted as winning. The Jape was a jester with what Joanne could guess as a black shovel head, or spade, hanging above him.

"Simple enough," Prince Gallium said.

Wobbles picked up the pile of cards and shuffled them. Joanne tried to follow where the Queen and Jape ended in the cluster, but, even drunk, Wobble's hands were a deft blur. Selene had returned with the serving girl who set down four mugs of frothy ale, before pulling up a chair and sitting close to Joanne.

"Should you drink that?" Selene asked.

"All in good fun," Joanne said, observing Wobbles deal out the cards until the small deck was gone.

"Everyone put in a pickle," Wobbles said.

"A what?" Joanne asked.

"A pickle is a small coin to start the round," Prince Gallium said.

Joanne found a few small coins in the purse he had given her. She placed one at the court in the center of the table, joining three more., two placed by Wobbles and another of greater value to make the number five.

"Since I dealt, Gothard here will place the first card," Wobbles said, thumbing at his friend.

Gothard brought up his right hand from beneath the table, tossing another coin in the court. The hand, Joanne noted, was deformed and it trembled as his fingers pinched the corners of a card. *So that's why he has them hidden. He doesn't want to show he's crippled.* After several tries, he managed to get it flipped over.

"A ten of hearts," Wobbles said. "A good sign."

"What would be a bad one?"

"Why, the Queen of course," Wobbles said. "Wouldn't want to steal the court before they have grown nice and plump."

"Plump as the royals who want war," Gothard said, staring at Joanne.

Does he know who I am?

"No need for that kind of talk," Wobbles said.

"War with who?" Joanne asked. "I thought we were at peace with Seaptum."

"Seaptum, aye, the bastards gave in like spoiled children when they couldn't get what they wanted," Gothard said, ignoring Wobble's glare. "But word is they got what they wanted in return to help our gracious lord fight his battles here in Nemus."

Prince Gallium tossed in a coin and flipped his card. The King of Jewels.

"Oh, so close," Wobbles said. "A King is no Queen in this squabble."

"But Seaptum will have a new queen, so I hear," Gothard said. "For our worse and their better."

"You have such big ears and a big mouth for one without the hands to support either," Wobbles said. "Your turn, lass. Drop in a coin to take the risk."

Joanne found one that matched what Prince Gallium put in. She flipped her top card.

"The Red Queen, though of love and not money," Wobbles said.

"Love doesn't count?" Joanne asked, looking at each of the men to gauge their response.

"Not in a game of coins," Wobbles said

"For the right price, love can always be bought," Prince Gallium said and drank from his mug.

Gothard narrowed his eyes, like Prince Gallium had stolen his words from him.

Am I the one being traded for coin? The answer was clear. Her father had traded her for peace among the nations. What about peace within their nation? Joanne tried the ale. It was bitter, but not too unpleasant. She preferred sweet wine that was sometimes served with her dinners. This place didn't look like they had much in the way of anything remotely sweet.

Wobbles dropped a coin and laid down his card. The court was looking more populated. The card he pulled was another ten. He groaned and the turn passed to Gothard. After a few unsuccessful tries at pulling a card, he managed to lick his thumb and drag one forward. Another ten. Odd, Joanne thought, how he should match his partner. Like there was some unspoken conversation she missed.

Prince Gallium dropped a Jack of Jewels; "the little brother to the Queen," Wobbles proclaimed. Joanne dropped her coin and flipped up a Queen with a diamond over her head.

"Janus bless you, Miss," Wobbles said. "Seems luck favors the beginner."

Joanne smiled. She had won! She dragged the coins to her purse.

"Another round?"

Joanne looked to Prince Gallium. He nodded, though Selene shuffled uneasily beside her.

"I would have my friend here shuffle, but as you can very well see, he lacks the dexterity for such endeavors."

"They were crushed by a Seaptum horse as I scrambled in the mud to avoid being trampled on while my friends held in their reeking guts or clamped onto severed limbs before they died in the bloody snow," Gothard said. "Guess I had Janus's lucky that day."

"Seems you paid the life price with your hands," Prince Gallium said, and then turned to Wobbles. "Is he always so pleasant?"

"The right conversationalist is my good friend, Gothard." Wobbles gathered up the cards and handed them to Prince Gallium. "Care to do the bidding?"

"I never turn down an opportunity to deal out good fortune." Joanne watched Prince Gallium deftly manipulate the cards. She would have dropped them all over the table. He was about to deal, when Wobbles placed his hand out.

"Cut, first, if you don't mind."

Prince Gallium handed Wobbles the deck. He split it in half, placing the bottom on top. Joanne drank more of the ale as the cards were delt. Her head felt lighter and she held back a giggle as the coin she used placed to pickle rolled around the group like a gossiping courtier. The first two rounds were played without a winner or loser. Gothard had grown silent, sullen, waiting on his turn and struggling with the cards. He spilled them on the floor and Prince Gallium watched him struggle to pick them up, before setting his cards face down on the table and kneeling to gather the fallen ones.

"Would be a shame to see our illustrious lord lose his place of power," Wobbles said. "All because some farmers didn't care to lose their voice in the council. Though, twin rivers run fiercer than one."

"I have no idea what you are going on about," Joanne said. "Nemus is better off under one ruler and soon, it will be twice as powerful."

"Like under Reuban?"

"Lord Desmond is nothing like Reuban," Joanne said, anger rising up. She had to watch her words and not give away that she was his daughter. *Gods be damned if I am going to allow this sot talk poorly of my father. After all he has done for Nemus!*

"A king is a king, even if they don't carry the title, they still carry the stick to strike down the people with harsh demands," Wobbles said. "Or has your life been made better by this king?"

"This *lord* has improved all of our lives," she said, growing louder and glaring at the man. She wanted to punch him at the accusations he was making.

Selene placed a hand on her arm.

"Forgive, my ward. She gets quite passionate under the influence of drink and lacks the proper knowledge of political matters to hold a sound discussion," Selene said. "Seems we may need to call an end to our games and be off to bed."

"Nay, stay and finish this round."

"We really should be—"

"No, I'm staying," Joanne said, her tone curter than intended. Her anger flared at Selene, and she backed away. *I won't let this fool best me!*

"Ah, I see our friend, Gothard, has found his hand," Wobbles said, grinning. Joanne found the jest inappropriate and rude. What else should she expect from such common rabble? "I mean, his cards. There, a nice one played. A ten, again! How fortunate in your unfortunate luck."

Prince Gallium dropped a coin and a card. The King of Spades.

When it came her turn to pull a card she stared at the Spaded Jape. His grin mocked her, laughing from its place on the card. In revulsion, she curled her fingers away and up to her neck where she could almost feel the noose. The same one that strangled Cook Mathers and sent his soul to Donn to be judged.

"Seems milady has found the hangs man, or rather he found her. Pay up twice what's accounted for to spare your life or be ousted from the game," Wobbles said.

Joanne placed the coins, all of her winnings plus a couple extra, into the court. She gave a sorry expression to Prince Gallium for losing his coins.

"All in good fun," Prince Gallium said. "Two faced Janus favors us with a smile while planting a blade in our backs."

"It's not over yet, you could still have the Jeweled Queen to bail you out." Wobbles flipped his card and gave a satisfying grunt. The Queen of Jewels smiled at him. "Appears she favors another." The coins were scooped up in a single gesture and disappeared into Wobble's pouch. "Shall we have one more go? Third times the charm, they say."

"Appears you have cleared me out of coins," Joanne said, holding up her empty purse. "That was a rather mean trick."

"Trick, Miss? Thramel plays no tricks with the cards." Wobbles gave a hurt expression. "I wouldn't want to tempt Janus's wrath."

Thramel. I will remember that name and get back at you for this cheat.

"Not as mean as the trick used by Lord Desmond to kill King Reuban and then the Wise Council," Gothard said. "After all the good they done to unify Nemus and bring us from the shitty swamp and desert dwellers to respectable folk."

"Would you shut your trap!" Thramel glared at Gothard. "Keep from mixing bitter opinions with our guests." Thramel returned a smile to Prince Gallium. "Besides, you never know who is listening."

"Father and Mother knows I'm tired of letting this bile rot my belly," Gothard said. "Best to let it leak out."

Joanne couldn't believe the outright treason these men spoke in public.

"I believe we are all tired and have imbued too much," Prince Gallium said. "We should retire to our rooms before another long day of travel."

"Where is it you are headed, strangers, should you mind my asking?" Thramel asked anyway. He drained his mug of ale, waiting for a response.

"North," Pince Gallium said.

"Cold there this time of year. I wish you happy travels." Thramel stood up and bowed. "May the Blades Man watch over you."

"Watch out for bloody Seaptums. They'll likely stab you as give you a kind word," Gothard said. He buried his hands in his pockets

"Selene, will you take our companion back to your room," Prince Gallium said. "I have something to take care of before I am able to sleep."

Selene curtsied and took Joanne by the elbow. At the stairs she leaned in close to Joanne.

"I do not like where tonight is headed," she said.

"I'm troubled as well," Joanne said. "Do all the people of Nemus feel the same about my father? Or are they a jealous few."

"War does strange things to people. Makes them bitter, hard to be around," Selene said. "My own father drank away our home and our land. That's why I was sent to serve at the Keep. To pay off the taxes."

"I never knew that," Joanne said.

"Plenty of parents had to sell their children in such hard times," Selene said. "Some go to the Keep and some serve in the markets, and then there are those who get sent to the backhouses to serve the lords of the land in their fleshy desires."

"I am glad you were given to me," Joanne said, and leaned her head on Selene's shoulder. "I mean, not that you were forced, but that if you had nowhere else to go, I rather it be in my bed than some scuzzy lord. Mother favor's the misfortunate at times. I am grateful not to have been sent away alone. I guess I'm just another currency to be traded in the name of my father keeping hold of his power."

For how long? If the people rise up against him, there isn't an army large enough to keep them in check.

Beaty was awake, reading a little book titled, *Teaching manners to the Ill-mannered.*

"Your little fun has ended so soon?"

Joanne yawned and began to undress.

"Very much," she said. "I've learned much about the people who live beyond the stone walls of the Manor and the Keep."

"An hour drinking and carousing tells you nothing about the people of the land," Beaty said. "They are low, base things no better than sheep who require the guidance of a shepherd to keep them from falling into the wolves' mouths."

"What are we? The shepherd or the wolf?"

"You smell of the nasty ale. Your head is cloudy. Come sleep it off." Beaty pulled the quilt aside. "You've had too much excitement after a long day of doldrum."

Joanne yawned again. She had no more fight in her as she slipped in beside Beaty. Perhaps she was right. Thramel and Gothard didn't seem the best examples of the people in the northern part of Nemus. There would always be veterans of war who believed they were treated unjustly without realizing that her father was safeguarding their future.

"I shouldn't have let you go," Beaty said, stroking Joanne's hair. "This is no place for a Princess to converse with the mud of the Kingdom. Especially with one who is not from here."

"It wasn't all bad," Joanne said. "I learned about a game called the Queen's Hangman."

"Oh, I thought you already knew that game." Beaty kissed Joanne on the cheek. "No more ale, no more cards. Until you are in the safety of your new home."

Joanne fell asleep, dreaming about the laughing face, the face of death. When she woke, she was choking, reaching for the noose around her neck, and instead found Beaty's arm holding her tight.

CHAPTER SEVEN: REVELATIONS

The more Gold they ripped from the water,
The more Red blood flooded the rivers.
The more Silver chiseled from stone,
The more White bone buried in burrows.
The more Jewels pulled from the dirt,
The more Hearts filled Donn's plate.
— From "Peasant's Lament"

They breakfasted on bread, butter, and nut paste along with temped tea. Joanne's mouth was dry, and her nose a little stuffy, but there wasn't the dreaded headache that told of a hangover. It was a little past sunrise when the carriages were loaded and they departed the Squealing Hog. A lone tree along the road caught her attention as there was something peculiar hanging from the branch. When they passed the tree, Joanne noticed it was a man dangling from the end of a rope. The hands stiff at its side gave away his identity. The fingers protruded at unnatural angles and they appeared shriveled. Gothard's hands were broken like those, in the war, he had proclaimed, and she had no reason to doubt him. A soldier serving her father against Seaptum.

Seems Gothard lost to the Queen's Hangman, afterall. Who would have done this to him and why? Joanne had only a single answer. Prince Gallium. He said he had business he had to attend before he could sleep. Now she understood his meaning. A nasty bit of work, and uncalled for, in her opinion.

Beaty lowered the shade over the window.

"Such an ugly view is not needed to ruin a beautiful morning," she said.

"Another cutpurse earned his reward," Fraum said, wheezing and wiping his nose on his sleeve. "I'm surprised that not more of your trees are adorned with such displays of lawlessness."

Joanne didn't know how to respond to the jab at her father's rule. She pursued her lips to hold back a harsh retort and earned a squeeze of the hand by Beaty. They rode in silence, Joanne's thoughts drifting to the card game and the conversation. Was it Janus's curse that everyone she met should suffer? What happened to Thramel? Was he dead somewhere in a back alley? Why was Gothard hung where she could see him, like some trophy kill? She would have to ask Prince Gallium about his actions and what they meant. It wasn't appropriate to goad the common folk with a game of cards, so they let down their guard and talk of things best left unspoken. They may have the intelligence of a sheep, but they wouldn't speak so plainly without care if they knew who they were, beyond a wealthy traveling merchant or something of the sort. At least she didn't think they would.

Joanne peeked out the curtain to get a sense of where they were travelling, that there was more to it than the annoying bumps and jostles created by what she presumed were ruts in the road. Why weren't the roads paved in stone like roads spindling north, south, east, and west? It would prove a quicker, more efficient travel with less bruising on the tailbone for those without the luxury of cushions.

Simple houses occupied barren ground far back from the road. Men, women, and children worked in the fields. Some moved behind horses, others had carts they tugged, tossing in grass and stone. They paused long enough to stare at the carriages and horsemen. Their faces dirty, weather worn, and weary eyes scanning the entourage, probably wondering what important figure moved through their otherwise quiet, uneventful sleepy little farms. Although, Joanne doubted they thought of anything at all beyond the sore muscles and bruised bone, except for the next meal and maybe some rutting if there proved enough motivation.

Animals had more life and expression than these peasants they had passed.

Sheep, Beaty had called them. Yes, they were sheep and their wool served their betters. Lord Desmond saw to their safety and they owed him their very lives. Soon, that responsibility would be passed onto her brothers.

What's my role in this game? A bargaining chip for their safety, and soon a lightning rod to ground the power of both lands into one.

They stopped for the first time that day, not too far beyond the last farm she had seen.

"Please stay," Fraum said after Beaty exited the carriage.

"Yes, my lord," Joanne said. "Is it proper we be left alone?"

Fraum gave a grinding laugh.

"More proper for a man and his betrothed to be together, than his brother and betrothed. Oh, I heard about your little adventure last night. Before you assume it was your lady who told me, remember, I have eyes and ears beyond the ones on my face. Did you have fun with my brother?"

"It was… informative, my lord," Joanne said.

"A little drink and some gambling," Fraum said. "Hardly the sort of actions a soon-to-be-queen should partake in right in front of her subjects. It will give them dangerous ideas. That she is of the people, rather than above the people."

"They didn't know who I was," Joanne said. "Otherwise—"

"They knew enough," Fraum said. "You reek of privilege. There's no hiding my brother's lineage with his pale and soft complexion. Do you really believe they took you for some common travelers? They may be filthy dogs fighting over fetid meat, but they have keen eyes and nose to smell coin. Even if you weren't waving it around like some whore showing off her tits."

"Your tone is not appropriate, sir," Joanne said.

"It is when one has to chastise a child," Fraum said. "If you don't approve of my tone, then change your behavior. Before I am forced to change it for you. It seems your maids, your ladies-in-waiting are too lenient, too fragile to stand up to an impetuous little imp. Any more nightly excursions and I will have them sold off in the chattel markets to serve the houses of lesser lords, and give you ones more suited for the Northern temperament."

Selene! You cannot have her, you monster! Joanne bit her lip, her cheeks burning in embarrassment and stinging of his words. He might as well have struck her.

"What do you have to say for yourself?"

"I…I made an error in judgement." Joanne clutched the seat cushions, her fingernails digging in. "It won't happen again."

"Words are empty," Fraum said, no longer looking at her, but out the side window. Prince Gallium walked by with his horse. "So many people make promises that are broken as easily as flower stems in the frost-bitten air."

"I have nothing else to offer," Joane said. "You hold everything, including my very person, captive, it appears."

"Yes, it appears that way," Fraum said. "I will have a guard stationed at your door. No one is to enter or leave except by my permission. Not without having consequences."

"Understood, my lord."

"Now leave me," Fraum said. "I rather not catch a chill."

Joanne knocked on the carriage door. It was opened immediately and she nearly tumbled out into Beaty's waiting arms. Selene stood beside her, hands wringing together. Beaty steadied Joanne as they moved away from ear shot of anyone who might possibly listen in and report back to Fraum.

"Did he hit you?" Beaty asked.

Might as well have.

Joanne let a few tears leak from her eyes and shook her head. "He threatened to send you two away."

"I knew letting you leave the room was a mistake," Beaty said, cheeks puffed and her back went rigid, chin raised, and she looked down her nose. An exact copy of indignation her grandmother used when Joanne annoyed her. Joanne thought about pointing out the resemblance, but it wouldn't improve the situation any more than stomping on Beaty's toes would have her dance better. Beaty shook her head. "I was derelict in my duty, milady, but I won't allow it to happen again."

Prince Gallium observed a gathering of servants, setting up the pavilion.

He nodded to Joanne and gave her his beautiful smile. Joanne released Beaty and raised her chin up. *Cannot show a sign of weakness.* Her heart did beat an erratic rhythm and her legs were heavier than she was used to.

"That one is trouble," Joanne said.

"More than that," Beaty said. "He wants what his brother has and will go about getting it by any means."

I want to be with him more than Fraum. Mother, not at the cost of Selene! She was certain he would take Selene away just to spite her. *"I will have to kill my brother,"* Fraum had told her. Such a declaration wasn't in jest or brotherly rivalry, but some sort of passage that she lacked the context of understanding. How could Fraum think of besting his brother when he could hardly walk in the light of day? He was so certain, and like the snake crawling from the rock to bite the dog, he must have some venomous plan to accomplish his task. Or why boldly share it with her? Unless it was a test of loyalty, perhaps. She frowned at all the unknown factors. A puzzle without a clear picture.

"We have entered into a different sort of card game," Joanne said. "We must keep our cards close to our chests and take no unnecessary risks."

Not until I can position myself into a better hand.

"I don't think you understand, milady," Beaty said. "You have no cards in this game, because, you are what they are playing with to gain everything. You are entering a foreign land and the people there will not trust you now, or possibly ever. You must be prepared for the role you will play."

"What role is that?"

"A vessel for children," Beaty said. "It is an honorable position, especially if you birth boys."

"What if I don't?"

"Pray to Mother that you are fertile and the fruit you bear is strong."

I'm to be nothing more than a field to be plowed and sowed.

The realization hit hard. She needed to sit down, to lie down, never to rise. This wasn't the life meant for her. Mother wouldn't be so cruel as to limit her to what her loins would produce.

"Sit, sit, milady," Beaty said. She stroked Joanne's hand. "I will see to it that they have a bath ready for you at the next tavern. Simple pleasures will guide you through each day."

Simple pleasures. I rather drown in the bath!

The Stone Creek Tavern was their next stop, the last overnight stay in Nemus, Joanne was told. Fraum didn't speak to her, hardly looked at her, while the carriage carried them through the empty roads. The occasions Joanne peeked out the window, she saw only burnt-down husks of what used to be homes. The fields were brown and populated by bramble weeds. Charred trunks of trees and shattered wagon pieces littered the land. This was the results of the war between Nemus and Seaptum. A war King Reuban allowed to continue for five years and claimed the life of her eldest brother, Henrick. All for protecting this place of stone and bones, though the mines beneath were more valuable than the flesh and blood sacrificed for it. Gold was found in the rivers, which were damned up to search the beds. King Dryd claimed the lands belonged to Seaptum and took offense to the damning of the river. The banks overflowed and flooded several farming communities to the north. What started as a squabble for land rights, turned bloody at the battle of Mouth of Noctis foothills. A hundred farmers and the noble lord Dremon perished in the fight, prompting a formal declaration of war from King Reuban to King Dryd.

Joanne hated the name of the tavern, since it was not whimsical, promised no mirth, and was too on the nose of a description—they were literally beside a stone creek that hadn't gained its water even after the dams were torn down. What brought her the most distress was, it was too close to the place where Henrick was killed.

She mentioned this fact to Beaty and Fraum smiled.

"Might have been a battle led by my brother," he said, and coughed. "Wouldn't it be divine if the reason you are marrying me is because your father didn't want to lose any more sons, so he gave me his only daughter."

"That wasn't very courteous," Joanne said. "Why do you even want to wed me?"

"I don't," Fraum said, his grin slipping and he glared at her face like she was the hideous one. Joanne felt a jolt in her stomach and heart at his sudden and bitter proclamation. "My father says I must and you know very well that you cannot deny our fathers. Not without paying a hefty price."

"Then let us at least be tolerable," Joanne said. "To spite our parents at the very least."

"I will be what I am," Fraum said. "You will be obedient. That's how this arrangement works."

"What if I were to tell of my poor treatment?"

"How, for one, would you get a message out that I wouldn't know?" Fraum asked. "I may appear weak, frail, sickly, but I know everything that occurs in my home. Second, as long as the peace holds, your father wouldn't care if I bound you naked in a cage. You are property and to do with as I wish."

"You could be nice."

"Where is the fun in that?"

"There could be much fun, if you allowed it."

"I do enjoy your spirit, girl," Fraum said. "I will enjoy breaking it."

We will enjoy killing him. A dark voice whispered in her ear. The Shadow Mistress. So much suffering came at her hand and Joanne's very own. *What's one more?*

Joanne closed her eyes, listening to Fraum's wheezing and imagined it to be a death rattle. Not yet married, and already she plotted her husband-to-be's demise. She couldn't do it alone, and despite having Beaty and Selene, she was alone.

Patience. Need to be patient and prove him wrong, Joanne said to herself, though her skin crawled and she itched to be away from his wicked and foul disposition. She would rather be riding with a snake. At least with that creature she understood why it would hiss and strike her. Fraum worried her the most, his venomous words and unpredictable violence. How would she be able to live being married and frightened for her life?

Beaty slipped fingers inside her hand and squeezed it. Joanne returned the squeeze.

I will outlast them all.

She lasted the rest of the journey in silence. As promised, there was a tub full of warm water waiting for her at Stone Creek. Selene helped her strip and scrubbed her back, taking care to massage Joanne's sore shoulders and neck, stiff from the journey. Joanne took hold of Selene's right arm and kissed the back of her soapy hand.

"I don't know what I would do without you." Joanne stroked Selene's fingers. "You are my little piece of home, no matter where I go."

"Thank you, milady," Selene said.

"Ugh, I hate that word. Milady! Milady! Milady!" Each time she repeated it in a mocking tone and smacked the water so it splashed both Selene and herself. "You need to come up with something else when it is just the two of us. None of this miss, milady, madame, or any other Donn stinking names. We have been together longer than I can remember. My constant playmate. My friend. My bedfellow. My, well, my dearest one! I haven't always been so kind to you, but that will change. I promise, you will have all my affections."

"Would that be appropriate?"

"I don't give a godsdamn what others think is appropriate." Joanne turned on her knees in the tub. She looked into those innocent brown eyes and wiggled a finger. "Come closer to me, please." Selene knelt to be on eye level with Joanne. "Give me your hands." She held out hers, palm upturned. Selene placed hers overtop Joanne's hands. "I want you to know this now and always. I love you, Selene. What you did for me with the tutor incident, I knew from that moment there's no one else I could ever trust. I love you and only you."

"Why are you telling me this?" Selene asked, her hands trembled, but she didn't try to pull away.

"I want you to be aware," Joanne said, the water cooling, but her skin was flush. "We can trust no one else, not even Beaty. We are alone in the wilderness."

"I'm scared," Selene said. "I never wanted to leave my home."

"I know, but I couldn't do this alone."

"Everything is always about your wants," Selene said. Her cheeks flushed and she tried to pull away. Joanne clamped down on her wrists. "I'm sorry, I...I didn't mean it that way."

"Don't apologize," Joanne said. "You are absolutely right. It's always about what I want and most of all, Selene, I want you." She crawled up the edge of the tube, hard nipples pressing against the metal, while drawing Selene closer. Their lips touched, soft, light as finger tips brushing together. Then they moved in closer, inhaling each other's breath and exhaling. Fingers intertwined and Joanne sank back into the water, carrying Selene to the edge with her. She wanted to drown in the moment. To feel the warmth of their bodies together as they drifted under. Selene squeaked as Joanne bit her lower lip and pressed her mouth harder on hers until their teeth mashed together.

There was a rattling on the latch. They parted quickly, Joanne's chest rising and falling, she smiled at Beaty who stood at the door, a little confused by what was happening. Joanne couldn't hide her blush, though it could be mistaken for the heat of the water. Selene on the other hand looked like a mouse caught with a cookie by the cat.

"I managed to find a warm meal, but I can see you are not yet ready, milady," Beaty said, holding a tray of what smelled like bread and vegetable stew. "I will set it down here while you and your maid complete your bath."

"Thank you, Beaty. We are about done. Selene was helping to sooth away the aches and stiffness from traveling."

"I can see, that." Beaty clasped her hands in front of her, though her facial expressions betrayed her disapproval. "Perhaps I should take it from here before your food and water grow cold."

"Yes, mistress," Selene said and bowed. Joanne noted the lack of eye contact and that her face was very red. "I didn't mean—"

"You have performed your duty well." Beaty held out the towel, a signal that the bath was over. Joanne stood, goose flesh prickling her skin and her nipples were hard. Her underbelly also throbbed and she took pleasure in Selene looking her over. Then she was standing on a wool cloth, toes sinking into the softness. Beaty wrapped the towel around her and patted her down. She put on a nightgown and was allowed to eat. Beaty kept her company while Selene went down to get a supper for herself and Beaty.

"You really shouldn't tease the girl," Beaty said. "She is new to all of this and doesn't understand social roles. Be careful of the power you hold over those who tend to your needs. Give them too much importance and you will be hurt."

"I'm not teasing her," Joanne said. "It's been a long day and we both have needs."

"Your biggest need is to be attentive to your betrothed."

"Who you know doesn't want to marry me."

"No prince wants to be forced into marriage. You get of the situation what you make of it."

"I don't want to talk about it anymore," Joanne said, staring at the plate in disappointment. She wanted more ale and perhaps to play a hand of cards with strangers. "I want to eat in peace and then go to bed."

"As you wish, milady."

Joanne cringed at the title. Selene arrived shortly after with a tray containing bread and stew. The flavor wasn't terrible and it was better than eating the same provisions brought on the journey north. Honestly, she didn't know how anyone could eat the same things day after day. She appreciated Cook Mathers more, and well too late, after just two days of eating outside the Keep.

Too bad you killed him.

"How many more days until we reach where ever this place is they're taking us?"

"We will cross into Seaptum tomorrow, or so I had heard," Beaty said. "Then it will be another three days before we arrive at the Argenti Lapisdom, where the Silver Throne of Seaptum sits."

"Sounds very grand."

"We will be visiting the houses of some minor lords of Seaptum, so this will be our last tavern," Beaty said.

How disappointing that no lords of Nemus would have us in their homes. Not after the Bloody Night with King Reuban and the destruction of the Wise Council.

From what she'd seen, there wouldn't be much left of any of the vassal's homes. The war had gutted the northern part of Nemus. Beaty brushed her hair while Selene quietly prepared the bed and one on the floor. Joanne wondered if Beaty would allow Selene to sleep beside her that night and she take the floor. That didn't seem likely. Selene was still lower in position to Beaty, though they were both her attendants. Besides, Joanne might be tempted to do more than sleep next to Selene.

Wouldn't want Beaty to be jealous of the moans and lecture us on the etiquette of pleasure.

Joanne giggled, though it was cut short by a tug from the brush.

"Tell me how your grandmother knows my mother?" Joanne asked more out of boredom than actual curiosity. There would be no cards and drinking—*or hangings*—this night.

"They are cousins," Beaty said.

"Cousins," Joanne said in disbelief.

"Yes," Beaty continued through the interruption. "King Reuban took away my grandfather's title and lands when he refused to send soldiers from the south to re-enforce the border between Seaptum and Nemus. Sending away his only son and his troops would have left his claims on the salt and copper mines unprotected. They were already disputed by the western lords who sought new areas of wealth. As my grandmother tells me, my grandfather called it a border skirmish that would break into all-out war if the other lords got involved. King Reuban sent his honor guard down to settle the matter and delivered a decree from the King that my grandfather was stripped of titles and lands immediately and from that day forth would be sent in exile to the south, or his family would be cut out of this existence root and trunk."

"He threatened to kill your entire family?"

"At the time my mother had died in childbirth, a son had gone to Donn with her, so my grandfather, in his grief petitioned Lord Desmond for help," Beaty said, stroking the side of Joanne's head. "In the battle to come, my grandfather was killed and my father also died. Our lands and titles were placed in trust until either Susan or myself marries into a noble family, which none here in Nemus feels inclined to it seems. We are adrift in the world and I am tethered to you, now, Joanne. That is how we come to this moment."

"How come you never told me we were related?"

"We were instructed not to say anything about our relations," Beaty said. "Grandmother didn't want us to sound like we were desperate. Besides, there should be a distinction between those who serve and the one employing them. I expect nothing except to see you well-married and guide you where I may to be a lady of the court and not some spoiled girl of wealth and privilege."

"I won't take those last words so harsh, because I know you mean well," Joanne said.

"See, you are learning."

"Well, my dear cousin, I appreciate your guidance." Joanne embraced her. "I will see you married to a lord of distinction, at least in Seaptum, if not in Nemus."

"Thank you, but please leave off the familiarity," Beaty said. "It will create unnecessary tension."

"Do these Princes know?"

"They weren't formally notified, but it wouldn't take much digging to discover."

They might use it for an advantage. Joanne knew she would have to be careful how much affection she demonstrated. It might be too late with Fraum. *He's as observant as a hawk watching the field for mice.*

Once more Selene was relegated to the floor while Beaty slept beside Joanne. Sleep was hard to find, since Joanne kept waiting and anticipating a knock on the door and another invite to drink and play cards while

92

observing her people. She would refuse, of course, or else suffer whatever demeaning consequence her husband-to-be designed. The knock never came and her eyes grew heavy. Pressed against her cousin who she couldn't acknowledge as kin, she laid an arm across her flat belly, and up to the swells of her small breasts. She'd prefer Selene beside her and more intimate caresses—Beaty was too boney for her liking. Warm, breathing in the lavender soap her cousin must have rinsed with prior to going to bed, Joanne slept.

In her dreams she was greeted by a third figure, stepping forward from his place between her tutor Teresa and Cook Mathers. His hands were mangled, hanging at his sides like little claws ready to clamp down. Gothard's neck had a slight crook to it and he smiled a lopsided smile.

"Seems the Queen's Hangman got me after all." He chuckled, but his brown eyes bulged and shot through with red, stared, lacking any mirth.

"*She* has a habit of following this one about," Cook Mathers agreed, pale hands holding up the braided rope around his neck. "How long before it catches this wicked lass and swings her into Donn's waiting teeth."

"Oh, she'll cut more throats and tear out more hearts long before a rope finds her," her tutor said.

"I…I didn't mean to—"

"Oh, she didn't mean to hurt us." Teresa pressed her lips into a big pouty face. "Drawing the blade across my throat and watching me bleed out was an accident. Forgivable offense for one who only intended to embarrass me."

"She was terrible at cards," Gothard said, holding up a deck in his right hand while attempting to peel the top one off with his left. His crab-like fingers refused to catch hold, so he shook his arm until several fell to the ground. Joanne noted they were all the spaded Jape and they were laughing at her. "Couldn't tell when she was played a fool. A fool and her coin are always parted. But the more fool I, since my soul and my body parted soon after."

"Red runs the blood of those unfortunate to cross her path," Teresa said in a maniacal whisper. "Blood will soak these lands and leave more innocents choking."

Call to me, child. Let me help you. A dark and seductive voice called from the shadows.

"I will not," Joanne said, falling to her knees. "I swear that I will be good and kind. To create a better place so no other must suffer."

"The Shadow calls to you," Teresa said, standing over her. "Beware that one who is far more cruel and wicked than you could ever imagine. Better to suffer in silence than pray to this one who has ruin on her mind."

Ruin? That is what I do to the people around me.

Ignore the dead, child, they envy the living and desire your soul to torment in Arula.

"Are you not innocent? Why do you not walk the green pastures of Nahrangi? Why must you torment me in my sleep?" Joanne begged for their answers. They gave her none, fading away into darkness. Before they left, their horrific grins changed to pity. Why should they pity her when she caused their demise?

"She will ruin all," Teresa said, her voice ending in a gurgle, lost in a mouthful of blood.

Around Joanne remained the fallen, stone-structures covered in dust and bones. A breeze swept away debris and there, bright yellow and red in the corner like a grave marker was a flower. Joanne recognized it as the Dragon's Vein. Beautiful, yet deadly. Untouched by the ravages of time. It was native to the north, to where she was heading into a new life. She would be like this flower. Must reign when all crumbles into nothing, a fire in the darkness, ready to ignite the rest of the surroundings. Ruin. Then so be it. Mother knew what awaited her, but she would not be ground into fine dust and swept away.

Pray to me, child, and I will give you everything.

Joanne shook her head.

The interference of gods in worldly matters was forbidden. She wouldn't invite that danger. She was marrying the mouth of the lion. One set of teeth against her throat was enough. Joanne woke with her fingernails digging into Beaty's breasts and her cousin, her lady-in-waiting, crying out, and hand closed over hers, trying to pry those fingers away. Joanne released her immediately and Beaty nearly fell off the bed to escape her, clutching at her chest.

"I'm sorry."

The dangers of sleeping beside a guilty conscious. She was lucky I didn't have my hands around her throat.

"Don't touch me!" Beaty nearly screamed.

"What happened?" Selene asked, sitting up from her make-shift bed.

"A bad dream," Joanne said. "I didn't mean to—"

"It's fine," Beaty said. "I was just frightened."

They dressed Joanne in silence, though Beaty was not very gentle with the hair brush, tearing out knots rather than teasing them out. Joanne sucked air through her teeth rather than scream out the pain and annoyance. Selene held a mirror up to her and the dark circles under her eyes marked the dark passage that her dream took her along. In the morbid light that the ash-stained window allowed, she looked as ghastly as she felt.

The meal was scant. Some burnt bread and weak tea that she chewed without pleasure and scalded her tongue because the water was too hot. The main room had a chill to it, made less comfortable by the silence of Fraum and her maids. Four men dressed in patch-worked outfits grumbled at the incursion of the private guard who had occupied the tables closest to the door, naked swords on the table and a loaded crossbow pointed at the newcomers from a stool at the corner of the bar.

"Why are there guards inside the tavern?" Joanne asked.

"There are always guards around," Beaty said, grimacing as she sipped tea. "You haven't noticed?"

"Not this blatant in the open," Joanne said. "I may not notice every detail, but these are as conspicuous as a swarm of flies on horse shit."

"Language, milady," Beaty said, but she gave a quick smile.

Prince Gallium dropped a plate of what might have been burnt bread and crusty cheese. He sat across from them. "You are absolutely correct, Princess." He nodded to the men near the door. "They are visible to remind the local, disgruntled peasants that we are not an easy target. It seems there has been talk of an uprising and that a member of the house nobility, nay, the daughter of Lord Desmond herself, was travelling north seeking Seaptum support in securing the throne and control over Nemus, since he is too weak to do it alone."

"What do they plan to do? Kidnap me?"

"More than that, Princess," Prince Gallium said, picked up the bread, examined it before tossing it back on the plate. "This here is an example of their hospitality."

"Burnt bread and tea that tastes like piss?"

"They are simple folk with simple means in which to fight," Prince Gallium said. "A spoiled meal is an insult to us, but may prove worse to those who may have only one meal the entire day. The worse this miserable filth will bring will be pitch forks, maybe a spear or axe, and a few hunting bows, nothing that we cannot stamp out. Best to show a little of the force we have so they may have second thoughts on watering the soil with their blood."

"Crude, I admit," Joanne said.

"Whatever keeps you safe." Prince Gallium said.

"Like hanging the card player."

Prine Gallium shrugged. "I would have cut off his hands, but that would have served no purpose than to anger the veterans. That cheat and cutpurse deserved punishment."

"Hanging?"

"I found this in his purse when I demanded my coin back." Prince Gallium tossed a card on the table. It was the Spaded Jape. "I took it as a sign."

"What of this?" Joanne tapped the burnt bread.

"The master of this house is fortunate I don't do as he has done to this innocent bread."

"I suggest we leave this town before inviting more trouble."

"As milady commands. The carriages are loaded horses hitched," Prince Gallium said. "I will pay our hosts the kindness they have shown us."

Joanne grabbed his sleeve.

"Don't hurt them."

Prince Gallium held up a coin bag.

"Do you take me for a vicious dog to bite every hand who does me injury?"

Not a dog, but more like a fox.

Secure once more in the carriage, Fraum smiled at her.

"Seems the travel is wearing on you," he said. "Dark circles tell of restless nights, though from what I hear you never left your room."

"I am not yet used to the noise," Joanne said. "Or the stiffness of the bed."

Beaty sat back straight, a mirthless smile on her face. She pulled her hand away when Joanne reached for it—whether from the nightmare attack or the talk of not seeming so close to give Fraum an advantage over her, Joanne didn't know.

"All part of the joys of travelling."

Joanne glanced out the window, looking back at the Stoney Creek Tavern. Smoke rose over its rooftop. The morning air had a chill, so a fire built in the hearth wasn't beyond imagining. *Neither is Gallium burning the place down.*

She let the blinds slide down and closed her eyes, carried away by the rocking of the carriage.

Loud noises woke her. Shouts, screams, and horses thundering past. Blurry eyed, Joanne blinked at the faces that were not in her dream—*the Tutor, the Cook, and the Veteran*—but were just as pale and frightened. Beaty looked at the carriage window, hands knotted together and writhing. Fraum sneezed, then grinned, spittle glistening on his wet, red lips. Joanne reached for the handle.

"I wouldn't do that," Fraum said, wheezing in excitement. "Seems like your people are upset?"

My people

"What's happening?" Joanne asked, looking to Beaty who grabbed her hand. Her mouth was drawn tight and she shook her head.

Fraum cocked his head and squinched his eyes, looking at her like she was an annoying child who should know the answer to such a simple question. "We are being attacked."

"Oh," Joanne said, her heart now picking up a beat of fear and anticipation. The fuzziness of sleep rolled away, leaving behind the picture of guards with naked swords and a crossbow back at the tavern. Prince Gallium's idea of a deterrent had failed to impress the masses who revolted against her, her father, and Seaptum. *The fools! Don't they know they will be slaughtered?* Something thumped against the carriage door.

"There would have been an arrow in that lovely breast of yours had you opened the door," Fraum said. "Best we wait it out inside. Shouldn't last longer than a few moments. The peasants are primitive in their tactics and weaponry. Field mice, really, attacking the cat with pointy sticks."

"Any idea how many are out there?"

Fraum shrugged his thin shoulders.

"I'm in here with you," he said, wrinkling his nose. "My loyal men clean up the mess others create."

Someone cried out, a loud, painfilled shriek that brought gooseflesh to her arms and neck. More death. It stalked her even out to the countryside. *Is there nowhere I can go where someone doesn't have to die?*

Joanne lifted the shade and her hand froze at the sight beyond. A man in a green cloak and dirty tunic gripped his gut, and was nearly doubled over. Red poured through his fingers and what might have been a pinkish gray rope dangled from a tear in his belly. The Seaptum guardsman stepped around him to engage another man, face red-blotched and scraggly beard poking a pitch fork at him. The Seaptum's sword slashed out, metal gouging a chunk of flesh from the peasant's neck. Blood spurted and the man fell, face contorted in agony as he desperately clung to his neck. It was too late, Joanne knew, she had seen firsthand what a wound to the throat could do to a person.

More keep coming. Why? Five, six, seven men appeared, overwhelming the Seaptum guard. Sticks, hammers, blades crashed down, stabbing the smashed and bloody body.

"They're heading for the horses," Joanne said.

Then the carriage jerked forward and Joanne gripped the bench to keep from falling face first into Fraum's lap. The shade fell, cutting her off from what was happening in the world outside her box. A box that might turn into their coffin. The carriage picked up speed, bumping along hard enough her teeth clicked together. Beaty wrung her hands, eyes closed, and whispered a prayer to Mother. Joanne knew Mother wouldn't be able to protect them. No god would intercede on their behalf. *Except there was one. She will stalk me to the very ends of the rope. No, I won't beg, not now, not ever.*

Fraum kept grinning.

"Take this," he said, handing her a dagger the length of her forearm. The handle was silver and vines spiraled around it. "Don't let them take you alive."

He held its pair in his lap.

"Aim for the vitals," Fraum said, "though you knew this already. I'm sorry, Miss Beaty, but I only have the two. Keep out of the way when the stabbing starts."

Beaty squeaked her affirmation.

The carriage soon slowed and came to a stop.

Joanne lifted the shade again. Barren trees and a burnt-out foundation of a home were visible, but nothing else. Sound of boots on the wooden bench where the driver sat. Joanne dropped the shade and held the dagger out. Whoever was out there would wish they hadn't opened the carriage door. Beaty placed a hand on her arm.

"You should run," she said, eyes wide and her hand trembled. "Do whatever you must to get away when the door opens. Then run and don't look back."

"No where to run to," Joanne said, annoyed at Beaty's cowardice. She was a Desmond and Desmonds fought on regardless of the circumstances.

Boots approached the carriage. Joanne resisted the urge to lift the blind. Best to not let them know she was armed. She took a breath in and sent out a prayer. Beside her the dark voice whispered. *Let me in and I'll protect you. They won't know they are dead until their body hits the ground, their life blood leaking out.*

"No," Joanne said.

"Hush." Fraum gave a low hiss, dagger held ready to jab anyone coming through the door. Joanne pinched her lips together, holding back her annoyed retort. The handle turned outside the door. Her arm tensed, ready to strike. The door opened. Joanne thrust her arm without seeing who as there. A killing blow for someone caught unaware. But the blade punctured air and a strong hand gripped her wrist, holding the dagger extended out and away from further harm.

"Let me go!"

"Woah there, Princess." A voice she recognized and a face. A handsome face spotted with drops of blood. Prince Gallium grinned at her. "This the way you greet people who rescue you?"

"Wouldn't need any type of rescue if you hadn't abandoned your post." Fraum scowled, nose twitching as droplets ran over his upper lip. "I would think the safety of your prince regent, and brother, was more important than running after some pig herders and boys barely out of their milk teeth. Was the slaughter worth endangering your brother and betrothed."

Prince Gallium laughed.

"Next time there's an attack by milk toothed-boys and pig herders, I expect to see you out here swinging a sword, brother."

"Are you hurt?" Joanne asked?

"This blood isn't mine," Prince Gallium said, dabbing at his face with a kerchief. "I see my brother is fine, sharp witted and vicious demeanor, but how are you two?"

"Shaken, but otherwise unharmed."

"Blades Man blessed your skill with a knife. If I had been unaware of your feistiness, Princess, Donn would be judging my misdeeds." Joanne blushed at the compliment. "At least I know my brother will be kept safe by his bride-to-be and her maid, while I will escort the carriage back to the remaining retinue."

"How many were there?" Joanne asked. "How many people attacked us?"

"The exact number will be figured once the bodies are collected," Prince Gallium said. "They were not your people, but traitors to both Nemus and Seaptum. They don't deserve your sympathies, or your mournful prayers to blessed Mother and merciless Donn. Arula's flaming shores await them for torment."

"I don't feel any remorse. I want to know the names of their families that dare attack mine so I can inform my father and have the rest of the traitors pulled out by the roots," Joanne said. "Master Elin wrote that "one cannot grow a garden without first removing all the weeds." They will creep back in and strangle all we hold dear, or worse, spread their seeds to infect other areas."

Fraum smiled.

"Very wise words."

The carriage rattled on and Joanne watched Beaty. Her cousin didn't look very good, though no matter how frightened she was, she didn't faint or throw up. Joanne felt a rush and wanted to go out and stab something. Instead, she waited until the carriage came to a halt and the door opened. Prince Gallium leaned in. "I beg my leave so I may gather up our fallen. A guard has been set to watch over you until we can continue moving north once more."

Fraum waved him away. Prince Gallium bowed and then closed the carriage door.

"The sooner we leave this dung heap festering with maggots you call people, the better off we will all be." Rheumy eyes glared at Joanne. He still kept the dagger in his lap. "Northern hospitality is not as cold as your people complain. They don't try killing their betters."

Unless it is my brother. Joanne pursed her lips to keep from speaking words she would later regret. They sat in uncomfortable silence. She had rejected the Mistress of Shadows, but the dark goddess hounded her like a hart. *Why does she want me? What do I have that she couldn't find in another?*

The longer she sat in the carriage with Fraum, the more she grew to detest him. It wasn't his weeping eyes and nose, the sallow skin or the constant sniffling. Those were merely physical revulsions. It was the sickness of his soul that caused her skin to crawl. Yet, here she was to be married to the man, to have him lay with her, violate her... but not yet. Not for another year.

He could die from an illness, or a sudden stabbing.

The carriage began moving and Joanne promised that although she was leaving her home, leaving Nemus and the misguided people, she would see to it that she would return with more than she left.

CHAPTER EIGHT: NEW TERRITORY

The ships landed at the eastern shores. The mountains glazed in snow.
Half-starved, thirsty from drinking filtered urine for nine weeks.
Victims of Moko and betrayed by Sin. Sails tattered and hold flooding,
Seaptum Ironwood led the last of the crew of Mother's Misery to the Stone and mountains and there carved out a kingdom in the hard land.

— from "Histories of Seaptum"

Joanne hated to admit it, but Seaptum was beautiful. The winter snows had melted, leaving behind a blanket of lush greens intermixed with the hard, gray stones. Vibrant, blue flowers floated like lakes along the green grasses with white laces creating the foam. In other areas, yellows and reds shone their fiery beauty. Joanne pressed her nose to the window, taking in the wonder of such a cold, hard place.

It won't last, she heard Fraum's voice, though he hadn't spoken more than a few words to her since they crossed the border into Seaptum—he was always such a such a storm cloud that she could feel his rumbling, even though she didn't see his lightning.

Burnt out farms were replaced by remnants of watch towers. Crumbling stones covered in vines and overtaken by weeds faded into the beauty Joanne admired. The road moved beside a river, swollen with winter runoff. Trees pregnant with white buds about to blossom lined the right side of the road. Joanne wanted to stop and leap out of the stuffy carriage, to strip down and bathe in the river, though the waters were probably icy fingers ready to snatch the warmth from her. Birds of various sizes and colors, as many as there were flowers, lined the trees and the bushes. Here was life outside the cold stone walls. Here the making of a new life. Here was a new territory to discover. To conquer. Joanne's heart thumped with the thrill of discovery.

Fraum's wet sneeze pulled her back into the harshness that awaited her.

"Lean any closer and you might fall out," Fraum said, wiping his nose on his already crusty and yellowed sleeve.

"I was looking at the flowers." *Which are far more appealing than what I find in here.*

"The bastards and their pollen make my nose swell and my eyes water," Fraum said, blowing his nose on a discolored handkerchief. That single piece of cloth probably held more liquid than all the streams in Seaptum, Joanne surmised, holding back bile wanting to creep up her throat. "I prefer the cold and the snow that chokes back all this beauty, as you might call it. A wooden floor would seem a comfort after wallowing in the mud, though it still makes the back ache."

Beaty frowned, patting Joanne's hand. She didn't need the assurance from her maid, knowing full-well to hold her tongue, or lose it. When the escort stopped later than she desired, Joanne stretched her aching back and cramping legs. Selene found her, hoisting her skirts as she ran to Joanne. Rather than give her a hug—Joanne wanted more in that moment, Selene stood in front, wide-eyed in excitement, examining her.

"Blessed be, Mother and Father, blessed be," Selene said, dropping the edges of her skirts and grasping Joanne's hands in her own, squeezing them from wrist to fingertips. Tears shimmered in her eyes and Joanne had never felt more desire for her servant and maid. "I thought I had lost you for good when the shout come that your carriage was stolen."

"I'm well. A little shaken, but nothing I won't overcome."

"Let's take this moment of relief somewhere private," Beaty said, motioning to a hedge of bushes.

"Not without some protection," Prince Gallium said.

"Are you going to watch over three women as they piss in the bushes?" Joanne asked.

"Of course not, but I will post a guard to be discrete, in case there are other dangers lurking about," he said.

"Brother! Come help me," Fraum cried from the carriage.

"The prince regent beckons." Prince Gallium bowed. He began to walk off, then turned back. "Eight, Princess."

"Eight?" Joanne asked

"The number of men who sacrificed their lives for your safety." Prince Gallium frowned and moved away to the carriage.

Eight didn't seem so many, but then again, they had a troop of less than thirty. Nearly a third were lost in a small revolt. That was too much. *How many peasants did they kill?* Beaty had her by one arm and Selene the other, guiding her away from the carriage. They squatted in the relative privacy of the bushes. The relief on her bladder nearly had her moaning.

"That man is a monster." Beaty whispered. Joanne didn't need her to clarify which man she referred to in the conversation. "I'm certain you will learn how to live with him, but stay little in his company. Respond only with pleasantries. If he strikes you, do not react. Let me know and I'll do my best to arrange the situation where you don't spend as much time in his company. Only what is necessary for a wife to perform certain obligations."

Joanne adjusted her small clothes and let her skirts fall back into place.

"After this journey, I believe I have earned a respite." *A marriage of power and not love. Nemus, the sacrifices I make to protect you, and then these pissants attack me!* She let the anger wash over her. Again, she was powerless, though she knew that she had great power. She must defer it, for now. "I want to wash off in the stream."

Beaty agreed, though her face was still flush from the outburst of contained anger.

"I'm going to get us something, first." Selene hurried away to the baggage carriage where their trunks were stored. She rode back there alone, like she was extra clothes to carry along, since all the Seaptum attendees had horses or wagons to use on their journey.

Fraum sat beside his attendees, a blanket covering his shoulders, and watched Joanne cross the road. She would keep her distance from him as long as she was free from her cell. With Fraum, she knew what it must be like to be imprisoned in a personal Arula. The gods despised her for what she had done. No other way to explain her betrothal to such a foul creature. *My journey to redemption.* She didn't believe in such things. Arula would have her and this was nothing more than the bitter taste before swallowing entire offal.

"I brought us some towels from the trunks," Selene said.

Beaty praised her foresight like Selene was a child who correctly named her colors. Selene didn't seem to notice the condescension in Beaty's words, smiling and moving along as though these were the happiest moments in her life.

I will need to protect her. What a mess my father sold us into. Again, she felt the rise of fury against Lord Desmond, against Fraum, and against the traitors who dared attack her. They splashed water on their hands and faces, wiping away the fear and exhaustion, watching their skin raise in goose flesh at the chill before drying themselves. Joanne sensed their guard standing within ear shot, but not being intrusive. *I'm sure he will report any conversation directly to Fraum.* She made certain not to speak of either prince, focusing on the clear blue sky and how green the grass was it didn't seem real, but rather sprang from a painting.

"Must be the minerals in the hills washing through the valley as the snows melted," Beaty said.

"Have you ever been in the snow?" Joanne asked.

"No, closest I've come was the frost that glazed the ground like icing on a cake. It didn't last long and served to kill some of my mother's flowers." Beaty frowned. "I'm sure you will get the full experience Seaptum has to offer."

They joined Fraum at the small table where hard bread and some nut paste waited for them. It wasn't a flavorful meal, but then Joanne wasn't interested much in eating—she nibbled enough to keep Selene and Beaty from bothering her about not eating. Then they were packed back in the carriage like luggage ready to be carted to the next destination.

Thatched-roofed houses sprung up among the flowers in the green fields. Men, women and children were out in the fields, scraping away at stone and dirt. They weren't dressed much differently than those in Nemus. Their faces weren't any less dirty, their hands any cleaner. They scraped their existence from the ground as any other peasant in Nemus. Working the soil seemed to make everyone equal. The houses had a slightly different design, with the roofs more slanted to keep from being crushed by snow, Joanne presumed. She felt the heat of Fraum's glare wordlessly telling her that she stared too long outside the window, allowing in too much light.

The carriage began to slow and Joanne lifted the shade again. There she noted a large stone wall and an iron gate. Two stone dragon statues, wings furled and eyes of some blue stone watched their approach. They had to be her size, if not larger. She had never seen a dragon before, though west of the Keep in Nemus, the Blackwyrm Marsh was rumored to have one.

A metal placard stood split at the top of the gate with two words: *Virtus Vivificat.* When the gates opened, the words parted. The dirt road had changed to cobblestones. The wooden wheels clattered across the stones into a large courtyard. At the enter stood a tall tree, its thick branches sprouting bright pink blossoms like it was holding out its victory over the harsh, frozen snow and winds. It was in stark contrast to the dull gray stone of the surrounding wall and the three-story manor house. The carriage stopped in front of the manor and the door was opened by attendants. Joanne stepped out, noticing how dark the windows were in the growing gloom. Like a sleeping giant. She was assisted by two serving men, each wearing a white uniform with a peculiar bit of color over their left breast that included bright orange petals, each marked by a red stripe down the center, like a flame. Joanne recognized it immediately.

Dragon's Vein.

She hadn't seen such a flower since the day she almost touched one and died a horrific death.

Why would that be their crest? It explained the dragon statues, but why was such a dangerous flower revered, and why would the King allow a house to bear it as their crest? Joanne figured it would be symbolic of assassination, since, as her once tutor Teresa had told her, the bristles excrete an enzyme that would melt away a person's innards. Did they not know?

The servants opened double wooden doors that were bound in iron. The hinges creaked and standing inside a dimly lit vestibule was an elderly man in thick robes of fur the color of flames, a silver band sat on his head in a puff of curly white hair. He had a white beard on a round face and blue eyes as sharp as ice shards taking in the faces of the newcomers. Beside him was a woman hardly older than Joanne, wearing a matching red and orange robe. Blonde hair cascaded over her shoulders and she wore a thinner silver band on her head. Her skin was pale like the sun hadn't kissed it in a year or longer and her eyes were a deeper blue, the kind Joanne might see in the sky after the storm clouds had passed.

Must be his daughter, or young enough to be his granddaughter.

Beside her, someone sneezed. Fraum took her arm and Joanne fought the urge to shake him off. She caught Beaty's expression, which mirrored her own revulsion, but her cousin smiled and nodded, telling her to go along with his game. *This is my life now, might as well get used to it.*

"A very warm welcome to the prince regent and his company," the older man said and gave a quick bow. The woman curtsied, her eyes locked on Joanne. "I see that Father has warmed your home. I heard you went to get a wife, but I didn't imagine you'd bring home the sun."

He took Joanne's hand and pressed a kiss to the back of it. His daughter didn't seem too pleased by this reception. A frown creased the lines around her pretty lips even further. Her father smiled, squeezing her hand a little longer than what Joanne deemed socially acceptable.

"You look in amazing health," he took Fraum by the arm and gave his hand a firm shake.

"Much better now I'm breathing northern air instead of that filth in the south," Fraum said.

"Oh, not in front of your new bride," the man said.

"She knows my feeling on this and many matters," Fraum said. "We are not yet wedded, but I bring her early to get accustomed to her new life as my mother advised and my father demanded."

"Fathers can be insistent, some more than others." The older man smiled at Joanne again. "Oh, where are my manners, we haven't been properly introduced. Time can be thief of many things, but one must maintain decorum or we might as well be nothing more than lizards crawling between the rocks. I'm sure by the way you are looking at me like I'm one of those moon-crazed men molesting you on the streets that Fraum hasn't told you where you are or with whom you will be spending the evening?"

Joanne shook her head, afraid to speak and upset her already perturbed betrothed.

"I'm Lord Hal Freeman, the second, and this tomb of a place is Dragon Perch," he said, then stepped back to the young woman's side. "This one scowling at us is Lady Helena Freeman, my wife."

Joanne nearly choked on her spittle.

Wife?

"Don't listen to this old fool," Lady Helena said. "I'm not scowling at you, just the break in hospitality by my husband. I am very pleased to meet you, Joanne, of Nemus."

"You know who I am?"

Lady Helena laughed.

"Of course, all of Seaptum knows who you are and why you are here."

"Then you knew long before I was informed," Joanne said.

"Come inside and we can talk about these matters with libations," Lord Hal said, waving to the open door. "You must be famished from the journey. Where's your brother?"

"Tending the horses and seeing to the men," Fraum said. "He insists on it."

"We'll welcome him once his obligations are completed," Lord Hal said. "I'll have my attendants show your attendants where your rooms will be for the night. Follow me to the main hall where I have had a little meal prepared for your welcome."

"That will be pleasant," Fraum said, taking Joanne's arm again. His hands were cold and moist, she could feel her skin chaffing under his grip. She was alone with him, Lord and Lady Freeman, and a man who led the way opening doors that separated the rooms. So many doors, Joanne marveled. Each room was sparsely furnished, but they had a fire place. Large, oblong windows were paired on the outer walls, though no sunlight would penetrate the thick drapes lidding the massive eyes, though they did emit a sense of warmth patterned in the familiar red and orange colors. Cushioned chairs occupied some space along with book shelves up to the ceiling full of bound pages. An oil lamp provided ligh, but not enough to do more than cast a shadow or two on the wall where they sat. Joanne noticed a lack of feminine softening of the rooms. They were hard and plain as the stones the manor was built on. Although, there were a few tapestries that depicted their patron gods: Blades Man, Mother, Father, and even one of Donn weighing a heart, his teeth red, streaked with gore from the many he had already eaten.

Fraum leaned on her for support more than a show of affection. Her shoulder began to ache where he pulled down on her. She sent a prayer to Mother when they reached the main hall and Fraum released her to be seated at the head of the table. Several candles lined the table and a large candelabra hung from the ceiling with at least a dozen candles lit. The "little" meal Lord Hal had prepared was enough to feed a dozen people, if not more. Joanne recognized several dishes of glazed fruits, various stuffed peppers, squash soups, roasted mushrooms, jams, breads, and boiled potatoes. Their smells were nearly overwhelming, his stomach growling in response to say how little she had eaten from the burnt bread that morning to the hard one at midday.

Joanne was seated to Fraum's left, a couple of chairs toward the middle of the table, designating position as less important that the Prince regent. A servant filled her crystal goblet with red wine. Lady Helena sat beside her on the left, leaving the right chair empty—this Joanne presumed was for Prince Gallium. Lord Hal positioned himself beside Fraum, opposite the empty chair. Joanne was happy with the arrangement, though she did miss the attentions of Beaty and Selene.

"How have your travels been so far?" Lady Helena asked, taking up her wine glass and sipping from it. "Being stuck inside a carriage for most of a day can prove challenging for one unaccustomed to such modes of transportation."

"There have been moments of discomfort," Joanne said. *And danger*, though she wouldn't speak of such issues with someone who didn't know. "I guess that is part of the journey."

Servants ladled up squash soup in bowls and placed them on the round, stone plates.

"Discomfort, that is a good word," Lady Helena said and spooned some of the yellow soup into her mouth.

Joanne followed suit, and had to keep from moaning at how good it tasted.

"When I first arrived at Seaptum, I came alone," Lady Helena said.

"You are not from here?"

"No, my father was a magistrate in Stoney Creek. I see you had passed through there to get this far. After the war, arrangements had been made to secure its safety. Fines paid and blood ransomed. It took some adjusting, but I rather like my new home."

"How long have you been married?"

"Three years."

The soup was finished and the next course of bread was started with a scoop of berry jam and butter. This, too, was delicious. Joanne forced herself to take small bites. In between she sipped the wine, which was also sweet, what she imagined how a frozen lake with a tang of grape would taste. She had finished the cup and her bread in the same course, though the cup didn't remain empty.

Lord Hal asked Fraum about the health of the king. A king Joanne had known by word of mouth and usually spoken of as the enemy. Dryd had caused her family and Nemus much sorrow. She wasn't certain how she might react around the person responsible for the death of her brother. *Civil and polite, unless you want your head returned to your father in a box*

"He was very ill, bed-ridden before we left on this excursion," Fraum said, though he didn't sound worried for his father. "I haven't heard word of his passing, so I assume he yet lives."

"That he does, that he does," Lord Hal said. "I was hoping for an absolution, but that may have to wait."

"Yes," Fraum said.

Absolution? From what? So many stories hidden in these stone walls. I wonder if Beaty learned anything?

"Were you able to bring anyone familiar with you?" Lady Helena asked. "If you are in need of a lady-in-waiting—"

Lord Hal dropped the knife he had used to slice up the stuffed pepper.

"Don't go pestering our young queen-in-waiting with your silly demands, girl," Lord Hal said, voice raising, but not yet a shout. "She doesn't need an empty-headed ornament to occupy space that a proper lady should due her."

Lady Helena's cheeks flushed and she bowed her head.

"I allowed her two of her choosing from her very home," Fraum said, "though, I may be in need of another should they prove lacking in our customs."

"I would get one of those old dowagers, like Lady Vulfshine, she's a widow now and her sons and daughters are married off to fine magistrates and lords."

"She's a mean bitch, I wouldn't have her within a league of me," Fraum said. "I won't say no to your request, Lady Freeman. But, she has no need of extra hands as of now. I don't need her getting fat and lazy. Perhaps when she is with child, she may need a third."

"Do you normally talk about a person in front of you like they weren't there?" Joanne asked.

The table went silent. Both men stared at Joanne like they had had never seen such a creature. Lady Helena held a hand up to her mouth. *Did I say something wrong?* Joanne was feeling giddy with food and wine. She shrugged, drinking more from her goblet.

Lord Hal smiled and laughed.

"This one has fire in her belly," he pointed at his wife. "Remember how you used to have the same fire, a tongue that could warm when she desired something, but burned every other instance. Oh, I remember well and how the lash cooled her. The heat of leather took the sting out of her tongue. Some women have a mouth and need to be taught when to speak and what words should be used around her lord and husband."

Lady Helena's cheeks burned red again and she folded her hands in her lap, head hanging at the chastisement. Joanne was about to respond, but the doors opened. Gallium entered in a flash of rain to wash away the tension in the room. He stopped beside Lady Helena and bowed, taking her hand.

"Greetings, beautiful hostess," he said and kissed her hand. "I see the Mother's blessing on such an extravagant table. Winter has been kind to you both. But the sun shines best on you."

"Ah, Prince Gallium decides to grace us with his presence," Lord Hal said. "Something is missing."

"Oh, what might that be," Prince Gallium said. He sat beside Joanne, winked at her, and began ladling soup in a bowl before the servants could do more than stand dumbfounded at how to react. One stepped forward and poured him some wine

"A wife," Lord Hal said.

"This journey wasn't for me, Lord Freeman, but rather to procure the future of Seaptum and Nemus in an embrace of peace and brotherly love," Prince Gallium said. "If you think I should take a wife, well, then I might take yours, Lord Freeman, only because my brother doesn't have one yet to take."

"I would let you have her, but she isn't the proper lineage for one in your position," Lord Hal said.

"My brother is being too forward," Fraum said. "It is a flaw in his personality."

"Yes, I seem to have many of those?"

"Flaws?" Lady Helena asked.

"Personalities," Prince Gallium said. "Mmmmm, this soup is divine."

Joanne laughed, which drew the irate glare from Fraum. *I'm going to suffer for this night. Might as well make the most of it.*

"I've seen a few," Joanne said. "And I've known of your existence for only a few days."

"I try to re-invent myself every day."

"Yes, you seem to have donned the fools cap," Fraum said.

"Someone needs to have a sense of humor, brother. Since I know you are too miserable to smile." The room went silent again. The mirth had strained thinner than a knife's edge and Joanne knew that to speak might draw blood. She pushed away her plate, appetite gone and her head hurt.

Prince Gallium ate like he hadn't caused the firestorm in the room. He sat back in his chair, as careless as a boy who yanked the braids of all the girls, finishing off a stuffed pepper and downing three cups of wine. Joanne wished she could leave the table instead of having her stomach turned into knots waiting for the next cutting word or degrading phrase. Finally, Fraum spoke up.

"I believe we need to discuss some business," her betrothed said. "It has been a very long day with much excitement. Are the rooms prepared where Joanne may retire for the evening?"

"Yes," Lady Helena said. "I will show her to them."

"Thank you, my dear," Lord Hal said.

Lady Helena took Joanne by the hand and they left the room together. They moved back through the rooms away from the dining hall. Joanne noted how the sky had darkened since they sat down to eat. Oil lamps still burned, but the gloom remained. The hearths stood cold, empty of fire that would warm the rooms. Lady Helena led her up a wide stairway, the steps carved from stone, and into hallway landing. A few tapestries covered the walls and, except for the length of doors, it was empty. A tomb that echoed their footfalls in solemness.

"Why does this place feel so empty?" Joanne asked.

"That's the way my husband prefers it," Lady Helena said. "Of course, when his first wife died, and he had no children to carry on, he made a choice to aide your brother during the war."

"He did what?"

"Your brother had pushed Seaptum troops back this far and took a wound in the side that nearly killed him. King Dryd had placed a spy in my husband's household, like he had in all the minor lords' homes. He was informed on. Your brother escaped and Lord Freeman professed he didn't know who had taken refuge in his home, but he was punished with a large fine that he must pay and forced to marry me so I can produce an heir for him to carry on with this generational burden. Everything of value was sold so Lord Freeman could pay the fees."

"Why didn't they execute him or exile him?"

"He is more valuable alive and produces more wealth working the silver mines," Lady Helena said, her voice full of sadness. "Soon we will have to release what few servants we have remaining. Well, all but the spy who tracks the ledgers of how much silver Lord Freeman pulls from the mines and sends off to King Dryd."

"I see," Joanne said.

The hospitality shown by Lord Hal and Lady Helena must have set them back quite a bit. To feed and house a small army would not be cheap. Joanne took in the clothes Lady Helena wore. They seemed to be worn and the color faded. Again, she wondered if they knew anything of how deadly the Dragon's Vein flower could be. Then again, it might be a mark of their betrayal. A symbol of how much King Dryd distrusted Lord Freeman.

No wonder she'd prefer to subject herself to the demanding task of lady-in-waiting.

If Lord Hal did indeed provide aide to her brother, then Joanne felt she owed him a debt. Perhaps she could get the fine rescinded and allow him a respite in his fading years. Any heir at least would be absolved of the sins of his father. She could offer nothing to the girl. Anything she might promise would get back to Fraum and then all of her plans would be ruined.

"I guess you could say I'm the spoils of war. Men fight and die, but we women pay the price," Lady Helena said. "It's not fair, but that is the role the gods have designed for us. We will always bear the burden. Here's your room. If you need anything, send one of your ladies. I will try to accommodate to the best of my ability."

"Thank you," Joanne said.

"It's real nice to meet you, Joanne." Lady Helena leaned in for a hug and Joanne allowed it. She then whispered in her ear. "These Seaptum men are cold as the ice and stone that marks this land. You must be colder to keep from breaking. No matter how long I live here, Nemus will aways be my home and you, my Queen." She placed a kiss on Joanne's cheek. "Sleep well."

Joanne watched her walk away down the dark hall, her yellow and red robe the only bit of light in the entire stone prison.

"How was it?" Beaty asked as soon as Joanne closed the door.

"The food was pleasant, the men, not so much," Joanne said. She saw the large bed with four posts and orange curtains, big enough to hold her, Beaty, and Selene. There was a wash basin with a jug of fresh water on a wooden pedestal. Their trunks were at the foot of the bed where her night clothes were set out, waiting for her. *Mother Bless you both, Selene and Beaty.* "Lord Freeman was rude and dismissive of his wife and the poor thing wants to escape so badly she nearly begged to be my lady-in-waiting."

"That must not have gone over well with the Lord or your betrothed," Beaty said.

"No better than if we had pissed in their soup." Selene giggled at that and Beaty pursed her lips together. "Besides, I heard an interesting story."

"Oh, what is it?"

"Lord Freeman had helped my brother, Henrick, in the war and the King found out. That's why he's being punished with hefty fines."

"That simpleton of a wife is also part of the punishment, I presume."

Joanne nodded, though she wouldn't call Lady Helena a simpleton. No, the girl was trying to survive. It wasn't her fault she was sold off like a prized cow. *Like me.* Joanne stripped off her dress and washed up before Beaty helped her dress for bed.

"The servants here also fear for their position," Beaty said. "From what you heard, some will require new employment. Before next winter."

"Sounds about right," Joanne said.

"Winter is a bad time to lose your home and station," Selene said. "They will starve unless another manor takes them in."

"Their lot is not my concern," Joanne said. "I barely hold onto a home and Donn knows my position here is anything but solid. I could be cast out by winter and then what? Go home and explain to my father that the snot-nosed Prince of the North couldn't stand me, so he sent me home. I hope this doesn't lead to another war!"

"Best you remember this," Beaty said. "As much as you may despise him, you pleasing him is what keeps Nemus from suffering the same fate as Lord Freeman and these servants."

"I'll do what I can once I have secured my trust here," Joanne said. "I may be about as useful as a talking chair for all these men listen to what the women have to say."

"Oh, they listen," Beaty said. "You have to speak their language."

Fear, bitterness, disgust and treachery. I know those words all too well.

"Remember, not all Lords and Ladies of Seaptum will be as accepting of this arraignment. Some will not see you as equal, but some peasant girl whose father won a rebellion to gain his rule. A traitor's daughter who is now betraying the land."

"They can sit on a hot spike and dance for all I care," Joanne said.

"You speak those words now, but you will need to seek allies among the enemies," Beaty said. "Remember, all who smile and praise your beauty are not your friends. Some hold a knife to your back."

"That's why I have you and Selene with me," Joanne said. "And we all get to sleep in the big bed."

"I was used to blankets on the floor," Selene said. "I guess I can accommodate you, milady."

"That is an order," Joanne said, bringing a smile to Selene's pretty mouth.

Joanne lay in the middle of both girls. She closed her eyes feeling the warmth of Selene and Beaty beside her, but kept seeing the slimy, sniveling face that would be her husband one day. His eyes leering at her nude form, both disgusted and excited by her. She reached out for Selene, leaning against her and gently kissing the back of her neck. Her right-hand cupped Selene's breast and she breathed in her freshly washed scent of lavender. Selene pressed her bottom against Joanne's hip.

I could lay like this forever.

But she knew one day she'd be like Lady Helena; a woman desperate to escape her husband. She wasn't even married and being away from him was a blessing from all the gods. How could one person leak out so much mucus and not be a shriveled grape? His touch lacked warmth; he could've been a corpse.

You can turn him into one.

The bloody knife was in her hand again. Her tutor clutched her throat where blood spurted and when she turned her head, it wasn't Teresa, but Fraum's pale face, red tipped nose, and his rheumy eyes rolled to stare at her, all the malice and contempt, twisting into a grin. *You had it in you, I always knew it.* He gave a cruel laugh, dropped his pale cold hand on her shoulder—the bloody gap in his neck had sealed. *You will never get rid of me. Never!* Joanne dropped the bloody knife.

Not without my help. A shadow dislodged from the corner. A dark cloak dropped to reveal a beautiful face. Raven-black hair cascaded over her shoulders. She smiled and offered up her hands. In her palms was the bright yellow flower, streaked with red.

"Dragon's Vein is poisonous," Joanne said.

Anything can be poisonous. One has to have the right imagination.

"I don't need you," Joanne said.

You will. We are destined to be together.

A sudden chill crept up her legs and she saw a pair of dark gloved hands gripping her thighs. Except she wasn't in bed, but standing in stone hallway. The hands crept from the shadows splayed by moonlight shining from the large window in the hallway. They crept up her night gown, squeezing her thighs.

"This is a dream," Joanne said, her words echoing back to her from the stone walls.

No. And yes. The sultry voice promised more as the hand worked closer to her underbelly.

"Release me," Joanne said. "I don't want you."

You refuse me twice, now, child.

"I refuse you a third and for a thousand more," Joanne said.

I am patient.

I await your cries.

When you need me, you will beg on your knees.

The hands slid down Joanne's legs from upper thighs, down her calves, ankles and stroked her feet, leaving her shivering. Joanne caught a glint of silver in the moonlight. She stared at the knife in her hands. The door she stood in front of was not one she recognized, but in her heart she knew that Fraum slept behind it, snoring his wet, squeaky snores. The knife was meant for him. But, was it her hand guiding it?

A dream, she told herself, but the cold on her bare feet distorted the illusion. She retreated back down the hall to her own room. Before she had reached it, a woman stepped from an alcove.

"Do you hear it, too?" Lady Helena asked, standing in her white night shift. Her eyes shone wild in the moon light. "The call to be released from the miserable world?"

"What?" Joanne asked.

Lady Helena touched Joanne's hand holding the knife.

"This," she said. "You'll carve out your soul before you could harm your husband. They sleep because others watch over them. Protecting them from harm. They hide in the shadows where we cannot see them."

"How do you know?" Joanne asked.

"I have felt them watching. Always watching," Lady Helena said. "Put that away before you slice us both with such ignorance."

"I didn't intend—"

"It doesn't matter," Lady Helena said. "Only what they say is real becomes reality. We are nothing more than these shadows to be shifted by their light. Learn that lesson and then you might achieve whatever it is you plan. Off to bed with you. No more night wanderings."

Lady Helena hugged her and then moved on down the hallway.

I am lost. How did I get out here and with such a strange encounter with that wretched woman? Is this a dream? The weight of the dagger was real enough. It was the one given to her by Fraum. She must have packed it away and forgotten about it. Back in her room, Selene and Beaty slept on. She wrapped the dagger in her dress and set it on the trunk—no one had died this night, none that she knew, anyway. Then she slipped between them, once again, folded in by their warmth. Sleep claimed her and she forgot about the strange dream that wasn't a dream, her night wandering, and talk with Lady Helena.

Lady Helena spoke very little to Joanne in the morning. She wore her sad expression like a comfortable gown meant for the most intimate guests. There was no hint of last night's wanderings. As far as Joanne was concerned, it was a dream, except the dagger was in the same place she had stowed it. Lady Helena sat beside Joanne, glanced at her a couple times in a way Joanne wasn't sure what she was trying to communicate, and they drank tea and a bowl of oats topped with cream and fresh berries.

Fraum appeared more refreshed. His eyes clear and nose looked dry.

Joanne almost found him pleasant to look at with his hair slicked back instead of a thinning mat that belonged more on an older man, than a young one.

"I trust that you slept well," Lord Hal said; the dark circles under his eyes told that he passed a restless, stressed-filled night.

"The most pleasant since I began this adventure," Fraum said and smiled, a genuine smile. Not one of his peevish, cruel ones that Joanne had weathered in the long carriage rides. "The weather is more agreeable and so was our host. I will not forget this visit, Lord Hal. My father will hear how you were most agreeable and amiable to the terms. Perhaps we can draw up other provisions in the future to lessen your burden?"

"That would be most amicable," Lord Hal said, and squeezed Lady Helena's shoulders. "Any way we can be of service to the crown."

Joanne didn't sense that Lord Freeman was pleased with the results of the post-dinner discussions. Not that he could do much about it. Especially if he was being punished for helping Henrick. *What else could Fraum have demanded from him? They had taken everything but this shell of a home and left him ostracized with a wife from Nemus? What fresh humiliation could he press into the man?*

Lady Helena didn't seem too pleased either.

"The carriages are loaded and we are ready to move on when you are, brother," Prince Gallium said.

"Seems we must take our leave, but not for long," Fraum said and clasped Lord Hal's arm in a friendly gesture.

"I wish you and your betrothed safe travels," Lord Hal said.

Lady Helena embraced Joanne and spoke a few words.

"Remember what I said about shadows. Call on me if you need me."

When you need me, you will beg on your knees.

Joanne nodded.

They parted from the Freeman estate. Joanne pondered what fate awaited her as the carriage rattled down the cobblestone and outside the gate. The blue eyes of the dragons watched them depart. Fraum's smile dropped and he glared at Joanne.

"Do not speak so willfully," Fraum said. "It may lead to you losing a friend. Gods know, you have very few of them here in the North. I would hate for you to be completely isolated."

Joanne knew he referenced their earlier conversation about Selene and Beaty, taking them away from her. She had no words to express her fear, her anger, so Joanne nodded.

"Not everyone will be as forgiving as I am, nor as understanding as that lump of mush, Lord Freeman. He owes us a very large debt, thanks in part to your family. He pays it without complaint and humors this marriage pact, since he himself understands the humiliation, I must endure for the sake of prosperity between our realms. But mark my words, no one else in Seaptum will be as tolerant of disrespect that you have shown for yourself and the family you are marrying into. You are in new territory, tread lightly."

"As my lord commands," Joanne said.

"You will find your life in the North much easier if you surrender everything," Fraum said. "Everything you once had. Everything you once were, is gone. You belong to me, now. You are mine to do with as I please, when it pleases me. I could have you stripped naked and riding atop the carriage like luggage. You are an extension of my will and I will break you, if I must."

"I will do my best to please you, my lord," Joanne said.

Until the time comes when I must kill you.

In the back of her mind, the Dark Mistress laughed.

I will be there when the time comes.

CHAPTER NINE: KNIVES LIKE SMILES IN THE BACK

Watch closely those who flatter, for they are the first to betray.
Power seduces even the strongest willed and brings them to their
knees.

—from "Matters of Friends of Enemies"

"Oh my, so this is the pretty little bauble you found on your
journeys!" A pasty-faced woman much older than Joanne, but younger than
her mother, clapped her hands together and smiled, white teeth showing
through pink lips. Lady Hawthorne stood in the vestibule, her round belly
telling how pregnant she was at the moment of near bursting. She wore
purple robes and white dress along with a golden circlet with a sapphire
jewel blazed in the light shining through the large window pane. "She is a
darling thing. Whatever swayed you to leave your home and follow this
handsome young prince all the way north?"

"My father commanded it," Joanne said. *Bauble! I'm no plaything for these vicious creatures.* Joanne smiled to hide her disgust.

Lady Hawthorne laughed, beaming at Fraum.

"She is so frank, so honest, I find that refreshing in a young princess. She will fit in well with the ice storms and frost melts."

"Like the weather, we don't always get to choose the conditions we want," Fraum said. The dark circles returned under his eyes and his hair was once again, a frumpy mess. He sneezed, wiping his nose on a kerchief. "She will learn."

"As long as she bends with the winds, and not break," Lady Hawthorne said. "Come, my dear. Take my hand and we will walk around the gardens while everyone else handles their business."

Joanne looked to Fraum.

"Go," he said. "Be careful not to wear yourself out, Lady Hawthorne."

"This being my fourth child, I think that advice is late in coming." Again, she tittered and took Joanne's hand.

Lord Hawthorne was a man twice the size of Fraum and even taller than Gallium. He also wore purple robes, a gold embroidered surcoat and black breeches. A belt with a gold buckle shaped as a raptor's claw, either hawk or owl, Joanne couldn't discern. He bowed to Joanne as they passed, brown curling hair parted at the center where he had a thicker, gold circlet with a bird's head and beak—Joanne would later learn it was a hawk. His face was lighter skinned and he smiled pleasantly, though said nothing more than, "enjoy, milady."

Three attendants followed them wearing purple dresses and white petticoats, bits of lace around their sleeves and the flower matching the one on her circlet was embroidered over the left breast. Two carried ceramic pitchers and the third held a crystal goblet in each hand. They were all young women around Beaty's age and silently followed Lady Hawthorne and Joanne out a side door where tall hedges marked the privacy garden.

"I'm sure this is all strange to you," Lady Hawthorne said.

"I've been in gardens before. In fact, the Keep held one larger than your entire estate," Joanne said. She didn't care for the woman's cheerful chatter or the way she slighted Joanne as some country peasant.

"I never presumed differently, milady." The lilt in her voice seemed affected rather than genuine. Again, Joanne recalled how the pretty ones were most dangerous. "I never took you for that primped up girl from the Stoney Creek Lord Freeman was *forced* to marry. Such an inconvenience for him. You know, he never had children with his last wife. I'm not so certain he will have any with this chickadee, no matter how fertile her eggs may be. No matter if they do have children, my second eldest boy, Geoff, will most likely inherit that hideous estate."

"How many boys do you have?"

"Two, so far," Lady Hawthorne said. "Mother willing, this will be a third. If all goes well between our nations, perhaps he'll be the first to establish the Hawthorne roots in Nemus."

"What of the girl?"

"Meridith will be married to one of the great houses here in Seaptum. Might even be one next in line to the High throne." She gave Joanne's hand a squeeze. "Depends on the children you have, milady. I wouldn't mind intertwining our family branches for the greater good of future societies."

There it is! This isn't some casual walk, but a preemptive matchmaking.

"I guess we will see what the future holds," Joanne said. "You don't seem upset about mixing the bloodlines between Seaptum and Nemus?"

"Not that I, or any other woman in the land, could have foreseen it, but here you are, the second Nemus lady to grace our stones and mountains. We northern people adapt to whatever the winds blow in our directions. We support King Dryd, may he recover swiftly, and the prince regent," Lady Hawthorne said, the lines coming out rehearsed. "Ah, Mother, but I do enjoy the fresh air. The masters say it is good for the child to walk in the outdoors away from the stuffy rooms indoors. Would you like a drink?"

Before Joanne could respond, an attendant presented her with a goblet full of amber colored liquid. It smelled sweet, but not like wine.

"Ambrosia leaves crushed and soaked in water," Lady Hawthorne explained. "Helps keep the eyes from watering and nose from dripping during the budding of all the flowers. It is good for a person who leaks too much from their nose and eyes."

She meant Fraum without saying his name, Joanne was certain. "I will keep this information in mind." She sipped the water. It tasted like sweet ice with a hint of fruit.

Lady Hawthrone drained her own goblet.

"The worst part about being pregnant is not being able to drink wine," she said. "It's bad for the baby, the masters tell me. How could something so joyful be bad for babies? Good clean water and plenty of fresh vegetables and fruits. I mean, wine is a fruit, isn't it?"

"I guess," Joanne said. "I've never seen a wine plant."

"Oh, you are darling," Lady Hawthorne said. "It grows on vines. Little grapes that need to be squashed and stored in a wooden barrel. I guess they didn't have grapes in your large gardens?"

"No," Joanne said. *It did have the Dragon's Vein*, she wanted to mention, but kept that to herself.

"I guess we all have something we need to learn. Here, let us sit until the bell." Lady Hawthorne pointed out a stone bench beside a cluster of red roses. "Another terrible part about pregnancy is the swelling feet. I feel like I'm walking on water bags full of stones. That is our lot in life. Suffering discomforts makes it all the more pleasant when the new life leaves your body."

"I've heard that isn't too pleasant, either."

"No, it's like being torn apart, but it makes us tough. Strong. Especially when we must make tough decisions regarding the beings who leave our bodies." Lady Hawthorne drank another goblet of water. "From what I recall, you had a brother fight in the war."

Joanne narrowed her eyes.

"I'm most sorry that he died fighting for a cause he believed in," Lady Hawthorne said. "I find that to be an admirable trait. Something I know that Prince Gallium shares, I mean, except for the dying part."

"No one particularly enjoys the dying part," Joanne said. She remembered the porcelain doll Henrick had bought her at the Sowing Festival at Foster Manor for her eleventh birthday. After Thomas sat her down and blurted out that Henrick was dead, she clutched that doll, the only comfort she had in that moment, crying for what seemed hours. Then in a fit of rage, she tossed it against the wall, cracking its pale face, and stomped it. Each splintering crack didn't ease the pain, and shame later weighed her heart after all other emotions bled from her. She would never again receive a gift from her eldest brother.

"I'm certain you will be together again in Nahrangi," Lady Hawthorne said, patting Joanne's leg. "By Donn's blessed judgement."

"By Donn's blessed judgment," Joanne agreed. Lady Hawthorne smiled and Joanne didn't trust it any more than she would trust Fraum or any Seaptum. She had more faith in the Dragon's Vein preserving her, than these northerners. They had what her father used to say, 'Smiles like knives in the back.' It was a mask meant to disarm her, while their true intentions were plotted—with Fraum, she already knew his intentions and rather have had the knife.

"I do hope they provide you more suitable dresses," Lady Hawthorne said. "That material you have on now will provide you with as much comfort as a hole in the wall during a snow storm. Also, the style is, shall I say, I've seen peasants dress better. I have a seamstress and a tailor who will transform your rather pedantic way of dressing into a Princess' choice."

"From pigsty to Princess," Joanne said.

"Don't be such a sulk," Lady Hawthorne said. "You'll soon learn the customs here and how to dress to your audience."

A bell rang.

"Sounds like dinner is served." Lady Hawthorne stood up from the bench and her ladies-in-waiting flocked around her to make certain she was steady on her feet. "I do hope you enjoy a good, hearty mushroom soup. It is Prince Gallium's favorite, and although I cannot eat it on account of being pregnant, something about the mushrooms might cause some unwanted discomfort to my belly and the baby, but I will satisfy myself with a plum pudding."

"What about Fraum? Do you know what he likes?" Joanne asked.

"Misery loves company," Lady Hawthorne said and laughed, a frivolous titter that grated on Joanne's nerves. "Fraum is most peculiar about his health and eats according to what his master physician says he must eat, never, from what I have learned over the last decade of his life, does he do anything for pleasure. You will find out his other appetites soon enough."

It wasn't the answer she had expected, but it matched up with everything else she knew about her betrothed. *I don't want to know about his appetites any more than a rabbit wants to know the tastes of the fox.*

"We all have our burdens to bear," Lady Hawthorne said, seeming to read Joanne's mind.

When they re-entered the manor, Prince Gallium was there to greet them. Lady Hawthorne made a loud noise short of an orgasm, arms held wide and embraced him, receiving a kiss on both cheeks, blushing as he held her apart while looking either at her swollen breasts or belly.

"You are radiant," he said. "Being with child only brings out your natural beauty."

"Oh my, you were always a charming one. Either your memory deceives you or you are just being polite," Lady Hawthorne said, gripping his forearms. Prince Gallium didn't resist, which got Joanne to wonder if there was an intimate past relationship with those two. She grinned, releasing him, well, almost entirely; her hand rested on his arm. "But I had cook make your favorite."

"Mushroom soup!" Prince Gallium was led down the hall, leaving Joanne behind, forgotten.

"This way, milady," one of the younger lady-in-waiting said, curtseyed, and, waited for Joanne to acknowledge her. She huffed and followed after the two without waiting to see if the girl followed. The main hall was warm, a fire crackled in the hearth, and smelled of wood smoke and nut spices. Chairs with swans carved into the backs lined a rather long table which was nearly full of platters and bowls and mugs. Lord Hawthorne and Fraum were already seated at the head of the table. Several other men and women had joined them, and by the cut and style of their clothes, they were not maids or servants, but probably local lord and ladies.

Heads turned and dozens of eyes licked her up like she was a flavor to spicy up their pallets. All the chairs were filled, except for the one at the far end of the table. There she would be on display for everyone to observe, every gesture, from what spoon she used for the soup to how she chewed her food. Women whispered to their partners, probably mentioning how young Joanne appeared. What did they expect from a fourteen-year-old? Wrinkles and graying chin hairs? But they were all full of smiles. There seemed to be an abundance of those. A male servant pulled the chair out for her and pushed it in when she sat. Down at the end of the table Fraum eyed her like some delectable treat he could eat later on.

I should be flattered, perhaps even curious, but I know what lies beyond those lips.

The idea of kissing the snot dripping mouth caused her to shudder.

"Seems my bride-to-be has decided to grace us with her presence," Fraum said. Laughter chimed around the table like an axe thudding against wood. Lady Hawthorne even gave a series of small claps, as though she hadn't abandoned her for Prince Gallium's company.

"She makes a brilliant entrance," Lady Hawthorne said. "All beauty and grace."

"Yes, she makes quite the entrance," Fraum agreed, though Joanne knew he had different intentions. "Since we are all well met, and our bellies are empty, I'm certain you will all introduce yourselves to the probable princess."

"Probable, very clever," Lady Hawthorne said. Joanne noted her left hand was under the table next to Prince Gallium.

"One cannot be too certain in these precarious times," Fraum said, wiping his nose on a handkerchief. "The wedding is a year out and we know how temperamental living in the north can be to those unused to her harsh climates."

A general agreement went around the table. Joanne no longer felt safe in this company of smiling gentry. All were knives honed and ready to stab her in the back. She never felt so isolated, so alone. Yet, she wouldn't give them the pleasure of knowing her discomfort.

"I welcome the change this new path offers," Joanne said. "This part of my journey may be more kind to me than my own father who had me witness the torture and hanging of the man accused of murdering my tutor. Or the callousness of two brothers who rather beat their swords on wooden men while their sister wept for the death of her favorite one. The snows and ice may be foreboding, but eventually snow melts and ice cracks, unlike my mother who acknowledged me only when duty called for it. I'm sure I will find warmer embraces here and the cold edges dulled, or if not, I'm used to the probable existence of being isolated with my thoughts as my only consul."

Wood crackled in the heart, occupying the silence following her response. But the smiles, oh the impeccable smiles, trained to be pleasant even when someone shits on their bread and calls it a sandwich, remained—though Fraum let his slip for a moment, and his weepy eyes were red with fury and his ailment. Joanne picked up her goblet and held it out for it to be filled.

A servant came forward and poured.

"I thank our host, Lord Hawthorne for his generosity. All that occurs at this meal will be remembered graciously and in-kind response returned to every guest here at this table," Joanne said, raising the full goblet. "I drink to the health of all."

"To Lord Hawthorne and his lovely lady," Prince Gallium shouted, raising his glass. "Let us drink to their happiness as well as my brother's and the Princess Joanne!"

Not a single glass went unraised. Fraum had his up, yellowed-teeth showing between what could be a smile to those not used to his snarl. *Not some timid little bird for you to crush.* She smiled and swallowed the sweet wine. She had played her cards and hoped the Queen's Hangman didn't wait for here at the end of the hand. *They will hate or love me, but I'll be godsdamned if they believe they could intimidate me!*

After they ate, musicians were brought in to entertain them with songs unfamiliar to Joanne. She hadn't had much opportunity to hear musicians, outside of the tavern visits, but she found their music dull. During the course of the meal, starting with mixture of greens and chopped fruit, Lady Willowcreek introduced herself. A pudgy woman who was Joanne's mother's age, though with a sweet, albeit simple disposition talked about the hundreds of acres of orchards of winter pears and apples that her husband received as a dowery. Of course, Lord Willowcreek didn't need such extravagance, because he owned and leased out the largest number of salt mines in all the three nations, his wealth was second to King Dryd, who of course taxed the salts and fruit orchards to maintain their rather large army, in which her eldest son was a captain.

"Perhaps he may have battled your brother in the field at some time," Lady Willowcreek said.

"Perhaps," Joanne replied. *If only he had killed your son, then we would have a conversational topic in common.* Joanne smiled at her, knowing they weren't the only ones who knew how to use knives.

When the breads with a savory dipping oil were served next, Lady Windridge stole her attention with her sweet voice and large round eyes. She was hardly older than Joanne, and had less life experiences. She was most curious about a particular flower that grew in Nemus. The blue bell, which was her mother's favorite flower and brought back from the war. Where they lived, on the stoney ridges, only tough thistles and deep-rooted shrubs would grow giving off whites and reds, but no blues.

"The blue-bell requires much love and tender care," Joanne said, making up the story. The flowers grew like weeds in her Keeps gardens. They covered most of Twin Rivers' basin, or so she'd heard. "If one loses their faith in Qetesh, the flower withers, the petals fall, and never more will grow."

"Oh, I've never heard that one before," Lady Windridge said, leaning in to Joanne, large wide eyes watching her. "That would explain why when my mother found my father filling my maid with his seed, the flowers died."

"A good test of a faithful spouse," Joanne said.

"Aye, aye," Lady Windridge said, then glanced at her husband who was talking to another woman, his face particularly close to her bosom.

"I would keep that a secret," Joanne said.

Lady Windridge placed a finger to her lips. *I wonder what she might do if she had someone bring her blue bells and they died? Would Lord Windridge expire, too?*

The mushroom soup came next. With it, Prince Gallium made a loud gasp and kissed his fingers, placing them on Lady Hawthorne's cheek. "My favorite meal! So divine! Mother, but you are too kind to us!" Joanne was certain at the way Lady Hawthorne blushed and leaned close to Gallium that plenty of blue bells died in their past.

Lady Willowcreek tasted a spoonful and beamed. "Seasoned with my husband's salt."

I should hope not. Joanne dared not speak the words aloud and perhaps give offense. She doubted the older woman would understand the joke. *I will save this story for Selene. She will appreciate it.* At the thought of her maid, she longed to see those beautiful brown eyes, innocent though they were, but full of kindness with nary a spark of ambition. Joanne could be her true self around Selene.

The musicians played moderate, sappy songs that didn't stir the foot or the heart. Joanne looked around the table, drinking her third goblet of sweet wine, her head full of conversations half-listened to and light on the fumes of good food and the sweet drink. She excused herself to visit the garderobe. A dark-haired maid with pale, smooth skin and brown eyes escorted her to the room. It was occupied and Joanne waited, pushing her knees together. In a nearby room, she heard two other ladies she had yet to meet gossiping about her.

"She is rather pretty for someone from down there." The phrase "down there" sounded like a dirty place, where you might carefully wipe so as not to get any on your hands. "I wonder if this a serious match or another Lady Freeman?"

"Oh, I wouldn't put much concern into her, just think how lucky our daughters were to avoid such a match." A short titter of laughter. "Seriously, I say before the winter ends, she'll be in the arms of Gallium. Then we will see who sits the throne and whose pretty head rolls merrily along."

The maid frowned, standing off to the side.

She knows they are talking about me.

Joanne went to the maid and took her by the arm. The girl jumped as though Joanne had hit her. Joanne smiled, leaning in close to the maid's ear. "Do you know these bitches?" The maid gave a small whimper and nodded.

"What are their names?"

The maid gave her their names.

The door to the garderobe opened. Another women who had yet been introduced to Joanne stepped out, adjusting her skirts. She was young and pretty, smiled at Joanne and gave a small bow. "Milday, I'm Lady Ironwood," she said. "It is a pleasure to make your acquaintance."

"Good to meet you," Joanne said, and glanced to the empty garderobe. "Wine is working its way through me."

"Oh, my apologies. I don't mean... please, don't let me hold you... I completely understand." She bowed and began working her way in the direction of the room with the two women.

Joanne entered the little room, barely getting her under clothes off to relieve her bladder. She dreamt of ways to make the two women suffer. Not in the house of Hawthorne, but later. They will suffer for their insults, even if they didn't understand the reason. When she finished and exited the garderobe, the maid waited.

"Not a word of what you heard," Joanne said. "Swear it."

"I swear," the girl said.

"Good, if you hear any more of these little twats speaking ill of me or my station. Whisper their names to me," Joanne said.

"I can tell you now, milady, that none of the women respect you. They fear your new found position and being from Nemus, what you might do to influence the course of their husbands' power," the maid said. "None believe that Prince Fraum will last long enough to sit the throne and so preen to his brother hoping to be the next queen."

Joanne's jaw tightened. It made sense the fawning of Lady Hawthorne over Prince Gallium.

"Does the Prince regent know this?"

"He'd be a fool not to know what the others think," she said.

"What do you think?"

"Milady?'

"What do you think of Gallium taking the throne?"

"It's not my place to have a thought on the subject," the maid said. "One ruler is the same as any other to me."

"Do you know how to write?"

"Yes, milady."

Joanne wasn't sure why she asked what she did, risking the wrath of Lord and Lady Hawthorne, and drawing suspicion to herself, and probable punishment from Fraum. With all these consequences weighed against her seething anger, like wrestling a snake that bore its fangs and tried to strangle her, poison her with its bite, Joanne made the choice her father would have: the right people for the right results. "Be my eyes and ears here, befriend my lady-in-waiting Selene and write her sweet letters and I will see you well rewarded."

"I don't know what to say—"

"Say nothing, but put it in ink," Joanne said. "I will let my girl know of the arrangement."

"As you wish, milady." The maid curtsied.

"What is your name?"

"Lily, milady."

"Well, Lily, this may be a chance meeting of a lifetime."

A sweet pastry full of some sort of nut paste sat on her plate when she returned. Lady Windridge and Lady Willowcreek chirped on about the delectable pastry, waiting eagerly for Joane to try it. "I doubt they have anything like this where you are from, my dear," Lady Willowcreek said. She was right and Joanne smiled as she bit into it. It had a burnt wood flavor that nearly gagged her, but she chewed. Chewed and chewed, watching the two women who spoke so poorly about her. They were thin little beasts with overabundant cleavage and eyes that flickered around the table, sometimes landing on Joanne, to give a quick smile, and scan along to their husbands, both older men with gray powdering their hair and beards. Men who had appearances of being important, but lacked the right birthing to be king. *Or the ambition to take it.* Lord Desmond took what he had to in order to protect Nemus from bleeding out. She paid the price of it. *None of these pampered girls and men will understand. I will have them on their knees.*

"It's good," Joanne said around a mouthful of paste. Lady Willowcreek and Lady Windridge both nodded as though they expected nothing less than this response. Did she trust their banality? Were they just another mask over cunning sneers? Joanne set the pastry down and took a hand from each of the women. "You will both have to show me more of such deliciousness. Perhaps we can celebrate more once I've settled into my new station."

"Yes! That would be most fun," Lady Windridge said, squeezing Joanne's hand.

"A dessert party for the princess," Lady Willowcreek agreed. "I will have it arranged and will invite the prominent Ladies for you to formally greet."

"Including those two," Joanne gestured to the two ladies who had spoken ill of her

"Lady Silversmith and Lady Foxglow?"

"Yes, those two."

"They never miss a social event of any importance," Lady Willowcreek said, her tone and demeanor didn't betray her affections one way or another to the women.

"They are moths to the fires of society," Lady Windridge said.

Then they won't mind having their wings singed.

"Excellent, then shall we set the date for a full moon from now?"

"So it will be, princess," Lady Willowcreek said. "So it will be."

CHAPTER TEN: COLD HOME, STONE HOME

"Silver steals the heart's warmth
Gold buys it back again."
—Seaptum proverb on wealth

Stuffed full of food and head spinning with wine, the musicians followed the women to a room set up with comfortable chairs and tables. They sat with cups of wine while the musicians played a dramatic overture and a woman spoke/sang a poem about Sin and her lost love, the Pirate Captain Hollister. Joanne knew the song, had sung it to Fraum not too long ago. Some of the words were changed to be more dramatic and less romantic, but some of the ladies wept and others nodded, their faces rapt in reverence at the sad story performed, to Joanne at least, in an over-rehearsed voice lacking in true emotion.

Joanne feigned interest and when it ended—Sin wept to Mother and Father who denied her request for the Pirate Captain to be Ascended, and the final monologue where the goddess of the moon and stars swore vengeance for the afront—she clapped along with the other women. Next up were two performers. One was dressed in obviously fake black armor, representing the Blades Man and the other was a young woman unknown to Joanne.

It opened with a long lament from the woman.

"They came at night, torches blazing like a hundred suns while we slept beneath thatched roofs, wood smoke fresh in bedded hearths. Mothers, fathers, sons, and daughters tucked away safely dreaming, when the nightmares came and lit our homes, our hearths, our beds on fire. They killed my father, stabbed him in his belly as he stood in the doorway, then another took his head."

Several ladies gasped at the revelation. The girl playing the part of whoever it was supposed to be, a tale that could be as old as yesterday or hundreds of years past. Men worked violence on other men, and when there were no men remaining, turned to violate women.

"My brother was taken next. Only five years old and they broke him like a disobedient dog, bashing his head until his cries ceased and fed his body to the flames. My mother they held down, gore-streaked hands tore her clothes and they grunted on her, strangling her, teeth biting and they beat her. Nothing remained, but her body, to be consumed by the fire. They turned to me, sweat and blood streaked, heat of violence smoking from them. I was ready to die. Ready to join my family in the fields of Nahrangi. But they stole me away instead."

Joanne leaned forward. She knew this story, but couldn't remember where she had heard it.

"The men took me to their village along with other young girls, many as young as my brother, and they fed us maggots and worms while forcing us to perform demeaning acts on knees and backs. Touched us in forbidden places and left us, stripped bare in the cold nights," the woman took off her black outfit and cloak, standing in only her small clothes. She knelt, eyes cast up, looking at Joanne. "I prayed, 'Blades Man, give me the strength to kill these men. Let me avenge my mother, my father, my brother, and these young girls. Let me kill my captors and free myself and these girls before I die.' For seven nights I prayed, the fire dancing in my words as my body shivered in the cold. Then on the seventh night he came to me."

The man in black stage-armor stepped beside the girl.

"Daughter, I hear your prayers. Let me aide you."

"Then he placed a hand on my shoulder and the weight of the chains broke"

The Blades Man actor helped the girl to her feet.

"You are free to go do as you please," he said.

"I want to kill them. Kill them all," the girl said.

The Blades Man placed a wooden knife in the girl's hand.

"Feed the steel and slack your thirst."

"I shall," the girl said, facing the audience of women, her face contorted into rage and fury. "I cut those men, sliced their souls from their flesh, casting them into Arula. Sliced throats, carved out hearts and tied visceral around their necks and hung them from the branches for the crows. My skin was stained with their blood, my hair thick with it. The steel drank until its thirst was slackened, the blade slick in my hands, and then I fed on their bodies. The other girls ran, frightened of the fiend who had freed them in the night. From then on, I lurked within the Shadows, killing all who offended, any who would lay a hand on the innocent girl or women. There I lurk to this day. Spirit of Vengeance and daughter of rage."

Mistress of Shadows! Joanne covered her mouth from blurting it out.

The actors bowed to the loud applause.

"Very daring," Lady Hawthorne said, dabbing her eyes. "Masterful performance."

The musicians played a happy tune and the woman talked about the song and the performance. Joanne approached the actress.

"Why did you act out the Mistress of Shadows?"

"It was requested," the girl said. "Did it not please you, lady?"

"All but the ending. How did she Ascend?"

"Why, from what I've been told she hadn't. She died, rejected by the other gods and goddesses and so her spirit wanders the night helping young women in need."

She stalks me in my sleep. No ghost, but a goddess.

"Thank you," Joanne said.

The night wore on and Joanne found herself drowsy. Many of the ladies had left already, leaving only the Windridges, the Willowcreeks, and some other names Joanne couldn't remember. Too many people and all the smiles they wore thin like wet parchment. Joanne was disgusted by it all. She was put on display, mocked, jeered, and yet, she found her opportunity.

She had to think of how her father might handle this situation. He was a strong, uncompromising man and she was his daughter. For now, she was saturated by all the oily affections, desiring only Selene's company. That was the security she trusted.

"I must bid you a good night," she said to the remaining guests. "My spirit may be willing, but my mind and body have reached the point of exhaustion."

The maid, Lily, led her down a long, dark hallway. They passed several closed doors and tapestries hanging on the walls. Joanne glanced at the soft light glow on the maid's face. There was something oddly familiar about the girl, though Joanne had never seen her before tonight, she could almost swear that they had met.

"Have you ever been to Nemus?" She asked the girl as they walked the hallway.

"Only in my dreams," Lily said, holding the taper out and pointed at a closed door. "These are your rooms. I hope you rest well, milady."

"Thank you, Lily. I look forward to your correspondence," Joanne said, giving her a warm smile.

Lilly curtsied and said, "I am in your service." The little candlelight floated down the hall, leaving Joanne to watch and wonder again why the girl was very familiar to her. She shook her head. *Must be the wine and exhaustion.* She entered the room.

Again, bed clothes were laid out for her. Selene and Beaty waited, chatting about some frivolous piece of gossip they had heard. Joanne was pleased they were getting along, but also a little jealous of Beaty. She got to spend more time with Selene than Joanne did. *Maybe Beaty will ride in the baggage carriage tomorrow.* That wouldn't work. Selene would be too frightened to be so close to her and Fraum. A mouse sitting too near the cats.

"I trust you had a productive visit," Joanne said, waiting for them to undress her. They bound off the bed and worked the laces of her dress.

"We have," Beaty said.

"I met a friend," Selene said.

"Oh."

"Yes, a Lady Lily who will be writing me correspondence regarding a certain condition that is plaguing me since I left home," Selene said. "I would do well to be certain that my mistress reads these letters so you may procure the proper ingredients to alleviate my discomforts."

"Sounds like you're either pregnant or bloated," Joanne said, though she was pleased that Lily spoke to Selene promptly rather than waiting. "It is all one and the same."

"Perhaps someone could teach me how to read letters and write them so I may respond properly," Selene said and blushed.

"I will take up that chore," Beaty said, lifting the dress over Joanne's head.

"Mother bless you for it," Selene said.

"I'm surprised at how bold our princess is becoming," Beaty said, taking away the small clothes that Joanne shed and helping her into the night shift. "Seems she is playing a little game with these houses."

"Why shouldn't I be informed?"

"As long as you understand who is informing on you, as well."

"Oh gods," Joanne said. "I'm tired of these false faces."

"Then smile and reveal nothing more than what they desire to hear," Beaty said. "Allow me to set up the little bird calls so no one comes back to blame you."

"Would you be so kind?"

"It is not out of charity, but more an act of necessity. My grandmother always said it is best to be well-informed to be well-prepared for any assault on you or your character. Since you are a Princess, it will not be proper for you to hop the branches of common birds, but rather, tease out what you need to know from the bigger nests."

"I know two birds I would like to throttle," Joanne said.

Beaty gave her a disapproving glance.

"They spoke foul of me and Fraum," Joanne said. "There is a belief that Fraum won't live long enough to sit the throne and that I would be sent back home like a little beggar girl. The way you two look at each other it is rather common knowledge. Is that what you heard as well from the other little birds?"

"Yes, and nothing more for you to be concerned over this night," Beaty said.

"It is time for you to rest," Selene said, helping her with her hair. She brushed it, her touch gentler than Beaty's. "I'm certain the prince regent is well-informed on who is planning what and is prepared to protect himself."

"Who will protect me?"

"That's why you have us," Beaty said. "We will build the goodwill of supporters, so, if anything does go sour with the prince regent, you will always have a sanctuary to retreat into before we can inform your father and get the necessary aide to see you home again."

But will my father care enough to bring me back? She hoped he would, but she had watched him torture an innocent man to confess to killing someone he had loved. Selling her off like an unwanted animal was one way he'd be finished with her, no matter the outcome. *I'm his sacrifice for a shot at protecting his interests.*

"Home," Joanne said. "These rocks and icy streams are our new home, no matter if we make them run red with blood."

She saw their worried faces in the looking glass behind her own certain grin. That night, both her ladies-in-waiting slept with their backs to her. Joanne dreamed something dark, something wicked, and the horrified expressions of Lady Foxglow and Lady Silversmith as Joanne stripped them of everything they owned, including their skin—she held it like a menstrual rag in one hand, knife in the other, their gristle-exposed mouths crying for death. Death she wouldn't give, because it was a mercy they had yet to earn.

A dark voice spoke: *Let them suffer as I had suffered. Let them ache and cry my name and I will turn a deaf ear to them. All for you, my pet.*

The morning found Joanne alone with Lady Hawthorne, stirring fruit into a bowl of hot oats seasoned with a sweet sugar. Syrup from the ironwood tree, Lady Hawthorne had called it. "One of the few pleasures allotted me. A dab in the morning, but not too much. Otherwise, it is bad on the teeth."

Joanne enjoyed the sweetness it brought to the bland oats.

"I have never tasted such a delight before," she said.

"I'm not surprised since the ironwood is indigenous to Seaptum," Lady Hawthorne said, sipping from a cup of mint tea. "Willowcreeks have the largest forest of ironwood that they tap the syrup from the trees and boil it to make it palatable. I'm certain Lord Willowcreek would be pleased to open trade in Nemus, since it holds almost no value in Seaptum. We are practically sticky with it." Lady Hawthorne laughed at her own joke. Joanne smiled and nodded.

As they were about to leave, Lady Hawthorne gifted Joanne with a ceramic jug of the syrup. Lily flashed her a quick smile which Joanne ignored. She couldn't let anyone suspect the friendship. Once again, she was settled into the carriage beside Beaty and across from Fraum. Her betrothed had a smile for her.

"I see you are enjoying these little visits," he said and didn't wait for her response. "Already have some foolish, dull-witted ladies of lesser houses fawning over your rustic charms. I think it is rather nice of them. Nice indeed. Having friends will smooth the stoney transition."

"I hope we can be friends," Joanne said.

Fraum laughed.

"I can have no friends, only sycophants bending and lapping the spittle at my feet. I can afford no comforts, beyond my duty to you as a husband," Fraum said.

For a moment Joanne felt sorry for him. He was as much a prisoner of his upbringing and station in life as she was to hers, bound by duty of different sorts. She reached out to touch his hand and he recoiled it, like she was a dog about to bite him. His smile turned into a snarl. "You may fool them, but I know what you are."

"What am I, milord?" Joanne asked, trying to contain her anger.

"A pebble in this game of crowns," Fraum said. "Cast to me and now I must play the role of protector to not only my people, but yours as well. Pebbles can be lost. Pebbles can be tossed away for a shinier one, or crushed into dust by larger stones. Oh, but pebbles are always a nuisance when tumbling around in my boot."

Joanne was close to tears at the harsh words.

"Why not cast away the nuisance?"

"I had rather a small pebble to pester me, than a larger rock to smash my toes," Fraum said. "If it pleases you, I would like silence, now that my pleasant mood has been ruined."

Joanne bowed her head, jaw stiff from closing her mouth and grinding her teeth. She pressed her hands between her knees, disgusted by his disgust. This wasn't going to work out. What was her father thinking that she could tame such a creature? Beaty took her hand, pried it off the other to calm her shaking leg. Joanne squeezed her fingers, the anger and hurt trembling in her limbs. She longed for Selene. With her she would find her comfort. Beaty was kind, but Selene was who she needed, but wouldn't have until they arrived at their next destination. Joanne laid her head on Beaty's shoulder, closed her eyes, and prayed they wouldn't be long.

They stopped once at midday and Joanne left the carriage without speaking to Fraum. He, likewise, didn't acknowledge her in any way. She could have been a clear glass for all he saw. She breathed in the fresh air and walked; Beaty tight against her.

"A beast. A common beast," Beaty said. "He doesn't deserve you or your affections."

"Yet I am tethered to him," Joanne said.

She saw Selene and grabbed the girl, producing a startled squeak from her. Beaty explained what had transpired in the carriage. Selene gasped, stroking Joanne's head and held her. It was a brief comfort. One where Joanne allowed the tears to slip down her cheek and soak into Selene's bosom. These would be the last tears she would shed for that creature. Husband in name alone, she would find her freedom from him. Let the gods damn duty and all men.

"They will all suffer," Joanne said.

"Be patient," Beaty said, rubbing her back. "Like he said, gather your friends, though they be simple and foolish. They have resources to support you."

Joane nodded. She couldn't afford to be rash. Think clearly and not allow emotion to rule her. That had been her detriment with her tutor. Yet, she couldn't be weak. She would set examples, but being a pebble in the game of crowns meant she had power, however slight it might be.

She had a blanket set up away from Fraum and Gallium. Eating some bread and nut paste, two men stood close watch over her. Even here in Seaptum, they were not free from the fear of treachery. She overheard Prince Gallium ask, "What did you do now to insult our little princess?"

"The truth is not palatable to everyone," Fraum said. His shoulders were slumped and his back to them.

"Ah, being your charming self as usual." Prince Gallium held a goblet up to Joanne, but she turned away from him. He was not much better than his brother. Charming, though he would kill just as easily as give a kind word.

Back in the carriage, Joanne stared out the window, making certain the shade wasn't raised too high to garnish a complaint from Fraum. They passed giant trees as tall as four Keeps, some with their tops out of view from her seat in the carriage. These giants cast long shadows over the road. Birds took light at their passage and several creatures hide in the underbrush. Then they were past this forest of giants and the carriage slowed, moving at an incline. The road narrowed, twisting like a slow slithering snake, with sharp turns coming without warning, making her belly queasy, and Joanne dropped the shade closed. She pinched her eyes closed and tried not to imagine the drop over the edge of this winding road. The coachman must be experienced enough, since there was no instance of freefall, though they eventually leveled again.

"That part of the journey always sickens even the most stalwart and iron-stomached individual," Fraum said. "I am used to the twists and turns."

The carriage picked up speed again and Joanne chanced a peek out the window. All the green faded into yellows and grays. Shrubs replaced the tall trees. Dust and stones took the place of grass, though the kind that did grow were long, yellow stalks. Dark purple flowers brought out the color of the mountain desert. Even the clouds seemed closer.

In the distance was a large rock structure carved into the peak of the mountain. An unfriendly, foreboding structure dug into the spine of the mountain itself. Argenti Lapisdom. Silver stone, though it didn't appear silver to her, but more like sterile rock lacking in life and attention. A tomb for the kings while they lived, though a defensible fortress that only a fool or a madman would try marching an army up the narrow paths to be slaughtered before they achieved the summit, the dreams of a siege dead and broken at the basin. Joanne felt the weight of it crushing her before the carriage arrived at the tall, stone walls. A large iron gate peeled apart, kicking up dust. Beyond the gates stood a sea of soldiers, bearing the Golden Sun emblem on their silver breast plates, holding up long halberds sharp-edged arcs. Some had banners that flapped in the breeze, again the golden sun overlayed the blue, like it was rising in the horizon.

Joanne marveled at the long lines of soldiers as endless as the blue sky. They reached an eventual horizon and the carriage rounded the turnabout. A dozen servants wearing purple and the golden sun over their right breasts, placed a foot stool and opened the carriage door. They assisted Fraum first, holding onto his arms as he ducked beneath the carriage door roof. A pair of hands offered to assist Joanne and she was swept up by them. They were gentle, guiding her to the proper footing and then she waited beside Fraum who was tugging his tunic into place. Beaty stood beside her. Again, the enormity of Argenti Lapisdom weighed on her. She craned her neck to take in the four stories of solid stone structure. Windows glinted in the bright light and more banners hung with the sun and blue horizon. There was no mistaking who resided here. Along the parapets archers stood, bows strung and fletchers full of arrows ready to rain down on any enemy below. Large constructs that appeared to be giant mechanical bows angled down over the line of the gate.

"Beautiful, isn't it," Fraum said. "No army has taken Argenti Lapisdom in over a century. It has stood here on Mount Victorious as an emblem to the realm. Seaptum will not be defeated. It will exist as long as this mountain exists. Root and stone."

"I see," Joanne said.

"Welcome to your new home."

A stone prison. Joanne's heart sank.

Attended by two servants, Fraum ascended the seven marble stairs leading to the double wooden doors bound in iron straps with spikes settled in inches apart, running vertical. Solid marble columns flaring out in sun beams where they reached the overlay marked either side of the doors. Joanne followed, stepping carefully and relying on the attendants to keep her balance. The doors were cavernous and she entered into the vestibule the size of several small homes. Her footfalls echoed as she entered inside, solemn as a temple of worship, and the ceiling itself was rounded. Four candelabras hung from them with a dozen candles each to light the room. Statues to Moko, the god of earthquakes, with his chiseled muscular form and stony legs, stood in alcoves, bent as though holding up the structure of the room. Tables ordained with lace cloths and flowers lined the walls. A marble staircase spiraled upward to the next floor lined with a banister of stone and gilded wood. Guards stood at every point along the way. They watched Joanne as she entered, standing at attention. Joanne was certain if called on, they would have her skewered like a pig roasting over a fire.

A woman dressed in purple with a long cape, golden stars pinning it to her shoulders entered from the next room. She shared similar features to Fraum, the same pale complexion and sharp blue eyes. Cold as the stone they walked on. Her bodice was tight, though modest, covering up her neck. Her skirt billowed out as she walked to Fraum.

"My beautiful son has returned," she said, holding out her hands. Fraum took them, leaned in to place a single kiss on her right cheek. "I was so worried the strain of travel would have an ill-effect on your health."

"I suffered a little from the foul airs, but the strength of the mountain runs in my veins," Fraum said. "How is father?"

"He is still bed ridden." Her scowl matched his. "I see your visit was a success, you have brought home a bride."

Fraum waved her away.

"My father commands and I obey."

Queen Galea, as Beaty instructed Joanne on the important names she should know, circled Joanne, appraising her the way she might appraise a sheep for wool. Her eyes worked up and down, taking in all her flaws or so Joanne assumed. What daughter could be perfect for her perfectly dreadful son?

"I assume you are unspoiled," Queen Galea said. "That is what your father promised."

"No man has yet touched me," Joanne said, looking into the cold blue eyes.

"What is your education, girl?"

"I can read and write. I know the history of Nemus, the cause of the war between our nation, philosophy, botany, and I know the stories of all the gods and goddesses," Joanne said.

"Needle work? Music? Poetry?"

"I am not as familiar in those areas," Joanne said. "My tutor was more into knowing things and less into creating things."

Then she died.

"You aren't as frivolous as I had feared," Queen Galea said. Joanne didn't know if that was a compliment or an insult. Not that Joanne wasn't used to veiled insults—her mother was a master of them. Joanne expected as much affection from Queen Galea as her own mother gave her. "Though I must insist you learn the true history of Seaptum."

"I am a quick study," Joanne said.

"Good," Queen Galea said. "You will need to learn much before you marry my son. Fraum will provide you with the books you need and a tutor to fill in the gaps. Your quarters will be in the west wing. There you and your retinue will reside. I will have a tailor come by the next week to take measurements and design for you proper attire. Meal times are sixth bell, thirteenth bell, and twentieth bell. You may find leisure in the gardens, between your studies. Fraum will join you on occasion so you may become familiar with his rather particular behaviors, and he yours."

Fraum scowled, but kept his mouth shut. She knew his opinion, anyway.

Queen Galea smiled.

"In less than a year, you will be married and perform the duties of a pious wife and princess. You have met most of the ladies who are of importance to Seaptum. Try not to be swept up in their curiosity. They will beg your favor and you should give none, unless it benefits your husband. All you are is an extension of Fraum."

"Yes, my Queen," Joanne said and curtsied.

"I have badgered you enough. Lady Hamlet will show you to your rooms." Queen Galea waggled her two fingers on her right hand. A blonde-haired woman wearing a white smock and purple bodice, adorned with the sun emblem on the shoulders, came forward. She was short and squat, though much younger than Lady Bodaline, but much older than Joanne. "Come, Fraum. I know you are anxious to see your father."

"Delightful, isn't she." A voice whispered from behind. Joanne startled, squeaked, and turned to find Prince Gallium standing there, watching his mother leave without so much as an acknowledgement. "I would be her favorite, but I was born second."

"Then the gods favored you," Joanne said and Prince Gallium laughed.

Lady Hamlet waited patiently for Joanne to follow her.

"This is to be my home?" *My prison of stone.* She started up the marble staircase.

"It isn't so bad, once you get used to the cold," Prince Gallium said. "Even in the hottest part of season, you may find your extremities a bit colder than usual. It is the mountain air. Get yourself settled and I will show you the most exquisite sight. There's nothing like it in the world."

"Have you travelled the world?"

"Much of it," Gallium said. "The perks of being the second son. I get to secure the trade rights from other nations, either by diplomacy or show of force."

"What did you use to secure me?"

"Both, princess. Both."

Lady Hamlet led her down an expansive hall, their footfalls echoing off the stone walls. They were not empty or impoverished like Freeman Hall. Brightly embroidered tapestries covered the walls, guards and servants moved around, paying her no attention beyond a cursory glance. Most impressive were the statues. Marble statues of the gods adorned alcoves along the way. Perfectly chiseled effigies that watched her as she passed by. The most disturbing was Donn, holding a silver platter, opened to reveal a heart waiting for him to sink his teeth into it. The stoney eyes followed her along and Joanne could sense her heart on the platter, bitter with the murder and deaths attributed to her. They say that soldiers could be forgiven for killing in war, self-preservation, but wasn't murder another way to preserve one's self? She slit her tutor's throat so she wouldn't get into trouble, though she doubted her father would have hung her like Cook Mathers.

I did them a favor. They are together as eternal lovers. Nothing could part them. Not age, not disease. Not jealousy. They are pure spirits there in Nahrangi for all time, unless there was more I didn't know. Perhaps they were treacherous. Perhaps Teresa was plotting to kill my family. Then my act was no more than a soldier's actions on the battlefield.

"Find me after the eighteenth bell in the east garden," Gallium said. "I will be waiting, princess."

He bowed and left her with Beaty and Lady Hamlet. She watched his swagger, knowing she had been promised to the wrong brother. A punishment for her sins. Joanne bit her lip and turned back to Lady Hamlet who gave her a knowing smile. She didn't say a thing, but she shared a similar opinion of the princes. They continued down a little way to a large double door.

"Here are my lady's quarters," Lady Hamlet said and curtsied. "If you need anything, send for me down the hall. I will take your lady with me so she knows where to find me. The halls of this great castle can be daunting, but you will get used to them in time."

Joanne entered the room and stood in awe. It was extremely large and very bright. Two framed windows were open, allowing in a breeze to pluck playfully at the gossamer curtains, flipping them like wings of a picture book angel. Joanne moved to the window and looked down at the parade ground where they had entered. The gate was far away, appearing as a small doorway to a vast empty space. The line of soldiers was replaced by footmen, unloading carriages. The cool breeze caused her to shudder and she backed away, pulling the window closed. At the far side of the room was a bed larger than the carriage, with four posts and purple curtains tied up. Adjacent to it was a large wardrobe, a chest of drawers, including a full-length mirror where Joanne stared at the simple girl lost in the grandeur. Several cushioned chairs were stationed around a round table. Bookshelves covered in leather bound tomes. There was even her own personal garderobe on the opposite side of the room. The hole for which dropped a distance into darkness that stank of old urine and feces. Vases of flowers adorned the side tables close by to cover the fragrance.

I could live in here and never step foot outside except for meal times. This could very well be my prison.

The fire place between the windows was clean and wood placed behind an iron grating. She was certain it would be used even in the warmer months to keep the drafts at bay. Another door led into adjoining rooms where presumably Selene and Beaty would reside when not attending Joanne and her needs.

"Mother bless us!" Joanne turned to see Selene standing in the doorway, brown eyes wide and the trunk she had been carrying dropped to her feet. "This room is larger than the house I was born in."

A footman cleared his throat and Selene moved aside, allowing the men behind her to bring in the rest of Joanne's belongings. Her two trunks hardly occupied any space. Her clothes would all fit in a corner of the wardrobe, not that it mattered much since Queen Galea would have more designed for her to fit the modest Seaptum court style, whatever that meant.

"That's the biggest bed I have ever seen," Selene said and jumped on it with her backside, kicking her feet that didn't reach the floor.

"I hope I'm not too alone in it," Joanne said.

"What do you mean? Aren't we sharing like before?"

"We don't have to," Joanne said. "You have your own room."

Selene's eyes grew larger and she clapped her hands.

"My own room?"

"It is much smaller than mine, of course, but it is right through this door," Joanne opened it to show Selene her modest-sized space. It was similar to the guestrooms they shared at the Freeman's and Hawthorne's estates. Selene giggled and spun around, her skirt showing her ankles and slippers. Joanne smiled, a stirring in her belly and a lightness filling her.

Is this joy? I haven't felt anything like it since— She had no memory of this feeling. Fear, sadness, anger, pleasure, and disgust. Those were known to her, but this joy was something wonderful. She went in and took Selene's hands and they danced around the room.

"What is this?"

Beaty stood in the doorway, arms folded and her mouth tight in displeasure. Selene immediately stopped dancing, her chest heaving, though her smiled remained, large and joyous. "My own room, Lady Beaty." She giggled at the silly sound of the rhyme and Joanne joined her.

"I see," Beaty said. Then she unfolded her arms and sighed. "Yes, it is a nice arrangement. I think it is best if we have quiet time to allow our princess time to rest before she must meet her obligations."

"Gallium wants to show me the most exquisite sight I have ever seen," Joanne said and yawned.

"I hope it isn't his bedroom," Beaty said.

"No, we are to meet him in the east garden."

"Then I suggest you take a rest."

I will try, though I am exhausted I feel as giddy as Selene.

The sky had a dark red streak with orange and yellow tendrils streaming to the east, like someone had lit it on fire. The breeze had given the air a slight chill that Joanne wasn't prepared for and she hugged herself though there was no warmth to be found. She didn't think a garden could be created on this rocky soil, but when Lady Hamlet opened a side door to a vast menagerie of bushes and trees, all budding and giving off such strong fragrances, she had found herself in awe for the second time since her arrival.

"All this beauty found in such a desolate place," Joanne said.

"Same could be said of you, Princess," Prince Gallium said.

Joanne blushed despite how foolish he sounded.

"Where is your brother? Why isn't he here to walk the gardens with me?"

"He refuses to leave the indoors until, as he puts it, the plants cease their fornication. The pollen pollutes his health and you have already seen him when he leaks from every hole in his face," Prince Gallium said and took off his cloak. "You must be cold, I can see the goose flesh popping up on your delicate skin, princess." He wrapped his cloak around her shoulders. His smell was pleasant and his own warmth caused her to shiver. "There, now I don't need to witness you suffering."

"What about my ladies?" Joanne asked, motioning to Beaty, Selene and Lady Hamlet.

"I only have the one cloak, but they are welcomed to be dismissed, if you would have them not be in discomfort. I have only good intentions for my brother's betrothed, and my soon to be sister," Gallium said and smiled.

Innocent and charming, like a fox in the parables Joanne had read when she was younger.

"We can endure this small discomfort, my prince," Beaty said and curtsied. "I thank you for your concern over our well-being."

"Very well then, follow me." Prince Gallium walked along the edges of the countless flowers. Some Joanne recognized, but many were unfamiliar. She wished she had Teresa's book on botany listing out the names of flowers and their uses. One flower she noted was absent was the yellow and red Dragon's Vein—*much too dangerous to be this close to the seat of power*. The wind howled a little, breathing its chilly breath on them. She heard Selene's teeth chatter.

"You can go back," Joanne said.

"N…no. I wannnna see this wonnnder."

"Don't complain to me later."

"Whennnn have I evvver?"

Prince Gallium unlatched a small gate at the far end of the stone wall marking the edge of the garden. Joanne sniffed the air. Another familiar smell drifted in and the sound it carried as well.

"Is that the sea?" Joanne asked.

"Follow me, princess," Prince Gallium said, exiting the garden through the gate. The ground continued on for a few more feet and then abruptly ended. "Watch your step. It is a rather long drop to a very unpleasant death."

Joanne stood near the precipice and stared over the edge. There the ocean foamed around several large, jagged rocks below. On the face of the rock grew hundreds of purple flowers with leaves thick and plump, as though they were sliced open and filled with the ocean. It was a beautiful sight, but not the most exquisite one she had ever seen. She was about to nod her head and ask to go back, when Gallium pointed out further in the sea. A large, scaly tail slithered from the water and dipped back into the waves.

"What is that?"

"Much like how Nemus has a dragon rumored to live in the black marsh, we have one in our ocean."

"Does it fly?"

"Not that I have ever noticed. It swims out in the sea close to our shores," Prince Gallium said, crouching down as though he could get closer to the creature. "I did watch it crush a small fisherman's boat when I was a child. A man and his boy had sailed this side of the mountain, seeking a larger haul I assume since no one ever fishes this region. They had cast their nets over the side. I saw the long, bluish gray neck rise above the water behind them. I cupped my hands and tried to shout a warning, but my voice was small compared to the vast sounds of the waves. The wyrm opened its large beak and snapped the mast mid-beam. The rest of the bulk crashed down on the vessel, smashing the father and sending his son overboard. The son dug his arms into the water, kicking his legs as fast as he could. I stood, shouting for him to swim faster, because the beast was behind him. I don't know if he heard, but he had almost reached the rocks. Had one hand on the slimy edge, when the beast clutched his right legs. The poor bastard had no chance, his life ripped away under the water. I waited to see if he might surface again, but like his father, he was lost. The sea wyrm retreated further away from the rocks, its long tail slithering along the horizon."

"That's horrifying," Joanne said. "Why don't you hunt it and kill it?"

Prince Gallium laughed. "Why would we? It is the greatest defense we have on the eastern shores. No one would dare invade us knowing that creature lurked to destroy their vessel."

"And it never leaves the sea?"

"No, princess, it won't sprout wings and fly up to eat your pretty self," Gallium said. "Rest knowing you are safe from sea and air wyrms. The greatest danger to you comes from within the heart of the stone itself. I will do my very best to protect you, though even my power has limits."

"What are you saying?" Joanne asked.

"That indifference may be your best ally," Prince Gallium said. "Be careful how much you place on the table when you gamble and watch out for the Queen's hangman. He'll take everything from you." He left her and her ladies, cold wind prickling their flesh.

That was the best proof to her fear that she was indeed not a bride, but a prisoner. A hostage never to be released or see her home country again. *How long would it take for my body to hit the water if I ran and jumped? How long might it take for me to die, smashed on the jagged rocks? Or a meal for the sea wyrm?*

"Let's go inside, milady," Beaty said, touching her on the elbow.

"It is cold," Joanne said and they entered the gardens and started her new life.

CHAPTER ELEVEN:
TO CATCH A FOX

The Fox is a clever creature and hard to capture
But when caught, it's fur makes a fine muffler for
Cold nights.
> —*from "Winter Wear" Seaptum's history of*
> *Women's apparel.*

Boredom wasn't on the list of Joanne's daily activities. As promised, books on the history of Seaptum were delivered to her room. A dozen large tomes written in small print waited for her stacked in two piles like twin towers on the table. She leafed through the top one, the paper crinkling in her fingers and it smelled old and musty. *Probably preserved in the tears of young children and adolescents forced to read them.* She sat in the chair and began to read. The stories were not as bad as she feared they would be. Some conflicted with what she was taught about Nemus, but she expected there to be discrepancies, especially since history was written by the survivors and not those who lost the wars.

At dinner, Queen Galea quizzed her on the readings the way a tutor would a pupil, asking for the details about how Seaptum was discovered, the first tribe of people, the unification of the three great lands, and the event which severed their unity.

Joanne had answered with confidence, spending her mornings and midday pouring through the books and working with the tutor they sent to her—a small, middle-aged man who lacked the excitement and energy of Teresa, but spoke in a monotonous tone, reciting almost verbatim the words printed in the actual books and she forced herself to stay awake during those sessions to prove that she was a diligent learner. Fraum would listen, never responding with a word of praise, nor one of spite. Indifference was cold, but it was the safest, according to Prince Gallium. She didn't complain, but ate her meals with Queen Galea, sometimes Prince Gallium joining, sometimes Fraum sulking over his meal. Not once did she see King Dryd. He was in his sick bed and feared to be growing worse, according to Beaty.

"A cold draft might end him," she said to Joanne. "Then Fraum will be crowned."

"A wedding and a coronation," Joanne said. "That would prove an easy celebration to coordinate, rather than two separate events."

"Don't be so callous."

"It's not me," Joanne said, slapping closed the book on the *Third Dynasty of Freemen*. "It's these stones. They harden me, locked away in their confines every day."

"The rock blaming the stones." Beaty said. "Be careful that you don't wear your edges smooth."

"I am my father's daughter," Joanne said.

Beaty frowned. "Unwise words, princess."

"Why are you calling me that name? I hate it. They use it to mock me, since I'm not married to the prince, and may never be." Frustration threatened scald and burn, her eyes tearing up, though she hated the tears so eager to boil over her cheeks when they were nothing more than a reminder of her lack of control. "Fraum never sees me outside of meals. Never says a kind word. I might as well be betrothed to a viper. Then I might know the venom in his fangs and end my suffering sooner than this slow poisoning of hate and boredom."

Beaty knelt beside Joanne, stroking her hand.

"You mustn't speak such words," she said. "No one knows what ears may be listening."

I wish it were Selene's ears. Her lady-in-waiting reverted back to her maid position, insisting on observing and assuring the cleanliness of Joanne's clothes taken away by servants to be washed. Not that it would matter if they used them for stable bedding. She would be fitted for new ones.

"Do you think they will allow me a pair of trousers?" Joanne asked.

"Oh, you are silly," Beaty responded. "You can't be serious. They would never allow such a travesty. You are not some whore, or one of those traveling performers, I mean even they only wear trousers as a costume."

"How would you know about whores?" Joanne asked.

"When I was younger, I've seen both men and women sell all that remained to them after the war. For some unfortunate ones, all they had were the clothes on the back and the flesh it preserved," Beaty said.

"Yet my father traded me like some expensive furniture," Joanne said, standing from the chair and stretching her lower back. "I might as well be nothing but flesh sold for others' freedom."

"Spoken like every other lady of wealth," Beaty said. "Privilege comes at a cost. Blame men for their terrible games, blame the gods for making men in their image. You'll be better off screaming at the wind to silence its howling."

Joanne clapped.

"Nice speech," she said. "A little rehearsed. Speak it from the heart, next time."

"I should take you over my knee and give you a good spanking for speaking to me like a child.

"You wouldn't lay a hand on your princess."

Beaty grabbed her arm and spun her to face the chair, forcing her to bend, face planted in the cushion. Joanne squeaked and tried to struggle, but Beaty had a firm control over her. Then Beaty lifted the edges of Joanne's skirts, and when she cousin struck her bottom, Joanne yelped.

"By you own admission, you are not yet a princess." Another strike on her bottom. It wasn't too hard, but it did sting despite her small clothes.

"Peace, cousin," Joanne said, though she was laughing. "I surrender."

"Also words you should never speak." Another light tap on her bottom. "You should be more careful, milady, not to allow your passions get the better of you." Beaty released Joanne, and helped her adjust her skirts. "Reckless words and behaviors will—"

Joanne wrapped her arms around Beaty's shoulders and kissed her full on the mouth. Beaty tried to push away, squirming and moaning. Joanne held her for a few heartbeats before pulling her mouth back, nearly panting in excitement. She laid a hand on Beaty's left breast, feeling her heart also beat in a sporadic rhythm.

"I will be as reckless as I desire. Princess or not, I will do as my father has taught me," Joanne said. "Power is a privilege that only a few are afforded. I may not have much power now, but I will purchase all I can, dear cousin. You will aide me, yes?"

Beaty nodded, her cheeks flushed.

"Speak the words."

"I have sworn to do my best to aide you," Beaty said and took a breath. "I'm to protect your interests and well-being with my life."

"Then know I love you more than any person here in this cold stone," Joanne said. *Outside of Selene.* "It is most important that others love me as much or more. If not love me, then fear me. Fear is a great motivator outside of pain."

"Seems I was too playful in my instructions," Beaty said.

"Oh no, I enjoyed your break from etiquette," Joanne said. "It proved to me that you are not some rotted old aristocrat like your grandmother. I shouldn't have someone that dusty and moldy stinking up my chambers. I love and cherish you, though we must not show any affections outside these chambers."

"My grandmother taught me well," Beaty said. "Social decorum is your armor against the lash of tongue and leather. Although, cousin, I do share your affections, I must warn you that I do not share your tastes in sexual preferences."

Joanne laughed.

"You're a little birdie who chases the worm." She held up her pinky and waggled it. "The kiss I gave you was just to silence your mouth, though I know you must've taken some pleasure in it."

"I was caught off guard," Beaty said, though her cheeks flushed again, betraying her deeper feelings.

"Kissing you was like kissing this wall," Joanne said.

"At least I wasn't some dragon trying to eat your face," Beaty said.

"I could warm up other areas should you desire," Joanne said. Before Beaty could answer, there came a knock on the chamber door. Joanne rolled her eyes and sighed. Of course, they would be disturbed when the banter heated up. "Enter!"

The door opened and Lady Hamlet filled the doorway. Her face was impassive, unreadable, though pleasant in a pasty sort of way when one desired bread without the jam. Lady Hamlet took in the room without betraying any thought or feelings of her observations. She picked up the edges of her blue skirts and curtsied.

"The tailor awaits, milady, in the Queen's chambers," Lady Hamlet said, speaking precise, clear words as though written by a cold hand on a smooth parchment.

Joanne glanced at Beaty, reading the same expression. She hadn't been to the Queen's chambers, yet. This was a new development in their adventure and perhaps one of greater enjoyment.

I guess I'm to be put on display.

Queen Galea's chambers were on the first floor of Argenti Lapisdom. They passed through several small hallways with multiple doors that were closed. Soldiers and servants moved about carrying out orders and chores without a second glance at Joanne. She was another fixture of the Argenti and none of their concern. The hallway widened into an antechamber where ladies in purple dresses mulled around, whispers like a strong breeze battering the stone walls. The tapestries were more formal. Mother and Father holding hands while standing in a palace very much like Argenti Lapisdom, stern and radiant in their wise assessment of the visitors. There was one to the Blades Man in his black armor, standing watch in the corner of the room. Vases sat on tables, flowers arranged for beauty and fragrance set in them. When Lady Hamlet entered the antechamber, the whispers ceased in a collective inhale. She tapped on the chamber door and waited. The door opened.

"Lady Joanne, my Queen," Lady Hamlet announced, curtsied, and stepped to the right side of the chamber.

The room was larger than her own. Tables laden with flowers which scented the room, platters of sweets and pitchers of wine. The bed was similar to Joanne's and there were twice the number of wardrobes. Queen

Galea sat in a gold painted chair with a rounded back. She wore a jeweled cornet in her braided hair, the purple dress darker than a bruise, collard up to her chin and lace fluffed around her wrists. A slight smile touched her pale face, but it was one of amusement.

"My Queen," Joanne said and curtsied. "Such a pleasure to have an invitation outside of a meal."

"This will be a feast, child," Queen Galea said. "A veritable feast, though you are the meal. Make certain not to squirm, or you may get stuck by needles and bleed over the fine fabrics that Master Tailor Woolsie has brought to design your new outfits."

Master Woolsie stood beside a trunk of fabrics. A thin man with sharp features, the shrewd kind that could snip a woman's image of herself like thin thread. He appraised Joanne's outfit, and from the disgusted turn of his nose and frown, she knew he immediately disdained Nemus's choice of style. Beside him were two women: one older and one younger. They all shared similar features, and hair color—brown, though the older one had streaks of gray— and they held long chords with marks on them.

"I will do my best to be still," Joanne said.

"Now strip, girl," Queen Galea said. "You are used to having little modesty, well, here you get to bare it all."

Joanne stood, barefoot and nude on a box while the women moved around her, cords stretching around her limbs and chest. Charcoal pencils scratched on parchment; notations Joanne couldn't comprehend.

"Right leg appears to be longer than the left," Master Woolsie said, looking at the parchment. "Hips are small, breasts are average. Her neck is thicker than typically found on a woman, but not manly."

Oh good, I'm a woman.

Next came the fabric wrappings. The women enfolded her like a present and pinned various colors while Queen Galea and Master Woolsie scrutinized. She heard how her complexion was too dark for such colors, that she needed time to fade, as though she was fabric hung out in the sun. Her feet ached and legs cramped. She twitched and they poked her in the side with a pin.

"Careful, look now she bleeds," Master Woolsie said. "Step down off the block, milady. Take a rest while we clean up the blood."

Beaty stepped forward with a robe they had given her and draped it around her shoulders. She was guided to a chair of lesser degree of prestige beside the Queen. A cup of water and watered wine was placed in her other hand.

"Looking beautiful is horrendous, isn't it?" Queen Galea asked, though not looking at Joanne but rather her other ladies-in-waiting. She frowned, though at what Joanne could only guess, probably the rouged cheeks, pink lips, pert breasts and thin waists. "So young and fertile. Yet, our seasons are short. We give all to the populace who will eat you up like vultures if shown a hint of weakness. That is why we must always, always give the perception of perpetual fruit, though the seeds have withered."

"I thank you for the gracious gifts," Joanne said. "I have never known such generosity."

"I wouldn't think so, child," Queen Galea smiled. "For the vast wealth of resources Nemus possess, it is woefully mismanaged. I'm surprised you are not wearing thread worn, homespun skirts. Ghastly, though your outfits were, they did serve a purpose for your status in your country. However, you represent a higher purpose and will be adorned accordingly."

Joanne nodded, sipping from the wine cup and then gulping the water. Her head and shoulders were sore from holding her pose for so long.

"Once these precious gifts arrive, would it be possible to host a tea gathering. I have met so many wonderful ladies on my course here in Seaptum, and they viewed me as this outsider in my homespun skirts," Joanne said. "I think it might be proper that they have a new view. A proper acceptance party."

Queen Galea laughed. "I'm sure you have met Lady Windridge and Willowcreek. What is your opinion of them?"

"They were genuine and nice," Joanne said. "Lady Windridge is a bit simple, though sweet. Lady Willowcreek is rather more serious and ambitious."

"Those two will drink piss from the palm of your hands and swear it the sweetest drink ever to grace their tongue," Queen Galea said, she drank from her wine goblet. "It is the other ladies you should be wary about, as you may have already perceived."

"I have seen the knives in their smiles."

"Yes, that is a good description," Queen Galea said. "I think a tea is a grand idea, though you cannot let them think it was your own. You don't want to seem desperate. That won't sheath any of the knives no matter the dress you wear."

"Oh, Lady Willowcreek has taken on the role of inviting every prominent lady in Seaptum," Joanne said. "I don't want to presume anything without first asking your permission, my Queen."

"Clever girl," Queen Galea said. "You will be a welcomed member of our household."

Master Woolsie clapped his hand.

"If it pleases the Queen, I would have the girl back on the block."

"Yes, and try a lighter blue. Blue like the sky," Queen Galea said.

"An excellent choice." Master Woolsie held up the fabric and pins.

"Beaty, would you prepare a letter for Lady Willowcreek?" Joanne asked, sitting back in her chair in her own room. She was exhausted! Who knew that being measured and prodded, tucked and pinched and praised and punctured more than she liked to think could be so tiring? "Let her know to schedule a tea for high planting, or whatever they call it this far north."

The door between Joanne's room and Selene's opened. Selene hurried it, holding up a letter. "Milady, milady this came to me from a messenger. I was instructed it is from a loving friend. I cannot read the name, but I assume it is from Lily."

"Oh, give it here!"

Lady Selene was written in neat, flowery script on the front of the folded envelope. Joanne unfolded it and began to read, excitement blossoming at the message.

My Dearest New Friend,

I thank Qetesh for our newly made acquaintance. Your beauty and charm have quite enchanted me. I can think of nothing but our conversation, brief though it seems, yet I hold it precious in my heart. I saw a little fox the other day. A mischievous creature that one can never truly trust. She was playing near the silver mines, making a den dangerously close to another creature's hollow. Also, of interesting note. A certain lady who shall not be freely named has suffered from episodes of illness. I do hope she gallantly fights through it and her constitution revives. I look forward to our next visit. Please write and send by my dear friend the cook.

Yours in duty and love,

Snow Drop

"Clever girl," Joanne said and gave Beaty the letter.

"What does it say?" Selene asked.

"I agree, this is a very interesting development," Beaty said. "How do you want to respond?"

"First, we will need to think of a way to thank our Snow Drop," Joanne said. "It seems Lady Freeman may be pregnant since our last visit and Lady Silversmith has more in common with Lady Foxglow than she is aware. We need proof of this dalliance before the tea. Would it be possible for her to acquire evidence?"

"I will write it immediately," Beaty said.

"Selene, my love, you must be careful when you deliver the letter.," Joanne said. "No one must know it comes from me."

"I swear by Mother and Father, I will protect this with my life," Selene said. "Besides, I like meeting new friends."

We will have plenty of friends and enemies before I settles into my role as Queen.

A dozen gowns arrived at the beginning of Sowing, along with the biting flies and humidity. Joanne tried keeping the windows closed, but the little buggers would squeeze through the frame work, forcing her to draw the curtains and prevented sunlight from entering the room, casting a deep gloom. Joanne had longed for her strolls through the gardens, no matter how wet it was outside. Not that she could escape the black swarms outdoors. Beaty and Selene would fan away the biters only for them to return in angry hoards, while she tried to read the history of continental warfare from when to deploy calvary and archers, to shield walls and how to rally troops to points of higher ground. Lady Hamlet informed her of the delivery and she hurried inside.

The gowns were made of heavier material than she was used to and the colors ranged from various hues of blues, pinks and purples, the lighter weight ones being the darker colors to hide the sweat stains around more intimate areas. She was grateful for them and planned out which one she would wear at the tea—invites were sent and Lady Willowcreek sounded like she received a marriage proposal rather than a guest list in her letter. It was all working out in her favor. Even Fraum seemed intrigued by the potential of the tea gathering.

"You have been a busy bee gathering your hive," he said and sniffled. He gave a wicked smile. "Beware their sting."

"I will take your precaution to heart, my prince," Joanne replied. "You know your people better than I. Are there any you wished won over, or that should be ignored?"

"None that your frivolous tea would bring to our side that are not already loyal," Fraum said, swiping at his nose with a handkerchief. "Unless you can put that Foxglow in her place. She is a spiteful cunt, from what I have heard."

"Consider it done." Joanne smiled. *With great pleasure.*

Lily wrote to Selene twice more about the illicit dalliance between Lady Floxglow and Lord Silversmith. The second letter included a signet ring bearing a willow tree and water with a lock of dark red hair matching the color of Lady Foxglow twined around it. *The perfect gift!* Joanne squealed once it was placed in her hand. *Should she complain, I have my husband-to-be's blessing to ruin her!*

Prince Gallium visited her once in the garden. "How can you be engaged by those awful books? I cannot believe my mother wanted you to read them!"

"They are not all bad," Joanne said. "I'm learning about our history that was neglected as part of my tutoring in Nemus."

"I wouldn't believe everything you read in them," Prince Gallium said. "History is written by the conquerors, not the defeated. Besides, I have a more vigorous activity for you." Joanne raised her eyebrow at the last part of his invite. "Before you let your imagination get the better of you, princess, I'm referring to sparring in the yard."

"That would be very unlady like," Beaty replied.

"I will join you," Joanne said.

She followed Pince Gallium out to the yard where men were stripped to the waist, swatting at each other with wooden swords. Prince Gallium proceeded to remove his tunic, revealing a lean, muscular torso that Joanne took some pleasure in ogling. Prince Gallium smirked, flexing his biceps and swinging his wooden sword around with ease.

"Do I need to take off my bodice?" Joanne asked.

"As the lady pleases," Prince Gallium said.

Joanne shrugged and tugged at her sleeves, when Beaty approached.

"Do not engage in this childish display."

"How am I to spar in a dress?" Joanne countered.

158

"Don't spar at all." There was an annoyance in her tone, knowing Joanne would ignore her advice.

A gathering of soldiers had circled them, some making wagers on how long Joanne might last, if she even took up the sword at all. *This is my chance to prove myself worthy of them. If I back down, they will see me as a weak woman and not a potential leader.*

"Fine. Hand me a weapon," Joanne said.

Shouts and cheers rose from the surrounding soldiers. A wooden sword was placed in her hand. She mimicked the stance she had seen her brothers use in the sparring yard at the Keep, the same one Prince Gallium displayed.

"I promise not to be too rough," Prince Gallium said.

He took an aggressive step and swung his sword in a lazy arc which Joanne batted aside easily. He spun as she swung for his arm, stumbling in her slippers. The men hooted and called out encouragement. Joanne held up her hand to create a pause in the fight. She took off her slippers and stripped her stockings, tossing them to a frowning Beaty, and walked bare foot in the dust of the sparring ground. Dust collected on the fringes of her gown and a strand of hair came loose, dragging in front of her face. She blew it aside, then resumed a defensive position.

Prince Gallium grinned and nodded his approval.

Joanne's heart raced when Prince Gallium rushed at her and she turned his strike aside again, but the encumbrance of the dress made it so she couldn't move easily and he swatted her on the backside. The soldiers gave shouts of disapproval and he shrugged.

"Milady must learn to defend herself from unwarranted advancements," he said.

Joanne lunged at him and he retreated from her reach while sliding to her left side, placing the tip of his sword against her breast.

"A strike to the heart can be deadly," he said. "Do you yield?"

"Only on Donn's silver platter." Joanne stepped away before he could press forward and slapped his left thigh. The wood made a loud noise that brought on more celebratory cheers. Prince Gallium limped away, though she could tell it was a false limp. She was right. He dropped the deceit and brought a flurry of backhanded strikes that caused her to stumble backward, landing on her bottom.

"How about now, princess?" Gallium said, placing the wood to her throat. The playfulness had left his face and was replaced by something more vicious.

Joanne stuck out her neck.

"Take my head, if you dare."

More hollers and cheers, most admiring her bravery and rest calling for Prince Gallium to back down. His grin returned and he pulled the sword back, bowing to her.

"I honor your bravery," he said and helped her to her feet. She handed him the sword. "Keep it. You will need it for your further training."

"I don't have a proper outfit."

"That can be easily resolved."

Beaty came forward, helping her place her shoes on and they left the men chattering about how she was unwilling to surrender in the face of death. Her legs hurt from the awkward movement in the dress and falling to the ground. Beaty leaned in as they walked.

"That could have been foolish," she said, her one shifting to a more agreeable one. "Though it seemed to have worked in your favor."

Joanne glanced back over her shoulder. Prince Gallium watched her, giving her a wink. She almost stumbled, but Beaty kept her on her feet.

"Remember not to incite any more gossip than you have created," Beaty said. "Fraum will not be pleased hearing of this activity."

Whether he was angry over the sparring or not, Fraum didn't comment. At dinner he mentioned the beauty of her dress and complimented her taste. Queen Galea smiled without taking credit for the choice of design. He invited her for an evening walk in the garden. Joanne accepted, not that she had any other choice.

"My father is dying," Fraum said. "The Masters Physic has no way to reverse the ailments brought on by age, but he lingers yet. A ghost trapped in his failing flesh."

"I'm sorry," Joanne said.

"If you knew him, the kind of man he is and was, you wouldn't be," Fraum said and when she reached for his hand, he didn't pull back. "He was wicked and cruel to even the ones who adored him the most. Though, I'm not sure how I'm to take my seat upon his chair. I must present a harsh hand, ready to strike, but it is very tiring. I feel like I have aged a decade over this last year."

"Your ailments seemed to have retreated and you have good color on your cheeks," Joanne said. "I think you have grown stronger under this new weight of responsibility. What may crush lesser men, you shoulder as though it were a pebble tossed in the stream."

Fraum laughed at that and gave her a shy smile.

"If only you weren't born in Nemus," he said. "But, I see you are shedding the old skin, molting the disease into which you were born, and will be one of us."

The sting brought a wave of anger that she let slide over her. King Dryd's hatred for Nemus was his failing, not his son's. She would have to prove his thinking to be inaccurate. From what she knew of her father, that may be a failing venture.

"I am your butterfly," Joanne said.

"Yes, that you are."

They passed the rest of the walk in silence.

Prince Gallium was true to his word. Lady Hamlet arrived at Joanne's chambers the next morning with a package. Joanne unwrapped it and found a small set of trousers and a tunic inside, along with a scribbled note from Prince Gallium informed her:

Princess,

Acquired these from a page boy who died from a blow to the head from a rather spirited horse. I hope these serve you better. Come find me at the yard by the fifth bell if you wish to learn to fight.

Yours in Service,

Gallium

"You can't," Beaty said, hands on her hips and glaring at her.

"I can," Joanne said. "I will."

"This isn't proper," Beaty said, her voice rising in pitch until she sounded like her grandmother. "You want me to protect you, but I can't do that when you willfully place yourself in positions to create a scandal! Might as well go ahead and tell Fraum you don't care about his reputation, nor your own. People will talk—"

"People will always talk," Joanne said, stripping down to her small clothes. "I need to learn to protect myself as well. You are welcome to come and be my chaperone."

"I'm not going to be a part of this gamble, go ruin it all!" Beaty said. "You had a good laugh the other day, please, Joanne, I'm pleading with you to let it go before you make a mockery out of yourself."

Mockery! Joanne pulled on the trousers, belting it, and tucked the tunic over it. The fit was good.

"You will address me as 'milady', if you believe what I do is a mockery!"

"Fine, milady," Beaty said and curtsied. "I hope you don't get hurt too badly."

Joanne took her wooden sword and stalked from the room followed by Selene.

"You don't think this is some jest," Joanne said.

"No, milady," Selene said, her eyes widening, "I mean princess, I mean…I don't know what I mean anymore."

"You mean more than the world to me," Joanne said, and kissed Selene on the cheek. "Let's go battle a prince."

They found Prince Gallium waiting in the yard with his wooden practice sword.

"I feared you would deny my request," he said.

"I would never turn down my chance to learn to fight from the Master Swordsman of Seaptum," Joanne replied, taking her practice sword from Selene. "One never knows when a lady will have to protect herself from brutish animals."

Pince Gallium grinned.

"Then let's start with your form. Right foot forward and left back, knees slightly bent. Good, good, now place your non-sword hand to the side so it doesn't interfere." Prince Gallium demonstrated the form and then pressed gently on her thighs, shoulders, and waist to help her adjust. He went through the basic motions of how to thrust, when to step back, and always to keep her guard up. "A dropped point leads to spilled blood."

They practiced until the sixth bell, when sweaty and breathing heavy, Joanne was forced to retire.

"Again, tomorrow, if you like," Prince Gallium said.

"I wouldn't miss it for anything!"

So began Joanne's training for physical combat. In the following week, the mental combat began. Lady Willowcreek and Lady Windridge arrived several days ahead of the event. Their joy at designing such a tea was delightful to Joanne. Quick chatter on what should be served and where to place the ladies to avoid disagreeable interactions captured Joanne's attention. She halted all her sparring and study of history. The lessons she learned about the various women of power in Seaptum were engaging enough to tire her mind and body with excess exercises. Of the twenty ladies from the wealthiest and most powerful houses, only eighteen would be arriving.

"Lady Hawthorne for obvious reasons of endangering the health of her baby," Lady Willowcreek said. "She's near ready to burst, poor thing."

"Who is the second?" Joanne hoped it wasn't either Silversmith or Foxglow. Their absence would ruin the entertainment she had planned.

"Lady Freeman, I have heard, is with child."

"How?" Lady Windridge asked.

"The usual way, my dear."

"Don't be a wet branch," Lady Windridge said, "you know what I mean. Lord Freeman has not produced an heir since his injuries."

"Injuries?"

"After he married his first wife and she was pregnant with his only son—"

"—who died at birth. Mother bless him. So tragic," Lady Willowcreek added in.

"Very tragic. He was never the same since," Lady Windridge said.

"How did he get injured?"

"Oh, he was out hunting on the eve of his child's birth," Lady Windridge continued. "He and his servants came across a wild boar. They had wounded it to death, but the boar had one last wicked trick. When Lord Freeman went in for the killing blow, that shadow blessed boar raised its tusked head—"

"Tusks as large as my arm," Lady Willowcreek added in. "Or so I was told."

"Very large tusks, and sharp as knives," Lady Windridge said. "The wicked creature, shadow spawned if nothing else, in its death throes, raised its head and lunged at Lord Freeman the same instance he thrust in his spear. Each punctured the other, though Lord Freeman took his in the rather painful danglies." She dipped two fingers down and let her wrist swing. "It was a mortal injury, it seemed, for both the boar and the lord."

Who's the father of the latest Lady Freeman? The question didn't need an answer. Joanne remembered the night Helena found her wandering the halls with the knife. Only one person in their retinue would have the power to take advantage of Lady Freeman. A very flirtatious prince.

"Who would be the father?" Lady Windridge asked, echoed her thoughts.

"A miracle of the gods, wouldn't you say dear?" Lady Willowcreek said, addressing Joanne.

"Mother's blessing," Joanne agreed.

Later that evening, she told Selene and Beaty of Lady Helena's pregnancy and how it occurred so close to their visit to Freeman Manor. She added in the story of Lord Freeman being gored in his manhood.

"Either she has a secret lover," Beaty said. "Or, it was a pre-arrangement that Prince Gallium sire a child on her."

"Or maybe not so pre-arranged." Joanne looked at the stack of history books on her table. There were plenty of bastard children who were accepted as legitimate heirs when no other natural child was born to the wedded couple—and a few battles fought over lineage.

The night prior to the tea, Joanne lay in bed unable to sleep. She opened Selene's door and moonlight shown on her maid's bed. Selene sat up, nightgown sagging, exposing her left shoulder. Her brown eyes shown in the light, exciting Joanne to their beautiful innocence.

"What is it, milady?" Selene asked. "Do you need something?"

"Yes," Joanne said and climbed the end of the bed, moving up Selene's covered body until their faces were close enough to reveal her soft features silver in the moonlight. Joanne leaned in, their lips nearly touching. "I want you."

She kissed Selene. Her hands ran through her maid's soft hair, gripping it and pulling her tight. Selene gasped, but opened her mouth for their tongues to touch. Hands reached for each other, searching and exploring, moving under night clothes and stripping them off. Lips explored exposed skin, tasting. Fingers pushed through folds until moans replaced gasps and they flowed like the rhythms of the night, giving and seeking pleasure until both sank into the bed, breathing rapidly, and giggled.

"I love you, Selene" Joanne said, wrapping her arms around the younger maid. "Qetesh, I'm selfish. This is why I brought you here."

"I love you, too, milady," Selene said, kissing Joanne on the forehead. "I'm happy you brought me. My hands were getting sore scrubbing pots."

"I will always have a better use for your hands," Joanne said, taking her right hand and placing it between her legs. "Soak them in me."

So the night passed quickly in passion and they collapsed into sleep, tangled and twisted together. Beaty found them in the morning, Joanne's leg tossed over Selene. Joanne opened one eye to see her cousin standing in the morning light cast through the window. She frowned and shook her head, then stepped forward, tickling the bottom of Joanne's foot.

"The day speeds along and you have guests soon to arrive," Beaty said.

"You do not want to join," Joanne said and grinned at her.

"Perhaps another time, milady," Beaty said. Selene, yawned and stretched, dropped her arm across Joanne's breasts. "I do not judge, but it is time to get up and dress you for the tea since you so dearly wanted to catch a fox by the tail."

Joanne wore a lavender dress with lace on the sleeves. A blue belt hooked with a gold sun buckle. Rings of fiery red rubies and deep blue opals adorned her fingers. On her head sat a gold circlet with rays spindling across her forehead and across her brow.

"This was a gift from Fraum," Beaty said. "He delivered it earlier, but didn't want me to disturb your sleep."

Joanne flushed at the generous gift, though she wouldn't betray her love for Selene. Not for all the jewels in Seaptum. Fraum approached her at the breakfast table where an array of fruits, breads, and jams awaited. He smiled at her entrance.

"I see you have found my gift," he said. "Do you find it to your liking?"

"Very much, my lord," Joanne said, curtsied and offered him her hand. To her surprise he took it and kissed the back of it. His lips were cold, though pleasant.

"I wish you a happy gathering," Fraum said. "I will be out for most of the day, but I should return before your little tea party has ended. I look forward to hearing all about the excitement."

What game is he playing? First he detests me, then he sends me gifts. Mother, I wish I could read his mind!

Lady Willowcreek and Lady Windridge bustled into the dining hall followed by Lady Hamlet. They gave quick curtsies to Fraum and Joanne. Fraum gave them an annoyed glare, exiting the room before they began their clucking. They fawned over Joanne's dress and circlet, then filled their mouths with fruit and munched bread slathered with jam.

"Beautiful," Lady Windridge said. "They will not recognize that simple girl from Nemus. Such a transformation! Too bad Lady Hawthorne will not be here to witness it."

"I'm certain she will hear soon enough," Lady Willowcreek said. "There will be much scrambling and flattery to gain favor with our new debutante Princess. Just you mark whose opinions will change as quickly as the seasons when the snows melt and the flowers bloom. Don't be taken in by all their words. The air will be thick with extravagance, but we will point out the sincere from the smoke and mirrors."

"I thank you for all your help and your generosity," Joanne said. "I count you two among my greatest friends."

Both ladies cooed and blushed.

I don't trust either of you any more than I would a fox around a chicken's coop. Joanne smiled and hugged them both.

Carriages arrived after midday and footman dressed in various uniforms from the roses, to crescent moons, tall mountains and vast rivers, blues, reds, greens, silver and blacks, escorted women in extravagant gowns, shoes, gloves, hats, circlets of silver and gold, slippers, and diamonds, sapphires, rubies around necks, on fingers, wrists, brooches, and hairnets. So much wealth Joanne had never seen. Faces young and fresh, painted, red lipped, cheeked, pink lipped, pale, others with wrinkles hidden, smiles revealing white teeth, grins, as real as the statues in the main hall. Names that Joanne would commit to memory. Lady Thornbrush, Lady Moonhollow, Lady Stonefield, Lady Meadows, so many ladies and Lady Willowcreek named them for Joanne as they peeked through a hole in the wall where they could spy the women gathering.

"Oh, there's Lady Foxglow and Lady Silversmith," Lady Willowcreek said. Joanne peered through and saw the two who had laughed at her at the gathering at the Hawthorne's. She twirled the little present given to her by Lily.

"Red hair," Joanne said, marking Lady Foxglow.

"A very distinct feature, isn't it," Lady Willowcreek said. "It appears all are gathered and you may make your appearance."

Joanne adjusted her skirts and straightened her shoulders. She had one chance at a fresh impression. If she could win a few to her side, then all the pokes and tight-necked dresses, the scheming and plotting, all came down to this moment.

Breathe, smile, and let them know you're a Princess of Seaptum.

Two of her own servants opened the large doors in the vestibule. Eager eyes turned to see who was waiting in the doorway. The echo of chatter becoming silent. Joanne marked their faces and reactions. Her heart pounded in her chest and she wished Selene was there holding her hand. *They still don't like me.*

Then surprise and grins broke across the faces, hands rising to mouths and quick head shakes of approval.

"Stunning."

"Beautiful."

"This can't be the same girl from Nemus."

A flurry of curtsies filled the room when Joanne entered and they created a path for her. Lady Willowcreek and Lady Windridge followed behind, acknowledging each guest. When Joanne reached what she estimated was the center, she clapped her hands together. "Welcome each and every one of you. Mother's blessing on you who have travelled so long and far to be here this afternoon and evening, where we can be properly introduced. I do hope you enjoy our hospitality, granted by the gracious Queen Galea, who will attend the events later. Please follow Lady Hamlet who will show you to the dining hall where the festivities will begin."

They moved along like a flock of birds, some still twittering about Joanne, but two she noted whispered and giggled. Joanne maintained her smile. *Oh, the things they will whisper about tomorrow!*

The main dining hall was set up with tables filled with cakes and sweet breads, ceramic jugs of spiced wines and teas were placed between the platters, mugs ready to be dispersed. Musicians played a cheerful, though quiet melody across the room. Gossip fluttered around the room on carless lips and Joanne stood at the center, smiling and returning polite small talk. She nibbled sweets and drank wine, while Selene and Beaty stood with Lady Hamlet at the back of the room, watching and listening as instructed by Joanne. Lady Silversmith and Lady Foxglow kept mostly to themselves, navigating around the fringes. They approached Joanne briefly to make some comment on her gown and their appreciation for the invitation to Argenti Lapisdom, which it seemed had very little visitors since Fraum and Gallium grew out of boyhood. They ate very little and at one point Beaty approached Joanne.

"Those two do nothing but complain about the treacherous road that bounced them around in their carriage just to arrive here," she said and took Joanne's cup, refilling it with watered spiced wine. "A few of the other ladies seem to agree, but no one is committing to them, yet."

"Take the ring and drop it by Foxglow when I approach," Joanne said and handed her a handkerchief. "I will wait until after the entertainment to create this stirring conclusion."

After the ladies had an opportunity to introduce themselves to Joanne—a long list of names she already knew, and even more boring details of their pedantic lives that she cared even less for— they retired to the gardens while tables were set up in the hall for card games. Lady Willowcreek and Lady Windridge remained at her side, a sign of their new prestige—this also brought a few comments from Foxglow and Silversmith, setting poison in the ear of the wealthier houses at the perceived power play, Beaty told her. Joanne grinned at the report, wishing to lead them all through the gate and push them over the edge to feed the sea wyrm below. After a stroll, they went back inside and sat at tables. Lady Foxglow and Lady Silversmith occupied one table along with two other prestigious ladies, Woodberry and Goldman. Joanne approached the table with Lady Willowcreek.

"Do you mind if we sit in this hand?" Joanne asked.

Lady Woodberry and Lady Goldman deferred, giving a bow and backing away. Lady Foxglow and Lady Silversmith gave uncomfortable glances to each other.

"Milady may find we are poor players at cards," Lady Foxglow said. "Such games our husbands excel at, but we find such strategies tedious and beyond our abilities to grasp."

"This one is easy," Joanne said. "It's called the Queen's Hangman."

She explained the rules and demonstrated a round.

"Very simple," Lady Willowcreek said. "Hope that Janus's luck keeps the jape away."

"They play this for money," Lady Silversmith said, sounding astonished that such an activity existed.

"Yes, but we will use buttons instead," Joanne said. "I would hate to have you pay more than you already do in taxes. From what I hear, your husband has had some good fortune of late in his silver mines."

"We are blessed," Lady Silversmith said, placing a silver button in the center of the table. Next, she placed a card. The King of diamonds. "He wanted to send a letter to the Master Tax Advisor, to pay a small advance against the new find, but he had misplaced his signet ring."

Joanne glanced at Lady Foxglow to gauge her reaction. She was reserved, giving no sign of her infidelity. *Probably doesn't know about the lock of hair tied around the ring.* Or, what if she were wrong and Lady Silversmith knew about the little triste, and participated in them? It was a gambit Joanne would have to play out. Lady Foxglow also placed in a silver button and dropped a card face up. The Queen of Clovers.

"Janus frowned on my Lord husband whose fields yielded lower crop last year due to an early freeze," Lady Foxglow said. "Though he did acquire more land from Lord Thornbrush, which is why Lady Thornbrush has avoided me all midday. He won it in a card game, much like this one."

Cheated away. Joanne smiled and nodded. She had heard Lady Thornbrush complain earlier about the marked cards. *A family of cheaters.*

"I'm certain there will be great surprises for you," Joanne said and dropped in a gold button. She flipped her card and it came up King of Clovers. "With trade to open south, there will be more markets for your wheat."

"Poorer markets, but I guess even poor people have to eat," Lady Foxglow said.

"Better some coin than to lose half your stores to rot and rats," Lady Willowcreek said. "Although, there are areas of great wealth in Nemus which our Princess will be well acquainted with and I gratefully welcome new custom. Oh, look I won!"

The Queen Diamonds sat on the stack.

"That was rather quick," Lady Silversmith said.

"Sometimes it is best when it is quick," Lady Willowcreek said and tittered her laughter.

"I guess it depends on taste," Lady Foxglow said. "Another hand?"

Joanne shuffled the cards and dealt them. This time several rounds passed and the pile of buttons grew. The conversation turned to the health of King Dryd which Joanne gave a non-committal reply. A brief remark on Prince Gallium from Lady Silversmith and how she was almost betrothed to him, except for the fact her family didn't meet the dowery demands. *Ah, another jab at my upbringing.*

They were growing comfortable around her and servants poured spiced wine. Joanne motioned for Beaty to approach. When Lady Foxglow laid the

Hangman's card, Beaty accidently bumped her, letting the ring fall in an audible sound and the signet ring rolled to Joanne.

"Don't be so clumsy," Lady Foxglow said. "Do they raise only milk maids in Nemus, lacking in grace and—"

"What is this?" Joanne picked up the signet ring. "Appears you dropped this on the floor, Lady Foxglow."

She held it so the willow tree and water waves were visible to Lady Silversmith.

"Is that...? May I see it?" Lady Silversmith asked, holding out her hand.

Joanne gave it, though she noticed Lady Foxglow grow paler.

"I've never seen it."

"Looks like a lock of hair twined around it. Red, very much like yours," Lady Willowcreek said, pointing out Lady Foxglow's hair color.

Lady Silversmith flushed, her mouth shrinking into a small slit. "If you would excuse me." She left the table.

Lady Foxglow glared at them and curtsied, following after her friend.

"Well, it seemed quite the scandal was uncovered," Lady Willowcreek said.

"You'll make certain that this doesn't spread."

"Not from my mouth," Lady Willowcreek said, and pressed her lips closed.

The fires are lit. Let the winds spread the tinder and burn them to ash in the very manner they wished to burn me.

Queen Galea joined them for the next phase of entertainment. The tables were cleared and the same troupe of performers from the Hawthorne's were employed for a special entertainment. Lady Foxglow stood apart of Lady Silversmith, a red glow on her cheek in the shape of a hand. Selene informed Joanne that they had a heated argument in the vestibule resulting in Lady Silversmith striking her former friend hard enough to rock her head to the side before marching back to the dining hall where chairs had been set up for the audience.

"She will not be a fan of this performance," Joanne said.

"What mischief has my daughter-to-be caused?" Queen Galea asked.

"None that was not already simmering unattended."

Queen Galea gave her a sideways glance that could have been a veiled approval or a reproach. The play started and Joanne no longer paid attention to the Queen, but to the two ladies who had insulted her. The woman actress who once played the role of a goddess, now was a fox who was employed to safe guard an important box by another woman dressed in silver.

"What's in the box?" asked the fox.

"None of your concerns. I can trust you to safe guard it when I am gone?"

"On pain of losing my head," the fox said.

Lady Foxglow was growing agitated.

Too on the nose? Joanne smiled.

When the woman dressed in silver left the fox sat by the box, pondering what was inside. Finally, it broke the lock, opened the lid, and pulled out a fake ring in an almost exact copy of Lord Silversmith's signet ring. There came a loud growl and the stamping of feet.

"You knew!" Lady Silversmith said, staring at Joanne. "You knew and didn't inform me in private but rather embarrass me in front of all these women. You swine. You dirty, filthy swine! You'll never have my support!"

"Nor mine." Lady Foxglow stood up. "Your sluttish Nemus ass should be returned in disgrace."

"She had nothing to do with the play. I set it up," Lady Willowcreek said. "You're the sluttish one whoring with Lord Silversmith while—"

Lady Silversmith took up a knife from the desert table and attacked Lady Willowcreek. The edge cut the sleeve of her dress, drawing blood. Joanne moved quickly, striking Lady Silversmith in the nose and forcing her to drop the knife.

"Guards! Guards!" Queen Galea shouted and the room became a frenzy of women leaping from their chairs and crying out. The actors ran from the room, and Joanne made note to pay them well after all settled down. She stood over the fallen Lady Silversmith, fists balled and ready to strike her again. Several house guards rushed in and seized hold of Lady Silversmith and Lady Foxglow.

"Escort them to their respective carriages," Queen Galea said. "Have all the carriages summoned. This gathering is over. It is supposed to be a celebration, not a blood sport."

Joanne stood, watching the ladies leave, a flurry of gossip slung around.

"You, girl," Queen Galea said. "You best remember that when you poison the well, you are left thirsty."

Part II

Secrets

CHAPTER TWELVE:
CORPSE CROWN

Great or small Donn weighs them all
Bitter or sweet death Donn eats
Innocence or guilt souls send to Nahrangi or Arula
No matter axe or sword, shovel or plow
Crown or beggar's cap, their heart on silver platter
Sits at the end and hope for a better afterlife begins
— from "Donn and Death"

King Dryd died.

Months after the scandalous tea party, Lady Hamlet came to her chambers, a dour expression on her face and her usually firm demeanor sunk, her hands nervously tapping on her thighs. A bright red harvest moon bled in the sky, which Joanne always felt was an ill-omen, especially after her brother died. *The blood of Sin warning of blood spilt.* Joanne didn't need to read the distress on the maid's face to know sorrow awaited the summons

Lady Hamlet gave. She, Beaty, and Selene followed the maid to the one room she had yet to step foot into since her arrival to Argenti Lapisdom. It stank of incense and camphor mixed with sweet herbs. The red moon hung outside the window, light penetrating the gossamer curtains. Queen Galea sat on the edge of a bed with Fraum. Prince Gallium stood beside an older man with wispy, white hair and a frizzy, white beard. The Master Physic and several assistants moved around the room, various bottles in hand and instruments to measure King Dryd's last moments in life. Joanne lingered quietly inside the door frame, not wanting to disrupt the solemn scene. A noise like a rumbling of an animal came from the bed.

"Are you sure?" Queen Galea asked.

More rumbling.

Queen Galea looked over her shoulder at Joanne. Prince Gallium also looked in her direction and gave her a smile.

"Come here, my dear," Queen Galea said, holding out a hand.

Joanne crossed the room and stood beside the Queen. She had not seen, nor heard, King Dryd before that moment and even now doubted his very existence. The man melting into the bed couldn't be King Dryd. That man had started a war that killed her brother over land rights, that man had forced Lord Desmond to sell his only daughter to them, that very same man had conquered continents and sired two brutal sons. This one was thin, sallow-faced, dark circles under his eyes more corpse-like than living. Tufts of hair slick with sweat stuck to his wrinkled forehead. He lifted a hand and Joanne took it, the skin rough as old parchment and bones that would snap should she apply any pressure to them.

King Dryd opened his mouth and a rattling cough rolled from his throat. His blue eyes, covered in a filmy white shroud, locked on hers. "Lovely lady," he said, words chasing the rattling cough. "You will do. You will do." A smile broke his cracked lips. "Obey. Rule." Though the last word sounded more like *cruel*. "Nemus free. Together." Then his smile dropped and his fingers gripped hers with a strength she didn't think possible. "Beware shadow. Death. Death. Death...."

He released her and his arm dropped onto the bed. His breathing became more ragged, filmy eyes closed. Joanne backed away, clutching at the hand that held death so close.

"Sometimes the patient relives past events," Master Physic said. "There is nothing for you to be concerned over."

Joanne nodded.

Mistress of Shadows stalks me still.

Standing beside Queen Galea, she watched and waited for King Dryd to complete his cycle of life. Fraum didn't say a word, nor would he look at her. He was focused on his father's slow rising chest.

He'll be king after this night

The bell tolled one when King Dryd slipped away to Gehenna where he awaited Donn's judgement. The Master Physic held a mirror under his nose and when it didn't fog over, laid an ear on the sunken chest. He stood up, back popping, and placed the coverlet over the body.

"He is gone," the Master Physic said and Queen Galea quietly shed a tear. After a few moments she was helped out of the chamber by Lady Hamlet. Prince Gallium patted Fraum's shoulder, but Fraum didn't react. His eyes remained on the thin form beneath the coverlet. Prince Gallium bowed his head to Joanne, and followed his mother out.

Joanne waited, watching Fraum for signs of what comes next.

"He was a bastard," Fraum said. "Always called me weak. He expected to outlive me, but one detail he didn't take into consideration was that I learned from him. I survived. Now he is dead and any commitment to his demands dies with him."

Joanne's mouth went dry. King Dryd arranged this marriage.

"Oh, don't worry. I'm not ending our engagement," Fraum said, looking at her. "I need you as much as you need me. If anything happens to you, I risk re-starting the war with Nemus and then I'll have my attention diverted between trying to hold back an invasion and my brother's attempts to kill me."

"Why would he kill you?" Joanne asked.

"It is part of the exchange of regency," Fraum said. "If I was an only son, there would be no challenger, but as long as Gallium lives and doesn't publicly abdicate the throne, then he is a threat. I don't see him giving up so easily."

"What if you convince him?"

Fraum snorted.

"He has the love and support of the soldiers. The army is his, though you do hold some perverse respect from them with your little training antics. They wouldn't dare harm you, though. I can only hope that will be my advantage as well." Fraum began to wheeze and wiped his nose on his sleeve. "The next biggest issue is that you have created a rift among the ladies, and therefore among the lords. Your petty display of petulance ruined the reputation of Foxglow and Silversmith, two very wealthy households here in Seaptum. Now they distrust us."

"The Foxglows are scoundrels," Joanne said. "They have cheated land—"

"I wouldn't care if they shat in the other lords' carriages and set them aflame," Fraum said. "Let them cheat land from weaker lords, fuck each other, since they are incestuous with their marriages the last century, or even speak scathing remarks about their little princess-to-be rutting with pigs in the mud. The more they gnaw and worry themselves, the less they bother with us. We get their taxes, their conscripts, their support when war breaks out. Now, you have left us with the Windridges and the Willowcreeks. Which means, you are going to have to find a way to mend the rift, or raise those other families to greater wealth and prestige. Might as well hold the wolf by the tail and not get your arm torn off."

"I will do my best, but…" Joanne had not seen any of the ladies since that evening. She knew of the distrust and anger from Lily's letters, though she was powerless to do so. "I think we should hold a trial."

"For Father's sake, a trial for what?"

"Treason, milord," Joanne said. "Lady Silversmith stabbed Lady Willowcreek, though it was an attempt on my life."

Fraum studied her, mouth pressed into a thin line. Then it curled into a smile.

"You are a devious and dangerous little bitch, aren't you," Fraum said.

The pretty ones are the dangerous ones.

"Only when my hand is forced."

"I will consider what you say," Fraum said. "Now leave me with my father. I have much to think about and don't need any more of your prattle to distract me."

Joanne curtsied and left the room. She felt relief at no longer having to be in the same space as the corpse and his son. Neither made for good company and both raised the hairs on her arms. *Obey. Rule. That I can do. Beware the Shadow, yes, that is sound advice.*

Beaty hurried to her side, leaning in close to avoid others hearing her. "Why do you insist on playing such dangerous games?"

"If I don't," Joanne said, "then someone else will."

The funeral took place a week later. It was small, took place at the base of the mountain where the chapel to Father and Mother sat a short distance from the main road in an idyllic tree covered grove. A dozen carriages from Argenti Lapisdom brought the mourning family, King Dryd's body, and several attendants. They crossed a stream to enter the wide yard cleared of trees and brush. The chapel was dark, cold, and smelled of incense to cover the rotting body stench. Joanne noted that there were equal number of lords and ladies of Seaptum who attended their king's funeral as those who had missed. Fraum listed the names of the houses who were absent: most notable, but not as surprising were Foxglow and Silversmith.

Those who did show wore an array of black and gray. Queen Galea led the procession of pallbearers as they entered the chapel and placed the coffin containing the remains of King Dryd on a stone table. The priest was an older man, black robes with hearts on the stoles and a headdress with a gold sun. He spoke in a reverent tone, emphasizing the great accomplishments of King Dryd, which included the ruining of Joanne's young life, and other political maneuvers, none more impressive than surviving three brothers to retain his crown, and other accomplishments which Joanne didn't much care about since they included winning the war with Nemus. Fraum sat stiff in his chair. Joane tried not to fidget, but the seats were uncomfortable hard wood and thin material to prevent her backside from getting splinters.

Queen Galea talked about her husband as a strong man and how much joy he had brought her, while dabbing at her tears with a handkerchief, though Joanne didn't hear much love in them. A duty of wife to her husband. That's what she sounded like, a person whose duty has ended, a relief, perhaps. *Or maybe she grew as cold as the stones she lived in.*

Prince Gallium spoke next about his father's lessons on strength and how to be a great leader and to inspire loyalty. People nodded, but no one else spoke at the funeral, not even Fraum. Joanne understood the man was feared and revered for his command of the kingdom, but not once did she hear a word about love. Not a single weeping or wailing. When they carried his casket to the mausoleum where his ancestors were buried and it was sealed up, there was nothing but silence. A strange exhale of breath. There was no celebration, no drinking and telling stories like at her brother's funeral. A line of finely dressed men and women returned to their carriages and then a silent trip back up the road to the stone tomb where she resided.

"The coronation will occur by Reaping's end," Fraum said. "You will need to be seen sitting at my side, though our marriage is not complete, it will be symbolic. Like the rising of Mother and Father to godhood. You may invite representatives from Nemus to bear witness to the event, though, my mother said you and your ladies would be enough."

"I will write to them immediately," Joanne said.

"Good. I will have a trusted messenger deliver it once you hand it to me," Fraum said. "I'm certain you won't have any concerns over me reading it before it is sent."

"None, my lord," Joanne said, though she would have to word it carefully. Especially since his paranoia would grow, seeing enemies and assassins in every shadow. The burden of every ruler. *Did my father worry?* She couldn't imagine him being so concerned, but then he was a hard man. Hard as the stone that would crush all who got it in its path. *Except King Dryd. He crumbled beneath his demands.*

"I expect you to continue your training with my brother as well," Fraum said. "In plain view of the soldiers. It is good for their morale and will aide them in their support during this rather difficult time of power transfer."

"As my lord commands." Though, that was one she would willingly follow.

The morning exercise was the one activity Joanne took real pleasure in. The histories and folklore of Seaptum quickly became dull in that they all showed the line of Kings in such favorable light and painted Nemus as the instigators of the separation and the several wars fought between the nations. Nemus history books would point at Seaptum as the culprit, when really it was greedy men who had vast amounts of wealth and resources, plus standing armies in which they didn't know what else to do with besides bleed and die over rocks and wood.

"*Silent Willow*," Gallium said, driving his blade forward.

Joanne brought her blade up to ward off the attack aimed at her chest—she had a bruise there when she was too slow to remember the defensive position. Pain was a good teacher, or so Prince Gallium told her. The crack of wood on wood was pleasant and she was happy she maintained her grip on the hilt, this time.

"*Dust in the Wind.*"

She whirled around deflecting his blade and tried *Plucking the Daisy*, but

Gallium danced away, *Slicing the Wind*, which landed a flat-sided blow on her bottom. Joanne squeaked and then growled, *Leaping Lilypad* followed by *Sowing Rain* to drive Gallium back. There were claps and shouts from several soldiers observing the sparring. *Broken Ground* slid Gallium's blade down hers, combined with his speed and strength, he had shoved her blade aside, holding the edge to her throat. Sweat glistened on his lips close enough for her to feel his warm breath.

"You are too aggressive, princess," he said. "Do not over-commit unless you know you have won."

"I yield," Joanne said, her chest heaving from the strain of the fight. *How is he not even winded?* "I have an important question."

"Is it something my brother has put you to asking?" Gallium stepped away, taking a towel to wipe sweat from his brow. "If so, then I want nothing to do with asking of questions and having to refuse to give answers I know not."

"This is purely my curiosity."

Gallium waved for her to continue.

"Will you abdicate your claim on the throne?" Joanne asked.

"A blunt question, princess," Gallium said.

"That isn't an answer."

"Again, you put me in a position where I haven't one yet."

"You haven't decided?"

Gallium shrugged.

"Time will tell what I may or may not do. Why, does he plan on having me murdered or exiled after the coronation?"

"Neither," Joanne said, though she wasn't privy to Fraum's plans during or after the crowning.

"Oh, my princess is worried about her place in the King's bed," Gallium said. "No matter the outcome, you will be safe. I give you my word. Besides, how could I harm such a great sparring partner. Who knows, maybe one day you might best me in a fight."

That midday, Joanne wrote a letter to her father.

Dearest Father,

I have settled in well here at Argenti Lapisdom. They have me learning the history of Seaptum to better understand my new people. I am certain news of King Dryd's death have reached you. Fraum will soon be given the crown. I would be grateful if you, mother and, perhaps my brothers, come witness the glorious event. I miss you all dearly.

Yours in Love,

Joanne Desmond.

Fraum sat at a large wooden desk, similar to the one occupying her father's office. He looked up, nose runny and eyes red, weepy, frowning at her disturbance. She gave him the letter before he could prompt why she was there. He scanned it, nodding in satisfaction, then placed it in an envelope, sealed it with wax and pressed the signet into it. He summoned a messenger, a young man with short cropped hair and a smudge of facial hair, and gave him the envelope. "Deliver this to the Keep in Nemus, urgent business. Hand it directly to Lord Desmond. Take an extra post horse and a rider that you trust. Bring back his reply as soon as you can."

"Aye, my lord," the young man said.

"Take this coin, but spend it wisely on food and drink needed to nourish for the trip there and back," Fraum said. "Do not splurge on woman or drink. Those will get you killed. Wear the badge of my house until you reach the border, then hide it. For now, it cannot guarantee you safe passage beyond our home country."

"I do my lord's bidding swiftly," the youth said, pocketing the coin.

"Does that satisfy my lady?" Fraum asked.

"I'm very pleased," Joanne said and curtsied.

"Now leave my presence since I have more pressing issues to resolve," he said and waved her away.

Joanne backed away from the room, annoyed at being dismissed like a child, but flush with hope of seeing her father again after so many months away. Back in her room, Selene paced back and forth, a worried expression on her face. Beaty sat in a chair, reading a letter, flipping the page over and over.

"What is the matter in here? You all look as though someone has died," Joanne said. Neither of her maids laughed at her dark humor. *This must be very serious business for Selene not to at least giggle.* "What do you have there, Beaty?"

"A letter from our good friend," she said

"What is the concern?"

"It seems Lady Silversmith has arranged for a divorce from Lord Silversmith," Beaty said.

"Justly so," Joanne said.

"Both are planning on petitioning the new king for a redress of damages caused by his new wife," Beaty said. "Otherwise, they will reclaim their regiment of ten thousand soldiers placed in the trust of King Dryd until these grievances are addressed."

"He couldn't."

"He can and will, even if it causes a civil war."

Joanne sighed.

"What grievances are there?"

She could guess about her complaint— Joanne did humiliate her and her husband in front of the Queen and the other prestigious ladies, though the indiscretion was most likely public knowledge.

"The willful slander of Lady Silversmith in a public-gathering that damaged the goodwill and reputation of Lord Silversmith. The loss of dowery and lands appointed him by Lady Silversmith as the bride price. The forfeit of children, since they had none," Beaty said. "In exchange for certain conditions will the grievance be dropped and the princess Joanne forgiven."

"It always comes down to coin, doesn't it," Joanne said.

"And land," Beaty handed her the letter. "They want a portion of land in Nemus that is part of your dowery to Fraum."

Anger flushed through her. *They want to take my land away from my family!*

"Donn can take the lot of them," Joanne said. "It says here they haven't petitioned yet."

"They will most likely wait until after the coronation when the decrees become official part of Fraum's rule," Beaty said.

"Anything about Lady Foxglow?"

Beaty shook her head.

"I wouldn't be surprised if she didn't submit a similar claim."

Wonderful way to start off a regime and a wedding! Starting a civil war!

"Send a letter back thanking Selene's dearest one for her concern," Joanne said. "I need another letter to go to Lady Windridge. I need a meeting with her regarding wedding plans and other issues."

They want to play games. Fine! Let's play the Queen's Hangman.

The date for Fraum's coronation was set for the first Harvest Night.

Joanne thought it an ill-omen to crown a prince king on the night typically reserved for honoring the dead in Nemus. However, traditions were different up north where the days shortened faster and the cold settled in. The messenger returned with her father's reply two weeks prior to Harvest Night. Fraum summoned her to his office, his face sallow and pasty again, eyes and nose weeping and he huddled under a heavy cloak, wheezing.

"This arrived for you," he said, tossing the opened envelope across the desk.

Joanne opened it and found the reply short and to the point.

My Dearest Daughter,

Your mother and I are most glad to hear of your smooth adjustment. I knew you would play your part well. Unfortunately, trouble has broken out here to the south. A minor rebellion has to be settled. Perhaps we will see you at Sowing for your wedding. Best regards to Fraum and our condolences.

Yours Under Mother and Father,

Lord Desmond

"Parents can be so very disappointing," Fraum said. "Not as disappointed as I will be if a certain suit against the crown isn't resolved. I am willing to give the Foster Manor and Blackwood to satisfy the complaint."

Joanne clenched her fists to hold back her tears.

"I will have it resolved, my lord." She curtsied and scurried back to her room, sealing it shut and refused to respond to Beaty's questions. Instead, Selene entered in. Joanne wept and told her everything in the letter and what Fraum had threatened.

Selene held her, stroking her head as she whispered.

"We won't allow that to happen, my love. Lady Windridge will help you, I know it."

Joanne reached up and kissed her. They stripped and stroked each other until the tears were swept away into moans of passion. Contented sleep claimed her and she dreamt of the Shadow looming over her.

You cannot avoid me forever.

Joanne woke up panting and sweaty. Beside her Selene slept peacefully. *I need a plan, in case Lady Windridge refuses my offer. I need to talk to Lady Helena. She'll have something I can use to be very persuasive with these Seaptum cunts.*

Joanne scribbled out another letter addressed to Lady Helena Freeman.

She would have Selene deliver it personally. Fraum wouldn't approve of this plan, or even if he did, she didn't need him mudding up the waters, especially if she required Lady Freeman for other purposes in the future.

The next morning, she sent Selene under the presumption that her lady was seeking to aide in fellowship of Nemus with the Lady Freeman. No one protested and Joanne kissed Selene goodbye and sent her with the letter. Later that day, Lady Windridge arrived. Her arm was in a sling and she had lost partial movement in her hand.

"It was worth it to spare you, my dear," she said, sipping tea in an awkward way using her dumb-hand as they called it in Seaptum. "I couldn't allow her to kill our Princess and start a war, gods no!"

"I'm glad you are healing well," Joanne said. "I have some terrible news, though."

She explained the grievance and the demanded reparations. Lady Windridge gasped and cursed at the various demands. Her expression that of disgust and she let out a long sigh after Joanne finished the details of the suit against her.

"He made the bed and now he wants to take yours," Lady Windridge said. "They need to be stopped."

Joanne smiled.

"I know how," she said. "A trial."

"A trial?" Lady Windridge sounded so much like Fraum that Joanne cringed.

"Yes, for attempted murder," Joanne said. In her mind she was placing her bet and flipping the card. "Not of me, of course, but you, my dear, brave friend. I think you deserve some compensation for your pain. Perhaps deeds to silver mines might ease your suffering?"

"They would," Lady Windridge said. "Wouldn't Lady Silversmith also be hanged for treason?"

"She could be, unless a display of clemency was made on her behalf by a certain princess-to-be," Joanne said. "To demonstrate good faith in the name of maintaining peace in Seaptum and the dowery kept in place."

"But I would have the deed?"

"Of course," Joanne said. "Lord Silversmith must be punished along with his wife."

"I will write my suit tonight!"

"You are doing such a great service, my dear Lady Windridge. I will never forget it."

Selene returned four days prior to the coronation. She brought with her a sealed box and was instructed not to open it. A letter accompanied it. Joanne read the note, then had the box filled with tea leaves and berries, specifically the favorite of a certain Lady Foxglow. The box was re-sealed with a houseless impression and sent to Lily so it would find its way to Lady Foxglow along with an anonymous note from a lesser lad hoping to curry favor by sending her tea to help her through these difficult days. Selene received a letter of confirmation that the box was delivered and the recipient in such a great mood, though she didn't open it in the deliverer's presence.

We wait for any sad news.

The days leading up to the coronation, Argenti Lapisdom was a flurry of activity. Extra rooms were prepared for guests arriving from the furthest points northwest of Seaptum. Flowers and food were delivered by dozens of carts, merchants and jewelers jostling to impress Queen Galea and Joanne. New dresses were commissioned, cut, sewn, and fitted. Bright purple petticoats and skirts with bone hoops stitched in the edges. White lace like sea foam curled from the sleeves, hems, and necklines. Matching purple slippers were cobbled in under a day. A new gold circlet was fitted on Joanne's brow. Every piece of silver shimmered in the light, fresh candles replaced the old ones in gold candelabras, sconces, and chandeliers draped in diamonds sparkled like stars in the sky.

"You look like rather beautiful. Try not to insult any of our guests," Fraum snapped at her after he approved of her outfit. "We cannot afford to lose any more support."

"I will be as civil as a flower," Joanne said, smiling at her own pun. *A bright red and orange one.*

Several of the ladies who arrived early found an opportunity to talk with Joanne in private. They professed her public shaming on Lady Foxglow and Lady Silversmith was a relief. They praised her shrewdness and cunning, hoping they never fell under her scrutiny, and swore their support to her. Lady Silversmith arrived separate from her husband, but Lady Foxglow was attended by Lord Foxglow, though he had a sour look on his face.

Neither woman spoke to Joanne, or each other. Where they went, a void happened in the room, until they found themselves occupying empty space while lively chatter embraced Joanne. Lady Windridge presented her with a silver bracelet with her household emblem etched in it: the sun flame and the rose. Others presented her with earrings, necklaces, and a silk set of handkerchiefs.

Joanne was flush with the attention, hotter than the fire which crackled in the hearth. It was all better than any name day celebration and she knew each gift came with a small web to grant the giver a unspoken favor. Nothing was ever truly a gift when one had power. She expected to her the secret wishes at some point. Tonight was for feasting. The grand hall was cleared of tables and the same priest who administered the funeral rites stood on a dais, making an announcement.

"Lords and Ladies of Seaptum. The gods have graced us with a life of service. A life to protect the innocent and powerless, to continue peace and harmony. One such life has passed beyond the realm of the living into the peaceful glades of Nahrangi where King Dryd awaits the loving embrace of his wife and sons. Where we will all one day walk for eternity," the priest said. "Until that day, we must protect this living realm and so Mother and Father have given us one such son. Fraum, son of Galea and Dryd, prince regent and first in-line to the silver throne. May long life and wisdom follow in his footsteps."

Fraum rose from the chair and he offered up a hand to Joanne who stood beside Queen Galea and Prince Gallium. Joanne ascended the three steps to the top of the dais.

"I walk in the light of the gods, but not alone," Fraum said, kissing Joanne's hand and holding it out, presenting her to the Lords and Ladies.

"We accept your sacrifice," a response came in unison, though Joanne noted some did not speak the line.

"With this acceptance and the blessing of the gods, I present to you, the new king of Seaptum! King Fraum!"

"May his rule be long and peaceful!"

A gold crown shaped like the sun with diamonds and rubies circling it was placed on his head.

"Rise, King Fraum, and let the people rejoice."

The room erupted in sounds of clapping and cheers, shouts of "Long live King Fraum" and a few "bless Princess Joanne."

A feast took place with barrels of wine and ale set up along with breads, roasted squash, nuts and a variety of savory dishes and desserts. Joanne ate a little and Queen Galea nibbled some, though she complained of stomach pains.

"What's wrong, mother?" Fraum asked.

"I was meeting with Lady Silverfox regarding her complaint surrounding the events from her previous visit, when I was not feeling myself. She offered me a tea that would settle my stomach and clear my head."

The cup froze at Joanne's mouth.

"I guess the pain is back and I might have to see her about more tea," Queen Galea said. *No!* Joanne wanted to grab the Queen's arm, to keep her from seeking death in the remedy, but if she drank the same tea that Joanne gifted her, it was far too late. Dragon's Vein swept through her body. "I feel warm. Too warm! I need air!"

Prince Gallium came to his mother's side and helped her from her seat. They hadn't walked more than a few paces when Queen Galea collapsed and began to convulse. Her eyes rolled up to the whites, bloody froth bubbled from her mouth and she gave an awful screech that silenced the room. She clutched her belly and began vomiting down the front of her new dress. Blood stained the white lace.

"Master Physic! Bring him here!!" Prince Gallium shouted. "The queen is ill."

The Master Physic made his way through the crowd and knelt beside Queen Galea. The queen had gone still by then. He touched her forehead and her chest, then shook his head. "The queen is dead."

"How?"

"Poisoned, it seems."

"Seal the doors, let no one escape until we find this poisoner!" Prince Gallium stood up. "Stay where you are, or prove your guilt by running."

Worried chatter rounded the room with a few whimpers and cries for the deceased Queen. Just like a year ago, Joanne found herself swept up in a search for a murderer. Lady Freeman caught her eye, her lips pressed together and hands folded over her belly.

She'd never tell. Not without giving herself away as an accessory to murder.

Lady Freeman lifted one finger and waggled it back and forth, a signal of sorts. One that Joanne would have to be contented with though both their lives hung by a frail thread.

CHAPTER THIRTEEN:
DONN AND QETESH
LOVE AND DEATH

Love is like death since where one begins life alone
they give up a piece of themselves to the ones they love.
Love is kind, love is cruel, love takes all, and gives
back none like death. One approaches it, knowing it
is the end of all they once knew and to suffer no longer
one must surrender to both.
   —from "Philosophia in Philio: Qetesh and the
    hideous love of Donn."
    Mathias Mathers. 2nd King of Nemus

People worried it was the wine. People cried out it was the food. But, it took a comment from Joanne to Prince Gallium to check one particular room. A wooden box was retrieved, which was taken to the Master Physic. He handled it with extreme care once he saw the crushed up yellow and red petals.

"Dragon's Vein," the Master Physic said.

"Dragon's Vein," Fraum repeated, nose wrinkled and lip curled to reveal yellowed teeth. "Who would be so vile to poison my mother?"

"Lady Foxglow has poisoned *our* mother," Prince Gallium said. "She has been taken below for interrogation."

"Why would she do that? What did she have to gain?" Fraum asked and looked at Joanne. "I fear you have something to do with this."

"What in the name of the Shadow would I have to do with Lady Foxglow poisoning your mother?" Joanne asked, trying to cover the flush she felt in the accusation. Especially since he was partially right, though it had all gone wrong for her.

"Peace, brother," Prince Gallium said. "Perhaps it was done in error."

"The queen told me she was feeling ill earlier and said Lady Foxglow gave her tea," Joanne said. "That sounds like malicious intent. Unless it is common for people to drink Dragon's Vein like it is stinging nettle for health benefits?"

"Dragon's Vein has no health benefits and it is not native to Nemus," the Master Physic said. "The place it could be readily acquired would be at the Freeman estate, though, why it is not eradicated is beyond my knowledge."

"Have Lady Freeman questioned," Fraum said. "Let's see what she has to confess."

She will confess to Lady Foxglow's unexpected visitation, to gain information on me and my family holdings. Joanne had noted this in the letter to Lady Freeman for this type of circumstance, only it was supposed to be Foxglow with her innards burnt out, not Queen Galea.

"Poisoning the Queen doesn't make sense," Prince Gallium said. "They gain nothing from her death."

"Unless it is to start a war with nobles and the King," Joanne said. "Perhaps create suspicion among you both as to what had happened and who might be the next target of poisoning? It was just Janus turning his head away from her that Queen Galea spoke to me of her stomach pains and getting tea from Lady Foxglow. We only have to turn to the event less than a century ago where Lord Ironwood poisoned Prince Valleum's paramour to start a war between he and his brother—"

"I am well aware of the histories," Fraum said, and dabbed his nose. Already his eyes were becoming gluey with film and he began to wheeze.

"It's time for milord's tincture," the Master Physic said. "Is there anything else needed from me?"

Fraum waved him away and he bowed.

"I know this has been a troublesome night," Joanne said, taking a folded parchment from her bosom, "but I have here a letter from Lady Windridge in which she wishes to submit a grievance against Lady Silversmith. For the harm caused to her when Lady Silversmith stabbed her, rather than me. It was an attempt on my life."

"Every one, leave me," Fraum said, pressing the handkerchief to his nose and blew a wet splatter into it. Joanne began to follow Prince Gallium out. He wouldn't listen to her, not after the unexpected loss of his mother, but she had to try——. "Except, you, Joanne. Stay here."

Alone in the room, she could sense his frustration, the wicked look on his face and the deep frown lines. This wasn't going the way she thought it might.

"What game are you playing?" Fraum asked. "My mother has just passed and here you are manipulating others, but for what reason? Did you have a hand in her death? Tell me the truth or I will have the flesh stripped from your backside."

"I knew nothing of the tea or Lady Foxglow's intentions," Joanne said, putting on her sternest look.

Fraum stepped close to her, standing a little above her in height.

"Did you murder my mother?"

"No," Joanne said.

His hand was quick, striking her on the cheek so fast Joanne only had time to squeak. The burn was instant and she placed her own hand on the mark, feeling the warmth. Fraum's cold, blue eyes chilled her.

"Before you came here, there was little strife among the lords and ladies. Yet you stomp in like a child dancing among an anthill. My mother is dead, two ladies stand accused of capital crimes and there is a rift among those in power," Fraum said, and grabbed Joanne's breasts. His fingers pinched her nipples, buffered only by the fabric of her dress. "This is your doing! I should have your tits removed and pieces of you sent home to your father in a box."

Tears burned Joanne's eyes and she tried to pull his hands off away from her. He pinched them harder until she dropped to her knees. *Tell him nothing.* It hurt bad enough she wanted to tell him everything. From the death of her tutor to having the box of tea delivered to Lady Foxglow. *Tell him nothing. Endure the pain.*

"Please," she said, lip trembling.

"I will not have my home torn apart by some bitch who doesn't know how to control her temper." Fraum gave one last twist and then released her. "You are my property. As my property you will follow the rules I establish. If I find that you break any of these rules, punishment will be swift and very unpleasant."

Joanne remained on her knees, staring at her skirts.

"I will look at the suit against Lady Silversmith, but you will have no say in how I deal out punishment to my people. After this mess you created is cleaned up, I expect you to be like a little lap dog," Fraum spun on her again, grabbing her chin. "Yap and I will have your tongue removed. Do you understand?"

Joanne nodded her head, though it was difficult with his hard grip. Fraum released her.

"Leave my sight. I don't want to see you until I summon you."

Joanne ran from the room.

"Princess," Prince Gallium said. "Did he hurt you?"

"I'll be fine," she said, anger rising.

"Are you certain?" Prince Gallium asked. "I could make it so he doesn't hit you ever again."

Yes! Kill him!

"We cannot have any more bloodshed this night," Joanne said. "Too much pain and death have happened." *More to come with the trials.*

Prince Gallium bowed.

"I will concede to your wish, for now," Prince Gallium said, though she could see he wasn't pleased by her response. "Tell me when you change your mind."

"Thank you." Tears stung her eyes at his kindness. She retreated to her room quickly, to avoid the curious glances of servants and soldiers. Selene and Beaty were changing her sheets on the bed, and stopped immediately when they saw her face.

"What happened now?" Beaty asked.

Selene poked her to check for bruising

"I'm alright. He is very upset and took his anger out on me," she said. "I just want to go to bed."

They undressed her, revealing the bruises on her breasts. Selene touched one lightly and Joanne hissed.

"Bestial," Beaty said.

"He shouldn't hurt you," Selene said. "Something should be done."

"I deserved it," Joanne said. "Worse. This is all my fault."

She broke down and wept. Selene took her in her arms and Beaty stroked Joanne's head. They help her strip, wash, and put her in bed nude without her nightgown which would chafe her bruised breasts. Both slept with her, to provide protection and comfort.

The next morning her bruising still ached and she was careful in how she dressed. Word had gusted through that Lady Foxglow confessed to the Queen's murder, though without giving an explanation as to why. The motive the guests passed along was that it was a move to dispatch the queen before she would take Foxglow's lands as part of the retribution to Silversmith for the infidelity.

"What do you think will come first, the wedding or the trial?" Lady Windridge asked.

"I don't know," Joanne said.

The coronation celebration turned into a funeral. The lords and ladies of Seaptum remained for the next two days, as much prisoners, since their carriages were forbidden to leave the grounds unguarded, as they were guests. A similar staging was done for the Queen as it was with the burial of Dryd. The priest, looking tired from all the events, read the same script. Prince Gallium spoke about how beautiful and kind his mother was to him, while Fraum brooded, wiping his leaky nose and stared intently at the casket holding his mother. She was buried beside Dryd.

"Together in the fields of Nahrangi where they await us," Prince Gallium said and placed white roses from the garden on her grave.

That night, two more arrests were made. Lord and Lady Silversmith were removed from their rooms under guard. They were escorted down the stairs into the lower chambers. Lady Silversmith glared at Joanne, but didn't say a word and if she had a knife, Joanne knew Lady Silversmith would try to stab her again.

Prince Gallium later approached Joanne and said, "Send word to your family that the wedding has been moved up."

"Moved up?" Joanne asked. *I won't be fifteen for a few more months.*

"The trials will conclude soon, and, since most of our guests will remain at the Argenti, Fraum decided to add one more event to the list of entertainment," he said.

"Why didn't he tell me?" Joanne asked.

"Because he is King, now. He doesn't have to answer to anyone," Prince Gallium said.

Joanne shuddered at the idea. *What other nasty surprises will he have for me?* She wrote the letter to her parents and Prince Gallium hired a messenger to take it. She hoped that her father would be able to come at such a short notice. Lord Desmond was preoccupied governing Nemus, but he wouldn't forget about her, would he?

I'll have to wait for the response.

Not that she was pleased with this sudden change in wedding date. Not like she would be less of a captive if she refused. Refusal was not something she could do, not after all the problems she had caused. No, she would see it through. The fate of Nemus depended on her being a good princess and becoming a Queen. Especially since Seaptum currently lacked one.

There were no late-night gatherings. Lords and ladies hid in their respective rooms. Fraum had dismissed them to go home, but no carriage left the gates. None wanted to miss out on the trial of their lifetime.

"This isn't good for Seaptum," Lady Hawthorne said, her belly near ready to burst. She moved around the garden at a slow pace, accompanied by Joanne, Lady Windridge and Lady Willowcreek. "A most suspicious way to begin a reign. The last king to subject his lords to unjust punishment didn't last longer than a moon's cycle."

"That would be King Bounty," Joanne said. "The end of the Goldvein line of succession."

"Someone has studied our history," Lady Hawthorne said.

"He punished the lords who tried rebelling and aiding his younger brother, Stiles, in his attempt to kill him," Joanne continued. "Stripped them of land and title, while forcing their wives into servitude and marrying their daughters off to farmers and loggers. I would say he's lenient."

"How so?"

"He left them alive and they gathered loyal citizens and soldiers to kill him." *Like my father had done with King Reuban. Possibly what Fraum will do to those who aide his brother when the time comes, unless I can persuade him otherwise.*

Lady Hawthorne frowned and looked back over her shoulder. Joanne followed her gaze to Gallium standing at the gate leading to the sea bluff.

The sea wyrm stalking the waters for unsuspecting prey.

That night, Lady Hawthorne went into labor and birthed a boy.

Master Tailor stood in front of Joanne who was nude and shivering in the cold room. He studied her neck, the curve of her shoulders and her hips. He clicked his tongue, and shook his head. Tossing down his measuring tape, he moved to the various textures of white fabric.

"None of this will work," he said, scattering the fabric.

"Why not?" Joanne asked, relaxing her shoulders.

"This was all her, hers and hers only," Master Tailor said, tears in his eyes. "The Queen had a vision, a style that was modest, but, look at you. The marks on your body." He pointed out the fading bruises around Joanne's nipples. "You must decide now how you want your dress styled. Or prance naked before the gods for all I care."

"Forgive him, Princess, he has been in his sadness since the Queen passed," the younger woman said. "We have your measurements and nothing has changed, except, you know." There was sympathy in her voice that Joanne was certain this woman had experienced similar humiliation at a man's abusive reactions. "Put your robe on, and we'll get you a dress the same as the others."

"No," Joanne said. "Master Tailor is right. The Queen is gone and so her choice of modesty must be interred with her. I decide style now for the court, and I say I desire a dress low cut on shoulders here and here." She pointed to a place below her collar bone and dragged a finger in a U-neck to where the dress would give a hint of cleavage. "I am a woman and not some priestess of Donn that must be stuffed inside a rough sack. Let them all leer and know that this Princess, this Queen-to-be, will not hide behind false curtains."

The woman curtsied.

"Hide behind false curtains," Beaty remarked when they left the room.

"It sounded good at the time," Joanne said, "could you do better?"

"Sure, this Sun Queen will let her beauty shine," Beaty said.

"Next time you write me the speech," Joanne said.

They laughed and dressed for the important event of the day. The trial and reading of Lady Windridge's complaint. The Grand Hall was warm with bodies gathered, standing apart to the various sides of the room.

Joanne entered, escorted by two guards to the front where a table and chairs were set in front of the same dais used at the coronation. Lady Silversmith, her hair ragged, face pale, eyes distant with shock and pain, and bruising around her chin and her lips rouged with blood rather than makeup, slouched in the chair. Her hands trembled, the small finger on her right hand appeared disjointed.

"What happened to her?" Joanne asked Lady Windridge who sat in a chair to the left of the dais.

"Fell down the stairs trying to escape the guard," Lady Windridge said, though the lilt in her voice spoke of a different sort of fall. Fraum entered the room with Gallium at his right. He was dressed in purple robes with the sun embroidered on the shoulders. Dark circles hung beneath his eyes and he scowled down at her. She hadn't seen or heard from him since after the interment of Queen Galea's body. He hunched over in his chair, the same miserable, petulant boy Joanne had grown to loathe in the carriage ride through Nemus and Seaptum. He lifted fingers, motioning for Prince Gallium to begin the proceedings.

"Lords and ladies of Seaptum, a grievance has been declared against Lady Silversmith regarding the injuries to Lady Windridge and the accused stabbing her in the right arm. The blade caused significant damage to her arm and Lady Windridge demands compensation in the form of land and wealth to be passed to her husband since the Lady Windridge took said wound in the service of the royal family. It is declared that she must delay having her third child because of the wound, give it a year to heal properly so as not to contract a blood illness to hurt or kill mother and child. This claim has been backed by our own Master Physic. Is all that I have stated true, Lady Windridge?"

Lady Windridge stood, making a show of adjusting her sling.

"By the Father and Mother, all is true. Most of the women here, including the Queen-in-waiting, herself, witnessed the attack, and was the object of assault until I stepped between them."

"Are there any here who would attest to a different course of events?" Gallium asked.

Joanne gazed around the room, watching all the faces look upon Lady Silversmith and then away. None spoke in her defense.

"What have you to say, Lady Silversmith?"

"I acted in anger due to my reputation being ruined and I was humiliated in front of these other noble women," Lady Silversmith said. "I ask for clemency and will do penance as the wise King of the land deems just."

"What say you, Queen-in-waiting?" Fraum asked. "Do you give clemency to this pitiful, broken woman?"

Joanne stood up, the memory of their mocking fresh and the savage demands for her land as a grievance they were going to pose against her. Lady Silversmith didn't meet her eyes. She sunk into her chair, her chin pressed into her chest, a vision of despair. Her life rested in Joanne's hands. She would set the tone and expectations with her words. She could draw favor with leniency.

"Clemency," Lady Windridge muttered beside her. "Give her clemency."

"Clemency is the wish and desire many here expect, for any could find themselves sitting in Lady Silversmith's place before a tribunal for acts committed in passion or ill-thought," Joanne said, the faces of the lords and ladies confirming her words. Joanne paused, allowing the moment to build to the expectations, because a benevolent queen was one they could love easily. *One they could betray just as easily.* "I declare Lady Silversmith's actions to be malicious and traitorous. Clemency is denied by me just as she would deny my right to live and recognized as one of the people of Seaptum. She attempted to harm me and so attempted to harm the king and the throne and all the good people of Seaptum represent."

Lady Silversmith whimpered at the refusal. Any hope that had lived had been snatched away like reaching into her chest and stealing her still-beating heart. Elation shivered through Joanne and she held back the smile that tried to force its way onto her lips.

Fraum leaned forward in the chair.

"No clemency?"

"No, my lord," Joanne said, watching Lady Silversmith diminish, a flower shriveling under the blaze of the sun.

Fraum smiled. "Then I declare Lady Silversmith a traitor to the throne of Seaptum. She shall be stripped of titles and land, her dowery will remain with Lord Silversmith, minus the deeds to half the silver mines, which will be forfeited to Lord Windridge as compensation for the injuries to his wife in service of the throne."

Agitated talks began around the room and a few protests to the declaration of traitor.

"As punishment for the attempted murder of a member of my house and betrothed, Marrium Silversmith, you are sentenced to death by beheading," Fraum said, looking to Joanne to signal this was her doing and she will bear the brunt of the complaints.

Marrium, former Lady Silversmith, dropped her head into her hands, and cried.

"Clear the room," Prince Gallium said. Then he and Fraum exited the dais, leaving through a back door where a dozen guards stood, hands on swords.

"Why didn't you give her clemency?" Lady Windridge asked.

"King Bounty," Joanne said. "Lessons in history."

"Oh, very wise, my Queen," Lady Windridge said, though fear lurked behind her gaze. Every woman in Seaptum would shudder at how efficiently she had destroyed one of their own. No matter how close to the crown they might sit, there would always be a sense of fear that a spark from the flame may burn them into ash, as well.

Let them fear me! When I do display clemency, then it will be a grand display and all will love me for it.

The executions were set for the morning.

That night, three visitors entered her dreams. Teresa grinned, neck dark with dried blood, and head eschewed. Holding her hand was Cook Marret Mathers, rope dangling and his face purple and bruised, and Gothard leaned on him, matching rope tight around his bloated neck and a card in his hand—Joanne didn't need to see it to know it was the Queen's Hangman. There was an empty space where the light didn't touch the ground and shadows angling to the side.

"Two more friends for us," Teresa said, maggots falling out of her mouth when she spoke. A worm crawled from her ear, dangling above the ear lobe crusted in dirt. She plucked the worm, watching it wiggle between her fingers before she ate it.

"Two more touched by death," Cook Mathers said.

"Death's shadow," Gothard whispered, tossing the card and it fluttered like bat wings and took off into the moonlit sky.

Queen Galea stepped from behind. Her mouth dripped bloody vomit, staining her purple dress a pinkish color. "We all wait for you, Joanne." She held out a yellow flower with red tendrils bisecting the petals. "We will feast on your blood. Eat your broken bones here in Arula."

I can protect you. The dark, sultry voice, tempting and yet Joanne was not ready to listen. In her dream, she turned her back on them, only to find them, her victims, there in front of her, though closer. Again, she turned and again they were closer, dead fingers groping for her.

Take my hand, little one.

Joanne reached for the black-gloved fingers.

"Don't," Selene said. A light shone in the distance. In that light stood her friend and lover. Selene's eyes shimmered, her mouth drawn tight. Joanne's hand yanked away from the glove which had changed to black smoke. "Wake up!"

"I can't," Joanne said.

"You must. It is time."

Joanne gasped, rising from the dream like a drowning person from water. Selene stood beside her, a hand on her shoulder.

"Time, milady," Selene said. "The execution is about to start."

"Where is my black dress?"

Joanne joined the rest of the crowd out in the parade grounds. The sound of metal striking metal, men grunting as they sparred, and the *thwonk* of arrows striking straw targets was silenced. A cold breeze blew through and Joanne tightened the black shawl over her shoulders. A platform was raised with a single block of wood on it. Selene pressed in close to Joanne.

"I thought they hung murderers?" Selene asked.

"Only if they have no title," Joanne responded.

Marium Silversmith and Freda Foxglow were led down the middle of the parade ground, metal shackles on their hands and feet. They clanked along at a slow pace, a spectacle for all to witness and draw warning from—this could be any of them who betray the King of Seaptum. Freda was nearly unrecognizable. Her hair was cropped, nose twisted and she limped like she had something crammed up an orifice, which Joanne wouldn't put it past either Fraum or Gallium to humiliate and hurt her in any way to get the answer they wanted. Blood streaked the back of her thighs and her hands were twisted. A doll mauled by dogs would look better than she did at the moment.

"It hurts to watch her walk," Beaty said. "Men are so cruel."

"If she were a man, they would have castrated her to get what they wanted," Joanne said.

"Do you think she knew about the tea?" Selene asked.

Joanne nodded at Lady Freeman who stood across the parade grounds, eyes wide, and hand on her belly where a noticeable bump had grown. Whatever they learned, Prince Gallium would protect the baby, wouldn't he?

"Foxglow knew nothing of it, so whatever they may have tortured from her wouldn't be of much value," Joanne said.

The two women reached the platform and stumbled up the stairs. Guards on either side of them gripped their arms, half-dragging them the rest of the way to their fate. Prince Gallium took the stairs next. He was dressed in dark blue uniform, a black cloak with the sun blazoned on the back. He stood on the right side of the block, face grim as he faced the lords and ladies. The crowd was silent and he raised his voice to be heard across the parade grounds, clear and unfaltering. "Freda Foxglow, you are charged with regicide. Rather than deny this claim, you have pled guilty. The penalty for your crimes is death by beheading. Do you have any last words?"

"I didn't know," she said. "Mother believe me, but I didn't know."

Prince Gallium motioned and the guards partially dragged her to the box. They forced her to her knees over the box. Freda whimpered, trying to pull her body away, but the guards held her arms out and she couldn't do more than turn her head from side to side. Prince Gallium drew his sword. "May Donn judge you fairly." He brought the blade down and Freda's head fell away from her neck, blood spurting across the wood and soaking into the dirt. Prince Gallium picked her head up, a surprised expression frozen in death. He placed this in a bag and tossed it to one of the guards behind whim while the other two dragged her decapitated corpse away. Marium vomited and pissed herself, urine pattering on the wood between her feet.

"Please," she muttered. "Please, please, please."

The guards picked her up by the arms and set her behind the box.

"Marium Silversmith, you are charged and were found guilty of treason against the royal family for attempted regicide and injuring a lady of good esteem. For this you are sentenced to die by beheading. Do you have any last words?"

"Don't trust her! The new queen will gut you all. Witness what happened here today and don't trust her or it'll be your head—"

Prince Gallium motioned for her to be dropped onto the block. One guard kicked her in the knees and she fell, words lost in a gust of breath.

Prince Gallium lifted the sword. "Dark mistress take you, you heartless whore. May your soul rot in Arula. May your—"

The sword fell, severing her head and voice. More blood gushed out and Marium's head spun, dropping over the edge and into the dirt. A guard stepped forward to retrieve it. In those dead eyes, Joanne saw the hatred the woman had for her. The fire was extinguished. There was nothing more she could do to Joanne. She had protected what was most valuable to her.

Let's see who rots in Arula now.

"It's over, milady, we may return inside," Beaty said.

They followed the silent parade of lords and ladies. Before they reached the doors to Argenti Lapisdom, Prince Gallium run up to her. He tapped her on the arm and she turned to see his blood speckled face. He held out a bloody rag, shaking it for her to take.

"Fraum wanted me to give it to you," he said, his face a bloody mask of rage and sadness. "It's the blood I wiped from my sword. He said those women may have died by my blade, but it was you who landed the killing blow by your indiscretions."

Joanne took the bloody rag.

"I will hold this most dear of the treasures you give me," she said.

"There will be more to come, princess." Prince Gallium bowed and left her to ponder his words.

More gifts or more blood?

Alfred arrived the day before the wedding. After the executions, Fraum declared the wedding would be a full quarter of a year early. She'd heard no word from the messenger Prince Gallium sent. She was nearly in tears when Alfred was announced by Lady Hamlet. Joanne rushed down the stairs and hugged her brother, placing a big kiss on his cheek.

"I thought no one would come," Joanne said, wiping at her eyes.

"I wouldn't miss my Joey's wedding," he said. "Though, because of the timing of events, I will be the only one here."

"Is everything well at home?"

"Nothing that our father cannot handle," Alfred said. "How are they treating you, little Joey? Do I need to sneak you out in my carriage?"

"I'd like nothing more than that," Joanne said, "but I have a promise to keep. Father is counting on me to complete this pact. For Nemus."

"Aye, for that rotten hole, Nemus," Alfred said. "We all have a duty, but I believe you are sacrificing too much. I heard a rumor that he has held all the lords and ladies captive here to witness an execution of two women?"

"I will tell you about it later," Joanne said. "For now, it is best we keep these feelings and thoughts for private discourse."

"Of course."

They dined in her chambers and she listened while he spoke of their mother trying to find a suitable match for Thomas and how Thomas has done his best to insult every family that offered a dowery. "Thomas being his charming self as always," Joanne said. Then there was trouble with some uprising in the east. A man named Thramel—*couldn't be the same one who cheated them at cards and then escaped hanging, could it?*— was stirring up a resistance around the Twin Rivers region.

"Should be over before the next Sowing rains."

"I pray to the Blades Man that it will be," Joanne said.

She filled him in on some of the events surrounding the deaths of the former queen, the stripping of titles and lands, and mentioned her sword practice with Prince Gallium. She tried to give a short version of the insults that led to her discovering the infidelity that led to the Silversmith attack on her.

"She is fortunate not to have lost her arm that very day," Alfred said. "Seems like you are doing everything right to make such powerful enemies and then crush them. Father will be proud."

The next morning, the day before the wedding, she took Alfred down to the training grounds. There she introduced him to Prince Gallium. She demonstrated her knowledge of forms with the sword and he accepted her challenge to spar. "I promise not to make you too sore for your wedding night," Alfred said, taking the wooden sword.

Alfred teased her with *Plucking the Daisy* and *Weeping Willow*. Joanne met each with a simple defense that quickly changed to *Raging Storm* where she nearly disarmed him. Alfred smiled, tipped her a salute and began his combination of cut, slash, parry, which Joanne danced away from the wooden blade like raindrop in a furious wind. Neither blade struck the opponent and it ended in a mutual draw.

"Perhaps, one day, you will lead the army," Alfred said, panting. "Gallium trained you well."

"When the pupil is willing..." Prince Gallium said and left it at that.

They dined with Fraum who was sullen, spoke little and ate less. Alfred gave him the dowery papers, which Fraum signed and left on the table. "A lovely fellow, so friendly and corrigible," Alfred said. "Like someone pissed in his soup and he found it too salty."

"That's how he is on a normal day."

"Maybe you can bring him a smile after the wedding."

I doubt it. I don't even want to touch him or have him touch me.

Thank the gods for Selene.

The morning of the wedding, Selene helped Joanne into her wedding dress. She quietly wept, the tears rolling over her cheeks. Joanne's heart ached and, when Beaty left the room to get a brush, Joanne grabbed and held Selene in her arms. "I promise, you will never be loved any less. You are my first and greatest love. My only one." She kissed Selene on the mouth, tasting the salty tears.

She waited, listening to the murmur of guests inside the grand hall, which had seen its fair share of events from feasts to funerals to trials and coronations. A wedding seemed like a small inconvenience compared with the events of the last month.

"Joey!" Alfred said, coming up beside her and taking her hand, astonishment on his face. "Qetesh would break a tooth in her jealousy."

"Thank you, you always were my favorite." Joanne kissed him on the cheek. *Besides Henrick.* Alfred's smile told her he knew that without her saying a word. Marrying into the family that killed him was very difficult, but she had already caused them pain unintentionally. *There's still time.*

"You will always be my little Joey, no matter how your head will swell with a crown."

The music began, signaling her entrance into a new phase of life.

The ceremony was unremarkable. This was the fourth meeting with the priest in the last two months—seeing him nearly as much as her betrothed. Fraum wore his Sun crown and a dress uniform that seemed too large on him. He wheezed as Alfred gave her hand to him.

Fraum leaned in and said, "You look like a whore in snow."

Alfred frowned at that statement, but Joanne played it off.

"Then you better pay me like one who'll melt the ice around your heart."

The priest coughed, regaining their attention. Words were spoken about union as the Mother and Father intended. About Qetesh and eternal love. About Donn and the union beyond this life. Joanne responded where she was requested and Fraum made a few comments that seemed non-committal. Their hands were bound in golden silk, his fingers cold against her warm ones. Joanne shivered. When the words had been spoken and a new gold circlet placed on Joanne's head, she was announced as Queen Joane of Seaptum. Auster music played as they passed the guests. Selene and Beaty were both crying and pressing their hands together when she passed.

The feast was rather plane and the wine watered. Having nearly forty lords and ladies and their compliment of attendants as guests over the last two months had thinned Argenti Lapisdom's stores. Lady Windridge complimented her dress. "I think I will have one in a similar style stitched for me, when the weather warms. Don't want to freeze my delicates off."

Lady Hawthorne was there with her new born son and Prince Gallium chatted with her, waggling a finger at the infant who lay in his mother's arms, oblivious to the events around him. Lady Freeman and her husband sat in the back of the hall, far from the center of attention.

I will need to speak to her before she leaves.

They ate and drank. Fraum took Joanne by the hand, leading her away from the festivities. "It is time we perform our duties, wife." She cringed at his words, but understood this moment was coming and there was nothing she could do to stop the inevitable. "It is traditional that there are witnesses from both parties to this act, but I don't want my brother's jeers or yours to see what we must do."

Joanne nodded, pleased that he broke this part of tradition.

In his bedchambers, Fraum stared at her.

"You don't really like me, do you?" he asked.

"What do you mean, milord?"

"You find me repugnant," he said, removing his belt from his trousers. "Don't speak. I refuse to listen to any filth that will fall from your mouth."

"I don't understand."

"Of course, you do. You are not a stupid child," Fraum said. "Take off your small clothes from under your dress."

Joanne hesitated and then lifted the skirts, having trouble keeping the bundle up and reaching beneath. Fraum stepped forward, his hand groping at her small clothes, pinching the hairs as he tugged her undergarment down to her knees. Joanne began to breath hard. No man had ever touched her below the waist. He cupped her between the legs, wiggling a finger

202

inside of her. She moaned at the painful insertion.

"You have not fucked a man," he said, drawing his finger out and sniffed it. "I'm surprised."

Joanne remained silent, observing him, and began to lower her skirts. Fraum caught her hand, squeezing the fingers painfully so she couldn't pull away. He stood close enough that his face was in hers, his rheumy eyes leaking at the corners, the string of saliva on his lips pressed against hers and he spoke, moist breath smelling of sickness and mold from mushrooms he chewed, caused her to choke back the foul air.

"Do not move unless I tell you to do so," he said. "Lift them higher. Very good, now sit on the bed."

Joanne did as she was instructed. His cold hands moved up her thighs and parted them. He kissed the inside of her left one, lips pressed hard enough to leave a bruise. And then he bit her. Joanne cried out and tried to shift her leg away, but he held her. Tongue moving along her flesh until it contacted her sensitive area, and again his teeth bit into her soft flesh. She cried out at the hot pain. He stopped short of drawing blood. This went on for far too long until he tore her small clothes completely off, dropped his trousers, lifted her legs, and thrust inside her. He pawed at her breasts, freeing them and pinched her nipples.

"It hurts," Joanne said.

"Not enough," Fraum replied, falling on her, crushing the air from her, and began to bite her nipples. He grunted, shuddered, and then crawled off of her. When it was over, he stared at her like she was some disgusting bug. "Leave me, now!"

Joanne held her skirts while she ran from his room and to her own. There Selene waited for her, a question of surprise and concern on her face. Joanne collapsed into her arms and without a word, helped her take off the dress, hissing at the bite marks and bruises.

"Looks like you were mauled by an animal."

Joanne nodded. She hurt and all she wanted was for the pain to be taken away. Naked in her own bed, Selene held her, rocking her to sleep as she sang.

"I met my love in the copse stand
Fingers entwined, her hand warm in mine
We walked the trees, eating sweet berries

Listening to the bees and dreamt of honey
And whey and of our wedding day."

It was the song she sang when Joanne found her in the kitchens. She cried until sleep took her.

CHAPTER FOURTEEN:
GUARDING INTRIGUE

Power is like life, temporary and fleeting.
One is born into it, but one does not die with it.
Power is a shackle around the neck of the lord or lady.
What leads you around will tell how long you maintain it.
　　　—King Bounty, rumored last words at his execution

After the wedding, the guests left. Carriages snaked down the mountainside from sunrise until after midday. Joanne watched from her window, wrapped in a blanket while drinking tea and Selene rubbing her back and shoulders. Beaty spent the day arguing with Lady Hamlet about the Queen's needs regarding her treatment by King Fraum. It was pointless, Joanne knew, sipping the tea, but Beaty had insisted to making her complaint heard. *Fraum will do as he pleases unless—*

A knock on her door tore her eyes from the window. She expected Alfred, but found Prince Gallium smiling at her.

"I have someone here who wishes to speak with you before she leaves," he said and moved aside for Lady Freeman to give her a kind smile.

"Of course, let her in," Joanne said.

Lady Freeman stepped in the room, giving a curtsy. "My Queen, I hope all finds you well."

Joanne was about to offer her tea. Then she remembered who gave Foxglow the box with Dragon's Vein. She didn't want to offend Lady Freeman and have her believe Joanne mocked her. Lady Freeman was a few of her remaining friends and, despite the pain and sorrow from last night's horrific bedding with her husband, Joanne was not in a spiteful mood. She invited Lady Freeman in and had Selene set up another chair across from her.

"The gods find me alive and another day older," Joanne said. "I am more fortunate than some other ladies here in Seaptum."

"Very unfortunate that Janus should turn his back on them," Lady Freeman said and touched her belly. Dark circles under her eyes told of how tired she must feel, not only from the pregnancy, but Joanne expected the constant questioning and suspicion was wearing. It wore her out. "Though, I expect a favorable eye has been cast on me. I hope our relations may continue and that I am not cast off to the far corners. One day we may be very close friends."

A favorable eye, indeed. He stands outside my door now.

"I believe we are close friends now. We are sisters of Nemus, if not by blood."

"Yet blood joins us," Lady Freeman said.

"Indeed, it does," Joanne said. "I pray we may ease each other's suffering with our companionship. There will always be a place here for you, Helena. One sacrifice to another."

"I thank you, my queen," Lady Freeman said and curtsied. "It seems many have profited from our new found relationships. I would cultivate those fields and remind them that the seed grows when properly watered."

"Speaking of seeds," Joanne said. "Who planted in your field?"

"My husband, of course." Lady Freeman rubbed her belly and smiled in a way to say that was the proper and only answer she would give.

"Well, that seed was not as impotent as I have heard," Joanne said and sipped her tea.

"Young and full of vitality, Qetesh knows," Lady Freeman said. "I cannot delay long. My husband awaits and I wanted to thank you for your kind gestures and not to forget the love I have for you always. Call on me whenever you need a pretty flower."

"The pretty ones are the most dangerous," Joanne said and Lady Freeman gave her a questioning look. "Something I once told my father about flowers. Same applies to people it seems."

"Always, my queen," Lady Freeman said. She knelt in front of Joanne and kissed her right hand. "I will be your pretty one, the most beautiful you could ever find."

You already are, Joanne returned her smile.

"Mother bless you," Joanne said, touching Lady Freeman's head. She lifted her chin and kissed her on both cheeks. "Bless your child, as well."

Joanne helped Lady Freeman from her knees, holding hands for a few intimate moments and then she was gone.

"That one knows much," Beaty said.

"Yes, and she bears a great burden," Joane replied. "I would have her in our service, but with a child, that no longer seems possible."

With Prince Gallium's child, that seems all too probable something will keep us apart until deemed otherwise. Poor woman is another vessel used until she was no longer of value to the schemes. I won't them discard her so easily.

That was one garden she would tend and cultivate with great care.

Alfred stayed on for a few more day. His presence was a great comfort, helping Joanne overcome the shock of the wedding night. He distracted her by illustrating his plans to train an army as vast as the one here in Seaptum. It seemed Prince Gallium had provided him with an idea on how to conscript soldiers from the local leaders, and since Nemus had few lords and more magistrates, this would be a way for them to check their own actions and put down a rebellion that was bubbling.

"I may not get the thousands of men from the area like King Dryd demanded, but hundreds of young men would be a start to flush out father's ranks," Alfred said over a midday meal in the gardens. "I think I might be able to convince Prince Gallium to send a contingent south should we need it. I told father the quickest way to end this rebellion was to carve out its leaders the way we would cut off a festering limb before it poisons the rest. The people care more about full bellies than they do with who sleeps in the Keep. Ending the malcontents would go a long way to bringing peace throughout the land."

"You might have to speak to my husband about any sending soldiers to Nemus," Joanne said, studying her brother who seemed to have gotten so much older since she had left. Had she aged any in that brief time? "I doubt he will grant you a single shield, since he doesn't hold Nemus in such esteem."

"Well, you're his wife," Alfred said, and playfully tapped her silver circlet sat, eschewing it. "Doesn't he hold you in high esteem?"

"He holds me in contempt." Joanne took the silver circlet off her head and looked down at it. It was along symbol of her bondage. A thing of cold metal, like Fraum. She dabbed at her eyes to chase back the tears.

"That's not very honorable of him," Alfred said, brow furrowing and he drank from his mug of ale. "It's not like you wanted to marry him."

"No," Joanne said, hating the whine she heard in her tone, "but I have a duty to perform for Nemus."

"Donn piss on this duty if he doesn't support you," Alfred said, and slapped the table, rattling plates and cups. Selene and Beaty began to move toward them, but Joanne motioned for them to stay.

"Please, keep your voice down," Joanne said. "I want no more trouble than I already must bear."

Alfred leaned in, lowering his voice. "Is it true?"

"What?"

"That Gallium could take the throne by, you know, killing your husband?"

So he heard some rumors buzzing. From who and where?

"Yes, but it would destabilize Seaptum," Joanne said.

"I don't see how. Seems that Gallium is more well-liked among the nobility," Alfred said. "We would have a greater friend in him, wouldn't we?"

"I don't know," Joanne said. "Fraum is honoring the treaty of peace, though he may not like it. His brother seems to have other plans."

"Is there a way to get him to favor you more?" Alfred asked. "You aren't ugly like the rest of these pale, frail Seaptum women."

"Stop," Joanne said. "It's not just him, but the support of the local lords. We, well I, have helped some of them gain more wealth and prestige. I don't know how long that will last, since I also gave them reason to mistrust me more than being an outsider in their inner circle, a pig among the party goers, as they might say."

"They are all swine as far as I'm concerned," Alfred said and narrowed his eyes. "Did he hurt you?"

"Who?"

"I swear by the Blades Man I will cut his throat if he harms you—"

"No," Joanne lied. "He barely touched me beyond his duty."

"By rights, I should return you back to Nemus for his disrespect," Alfred said and chewed on some olives. "That might provoke more hostilities in a time when we need peace on our northern borders to take care of our east. But, my dear sister, I won't have them take another sibling from me. Not without retribution."

"Thank you, Alfred, I love and appreciate you more than you know," Joanne said, taking his hands. "I will satisfy my duties and be certain, no harm will come to me. I do have friends here in the north."

"Good," he said. "I must leave after today. Father gave me permission to attend your wedding only if I learned something of value. He wants me to help train his army, which doesn't please Thomas any. But before I go, I have gift for you." He set a wrapped dagger on the table. The handle was silver and had a wolf's head on it. "Cut out the heart of any who will try to do you wrong."

Learn something of value? Not that his daughter is being abused by the monster he sold her to, isn't that value enough? At least my brother cares about my well-being!

"I'll leave nothing for Donn to taste," Joanne said, tears flooding her eyes. She hugged Alfred with all her strength. "I love you all dearly, let them know that please."

"I will pass it on."

Alfred left the next morning.

"Your brother is very wise," Prince Gallium said, glancing down at the knife on her belt. "He will make a fine general one day."

"He admires you," Joanne said.

"Only because I respect you," Prince Gallium said.

That night Fraum sent for her. The biting and pinching continued until he drew blood from her. Joanne slapped his face which Fraum reacted by snarling and tossing her on the bed, whipping her bottom and thighs. The flesh mottled in various shades of purple to match her dress. Then he lay on her, pressing his member into her bottom and stretched her in a way that burned and bleed. For days after it was difficult for her to empty her bowels properly without blood and pain. After he grunted and came into her, he shoved her to the floor like a doll he no longer desired to play with.

Again, Selene held her all night as she cried.

The next morning, she turned down Prince Gallium's invitation to spar, sitting on a pillow and trying not to cry out after every tiny adjustment. She thought of the dagger Alfred gave her. Imagined digging it into Fraum's gut from his holes, feeding the wolf his viscera. The idea of moving was so painful she broke down into tears until Selene comforted her.

Snow soon came to Mount Victorious and the windows were shuttered. Joanne spent her those fridged days reading and fearing a summons to Fraum's chambers. When they chanced passing in the halls, he didn't speak directly to her. Though she would catch him glaring down his nose at her, as though she had caused his misery, his sneezing and wheezing. Selene warmed her beds most nights, sang and stroked her after her duties with Fraum. She played the docile queen, meek and mild, moving about the Argenti like a mouse avoiding the cat's attentions. She performed her duties on her back, letting her mind wander while her body was used.

The weather lightened and her fifteenth birthday—the day that marked her original wedding day—came, and went with little acknowledgement. Lady Windridge and Lady Willowcreek visited her after the snows melted, freeing up the passage to Argenti Lapisdom.

"Such a quiet place without all the funerals and weddings," Lady Windridge said, sitting in a chair, taking in the brisk winds of the gardens. "I have never dreamed that such an upheaval would shake our land like Moko having a temper tantrum. I'm surprised this mountain still stands with our new Queen Joanne sitting proudly on the throne."

"This coronation and wedding are one the historians will argue over for generations," Lady Willowcreek said, sipping tea and then nibbling a cracker with bean paste. "Some blame Gallium, believing he meant to poison his brother, whereas others thought this was another King Bounty uprising which your husband meticulously crushed."

"Lord Foxglow has already taken a mistress," Lady Windridge said, snapping a stem off a pear. "I heard it from Lady Sweetwater that it is her cousin, Evelyn, warming his bed this past snowfall. A pretty girl, though shrewd. Mark my words, she will be the next Lady Foxglow."

"What of Lord Silversmith?" Joanne asked. *He was going to sue for my lands, the bastard!*

"No one has heard a single word. Not since he forfeited the mines to my husband," Lady Windridge said. "We are very much in gratitude for your kind gesture."

"I'm grateful for your love and support," Joanne said. "Not every day a Queen gets stabbed." *Or poisoned.* "Mother bless me, but you were in the right place to prevent her madness from inflicting me. How is the arm?"

"Scarred, but nothing a silver bracelet cannot conceal." Lady Windridge laughed, holding up the large silver circlet engraved with her family crest, two large ever grows encircled by the sun.

"I'm grateful he has yet to recall his portion of soldiers," Joanne said.

Lady Willowcreek and Lady Windridge looked at each other.

"What is that concern I see on your faces?"

"Well, strategic though your husband's blow may have been, I do not count him safe from certain forces, my Queen," Lady Willowcreek said. "There is the matter of his brother who is beloved by the same troops—"

"Oh, you, yourself, my Queen, have made quite the impression with your studious efforts to master the sword," Lady Windridge said.

"I fear that the bloodshed has not yet ended," Lady Willowcreek said. "Not unless you can convince Gallium to publicly declare for his brother, then I fear for your husbands reign."

"What of my life?"

"None dare harm you, my Queen," Lady Windridge said. "Seaptum cannot afford a war with Nemus in these delicate times. If anything should befall your husband, well, the Lords would support Gallium, though I think they fear you. Given more time, they would accept you, but under the shadow of the events that transpired last Reaping, you would be exiled."

"Whose support do I have?"

"Besides us," Lady Willowcreek said, "I can only say Lady Freeman because of her kinship to your land."

None of the other lords and ladies, despite their outward declarations during their captivity, would support her. This wasn't surprising, though it was disappointing.

"I thank you for your candor," Joanne said. "I will have to find a way to keep my husband from an untimely death." *I would kill him myself, if that wouldn't mean thrusting Seaptum and Nemus into chaos. Father has his own problems keeping his hold on the land.*

"You'll find no greater friends than us, my Queen," Lady Windridge said, sipping her tea.

Joanne thanked them knowing she couldn't trust either any more than the sea wyrm swimming along her shores. They would eat her up if it profited them more.

Later that night a letter arrived from Lily. Selene held it out to Joanne in her room. Beaty stood beside Joanne as she read it.

My Dearest Friend,

It seems that Gold is precious, though Silver is deadly. Resentment builds against grievances usurped. Caution must be heeded when the winds in the caverns grow silent. Death lingers in the shadows to snatch unwary sojourners. I pray for our love's safety.

Great Love,

Snow Drop

"This confirms what Lady Windridge and Willowcreek revealed to me," Joanne said, biting on her thumb nail. "Lord Silversmith holds a great number of troops here and they demonstrate more loyalty to Gallium. Fraum cannot move against his brother, not without military strength. It seems the reason Gallium has yet to move on his brother is because of me. For as much contempt that he holds to me, he owes me his life."

"Yes, and he knows this," Beaty said. "It would be best not for you to remind him, though I understand the precarious waters you must tread. As distraught as you might be at becoming a widow while so freshly wed, it might improve your health."

"At the expense of my family in Nemus," Joanne said. "Gallium wins and I'm sent home without support of Seaptum's forces to crush the uprising, should my brother not find success. Then I will still be in peril."

"What are you going to do?" Selene asked.

"Hold on to my fingerhold here like I am going to drop into the sea," Joanne said.

Fraum summoned her again that night. Joanne showed, ready to endure the pain and humiliation of his teeth and fingers. Instead of his contemptuous violence, he was sweet, tender. Afterward, lingering in her embrace.

"I must leave you for a short while," he said, his wheezing, though not as bad as some days. "One duty of the King is to tour my resources, like the silver mines and the grain fields, to treat with the lords and demonstrate my generosity."

"I follow where my lord commands," Joanne said.

"I must go alone, which means you will take care of Argenti Lapisdom." Fraum stood up and began pacing. "I dare not leave the throne unattended, knowing the temptation for my brother with a full contingent of loyal soldiers here in our home."

"Why not take him with you?"

"I do not need Gallium with me everywhere I go," Fraum said. "I'm not a child and the lords need proof that I do not fear losing my position. They already see me as weak in this godsdamned diseased body." He stood with his thin frame, chest rising and falling. A cough rattled up his throat and he spat phlegm into the hearth where it hissed in the fire. "This is the duty of the Queen. To be where her husband cannot. You are not just a vessel to my children. As much as I detest relying on you, I find that I must in this instance, and possible future ones. My father wasn't such as fool in this pairing as I had originally thought."

"I am glad that I have satisfied your requirements," Joanne said.

Though, we are both a prisoner of this marriage contract and must do what is expected to survive it.

"Do your duty well and I will know our regime will be one for the history books," Fraum said.

"I will always do my best, my lord," Joanne said, putting her robe back on.

"You may stay, if you li—" coughing took his words.

"I do not want to be a burden. I'll send for the Master Physic," Joanne said.

"Don't bother summoning that fool. His treatments nearly kill me," Fraum said. "I have my own masters. Oh, and Joanne. I believe you are right. Sleep well, my queen."

Joanne stood outside, listening to Fraum cough and curse. This was a new feeling. One where she didn't want to scrub her skin or have Selene sooth away his brutal touch. He was almost kind. She moved down the stairs to her chambers. Selene waited with a glass of wine and a basin full of water and lye soap.

"Something is different," Selene said and Joanne took the cup of wine.

"Did he hurt you?"

Joanne shook her head.

"He was gentle," she said. "Because he knows I help him hold his throne against those ready to pry it from his cold, moist fingers."

"Then you won't be needing me tonight." Selene sounded disappointed.

Joanne dropped her robe.

"I always need you."

She wrapped her arms around Selene, holding the cup of wine for them both to drink out of, before tasting it on her lips, and swallowing it from her mouth.

Fraum's coach left the next morning and Joanne saw him off. There were no long hugs, no kisses or declarations of love or that she would even be missed. She might as well have been a dog he was leaving behind, though he might have shown a dog greater affection.

When his carriage exited the front gates, Joanne went back to her room and dressed in her sparring outfit. Beaty said nothing, though Joanne knew she didn't approve—it was by the King's decree she continue this unladylike activity. Prince Gallium was on the parade grounds with his men as usual at this hour. The wolf's head dagger bounced on her hip as she stepped into the dusty ring, picked up a wooden sword, and took up *Weeping Willow* pose. Prince Gallium smiled, sweat glistening on his nude chest, arms held out as he bent at the waist in a bow. *Thrashing the Bushes* tested her defenses and her foot work suffered slower steps, allowing Prince Gallium to get an inside blow glancing off her outer thighs.

"You've lost a step in the winter snows," Prince Gallium said, turning her wooden blade aside in *Sower's Rain*, before poking her in the breast with *Thorn in the Petals*. "I feel like I am taking advantage of a child."

Joanne halted, rubbing the spot on her breast where he had jabbed her.

"You don't need to play so rough," she said.

"How else will you learn not to be slovenly in your practice habits," Prince Gallium said. "I could have turned you around and stabbed you in so many places."

"With such a blunt blade, the memory would have been forgotten," Joanne said.

"My Queen cuts me with her sharp tongue."

"A wound you should never forget."

"With my brother gone, I am always at my Queen's service for all her needs," Gallium said.

"There is one, I must ask of you," Joanne said.

Prince Gallium's smile faded.

"I fear I know what it is she will ask." He stepped up to Joanne, walking with her away from the parade ground. All sense of joyful banter gone. "This is not the place to be seen discussing such business out in the open. I will have to refuse you outright in front of the soldiers and then toss all my coins and cards on the table, forcing a hand that should never be revealed, by Janus' luck."

"You must commit one way or another," Joanne said. "The sooner the cards are played, the sooner the game ends."

"In bloody civil war," Prince Gallium said. "You are young and impetuous. It would cost your husband's life and you would be cast adrift. No, you have far more enemies than friends here in Seaptum. That you have done to yourself."

"Then give me your word that you will not try anything while Fraum is away," Joanne said.

"Where's the fun in that, my Queen?" He gave her a wide smile. "Besides, I must play my part as much as Fraum and you do. This game we play is to keep the lords in line as well as the soldiers. If they do not know the outcome, but think they do, that they support the winning position and gain favor, then we keep their curiosity fed and they don't try to eat us."

Joanne nodded.

The rules for this game became clearer, though she didn't entirely trust the bluff Gallium gave her. He was shrewd and played this longer than her.

"You could wait," Joanne said. "He is ill."

"Is he?" Prince Gallium asked.

Joanne didn't know how to respond. She wanted to talk about how he coughs and wheezes, though she didn't want to weaken him anymore than what others have seen. It's not like Gallium couldn't witness it for himself. Or was there something the Master Physic wasn't telling her or Gallium?

"We are not brutal savages who kill a king and hope everyone will rejoice us," Prince Gallium said. "There is more to this ruling than sitting pretty on a throne and commanding taxes and conscripts. I hope you learn how to do this better before you lose more than your place, my Queen." Gallium bowed, then speaking loudly for all to hear, said: "I will gladly join you for supper this evening, your majesty."

"Your brother will be pleased," Joanne said. "That I wasn't left to eat with his attending servants for my only company."

"It will be a pleasure." Prince Gallium bowed, lingering enough to show off the contours of his muscles. Then he grinned and walked back to the training ground.

She spent the rest of the day reading and lounging before the evening. Again, the history books provided all sorts of information on Seaptum's brutal past that they try to hide away beneath false modesty and a sense of decorum, but Fraum was no different than the rest of the bloody and abusive kings of old. She was going to dine with his brother.

"Are you sure this is what you want?" Beaty asked, tightening the corset ties. Joanne grunted and closed her eyes. The price of beauty. Not that she wanted to seduce him, unless it would change his mind.

"Of course," Joanne said and winced at the pain in her ribs as Beaty gave another tug. "How else am I going to protect my husband's throne?"

"There is the Dragon's Vein," Selene said, mixing the rogue in a pot.

"Please, don't, not even in jest," Joanne said, fitting her knife in the belt around her skirt. "Bad enough their mother died because of the careless risk. Do we really want the entire Argenti to crumble on our heads? Fraum will know it was me. He already blames me for the deaths of the ladies. I am just building a relationship where I won't be punished every time I'm alone with him."

"Then you better keep up your guard," Beaty said. "Don't flirt too much with him."

"You will be in the room." Joanne watched Selene paint her cheeks in the mirror. "That's plenty. It's a meal, not naked wrestling."

"Naked wrestling would be interesting to watch," Selene said, setting the pot of rouge on the table. "Perhaps you could convince him to advocate if he can stop himself from getting an erection."

"It does seem every lady he gets around catches pregnant," Beaty said and adjusted the golden circlet in Joanne's hair. "I wouldn't advise it, until your husband returns."

"Qetesh knows, I love no man," Joanne said and glanced at Selene. Her former maid blushed.

"Love doesn't matter when it comes to who gets whom pregnant."

"Once upon a time, I may have wished I was betrothed to Gallium," Joanne said, "but I know the waters of the wyrm where I dip my toe. He may try to nibble, but his teeth won't taste my flesh."

They ate in one of the smaller rooms. A table was set up near the kitchens and a fire burned in the hearth to keep the late winter's bite off the room. Beaty and Selene kept watch from a small table and Lady Hamlet stood against the far wall. Joanne assumed Prince Gallim invited her, since she had not seen much of Lady Hamlet since the former Queen, Galea's funeral. The meal wasn't elaborate. Cooked squash and some bean curd with syrup and butter to add flavor. The wine was dark amber colored, bitter to the tongue.

"You look rather radiant, my Queen," Gallium said, giving her a charming grin. His blue eyes were bright and his hair slicked back. He wore a purple vest embroidered in gold sun beams around the shoulders. He sat so his broad chest and muscular arms caught the shadows from the firelight.

"Thank you," Joanne responded. "I appreciate this meal with you while my husband is away." Not that she ate often with Fraum, who took his meals in his office, and which Joanne thanked the Father because he ate some strange, smelly foods that stank of old farts.

"I couldn't let you cause a rift out on the practice grounds," Prince Gallium said. "The men are always watching, spying for Silversmith, especially now you cost him a wife and some of his mines. He's waiting for any excuse to expel you from Seaptum, even if it means splitting it by war."

"Greedy bastards, aren't they." Joanne sipped the wine.

"When you know nothing but wealth and privilege, you will fight any way you can to keep hold of it," Prince Gallium said. "He has two sons, you know."

"I didn't," Joanne said.

"He believes you are going to steal their inheritance and is ready to pull his ten thousand troops. The other day he complained that since Windridge owns the stake in the mines, he should contribute more soldiers."

"Wouldn't that offset Silversmith's power?"

"No, because Windridge doesn't have the man power to spare for soldiers. With his new mines now and other business." Gallium nibbled squash from his fork. "Again, he will complain and seem like he is doing nothing, but all this time there are maneuvers against Fraum and myself."

"Isn't Foxglow countering him?"

"Clever queen," Gallium said. "Yes, but his forces here are but an eighth of Silversmith's contribution."

"What of the other troops? Don't you have nearly fifty-thousand at your command?"

"They are mixed. Some support Silversmith. Some support Fraum," Gallium said.

What number of those support you? All? Most?

"Seems we are at an impasse," Joanne said.

"Unless," Prince Gallium said, "unless, you were able to convince your father to send Nemus troops to support Fraum."

"I could send him a letter."

"That would be one way to tip the powers away from the angry lords and into our hands once again," Prince Gallium said, sat back and gave her a curious look. The one he gave before making his strike. "I know you don't believe me when I say I support my brother in retaining the throne."

"You have to speak such words in front of me," Joanne said. "Otherwise, it would be treasonous. I would have your head waiting for him when he returns."

Prince Gallium laughed.

"You are something special. God-touched, I'd say." He leaned forward. "I promise you, my queen, should anything befall my brother, you will not lose your station."

"I believe you," she said. "They will have to carry my body out of the throne room and then wait for my father to burn down every city in Seaptum."

"Too bad he didn't do that for your brother," Prince Gallium said.

"Well, that was war," Joanne said. "This would be retribution."

Which is what I have started for you, Henrick.

CHAPTER FIFTEEN: A UNION TO THWART LORDS

When one is in power, one marries not for love,
But to gain more of an advantage in wealth and status
—From "Marriage among Kings and Queens"

Fraum returned before the first Sower's rains. Gray clouds and a cruel breeze buffeted Argenti Lapisdom. Angry waves tore at the edge of the mountain, clawing it, but no more than a child pawing at her parent's leg. Mount Victorious remained, steady, firm, strong like it had since Moko first ripped it from the sea. Despite the fires burning to chase away the chill of the stone, Joanne wrapped herself in a shawl and waited in the vestibule. She was both feverous and cold, though she didn't feel ill. The anticipation of her husband's return coursed through her mind and her heart fluttered. She missed him. A strange feeling of loneliness—when she had anticipated relief—hung on her like a heavy cloak she couldn't shrug off. The door opened, two footmen held them, and Joanne shuddered at the breeze.

Fraum followed up the steps, wrapped in his own cloak, a creature hiding away from the light. Behind him followed two more footmen and four soldiers.

"My lord, Mother bless your safe return," Joanne said.

"Cursed," Fraum said and lurched past her.

Joanne turned and caught up to him.

"Your visits did not go well," Joanne said.

"Very observant," Fraum said, and dragged a chair to the fire. He leaned in close to the flames, steam rising from his damp cloak and the fire teased its edges in a bright orange and red light. Joanne could nudge him and he might catch fire like some old, dried out tinder. Fraum snapped his fingers and glared at the first servant to run afoul of his vision. "Bring me wine!"

Doors opened and slammed. Pounding feet went off to the kitchens.

"Which lord was it?" Joanne asked, standing behind her husband, out of his direct view. *Last thing I need is to be the object of his ire.*

Fraum stared into the flames and frowned. Hunched over as he was, she could guess which lord had vexed him. The same one who had complained about losing his mines and his wife, though the loudest to squeak was the first to bite his own tail. *The cheating, lying bastard. Should have had him join his wife and mistress on the trial to commit conspiracy and attempted regicide.*

"What did he want now?"

"Compensation from Foxglow. Since that bloody, bastard Silversmith watched his wife's execution, he didn't dare submit a grievance to me about you. He's worried I'd take his head next and then strip his children of their inheritance," Fraum said. "In truth, he owes Foxglow compensation for fucking his wife, but they never see it that way. I should fault you for the problems, but they brought it on themselves. Their disloyalty to each other was a symptom of a greater rot in Seaptum. Best to cut it off before they poison the rest of the lords."

"I'm sorry my king didn't have a pleasant visit," Joanne said, wanting to comfort him, but she knew if she touched him, he might nip her like a wounded dog.

"Oh, it only grew worse from there," Fraum said. "Where's my godsdamn wine! The thorns grow thick on these brambles!"

Joanne could imagine. From what Prince Gallium had informed her about the court politics and how each lord was responsible for taxes and providing men to serve in the Seaptum army—the more wealth and land a lord owned, the more they contributed to the king's treasury, which were then used to protect the lords and the nation from their enemies or in time of great need, like when the frost came late and killed the majority of the crops and they had to open the reserve granaries and then purchase more from southern islands of Creatos at a premium. Rather than be made a fool and pay, King Dryd invaded the islands and killed their chieftains. He took what grains Seaptum needed, while conscripting the Creaton islanders into his naval force.

A man servant brought him a mug of wine and stood by, holding the carafe when Fraum would need it refilled. He sucked down the mug in a couple of gulps, and held it out to be filled. The corner of his lips ran red with it.

"Silversmith demands his tribute be reduced," Fraum said, staring at the red wine, "but that is not all. They worry about my brother. They worry that he will gain favor from the other lords by marrying their daughters, sisters, cousins, or anyone else who has a slit instead of a dagger."

Joanne clicked her tongue the way Beaty would when she disapproved of Joanne's crass words.

"Did I offend, milady?" He snorted laughter, then took a gulp of wine, wiping his nose and mouth on his sleeve. "Gallium will have to marry someone without any connections. Someone insignificant to Seaptum in the eyes of the lords. Poor bastard won't like it, but we all have to make sacrifices." He paused, looked at the servants, and waved them away. "Everyone out, except for the Queen. Leave the wine, I'm not through with it."

They hastily made their way from the room. Fraum stood and checked the doors to be certain no one spied on their conversation. Joanne's heart began to race. Who could he be hinting at, other than Lady Helena Freeman who suddenly got pregnant on the night of their visit? Lord Freeman would be forced to dissolve the marriage, which might be what they had talked about on that night. A ploy to appease the demands of the lords, by angering them all. The new marriage would be a rise in Helena's station. Joanne could support—

"Beaty," Fraum said. "She is your cousin, is she not?"

"Yes," Joanne said, taken by surprise. *Why would he want to know about Beaty?*

"Then I believe that arrangement would be beneficial for us," Fraum said.

He handed the cup to Joanne. "Drink, you look pale."

Joanne drank. It was very bitter.

"What are you suggesting?"

"I am not suggesting anything," Fraum said. "This will happen. Your lady-in-waiting, Beaty, will marry my brother. Again, Gallium will not be pleased with this proposal, but he won't decline."

"What about Beaty?"

"She should be thrilled," Fraum said. "Wait a day before you blab this to her. I don't want her stirring the other servants around Argenti Lapisdom until I have talked to my brother. He will be difficult at best to convince, but he will see the logic behind the marriage. In a way, it will mirror what I was forced into."

He plucked the cup from Joanne and hurried away.

"Oh, I'm pleased to see the place as I have left it, wife," Fraum said. "I expected to return to a body or two hung from the parapet."

Back in her room, Joanne tried not to look at Beaty in the mirror while her cousin brushed her hair. It was difficult not to speak, but she knew it was best to keep words at a minimal in case she accidently let the secret out.

"Are you displeased that he forgot you name day?" Beaty asked. "Your shoulders are tense and your mouth has a curious line that it gets when you are upset, but don't want to talk about it."

"I can't," Joanne said.

"Men can be callous, my grandmother often told me. They get a bug on their mind and spend the rest of their time scratching it off that nothing else matters." Beaty smoothed her hair. "At least you had a nice meal with Gallium and he got you a pretty bracelet. I shouldn't expect anything from that husband of yours, except disappointment."

What until you hear what he has planned.

"Ouch! Watch how you are trying to pluck me bald," Joanne said. "I would be careful how you speak of Fraum. We both know you don't care for him."

"I care for my queen. The way he treats you is not acceptable," Beaty said.

"I'm grateful for your loyalty and your love," Joanne said. *I hope you remember both when you are directed on a similar path as mine. Qetesh is cruel. At least you get the handsome one.*

Beaty might be queen one day if Fraum should be deposed. The idea crossed Joanne's mind more than once. Fraum was cruel. Not only was he taking away her cousin, he was also setting her up as a potential rival. It would look good for Nemus, in the same instance create more tension among the lords and the Silver Throne. Fraum would be dealing a devastating blow to his brother and put Beaty at risk.

"I'm sorry, cousin," Joanne said. She rose from her chair and threw her arms around Beaty. "None of this was my intentions or plans. I'm just so tired of being caught up in the swells of everyone else's winds."

"What are you talking about?" Beaty asked, thumping Joanne on the back with the brush.

"You will know soon enough." Joanne wiped a tear from her eye.

"Gods! Are they planning on deposing Fraum?"

Joanne shook her head.

"I cannot say anything."

"But you already have," Beaty said. "Just finish your thoughts."

"Fine, now, don't be too upset." There came a knock on the door and Selene answered it. Lady Hamlet stood in the doorway, a mute expression on her face. "Seems I am summoned by my husband."

"Not tonight, my Queen," Lady Hamlet said. "The King requests Lady Beaty."

Beaty set the brush down, giving Joanne a nervous look.

"It's nothing too serious," Joanne said. "Don't keep the King waiting."

Beaty curtsied and bowed her head.

"I do as my Queen commands." Then she followed Lady Hamlet.

More like the King commands.

"What is that all about?" Selene asked. "Is she in trouble?"

Depends on how you define trouble.

"Fraum wants Gallium to marry Beaty," Joanne said. "It's a move to displace power from the lords. By marrying an outsider, they won't gain any sort of advantage over either brother. It's what Dryd did to Fraum to prevent any one lord from rising above another."

Selene shuddered.

"It's treating women like cattle traded among the farmers so the other won't cry he has a greater hold. I don't like it."

"Neither do I," Joanne said. "One day it may change."

They waited, sipping glasses of wine, trying not to think about how Beaty must feel, stuck in the room with both brothers, talked over like a piece of furniture, or as Selene put it, a cow. Prince Gallium wouldn't have to agree. If he didn't, then Fraum would guess his hand and start to denounce him. Beaty certainly didn't have a say. She was a face card, but not one of importance. A distraction at best. The moon shone through the windows, casting shadows around the room where Joanne had one lamp lit for reading. Joanne kept reading the same words about why using a light calvary was more effective against lancers since they could quickly adjust to position and the terrain, when the door opened. She sat upright, shutting the book. Selene stepped beside her while they waited for Beaty to enter. Her steps were unsure and Joanne hurried to embrace her cousin whose legs gave out.

"Help me get her to the bed," Joanne said.

Selene shouldered Beaty on the left while Joanne carried her right. They got her on the bed and began to loosen her dress. Beaty returned to her senses, giving a horrified cry.

"Did they hurt you?" Joanne asked, searching for bruises or bite marks.

"No," Beaty said, staring at a spot in the far corner. She blinked, looking at Joanne as though she had noticed she was there. "I'm sorry. It's just..."

"Water, Selene," Joanne commanded, then took Beaty's hands. "They are forcing you into marriage."

"Yes," Beaty said. "I... I don't know how I feel about it. I never expected this."

"I don't think anyone did."

"And Prince Gallium—" Beaty broke into tears. Joanne held her cousin, rocking her gently. She caught her breath, taking the water offered from Selene and drank it. "Prince Gallium was upset. No, he was furious. He called me plain and my bloodline tainted. He said he'd rather marry a sow, which the King said that could be arranged if he didn't accept the proposal. Why didn't you tell me this was his plan?"

"Fraum ordered me not to say a word," Joanne said.

"Well, it doesn't matter," Beaty said. "The match is made. Gallium marched from the King's chambers without a word or one glance to me. I might as well not have been there. After Gallium left, the King looked to me and asked 'do you share the same opinion?' I told him I held no opinion on the matter one way or the other. 'You should thank the Father, you are rising well above your station. Higher than if you remained in the backwoods of Nemus.' I bowed and thanked him, instead. The gods laugh at me, at us, Joanne."

All but one. She wants me for some other reason I'm afraid to seek out.

"One positive take is we will no longer be cousins, but sisters," Joanne said, pushing a strand of hair that fell across Beaty's eye. "Nemus will have greater ties to protect our people."

"Sisters." Beaty laughed, more from exhaustion and the strangeness in how it sounded. Joanne was still in disbelief herself. "We will rule the country and make them pay for what they took from us."

"Yes," Joanne said. "We will shape it in our vision. Just need to be careful in how we proceed."

Or our heads will be on the chopping block.

The wedding took place at Midsummer. Lady Bodaline and Susie arrived with a great number of tears and embraces for Beaty. They marveled over how much she had grown, her flattering dress cut by the same tailor who designed for Joanne. They enjoyed several meals out in the gardens, expressing how vast and lovely it was for the placement.

"I wouldn't expect much to grow this high up or thrive on such hard stone," Lady Bodaline said, sipping hibiscus water. The woman who had once annoyed Joanne so much, seemed content. There were more wrinkles and strands of gray hair sticking out from her ridiculous hat. But, she was no longer the figure of authority. Lady Bodaline was just another aristocrat, a distant relative though Joanne never brought it up. She seemed at peace. That's better than what Joanne could hope for. "Even in the harshest conditions life finds a way."

"It does," Joanne said. "It always does."

They celebrated Beaty's nineteenth name day the night before the wedding. Lady Freeman joined the private affair, nursing a baby boy. No other lady of Seaptum made an appearance—given what happened to two of their own, Joanne didn't blame them. She was disappointed in Lady Windridge and Lady Willowcreek, who both sent condolences about their delay. Joanne figured they didn't wish to damage their reputations by being perceived to acknowledge this union. Along with Selene, there were six women from Nemus.

"Probably the greatest number of people from Nemus ever to peacefully gather in Seaptum," Joanne remarked.

"We have conquered your rooms," Lady Freeman said, rocking the baby. "Call this the Desmond Manor rooms. Hole up here until they give into our demands for syrups and sweet wine."

"I wish I could bring you a better gift, my dear child," Lady Bodaline said and handed Beaty a small bundle. Beaty unwrapped it, revealing a golden brooch shaped like a bird. "It was your mother's and she wore it until the day she died."

"I remember it," Beaty said, tears blurring her eyes. "It is the greatest gift I could receive."

"How are events in Nemus?" Joanne asked.

"Your father and brothers busy themselves with gathering conscripts to deal with the insurgents. For every one they get, three more join the traitorous commander Thramel in Twin Rivers. They haven't declared war, yet, but they do harass merchants and farmers delivering goods to the Keep. I fear it may lead to bloodshed before the season ends."

"Perhaps we could send some soldiers to assist," Beaty said, looking at Joanne for confirmation.

"I doubt my father would welcome them, seeing as how he married me off to end the previous invasion."

"Lord Desmond has his pride," Lady Bodaline said.

"It goeth before the fall," Susie said.

"Hush, child. Politics are not supported by philosophies. The arrogance of men outweighs the good sense they once preached," Lady Bodaline said. "Besides, the princes, I mean the King has problems here to maintain peace. He has unwittingly set our former ward and my granddaughter at odds."

"Oh no, he used his wits," Joanne said. "He had to protect his own interests."

"Will you protect your cousin?" Lady Bodaline asked.

Joanne was surprised to have Lady Bodaline bring the familiar relations up. All pretenses should be dropped, Joanne smiled. *She is still a shrewd woman.* All women had to be in order to survive the society of Kings and Lords.

"I will allow no harm to come to her," Joanne said. "She is to be a sister to me and we are bonded closer than blood."

"Watch for the knife which may sever it," Lady Freeman said and the baby began to fuss.

"Well, I can only pray to the Mother you will remember your true family and loyalties," Lady Bodaline said. "Enough dour talk of politicking. Where is the cake?"

There was plenty of cake to eat and not enough mouths to fill.

All but a few lords and ladies arrived for the wedding between Prince Gallium and Lady Beaty. The ceremony was brief, the conversations light, especially around Joanne, and none stayed beyond the feasts. Lady Beaty became Princess Beaty with a few words, tying of knots, and a kiss. A magical transformation that stole her from Joanne, leaving her room bare and Selene alone to tend to Joanne's needs. Lady Hamlet asked if the Queen would like another lady-in-waiting, but Joanne declined, though there were plenty of daughters of age to come to court in the Windridge and Willowcreek family. Lady Freeman offered her service, formality that must be declined due to her childrearing—Joanne itched to ask her who the father truly was, but didn't wish to put Helena in the position to lie to her. Not when there was so many other secrets they must keep for the preservation of the other.

Selene spent most nights in the Queen's bed, tending to needs the King could never fulfill. His attentions waned and when he did call on Joanne for duty's sake, his desire to pinch and bite returned as well, combined with severe slaps on her bottom, thighs, and once leaving a bruise on her cheek that Joanne feared leaving her room for three days.

Her training with Gallium all but ceased. Instead, she chose a different sparring partner, until she bested them, one after another, and they were too embarrassed to fight her, and lose.

The greatest loss came to her over the next two years. From it, an even greater gain. Not long after Joanne's seventeenth name day, Gallium placed his bet and played his card. Joanne watched a country fall to the brink of civil war, and she played the role of the betrayed and the betrayer. Leaving her with nothing to turn to, nowhere left to go, but to the shadow.

CHAPTER SIXTEEN:
BETRAYAL

"Trust is like a knife held at your throat
While you hold one to the back."
—Quote from King Bounty

There's nowhere to run, child. *Nowhere left to hide.* The dark, seductive voice whispered in Joanne's sleeping ear. Caught in the land of dreams, paralyzed by fear, dark hands encircling her, Joanne was helpless—a rabbit trapped in the snare and waiting the teeth to close around her throat. Beside her, Selene groaned. *Ah, that simple maid you made a lady is all you have left.*

"My father, mother, and brothers remain in Nemus," Joanne said, her voice small, unconvincing even to herself.

The Mistress of Shadows tsked and her cloaked head moved slowly back and forth. *A wise warrior knows when to use the sword and when to offer the white-laced lily. Impatience leads to many a strong, hard-hearted, and hard-headed man's demise. This is the plight of your family, caught in the axe man's bind and will find itself cut off at the roots. Question stands now, do you wither with them?*

"My father defeated King Reuban, he can handle some thief and vagabond in the backwoods."

Oh, the confidence in the man who once terrified you. The field mouse believing the cat a vicious monster until the fox catches it. When the cat is eaten, who will be there to prevent the fox from swallowing you whole? When princes clash and crowns fall and there are no walls left standing to hide behind, who will stand by your side? Bring you succor?

Joanne glared at the smoke and shadows. The answer the goddess of darkness wanted was so simple that even a child could respond. Yet, no deal would be completed, no card placed without a pickle placed to bet against the Queen of Diamond, or the hangman.

"What do you want? What can you offer me?"

The dark mistress laughed. *Let me in and I can give you it all.* From the shadows crept a man, but it was only the body of a man. The head was a wolf. Blood red moonlight shone off what appeared to be a metallic surface. *I only ask that you bring me a child of Sin.*

A game among gods? Joanne was to play the fool and do the biding and reap the consequences?

"I don't know what that is," Joanne said.

You will, when the time comes. The wolfman retreated into the shadows, fiery eyes floating in the darkness. *In return for your services, I will have you ascend into godhood. here and beyond. A huntress for all who desire revenge to fall upon their knees and cry out to you!* A vision of thousands of people prostrating themselves before her danced in the shadows. They dissipated as though a wind blew them away. *Otherwise, you will be left to the whims of those you murdered.* Headless shapes stepped forward, followed by the bloated Queen, and hung cook and card dealer, and last of all, the tutor who taught her that death was permanent, only when you yet lived.

They will have their revenge. Cold fingers scraped across her flesh, tore the fabric of her dress, shredding it until her breasts hung loose and the nails continued to bore through her flesh, tore bone like it was thin parchment, seeking her heart. Joanne screamed, trying to escape.

"Wake up!"

"I can't! They are killing me!"

"Wake up!"

Joanne opened her eyes and saw the frightened face of her love. She had grabbed Joanne's arms and tried shoving her off the bed. *Selene?* Realization struck like cold water. She was no longer in the dream. It lingered on her, a sticky residue promising to be a reality one day. Unless she did as the goddess asked.

"I can't…" Joanne sank into Selene's warm arms and wept. "I'm losing everything."

"Not me," Selene said, stroking her head. "You always have me."

In the early gray morning light, Joanne surrendered to Selene's kiss and caresses. She had never felt more loved, yet, more insecure. Her seventeenth name day had come and so did the letter she had feared.

"What do you dream about that causes you such terrors?" Selene asked as they were eating breakfast. It still felt strange not having Beaty in the room instructing her on proper dress or behavior, warning that Joanne was about to piss off her husband or another man with her actions—which encouraged Joanne to act on it, rather than prove a deterrent.

"Shadows," Joanne said. "The innocent sleep peacefully, but my dreams are not peaceful."

"Do you ever dream of her?"

Joanne knew who Selene meant, though almost four years had passed since her tutor's murder. She nodded, sipping a cup of warm hibiscus tea sweetened with syrup. It was a pleasant day and she had almost forgotten it was her name day. Not that anyone else chose to remember. The only ladies to call on her were Lady Freeman, though not so much of late. Last harvest her husband died in his sleep from a weakened heart caused by stress of ever burdening taxes, or so the letter from Lady Lily hinted. Even Princess Beaty found her days filled with raising two sons, a toddler and an infant. Joanne had yet to get pregnant and rumors fluttered about that she was barren. Of course, none of them mentioned that her sickly husband's shortcomings may be the reason the throne had no heir, but the burden of babies was the woman's to bear, no matter the stature of the man.

"The dead want their vengeance," Joanne said. "They will have to wait. I have much more living to do." *Perhaps add some more bodies to their numbers before I'm done.*

"Do you regret any of them?" Selene asked.

"A few." Joanne smiled, remembering Cook Mather's stupefied look, the horror of the accusation, and his mangled face. All because of Joanne.

Some I would kill over and over again if I could.

Footsteps approached and Joanne saw Lady Hamlet lead a man dressed in the gray uniform of a man from Nemus. The uniform had dark stains and was rumpled like he had slept in for many nights. The messenger didn't look any better with dark circles under his eyes and a scraggly beard.

"My Queen, this man came with an urgent letter for you," Lady Hamlet said. As always, her face was impassive. Joanne could never figure out where the woman's loyalties lay, but if she spied for Fraum, she never let on.

"My Queen, forgive my unkempt appearance. I've traveled nonstop o bring you this," the man said, bowing, and then pawed through his parcel bag. He retrieved a letter with her father's seal unbroken. "I'm to wait for a reply."

"Lady Hamlet, please see our guest is fed and given plenty of wine. Prepare the room where Princess Beaty resided and let him rest there," Joanne said.

"You are, too kind, My Queen." The man was near trembling with exhaustion. He nearly fell over as he bowed again. Lady Hamlet held him by the arm as she led him from the room. After they left, Joanne broke the seal. Her fingers trembled with anticipation of news. Selene placed a comforting hand on her shoulder and Joanne covered it with her right. She gave a small whimper at her father's words..

My dearest daughter,

I hope this letter finds you well. Unfortunately, the situation at home has worsened. The rebels have grown stronger than we had imagined. The skirmishes have grown into battles where we lose more soldiers every encounter. I will soon dispatch your brother, Thomas, with a contingent of soldiers to burn down the Twin Rivers, but I fear we lack the numbers for a decisive victory. Our scouts are unsure of the enemy's exact numbers and I cannot trust the fate of our nation to hypotheticals. I have petitioned King Fraum for assistance several times over the last year, but he has ignored my requests and broken our agreement. I ask, no, I urge you to persuade him to send a minimal of five thousand soldiers, twice that would shorten the campaign. Otherwise, I fear Nemus will fracture and fold, which may be the intentions of your husband. To wait until our corpses cool before looting us, but I pray to the Blades Man that is an empty fear. I await your timely reply. Otherwise, I will have to send your brothers before the Sower's Rains make the roads impassable. Your family is at your mercy and I implore you use whatever persuasive means you at your disposal.

With great love,

Lord Desmond

"I have heard nothing of these petitions," Joanne said. She shouldn't have been surprised Fraum had prevent a missive from her father getting to her, but fury built like an inescapable storm, her thoughts a flash of lightning ready to engulf the Argenti, destroying stone and wood and flesh. *How dare he hold this information back from me! How dare he not honor the contract! All I gave up for Nemus!* She jumped to her feet and grabbed a shawl.

"Where are you going?" Selene asked, setting down her cup of tea.

"To demand answers from my husband."

"Are you sure that's a good idea?" Selene asked, her voice rising in concern, and followed behind her.

I'm out of all ideas, but I will give my husband some so he doesn't forget to tell me about my father's troubles.

Two guards barred Joanne's entrance to Fraum's office. They were older, and not ones she recognized from parade grounds or exercises she took, laughing and cheering her on while she sparred with Prince Gallium. These were mute predators. They glanced at Joanne, frowned, and then dismissed her presence. They didn't bow or shift on their feet. She could have been a gnat buzzing about in annoyance.

This gnat will bite if she must!

"I demand to see the King," Joanne said. "It is an urgent matter of state security."

No response.

"Rude and despicable creatures," Joanne said, her anger lashing out. "I'll see you whipped and removed from your posts at once!"

Again, no response.

Are they made of stone?

They didn't flinch when she reached for the door, but their bulk prevented her from touching the handle. Joanne gave a screech and grabbed the wolf-headed dagger at her hip. She drew it and placed the blade to the throat of the guard closest to the handle. His eyes moved to her, but there was more amusement in them than fear.

"I should kill you for your insolence," Joanne said. "I understand you are doing as my husband commands, so I will forgive you this fault if you move your ass now."

"As my Queen commands," the man said, still smiling, and stepped aside.

"Wait here," she told Selene and sheathed her dagger. If she kept it in hand, she might've stabbed her husband as soon as she entered his office.

Fraum jerked his head from the paper work he was staring at, the paper crumpling in his hands and a snarl curled his lips. "What... are you," he wheezed, took in a shallow breath, coughed, spat out green phlegm into a section of discarded parchment, and tried again. "What are you doing in here?"

"I've come to see my husband on an urgent matter," Joanne said. "A letter has come into my possessions regarding a great concern."

Fraum sat back and wiped his brow. He waved for her to continue. Joanne tossed her father's letter onto the desk. Fraum stared at it as though it was some disgusting, slimy goo that she spat at him.

"Why is this the first I hear of my father's concerns?" Joanne asked, folding her arms over her chest. "Why haven't you told me of his request for aide?'

"It is a matter of state business and not a social one for you to be concerned over," Fraum said. "I have tried to send messengers to explain our precarious situation here with my brother gathering aide to move against us, but it appears none have survived the journey due to this insurrection he has devised. One which he should have stamped out like a camp fire before it consumed his entire backyard."

"Gallium is not moving against you," Joanne said. "We can spare five thousand spear and light calvary. Send them by the boat and they could meet up with my brother's forces from the west and march inland from the east coast."

"So, you are a master tactician now," Fraum said and laughed. "Tell me, general, what would we do if we lose those five thousand to inclement weather or Janus's ill-luck, they are ill-timed in their assault because your brother bungled the attack with impetuous need to prove himself superior?

What do we do about our weakened positions should the lords demand an explanation for sending their sons and conscripts into a foreign war?"

"My father arranged this marriage—"

"To end the war with my father," Fraum said. "I owe him nothing more. I will not weaken Seaptum to make up for his inability to control his own people, nor for his greed."

"Then do it for me," Joanne said.

"For you? You who haven't given me an heir in three years of marriage. You who rather fuck her handmaid than your own husband! You, who nearly sent my nation into a civil war!" Fraum tore the pages in his hand and slammed the desk. Joanne winced at the violent outburst. "Tell me what have you ever done for me other than bring ruin and heartache into my home?"

"It's not my fault I'm not with child."

Fraum stood from his chair and moved quicker than she thought him capable, his hand smacking her face. She drew her dagger, but he caught her arm and twisted it. "You may have trained with soldiers, wife, but you are still a weak woman." He shook the dagger from her hand where it clattered to the floor. "I would have your hand removed for attacking your king, but that would only anger the soldiers even more and provide my brother a stronger reason to attack me."

He turned her around and bent her over the desk.

"Instead, you will learn your place, once more." He tore her skirts and small clothes. Spreading her bottom, he thrust into her. She cried out at the tearing pain. "You do not dictate to me. I am head of state and military. I decide who gets my aide and who must suffer due to their inadequacies." He thrust into her, punctuating each point. Finally, he shuddered, spending himself and collapsed over her back. He bit her ear lobe and whispered, his breath smelling of rot. "If you ever disturb me again with these idiotic demands, I will beat you senseless. Understand?"

Joanne nodded, not trusting her words with her tongue thick with tears.

"Now get the fuck out."

Joanne snatched up her dagger and stumbled from the office into Selene's arms. The guards laughed and leered at her exposed bottom in the torn dress. She held back the tempest which had turned into a rain storm of salty, hot tears, burning her flushed cheeks. Selene held her all the way back to their room. There, Joanne stripped the clothes off.

"Burn them," Joanne said. The stink of his sweat and semen was too much.

"Milady?"

"Just do it!" Joanne threw the dress and undergarments at Selene's feet. Her maid looked so much like a hurt, dumb cow, eyes wide and mouth gawping open, that she wanted to strike sense into her. Then Selene gathered the clothes.

"As milady wishes." She left the room.

Alone and naked, Joanne knelt and prayed.

"I know you have visited my dreams and I have rebuked you, Mistress of Shadows. I beg your assistance, if you can hear me. I will do your bidding if you fulfill your promise. I will bring you every child in Seaptum and burn them at your altar if you command it. I am ready. Take me and do your bidding."

She waited, but there was no response, not that she expected anything. Her skin was cold and prickled with goose flesh. She got to her feet, ready to climb into bed. A gust of wind blew open the window, wrapping her in the cold. Before she closed it, she thought she heard, swirling in the cold wind, a dark laughter.

"I need an answer, my Queen," the messenger said. The sleep and food gave him back some sign of life. His clothes were clean and pressed. The worry lines creased his brow and mouth. "Every day is precious and I cannot keep Lord Desmond waiting. Does your husband consent to his requests?"

"I wish I could do more," Joanne said, frowning at her feet. She had failed at the one duty she was supposed to complete here. To protect Nemus. "My husband is stubborn and fears his brother. As long as that threat remains, he will not send a single soldier to aide my father."

"I am sorry, my Queen," the man said. "I had hoped for better news to report."

"Tell my father to delay action until after the Sower's Rain. I will see if maybe I can muster a force from my friends, if not from my husband."

"I will relay your words, but I can promise nothing. Not to speak ill, but your father and brother are not the patient sort of men"

"You tell nothing I didn't already know." She gave him some coin for his travels.

"Mother's blessing on you, my Queen." He bowed and left.

Joanne immediately wrote letters to Beaty, to Lady Windridge, to Lady Willowcreek, and to Lady Hawthorne in her desperation. Lady Lily had gone silent since the last letter about Silversmith's intent. The eyes and ears Beaty promised she would acquire never materialized. She received only the few letters from Beaty about her children and Lady Freeman. It was as though Lily disappeared. Out of concern, when Joanne saw Lady Hawthorne a year after Beaty's wedding at some formal gathering, she asked about a maid in her service named Lily.

"My own lady had a special interest in this Lily and she has been pining and moody for a while," Joanne said, choosing her words carefully.

"Lady Lily," Lady Hawthorne said, tasting the name. "I do not recall anyone in my service by that name, but that doesn't mean much. They grow up, get married, and are gone before I can recall if there was a Daisy, Jasmine, or even a Lily."

She prayed to the Mother that what Lady Hathorne said were true, but, if Lady Lily had been found out, Joanne was certain she would be having a different conversation with Fraum. Without Lily's eyes and ears, Joanne was deaf and blind to the world outside of Argenti Lapisdom.

This missive held great importance. Joanne understood that her very life and safety were at stake with Fraum. Not just her own, but possibly Nemus. She sent Selene out to personally deliver the letters, which would also protect her from any retribution Fraum might take against her in his anger with Joanne.

The godsdamned fool won't be happy until he has isolated me away from everyone I love. Oath breaker. I'll break him!

Her anger and annoyance mingled with worry while she crept to the stables before to have a horse saddled. The air was damp and musty with the stench of straw and horse dung. Selene wore a blue dress with a split up the side for her to ride comfortably. The saddle bags contained the letters asking for assistance—each house had a private contingent of troops that they kept for security. These were rotated with the ones at Argenti Lapisdom and she hoped they could siphon some off from the rotating numbers and send at least five thousand to her father. It was a risk, but one she had to take. Donn take Fraum if she was going to stand by and watch her father and brothers fail.

Selene knew the importance of the letters content. Knew the risk of failure on all accounts.

"Be swift, my love," Joanne said, and kissed Selene on the lips.

"I will do my best," Selene said and climbed the block into the saddle. Joanne watched her leave out the gates before returning alone to her room. She remained there, writing out a letter which she would take to Beaty to hand to Prince Gallium. It was her last effort plea. An act of desperation which could be seen as treason. A declaration of war. *I won't lose my family like I lost Henrick.*

Without Selene, the Argenti was a lonely, desolate place. The weight of the stones seemed crushing in despair. This was what her life would continue to be without Selene. Until they buried her in the stone tomb with the other kings and queens, lost to the pages of unwritten history. An obscure mention of the girl from Nemus married to a Prince, but died before she could bear anything of note, or serve as a warning to future kings about marrying Nemus peasants who will ruin the court and sow dissent among the lords. The history books brought no comfort and she stared at the dried, dead words, and the day passed and she ate very little, though no one was there to note what and how much she ate.

That night she had trouble falling asleep, fearing a knock on the door and a summons by Fraum—another punishment session before he spilled his dead seed into her. His illness was what prevented her from being pregnant. He could bite, hit, tear her open and rut around, but her eggs would never be fertilized by him. He wasn't a true man and didn't deserve to rule.

Mistress of Shadows give me the strength to do what I must for the good of both nations.

Even the dark goddess was silent.

The next day, Joanne left a note for Lady Hamlet addressed to Fraum. It was short, explaining that she went to visit her cousin and since he didn't want her to disturb him, she left him that note. She would return in three days' time—with an army to attack Fraum and usurp the crown, but that intention she kept off the page.

Without any further word, she gathered her belongs, had a man carry her trunk down to the carriage, and left. Prince Gallium and Princess Beaty were a few leagues away in a Moonglow Estate that once belonged to Lord Foxglow, but was "gifted" to the newly wed as a show of good faith to the

King. Joanne had a carriage take her there attended by a small number of troops and servants. She had made such excursions several times after their wedding and while Beaty was at the end stages of each pregnancy, staying to help tend to the babies and Beaty until her cousin was out of bed. She hoped that such a visit would not draw suspicion from Fraum.

Moonglow was named after the type of grape which grew at the estate. It was nearly white and, when ripe, at night would capture the moon's radiance and they would give the appearance of glowing. The house was two stories and of moderate size. There was a copper statue to Qetesh, kneeling half-nude with one breast exposed in the water where lily pads floated around her bare feet. The carriage pulled up to the font of the estate and the servants placed a foot stool down for her to climb out. The door to the estate opened and Beaty stood in a white gossamer dress, flowing like moonlight itself.

"Joanne?" Beaty said in disbelief. "I wasn't expecting you! Why didn't you write ahead?"

"I thought I would surprise you, cousin." Joanne took Beaty's outstretched hands. "It's been nearly four months since our last visit and there are some issues I would rather speak to you about in private, rather than trust to ink and parchment."

"Come inside," Beaty said, leading her by the hand. "Gallium is away on a visit to encourage the lords to contribute more troops to train. Something about wanting to secure our boarders because of the conflict with rebels in Nemus. I wrote to my grandmother, but I have yet to receive a response on what is happening at the Keep."

The interior to Moonglow was bright. Large windows were open, allowing for a cool breeze to blow through the rooms and sun light to shine on the gold embroidered carpets, the marble inlays around the hearth and paintings of the gods in gilded frames.

"That's also why I have come," Joanne said.

They went to Beaty's private room with a chair set up for nursing and a settee where Joanne often sat to keep her cousin company while the little babies fed. Beaty sent a maid for tea and bread. Then she sat close to Joanne on the settee. There was a tremble in her hands.

"Is there a war?"

"Not yet," Joanne said.

Beaty closed her eyes and let out a small sigh from pursed lips.

"Oh, where is Selene? I've never seen you travel without her."

"On a similar visit," Joanne said. "My father had sent Fraum several requests for assistance in putting down the rebellion. He never told me of these letters and when I confronted him about it, he…he…" Joanne wiped at the tears in her eyes.

"That bastard hurt you, again!"

"Yes, he hit and hurt me in humiliating ways," Joanne said, unable to keep the fury from her voice, her bottom aching as she recalled his penetration. "I can hardly sit without the pain burning my insides. Then, he told me he wouldn't send a single man to help my father and he was too weak to waste the resources on him. I hate him, Beaty. I hate him worse than anything I've ever hated. He is more beast than man and he needs to be destroyed."

"Destroyed!" Beaty placed a hand to her mouth.

"What has Gallium told you of his plans?" Joanne asked.

"Nothing," Beaty said.

"I don't believe it! You've been married to him for two years and he has not spoken of his plans *once*? Not a single slip where he said he'd kill Fraum or maybe a joke about sitting on the throne and you being a Queen?"

"Not once. He doesn't talk about state business with me," Beaty said. "In fact, he has been away on duty for your husband, sailing to the islands to continue trade and returns with fresh troops which he no longer trains or commands."

That can't be true.

"What does Fraum fear from him if he no longer commands or trains the soldiers?"

"Nothing, that I am aware of, unless there has been some change which Gallium hasn't told me about, other than the Master of Arms is Hollister. He took over the day we left Argenti Lapisdom. I'm surprised that you didn't know," Beaty said, taking Joanne's hands She frowned in her concerned way. *Probably thinks that I'm still a naïve child no matter the color of the crown I wear or how close to the throne I sit.*

"I'm a fool. I thought he was upset with Fraum and decided to punish me by refusing to continue his training with me," Joanne said.

"Seems to me you should be more aware of what your husband plans."

"He refuses to send aide to my father," Joanne said, ignoring the criticism and taking her hands away. "If he loses, then so do your grandmother and sister. They will be strung up in the streets for the crows to peck at their corpses."

Beaty said nothing for a few heart beats, but Joanne could tell there was something weighing on her cousin's mind.

"Why are you so quiet?"

"I have sent for my sister to be my lady-in-waiting," Beaty said. "She should be here with-in the week. I'm sure she would have told me everything, but now I worry. Should I have a guard sent to escort her?"

"I don't know," Joanne said. *Don't reveal all your cards. She knows more than she lets on.* "I have no idea where the fighting is happening. What I do know is that my father is about to confront the rebels after the sowing rains. He will be going into the battle practically blind. I think if we were able to capture the throne before the year ends, we could send our forces down to support my father—"

"Why? What has he done for you?"

Joanne took a breath. She wanted to tell her how she would have nothing and nowhere to go. Nemus was her home.

"I don't want to lose everything," Joanne said. "I already lost one brother to these beasts. I won't lose everyone else. The only reason my father married me off was to protect Nemus. I won't be sacrificed for nothing."

The servant arrived with the tea and a plate of bread. Joanne watched Beaty instruct the servant on where to place the items. She was more prepared for this type of life than Joanne was and would make a better Queen. With Fraum gone, perhaps she could go back to her home with Selene. The servant left and Beaty turned to Joanne.

"I understand your concerns. I do not like Fraum any more than you do, but I don't see how we could accomplish what you are asking without further support," Beaty said. "The lords are divided and Gallium doesn't have any more of an advantage, since he married me and was removed from commanding the soldiers. They will be loyal to their lords at best, but Fraum has balanced the power by taking it away from everyone. So, unless you can get Lady Willowcreek or Windridge to commit to what you are asking, your best bet would be to wait out your husband's illness and see if he survives the winter, like every year."

Beaty spread the jam on the bread and nibbled it.

"Here, eat and drink some tea," Beaty said. "Stay here for a few days and when Gallium returns, maybe he could think of a solution."

"As long as we don't bring up the topic that I tried to start a coup."

"I wouldn't dream of it, cousin," Beaty said. "We need to protect each other. That cannot happen if either one of us is put to death for treason."

That night, Joanne prayed again to the Mistress of Shadows. There were no dreams, no response. She woke up and didn't sense any difference, not that she knew what to expect. There were no books written on what happens when a god takes over. Stories and myths of people who were thought to have been possessed, but those turned out to be cases of madness. Joanne imagined it would be like an unseen force guiding her hand. An extra nudge. She woke up more anxious than she felt going to sleep. Another day passed and she wasn't any closer to gathering the support she needed to help Nemus.

Two Princes controlled the fate of the continent and she was a helpless puff of dust caught in the wake of their sails. She ate breakfast and tried not to think about it. She listened to Beaty talk on and on about motherhood, cradling Philip in her arms while watching Henry crawl around on the floor. She was as needy as these children, and as helpless to get those needs satisfied.

Soon Beaty would have Susie here to help, leaving Lady Bodaline the only remaining immediate family to the south—or perhaps she would follow Susie north. Beaty wouldn't have anyone left in Nemus to worry about. It wasn't any wonder that her cousin could be so casual about waiting. Joanne didn't bring this up. Again, she wondered how much she could trust Beaty.

We cannot trust her. She remembered telling Selene on their journey here, which seemed a lifetime ago. Her cousin had risen in stature and position since her arrival. Was she still the rival? She did have heirs, should Gallium inherit the throne, or take it by force. She was in a much better position than Joanne who was Queen.

Two more days had passed and Gallium still hadn't returned. Joanne called for her carriage.

"You could stay an extra few days," Beaty said. "I enjoy your company, especially since I don't have to dress you or brush your hair any longer. Not that it was such a horrible task, but you were not the easiest person to be around when in your moods."

"Now you have two little ones to dress and brush. I have seen them in worse moods than what I gave, well, maybe not, but you didn't have to breast feed me," Joanne said and gave a wicked smile. *Not that I didn't try.* "Besides, Fraum will be expecting my return or he'll grow suspicious" *If he even noticed I was gone.*

"Please take care and don't make any rash decisions," Beaty said.

"I haven't had anyone killed in two years."

They shared a laugh, though it was uneasy. Especially since the conversation where she talked about having her husband killed wasn't that long past. The carriage ride back to Argenti Lapisdom was long and lonely. *Are you having better fortune? In Janus smiling on you, Selene, as he frowns upon me?* She wouldn't know for at least a week.

Argenti Lapisdom was quiet. Entering was like stepping into a tomb. The occasional servant scurrying from the room was the sign of life not much better than a mouse in the graveyard. The footmen took her trunk to her room while Joanne went to the gardens. Lady Hamlet found her lounging in the chair, eyes closed and basking in the limited sun that would soon be covered by clouds.

"The King requests your presence," Lady Hamlet said.

Now I will hear his complaint!

She went to follow her inside, but Lady Hamlet moved further along the garden. *Why would Fraum be out here and not in his office? The pollen was thick and would choke him, even though it was nearing the end of the season.* The medication the Master Physic gave him delayed the symptoms, sometimes suppressing them and making him look and sound almost human.

"Where is my husband? Hiding among the roses?" Joanne asked.

Lady Hamlet didn't respond, but went out the garden gate to where Gallium had shown her the sea wyrm. Joanne paused, her heart pounding at why Fraum might be at the sea bluff. He had never mentioned coming out here.

Perhaps he wants to toss me in and say it was an accident.

She swung through the gate and a cold wind stilled her. Fraum stood at the precipice, purple cloak flapping in the wind, like dragon wings. His chin was raised as though he was enjoying the breeze, but his expression was hidden with his back to her. He wasn't alone. Two guards stood on either side, swords drawn and hands on the shoulders of two, kneeling women. Lady Helena Freeman's eyes widened at Joanne, but her mouth was gagged and her hands were tied. The other captive was Selene. She moaned against the rag and tried to stand, but the guard shoved her back down.

"What is the meaning of this?" Joanne asked. "Why have you imprisoned my lady and my friend?"

"Am I really that stupid? Do you think so little of me that you could go behind my back, disobey a direct command, and I wouldn't know," Fraum said, voice raised as he spoke to the side, not dignifying her by turning around. "I have been lenient with you child."

"You call raping me leniency? Biting and bruising me?" Joanne asked, balling her fists, she reached for the wolf-headed dagger at her hip. How far would she get before the soldiers drew the swords across her friend and lover's throat? How many steps to strike Fraum in the back before the bloody swords struck her down?

"Yes, because you still live." Fraum turned slowly. His eyes oozed and nose was bright red, skin pasty, and he sniffled. "I should have had you removed on the night of the coronation, allowed Silversmith and Foxglow to tear you apart, legally. Cast you broken, bleeding, and naked back to your father, a sign labeling you as damaged goods and then attacked his Keep myself for breach of contract. Blades Man knows I was within my rights. But I didn't. I allowed you to play your courtly games, and this is what I get. You sent your maid with a letter to Freeman requesting assistance."

Joanne remained silent. She didn't know what Fraum had discovered, nor was she about to give him more fodder to be used against her.

"Don't tell me you didn't know what she was doing delivering letters to your 'friends.' I figured by now you would have learned how few people support you," Fraum said, mouth curling into smile. "Oh, but you are stupid aren't you. There's no virtue in you, no matter how you pretended to be like one of us. You and your ilk are nothing more than cows chewing their cud in the back fields while the farmer sharpens his knife for slaughter."

"What do you want, my King?"

"Oh, it is my King now!" His eyes blazed and he clapped his hands together.

"Why won't you support me?" Joanne was nearing tears, the words trembled in her mouth.

"Because you never supported me," Fraum said. "My brother has two children, but where are mine? My brother has a wife who wouldn't betray him, yet here you are, plotting my death as we stand here. Would you like to shove me off the cliff? Feed me to the fish below?"

"I only wanted to help my family."

"I am your family!" Fraum stepped beside Selene. "This girl warms your bed, doesn't she? Provides you with physical comforts? Holds your secrets. Yet she cannot even read! This poor, simple creature you twisted around your finger now has to suffer for your actions."

Fraum lifted Selene to her feet and began to drag her to the cliff's edge.

"No!" Joanne shouted. "Don't harm her!"

Fraum threw Selene forward, where she began to inch across the stone like a worm dropped by a bird.

"What about this one, then?" He grabbed Lady Freeman by the hair. "What value do you place in her? As far as I know she knew nothing of the plot to displace me or siphon off troops, which I admit is a clever plan if poorly executed."

"How did you find out?"

"I read your letters." *Who betrayed me? Lady Windridge? Lady Willowcreek?* "So, I'm going to give you a choice on which one gets to live. The maid or the mother of two children. I will give them a chance to speak in their defense before they die."

Lady Freeman knew Joanne killed Galea with the tea. Selene would never be safe. He'd marry her off to some lord he wanted to punish, or worse, rape and murder her in front of Joanne as punishment. Selene was her love, and Joanne promised to protect her.

"Please, Fraum," Joanne said, falling to her knees. "Let them go. Punish me instead."

"That's what I'm doing," Fraum said and knelt in front of Joanne, lowering his voice. "You need a punishment that you will never forget. Who will it be? Your lover"—he motioned his head toward Selene— "or the mother?"

Joanne looked Fraum in the eyes. The filmy white had nearly blinded him and there was nothing she could do to change his mind. He would kill them both if she didn't decide. She clenched her fists into her skirts, lowered her head as the tears began to fall. *I could confess it all and die with them.* That would be a foolish waste. Joanne lifted her head and spoke one name. Fraum patted her on the shoulder.

"A tough choice," he said and backed away. His motion took him close to Lady Freeman who began to shake her head. "Seems your Queen has spoken! She has made her choice." The tears ran down Lady Freeman's face and she urinated on the ground. Fraum stood up and made a face of disgust. "The Queen has chosen you… and you are indeed, free."

He moved quickly and gripped the gag in Selene's mouth, and yanked it out.

"Anything to confess or speak in your defense?"

Selene stood, her brown eyes wide and distant, almost glassy as they gazed on Joanne.

"Only that I loved my Queen and I'd do anything for her."

Fraum slowly clapped.

"I commend your loyalty, but look at where it has led you."

He spun Selene around and then shoved her to the precipice. She swayed in the breeze, seemed to get her balance for a moment. Selene looked back over her shoulder and shouted, "I love you!" Then toppled over the edge.

"No!" Joanne reached for her, crawling along until the water and rocks were in view. She swept her gaze along the frothing waves, but didn't see a thing except… there, close by, the serpent's tail sank beneath the waves.

Rough hands grabbed her under the arms and dragged her away from the edge.

"Lock her away in her room," Fraum said. "She is neither to leave, nor have any visitors."

Selene! Selene! Oh, Mother what have I done!

They forced her through the gardens, fingers digging into her flesh as they easily lifted her. More soldiers followed her to her rooms, tossing her to the hard floor, and slamming the doors shut. Joanne wept and tore at her bodice. She beat her fists on the floor until the skin broke and mingled with the tears and spittle and snot streaming from her face.

When darkness came, she stripped the ruined dress off her aching body and climbed into bed. There she shivered, convulsing into whining and weeping, face pressed into the pillow. She was now alone. Completely alone.

A dark voice whispered to her.

Now you are ready for me.

CHAPTER SEVENTEEN:
MISTRESS OF SHADOWS

Be careful of what you wish for
Hold tight onto your desires
Whisper not to the night nor shadows
Or she will snatch your dreams away
She cares not for love, she cares not for you
She desires only to steal away your soul
So, forever be true.

Be careful of what you wish for
Hold tight onto your desires
Whisper not to the night nor shadows
Or the Dark Mistress will snatch you away
            —From, "Dark Mistress" nursery Rhym.

Joanne sat naked on the coverlet, her legs drawn beneath her. She stared into the empty hearth, loneliness binding her heart and she willed a fire to appear. One where she could burn away the coldness deep in her body. The coldness would never leave it. It was a fire in and of itself. One that burned with hatred of the man who had killed her love. Hatred of herself for choosing her. She had no other choice. Selene would have died after Lady Freeman confessed it all, the killing of Queen Galea and the conspiracy against Fraum. She stared at the black soot, so hard her eyes were beginning to play tricks on her. The soot seemed to swirl, the shadows bent. It took shape, a corporeal form gathering from the shadows, peeling them from the stone and metal grating. *It's my imagination.* But the shape of a woman formed. For a moment she thought it might be Selene returning and tears blurred her vision,

I prayed and you have returned!

"Selene." Joanne unfurled her legs.

No, it couldn't be her. Her love was gone. A hard question teased her. Did she really love the scullery maid, or was she nothing more than a distraction from the pain? She couldn't, wouldn't answer it, because no matter what it was all a fog of confusion and loss. Joanne had prayed for the Mistress of Shadows to intervene. Once a god was involved, the stories always told, the path was laid and the consequences met. Whatever happened at this point, she would accept it.

The shadow took final form. A woman all in black with a hood covering her head. Raven black hair flowed like smoke from the edges of the hood. She was not much taller than Joanne, but she did wear black boots with a heel that added to her height. The Mistress of Shadows had an attractive form the way the Dragon's Vein once tempted Joanne to touch its petals.

"You pitiful creature," the Mistress of Shadows said, stalking toward the bed, her hips moving in a mesmerizing sway. "Look at what you have been reduced to, all because you wouldn't trust me."

"I still don't," Joanne said. "I'm not certain who or what to trust. Everything I touch turns to rot."

"People close to you do have tendency to end up dead." The Mistress of Shadows laughed, teasing and seductive. "Great leaders are created through a little spilled blood. There's so much more to rain down on the people. A baptismal cleansing unlike any in history. These lords and ladies, kings and stewards, have all grown complacent, weak, and are ready to snap like twigs when stepped on. You have already heard them crack under a little pressure."

"The greedy ones took themselves out," Joanne said, watching the Mistress of Shadows crawl up the end of the bed.

"They fear you," the goddess said. "They fear you like no one else in their history. You know why?"

"Because I'm an outsider."

"You are a woman." The Mistress of Shadows touched Joanne's arm. Goose flesh raised up across her skin. "This cold, hard place has created weak men afraid of their women. That's why the ladies were punished by beheadings or shoved into the sea."

Joanne gave an involuntary cry voice at the last part. She hated the sound of the whimper, dragging her back to her childhood, but—

Selene

"Prince hasn't moved against Prince, because they know that neither is strong enough to keep this piece of rock from crumbling," The Mistress of Shadows pulled Joanne's arm away from her chest and touched her breast over her heart. The touch was cold, tough, firm, as solid as a block of ice. "Here is where you win wars. Here is where you conquer kingdoms. Here is where you rule everything and everyone. You have shown you have the ability to turn flesh into stone. I will teach you how to forge it into metal."

Flesh into metal? Anything so I may get my revenge.

"What do you need me to do?" Joanne asked, her lips trembling. Not from the cold touch alone, but also the thrill of what this goddess promised.

"Surrender to me." The Mistress of Shadows leaned close to her face. The hood dropped revealing a young face, pale skin, and piercing green eyes that burned like Arula's fire. Her breath was frost on Joanne's lips and then she kissed her, the cold ice slipping inside her. Joanne wanted to scream, but it froze in her throat. The coldness soon warmed, fingers caressed her body, pressing into intimate areas, fondling and squeezing until she moaned and her body shuddered. Her thighs quivered and she collapsed backwards onto the bed. She opened her eyes to stare up at the canopy. The Mistress of Shadow's touch had disappeared as well.

Did I imagine it all?

She was sweating, panting, the taste of ash on her tongue. She ran her hands over her body, down her belly and found between her legs was wet. No, she didn't image it. The room took on a sharper edge. Everything around her was brighter and she saw the dagger her brother had given her, the wolf head on the hilt staring back at her.

They will pay for what they did to us. She grabbed the dagger and pulled it from the sheathe. "I swear my body and soul to you, my Dark Mistress. My blood running through my veins is yours to command." She drew the blade across her right palm, squeezing it until droplets of blood stained her sheets. "I am yours."

We will rule it all.

Joanne lay back on her bed and smiled. They could keep her locked up, but she was free. She fell asleep and woke up to a knock on her door. Lady Hamlet entered with a tray of food. She glanced at Joanne after setting the tray on the table.

"It's not good to stay in bed all day," she said and opened the shades to allow in sunlight. *When did it become morning? Did I sleep that long?* "You are still Queen and need to act like one. For Mother's sake, wash yourself and put on some decent clothes."

"I thought the King desired me to be locked away," Joanne said.

"The King isn't around presently," Lady Hamlet said, "which will be a perfect time for his Queen to stretch her legs around the garden."

Burn it all for what I care. I never want to step foot in there again.

Selene!

"Won't you be punished for this defiant act?"

"What the King doesn't know won't hurt either of us," Lady Hamlet said, giving the first smile that Joanne could ever recall. "I will have a tub and hot water brought up presently, my Queen. It will do you some good to wash away the sorrows."

We keep that one alive, the Mistress of Shadows spoke in her head.

"Yes," Joanne agreed. She slipped on a robe and her stomach growled at the sight of the meal left behind. A large chunk of bread and nut paste and a bowl of jam and some late harvest fruits, along with hot tea. Joanne tore a chunk of bread and her mouth salivated at the flavor. *How long had it been since she last had a meal?* She shifted the bowl of fruit and discovered a note beneath it. Joanne hesitated, looked around to be certain that she wasn't being watched like in some sort of test of loyalty. Then she unfolded the note.

My Queen,

I pray to Mother this note finds you or else your sacrifice was in vain. I know the difficult choice to spare me came at the cost of one who loved you dearly. I am to be sent home soon, but it is no longer a home, never truly was a home, but a desolate place of despair and enemies surround us, betray us at every opportunity. My very child is that of an enemy set to inherit the place of punishment and I will be sent away to my father's when the boy comes of age. I no longer care what befalls my being, as long as it is in service to you. Should you require my special tea which your beloved inquired after, place a red rag out the window and I will spot it, sending you my warmest brew that will keep a fire in your belly this long winter. Sip it slowly and it will draw out the warmth.

Yours in Loyalty and Love,

Helena of Nemus.

"Strange that she dropped her title and husband's last name," Joanne said, crumpling the note and placing it under her mattress to later burn in the fire. Helena confirmed that the child was Gallium's and not Lord Freeman's heir. Not that it mattered any. The tea would be the prize Joanne sought.

A devious ploy, but one you must exercise caution in who drinks your concoction. The Mistress of Shadows whispered. *Too fast and Gallium will suspect you. Then you will build a different cage.*

"We need to force his hand," Joanne said, spreading jam across the bread. "Set brother against brother. Then to get control of the lords and their soldiers."

Brew the plan and I will help set the trap. The biggest concern is your cousin. She no longer seems to be an ally, as you once warned Selene, she cannot be trusted. She has the power and position many women in Seaptum dream about.

"How do you know what I said to Selene?" Joanne asked.

Think of my name and know that it is truth.

There came another knock on her door. Joanne told them to enter. Two male servants carried a metal tub into the room followed by several others with buckets of warm water. They set the tub across from the hearth and emptied the buckets into it.

"Has Lady Freeman departed yet?" Joanne asked one of the maids.

"No, my Queen," she responded, curtsied, and hurried from the room, bucket clanking against her leg. The others left as well, with one inquiring if the Queen had any further needs. *My husband and his brother dead.* But she declined and was left alone. She slid into the refreshing warm water and plotted with the goddess in her head. If all went well, she could be the sole sovereign figure and send aide to her father. The entire force of Seaptum if needed.

And the wolves will howl to celebrate their new master. A singular Queen to ruin them all.

Joanne stuck a red stocking out the window, tying a knot in the end before closing it in the frame and hoping Helena saw it before she went back to her desolate home. Part of Joanne wished she could stay on as her new lady-in-waiting, but Fraum would never allow it. She wasn't sure how much she could trust Lady Hamlet, or if the only reason she took pity on Joanne was to spite the overbearing King. His harsh treatment of her was known by all the servants, and they looked upon her with pity when they dared to look. She dressed in a light gown and moved to gardens. A few days ago, she had been summoned from them to watch her lover die. Now, the fading warmth of the sun felt good on her refreshed skin.

I will strip the ground bare and plant Dragon's Vein.

Go the training grounds, the Mistress of Shadows said. *Choose one of the biggest, strongest men.*

Why?

I will show you how to use shadow magic to convert people to your needs. It starts with one. Then the rest will fall in line. You will have your army, so I will get mine.

What do you need an army for? Joanne asked, holding her arms out as though embracing the warmth of the sun. She wanted to strip and run naked beneath it, absorbing all of its blessings before the winter clouds stole it away.

When gods war, we need every resource at our disposal.

"You are at war with the other gods." Joanne opened her eyes and stared down at her shadow. It was no longer hers. The fringes of the cloak billowed around the legs which were not her own. An idea came to mind and before she could speak it, the Mistress of Shadows answered.

Yes and yes.

Then we have much planning to do. Joanne smiled, though she didn't know if it was her who moved the muscles around her mouth, or her new Mistress.

Joanne moved from the gardens, passing through the halls of Argenti Lapisdom. She expected someone to halt her, to question why she was leaving the gardens, and force her back to her room. She went through the main dining hall, footsteps echoing in the silent room where food and drink used to be enjoyed in company, if not always friendly, then at least mutually entertaining. Beyond the main hall she passed some servants mulling around, dusting and sweeping. She was more ghost in the room—*Shadow*—than anything of substance.

Out the east door, she moved alongside Argenti Lapisdom to the barracks. The sound of officers shouting orders and men marching in squadrons, banners raised with the sun emblem flapping in the wind. Drums pounded out a rhythm to which they moved in time, a singular entity shining in metal and bristling with sharp edges.

The Mistress of Shadows sent out an admiring hum. The vast numbers and order were impressive. A terrifying sight to be on the opposite side of such force. *Who do you want?* Joanne asked, staring at the numbers, but unable to pull one from the many.

Take me closer.

Joanne hesitated. Lady Hamlet may be lenient with Fraum's orders, but she didn't know what her husband instructed the captains of his army. *I can't keep hidden in my warren, all timid. Fraum has stripped everything else from me. I'll have to risk it.*

One of many you'll take for me, the Mistress of Shadows confessed.

As long as the reward is great!

More than you could ever dream about, the dark goddess said. *Move along like you belong here. In essence, all of this is yours. Just seize it and don't let go!*

Joanne moved through the parade grounds, keeping to the peripheral and allowing the goddess to assess those she passed. She spotted Captain Hollister, Master of Arms—an unfortunate name shared with the legendary pirate and lover of Sin. He was tall, talons of the golden sun bright on his shoulders. A long, purple cloak etched in gold and helm in hand, he bowed and knelt at her approach. The entire army bent their knee as one. It was breathtaking how they went from a dangerous force standing, to knee as one, like the bending of grass in wind, or beneath her foot as she crushes it.

"My Queen," he said. "What brings you out here? Was there an inspection that I was made unaware of? If so, please forgive my negligence."

"Rise, Captain, you have done no wrong," Joanne said. "I only come on a whim, though now I have seen your impressive work, I will need to visit more often."

"You flatter me, my Queen," Captain Hollister said, puffing up his chest.

"Not at all," Joanne said. "In fact, pretend I am not here at all and carry on with your exercises."

"As the Queen commands, so it will be."

"Thank you, Master of Arms." Joanne gave him her friendliest smile and touched his arm lightly. He straightened, tugged his uniform, and began shouting commands. The drums picked up the beat and the troops moved in unison. Joanne walked along the east edge where the infantry carried long spears five rows deep. Bannermen were sprinkled among them. Another eight rows of shield bearers completed the formation. Behind them were long bowman, directed by another captain, commanding them to draw and loose, draw and loose, without actually drawing the string. Several spotters were correcting the angels of the bows. Calvary was the only piece missing, according to the Mistress of Shadows. *The parade ground's too small for that type of exercise. They would require more space.*

Thomas and Alfred would know more about this than she did. Book learning was one aspect, but live instruction, with the beast before her, well that was something entirely different.

There, that one.

Joanne's head turned and she spotted the shield bearer. Not that she could very well miss him. The man was taller than his shield mates, broader in his armor, occupying nearly two spaces, though his movements were synchronized with the others, legs arms, head, all moving as one body. Joanne could see his appeal to the Dark Mistress. *Do you want me to pull him from the line?*

Not, yet. We have one more task.

Do you think we will be able to find this boy later?

I don't think it will be a problem.

They left the parade grounds and the Mistress of Shadows instructed her to move to the barracks. Passing the stables with over a thousand stalls, the smell of horse, straw, and leather was strong. Dozens of groomsmen and women hustled around, carrying various accessories from buckets to blankets. Beyond the stables she heard the clank of metal striking metal. The smell of smoke permeated the air. Smoke not from cooking fires, but the acrid burning of coal. Men in aprons beat hammers against metal, carried tongs to place chunks in the fire, while dirt-streaked boys worked the billows.

What are we doing here?

The Mistress of Shadows moved past the rows of horse shoes, nails, tools and other daily necessities. Joanne spotted the knives, swords, spear tips, and arrowheads, but they went to the next area where armor, shields, and helmets were stacked. *This is where I need to create the ideal insignia for your personal guard. Something to strike terror in those who stand against you.*

What will it be?

Patience, my dear one. You will find out soon enough.

They returned back inside Argenti Lapisdom. Lady Hamlet waited for her in the dining hall. She had a concerned look on her face that changed to relief when Joanne entered the room. "Did you have a nice stroll?" Lady Hamlet asked, examining the table settings. It appeared she wasn't sending her back to her rooms at this moment.

"Yes," Joanne said. "Just stretching my legs. I cannot linger in a place of bad memories for too long."

"Nor should you," Lady Hamlet said. "You are the Queen and can go as she pleases."

There was the unspoken condition underlying her words. Joanne was free to go where she pleased as long as Fraum didn't find out, or wasn't around to restrict her. "Now you must eat." Cooked squash covered in syrup and roasted nuts with a side of sweet berries covered the plate and a small mug of cider consisted her meal.

"I will not forget your kindness," Joanne said, sitting down and tasting the meal. "Seems like I haven't eaten in days."

"You haven't, really, outside of breakfast" Lady Hamlet said. "I'm surprised you were able to move about as much as you have on such an empty belly. I believe our King will be returning in the morning or midday, so I may not be as accommodating, tomorrow."

"Understandable," Joanne said, "unless the King takes pity and changes his mind."

Which we know he won't.

Joanne returned to her room, which had been cleaned and aired. She sat down with ink and parchment, allowing the goddess to dictate a letter, which she sealed and set aside. Joanne had no idea how it would be delivered, since she didn't trust any of the servants, despite the kindness Lady Hamlet displayed. The goddess assured her it would be done. The sun went down early and with it, Joanne. The empty side of the bed brought on tears. No matter what she did, if she conquered kingdoms or failed, her love was dead and it was her fault.

Yet she dreamed.

She was back at the wood pile. The same axe was stuck in a log, the same little fox hole where she had once hid trying to escape her ghosts and the Dark Mistress. A childish game she had lost even before she knew it had begun. The air was strangely cold and she shivered. She stared at her hands. Blood stained them, but it was old, fading. The ghosts of murders past.

Don't worry, my little love, a dark and seductive voice spoke from the shadow of the woods. *There will be plenty more to bathe in if you like.*

"I don't," Joanne said inside the dream. "Will I ever be free of it?"

You will never wear white. The Dark Mistress walked from the woods, though walking was not the right word. Materialized the way smoke drifted from the flame. She was beautiful, so much it hurt Joanne's heart to look on her slender form.

Selene!

Are you still crying over that one? She only held you back, the Dark Mistress said. *A pretty thing she used to be, but she belongs to Donn and his judgement sends her onto her next path. Like you have entered a new path.*

"Where will it lead me?"

Look. The goddess pointed into the shadows. Red eyes glowed and a creature emerged, silver and sleek. A wolf, though not a natural one. This one was alone, powerful muscles writhing beneath the silver fur. The wolf stared at Joanne, then turned.

"It wants me to follow," Joanne said.

Then follow.

"I'm afraid."

You would be a fool not to be afraid.

"Fine," Joanne said, taking the axe from the log. She stalked into the dark woods. Mist shrouded her and she shivered in the damp, coldness. *Why couldn't my dreams be warm and sunny and full of fuzzy bunnies?* The trees were bare, dead branches reaching for her like the hands of the condemned to steal her away and suffer with the souls she'd already sent on their path in the afterlife. They didn't touch her, but she could feel their anger, their bitter desire to destroy her.

In the moonlight, she caught the glimmer of silver. Only this time it wasn't at ground level, but rose up taller than her. It stood on two legs, the naked shape of a man standing before her, but with the head of a wolf and red glowing eyes. Silently snarling not more than a few feet away, it could tear her apart in less time than it took her to breathe. It didn't move. Joanne raised the axe, but doubted it would do the creature much harm. While she waited, watching this man and wolf, more appeared. A dozen she counted, hard muscled and nude, bare feet shuffling through the underbrush. They encircled her. There was no where she could run.

The Dark Mistress has abandoned me. I'm alone here and—

As one, the wolf men dropped to a knee, presented their arms, palms upward. Those metallic masks still stared at her. She moved in a circle and hesitantly touched each palm, waiting for the hand to close on her and drag her to a death she couldn't imagine. None did. When she got to the last, they stood up, took a step back, lifted their heads, and howled.

The name came to her. One older than the stones where they stepped.

Mors Faunis.

Death Howler.

When she woke, her body was sore, as though she hadn't slept at all. She turned to her side and let out a screech. Inside her mind, the Mistress of Shadows laughed. *What do you think?* Lying on the pillow beside her was a metallic wolf's head staring empty-eyed at her. It was authentic in design and craftmanship as far as Joanne could tell. Even the mouth drawn back in a perpetual snarl, the wrinkles in the snout and gum lines seemed it would bite her hand if she put it too close.

Where did it come from?

I...well you made it last night at the forge, the Mistress of Shadows said. *You may have startled one of the blacksmiths awake to fire the forge. Don't worry, we paid him off well.*

Joanne didn't bother to ask how or with what coin.

You never answered me. What do you think?

I think it is horrifying.

So will your enemies.

CHAPTER EIGHTEEN:
QUEEN'S HANGMAN

War is like a card game,
Don't gamble with what
You cannot afford to lose.
                    —*Seaptum Military proverb*

With a break in the winter storms, a box arrived for Joanne. It was small, no larger than a boot box, but made of heavy wood and contained the dagger and throne crest burnt into the lid. Desmond's crest, though Joanne knew her father didn't send it, but rather another, former Nemus resident. It was similar in construction to the one delivered to the former Lady Foxglow. No note arrived with the box, but once Joanne opened the lid and saw the dried leaves, she knew the identity of the sender. She pushed through the tea leaves and berries, discovering a false bottom. Carefully removing the wooden wedge, Joanne spotted the yellow petals with red veins. *This will warm the cold-blooded bastard.* She replaced the false bottom and set the box beside others in her collection so it would be inconspicuous, hiding in plain sight.

Fraum had spent most of the cold weather locked in his rooms and refused to see Joanne, not that she had gone seeking his attentions. Since Selene's death, she had seen him once and that was a disaster, ending in bruises and a split lip for Joanne. She ghosted through the Argenti unnoticed and at her discretion. No one spoke of her strange, nightly visits to the forge. Or the creepy masks that she created, waking to sore arms and a snarling wolf's head. Two dozen in all were forged.

What are we going to do we with these? Joanne asked

Fill them, the goddess replied. *Oh, you have another gift. On the table, under the red cloth.*

Joanne hesitated, not knowing what to expect. A tongue of a particularly nosey and talkative page boy, perhaps? She removed the red cloth and gasped. Tears filled her eyes at the beauty of the dagger on the table, a perfect match to the one Alfred had given her. The wolf's head on the hilt shone in the light of day.

You deserve a little reward for all your hard work, the Mistress of Shadows said. *Besides, two daggers are better than one.*

From that day, she wore a dagger on both hips. No one noticed the new decorum added to her dress, or if they did, thought better than to speak a word against it. Joanne added another duty to her daily schedule, visiting the barracks during the cold, snowy season, and bringing a variety of goods to the soldiers, from sweet, syrup candies, to warm blankets. She gave an extra blanket to the soldier the Dark Mistress had marked out.

"One won't be enough for someone your size," she had said, handing him the second blanket. He smiled, dimples forming in his smooth cheeks. His blue eyes lit up when he took the blankets, two large hands swallowing them as though they were nothing but rags.

"You are very gracious, my Queen," he said.

"What is your name?"

"Iphan," he said, his voice deep and smooth. The way she imagined a young adult dragon might sound before he ate her up.

"Well, Iphan, I thank you for your service." She placed a hand on his forearm, which was as big as loaf of bread. It lingered enough to hint at something more than friendliness. His expression changed to one of confusion and surprise. To finish the teasing, she gave him a coy smile full of meaning to bait the trap.

He's watching you as you walk away.

Let them all watch.

Every visit she would give him a little extra and even heard some of the other soldiers remark on this with pokes and jabs, winks in his direction, though none would be crude or crass about her in her presence—since she was the Queen and Fraum was not a King known for his kindness— she imagined they would speak all sorts of bawdy language, allowing him to soak it up and fill his fantasies of her.

"You are investing some time at the barracks," Fraum noted once.

"Fostering goodwill and sowing seeds of loyalty and moral among the soldiers, my lord," Joanne told him. "I read that was how King Jasper prevented his soldiers from mutiny when the Sowers Rain brought ice storms and killed the crops and created a great famine."

"His pretty little Queen ogled the men and waggled her ass at them," Fraum said, though his interest fell on a paper one of his councils gave him. Lesser lords had arrived at the Argenti after Fraum returned from his last visits. There were whispers of war. He frowned at the paper and walked away before she could reply.

He either lost interest or accepted her response, but didn't bring the subject up again. Nor did he ask about the nights at the forge—which would have been an awkward conversation regarding her obsession with wolves, but whatever kept her from killing the Lords and Ladies of Seaptum, would be an acceptable hobby.

Plotting his death probably wouldn't be welcomed. Joanne smiled at the idea of being free from him. He may have assumed she was done with her ploys. She'd given him no other reason to question her loyalty.

Not much longer, the Dark Mistress said. *Then we start creating your new guard. Your* Mors Faunis.

Death Howlers. It was as good a name as any Joanne could've picked.

As the snows melted, she went to the kitchens to observe a particular routine the Master Physic performed with his assistants. They didn't say anything of her presence, but allowed her to watch in silence. Water boiled over the fire while they mashed up dried leaves, dropping them to soak in a pungent oil. The concoction was then scooped up by a tiny spoon and emptied into several small glass vials. Last came the partial ladle-full of hot water. They sealed the glass with wax and shook it vigorously afterward.

"Is this the King's tinctures?" Joanne asked, finally, though she knew the response.

"Yes, my Queen," the Master Physic said, as though responding to a curious child. "It is a rather delicate process and requires precision in measurements."

"How come they haven't healed him?" Joanne asked

"Oh, there's no cure for his ailment," the Master Physic said. He held the tincture to the window where the sunlight shone through the greenish liquid. "This is to ease the symptoms. He will gradually worsen."

"How long does the King have before—" She let the word "die" drop, knowing they would take it for an emotional lapse rather than the calculated risk she was taking. Although she had seen the tinctures administered to Fraum, she hadn't taken an interest in their preparations, assuming their purpose was to help him go about his day with his symptoms eased. Should something horrific befall to her husband, she didn't want the suspicion to fall on her.

The magistrate gave her a sympathetic look. "We do not know. He has lived with it for two decades, but beyond that, it is in Mother's hands how long the thread grows before it is cut."

"If you wish to maintain the order," one of the assistants said, "then you best pray for an heir."

She watched them close the container of dried leaves and place the jar of oil into a wooden box with steel clasps and then lock it. The box was placed in a cupboard, which another key locked. Both keys were attached to a chain around the older man's neck. This was a small obstacle, but one Joanne would discover a way to overcome.

All we need is an impression.

"I don't know how that will—"

Leave it to me!

Lady Hamlet approached her when she left the kitchens, wearing a look of concern. She handed Joanne a letter, the wax seal was broken, but she recognized the sword and the roses.

"I found this, milady, while cleaning the King's room," Lady Hamlet said, a tremble in her voice.

My Dear Daughter,
Conflict has found us here at home and violence has escalated.

Thomas has dispatched to put down the instigators of this rebellion, while Alfred helps me handle the raids on our goods here at the Keep. Any aide you can send will be a great welcome. May the Blades Man guide you in your wisdom.

With great affection,

Lord Desmond

Joanne noted it was dated several weeks ago. *How long has Fraum known?* Obviously, her father was wise enough to make it seem like he was talking to her, but in reality, he was asking King Fraum. Pleading, even. He had no more daughters to give or anything of value to Fraum. Fraum didn't even want her. She was about to crumple the note, but notice Lady Hamlet standing there, hands writhing together.

"Put this back where you got it," Joanne said, and wiped at her eyes. "He can never know that I know. When a messenger comes again from my father, tell me immediately."

"Yes, my Queen." Lady Hamlet bowed, and then gently touched her arm. "Pray on the manner. I wouldn't worry about your brother. I'm sure he is a fine commander and will easily disperse the malcontents."

"Perhaps," Joanne said.

He will be overwhelmed, the Dark Mistress said.

We need to kill Fraum tonight! To take over the army and march south!

No, the Mistress of Shadows said, though there was sympathy in her voice. *The army won't follow you, not yet. Nor will killing Fraum in haste save your brother. We must continue the plan.*

Is there nothing we can do?

Their army will be near Twin Rivers by now. Should you murder everyone and gain command, the battle would be done and over before you could muster the forces. Best course of action is to continue the plan.

"Fraum will suffer for this," Joanne hissed between her teeth and slammed her door. "He will die a slow painful death." She took out the tea box, put on a pair of thick leather gloves. And removed the false bottom. There was the dried Dragon's Vein, orange and red. She lifted it up, careful not to let it touch her skin or get too close to her nose. She crumpled it up and mixed it in with the rest of the tea leaves. Then she closed the box.

We get the key impression tonight.

The room was silent except for the occasional snore. This took her back to nearly four years when she had entered her tutor's room with the fateful knife. *Let's not have a repeat of how that night ended,* the Mistress of Shadows warned. Joanne agreed and removed her slipper shoes. She crept in the room, moving on her toes. Moonlight shone through the window, revealing the Master Physic's room to be rather sparse. There was a dressing cupboard, a desk, and a bed. Joanne went to the desk first, examining its contents. Papers and ink blotter were set out meticulously, but not key. She checked several drawers, but again, only quills, a small knife to sharpen the writing device, and blank parchments.

Where would he keep the keys? Locked away in another box full of keys that required more keys?

The master turned in his bed. There, around his neck, she saw the glint of metal.

Of course it would be there.

Again, Joanne was taken back to the night, slicing her tutor's hair and then her throat. She approached the older man's bed, which smelled of camphor and other strong herbs. She recognized them as sleep aides and pain relievers. A blanket covered his nude upper body, tucked under his arm. Joanne stood by the bed, searching for a way to get the keys without waking the older man, thus repeating the actions when she was thirteen. The chain around his wrinkled neck disappeared down his front. The keys were trapped under him.

I can't get it. Frustration built in Joanne. *We have to come back a different time.*

Let me handle it, the Mistress of Shadows said.

Joanne blinked and what felt like an instance later, she was holding one key and pressing it into wax. She did the same for the second key as well. Then she gently returned the keys to their sleeping master. Joanne slipped beyond the door, heart pounding as she moved briskly down the hall, the wax impression of both keys wrapped in a cloth.

How'd you do that?

I waited until he turned over, the dark goddess said. *It was much easier for me, since I'm used to patiently waiting in shadows.*

Where did you learn it from?

An unlikely source, she said. *The Blades Man.*

I'm not surprised.

The wax dried while Joanne slept and the next day she visited the forge, molding the two keys. She returned to the kitchens and found the box the masters had taken the supplies for Fraum's tinctures. She tried the one key. It didn't fit.

Try the other.

Joanne did and there was a click. The lid opened. She tried the second key and it opened that lock as well. There was the vial of oil and the box of dried leaves. Joanne took out an envelope, shaking in the crushed, dried pieces from her own box of tea. A pinch was enough to kill Queen Amaria in one cup of tea. She shook it so it was fine enough that only a small portion would get into his tincture. Enough to sicken him, not melt his insides like it did to his mother. Joanne closed the lid, locked it, and placed it back on the shelf.

"What are you doing up so late, my Queen?" Lady Hamlet asked, holding a taper.

She startled and lost her hold on one of the keys. It made a small metallic sound when it landed somewhere in the shadows. *Kill her!* The Mistress of Shadows whispered. Joanne ignored the seductive voice. Her hands twitched into a fist and she forced it open, making a show of examining the shelves. "I was a little hungry and wanted to see what was available for a nibble."

"Does my Queen wish for me to make her a small plate?"

"No." She grabbed a container of dried fruit. "This will suffice. That is all, Lady Hamlet."

"As my Queen wishes." The older woman didn't seem entirely convinced. As Joanne walked away, Lady Hamlet cleared her throat. "You dropped this."

Joanne turned to see the key she had crafted to access Fraum's tincture box pinched between Lady Hamlet's fingers. "How clumsy of me," she said, and took the key from Lady Hamlet.

"Sometimes we get careless in the dark," she said. "Take care, my Queen. You don't know what evils may lurk in the shadows."

If she only knew, the Mistress of Shadows grinned and Joanne smiled.

Back at her room, Joanne took out parchment and ink. Events were in motion and she couldn't stop them even if she had wanted. She wrote two separate letters. One to Beaty to express her concerns over Fraum's health, and another to Helena, thanking her for the tea.

She placed these notes aside and sleep took over before dawn.

Midday she woke and made her way to the parade grounds. Iphan once more was in the front shield line. The Dark Mistress took note of several other of his companions that would soon form her private guard. *Mors Faunis.* She didn't understand the Dark Mistress's plan for convincing them to wear the wolf helm, or to serve her, but that was a surprise the goddess promised would be personally handled by her.

Soon enough.

She went to the stables and found a young boy. She promised him several gold coins to deliver the one note to Helena. The other note would have to wait until the right time. She would observe what happens when her husband was given the extra additive.

That night she was summoned to Fraum. He stood with his back to her, a robe covering his thin shoulders, and he stared out the window. Silver moonlight wreathed him. His hair seemed to have thinned more, almost to the point of balding. If she hadn't known better, she'd think he was dying now.

"There's a problem," he said and wheezed.

Joanne's heart raced at the words. *He knows? But how?*

"What's the problem?" Joanne asked.

"The Master Physic told me that my condition is incurable," Fraum said, still not turning away from the window. "If I am going to get an heir, then I must do it soon. I know the act is detestable to you, but either you get pregnant or we lose all connection to the throne. I am not getting any healthier and…."

"We'll do what we can," Joanne said, keeping the disgust from her voice. The image of him throwing Selene over the precipice dug at her like a knife in the heart. "No one will take the throne from us."

Fraum turned and for the first time she saw tears on his face.

He's facing his own mortality.

His body was very thin and when he released his robe, she could see the outline of his bones pressing against his skin. He walked to her, his body trembling, and took her by the hands, almost tender. His skin was pale, his touch like ashes in the fireplace. He led her to the bed and disrobed her. Spreading her legs and laying on her, she could smell an old, musty odor— an old man in a young body, one which seemed to be rotting. He didn't last long, nor did he kiss her. He rolled over, chest heaving and air wheezing like a creaking tree limb.

"I'm going to get the Master Physic," Joanne said, putting her dress back on.

Fraum nodded.

In the hallway, the Mistress of Shadows gave a disgusted sound.

You pity him! This murdering bastard! He doesn't deserve anything more than a knife to his balls.

"Who will pity me when I'm dying?"

No one! When you die, you will ascend to become a goddess.

Joanne knocked on the Master Physic's door and told him that Fraum needed his tincture. She followed him to the kitchens where he prepared a fresh one. There was no indication that he noticed any tampering with the herbs and oils. He ground away and boiled water over the fire while the leaves soaked. He poured it altogether in a vial. Joanne couldn't tell if any of the Dragon's Vein made it inside, though the Master shook it up.

"I will take care of him, my Queen," he said. "Try not to worry yourself and get some rest."

Joanne thanked him and returned to her room.

It's time to begin the next phase.

"You wanted to see me, my Queen?" Iphan asked. He stood in the vestibule, looking rather uncomfortable to be inside the Argenti. He looked around at the statues of the gods and blushed when he saw her in the low neckline, trying not to stare at her cleavage.

"I did," Joanne said. "I am in need of a service only you can provide. Let's not speak of it here in the open."

"Would it be prudent for me to be seen by my Queen alone?" Iphan asked. *He is a wise one. Loyal and yet desires to be obedient.* "Won't others speak of indiscretion to the King and my commander?"

"Any who do will lose their tongue," Joanne said. "Follow me, if you would."

Iphan hesitated, but Joanne didn't give him a chance to protest further. She climbed the stairs to the second level and continued without a word to her chambers. There were no servants around to witness, since she had instructed Lady Hamlet to keep the area clear and that no one was to disturb her chambers. The desperation by which she had believed Joanne faced to conceive a child, no matter with who, led to the older woman to consent. She entered her chamber and instructed Iphan to close the door.

"My Queen, I mean to serve—"

"Close the door and quit blubbering," Joanne said, sitting in her chair where she used to read the histories of Seaptum, beside a table with a carafe of wine and two glasses. She poured two glasses. "You will disobey your Queen?"

Iphan gave a helpless smile and bowed. Then he closed the door.

"Take this and drink," she said. "I have a proposal for you."

Iphan took the glass in his hand. It was tiny by comparison, a thimbleful rather than a goblet. He held it and when she motioned for him to drink, he did so. The graceful and certain movements she witnessed from him on the parade grounds were missing from this man-child. *He acts so skittish; I wonder if he has ever been with a woman. A pity to take that away from him.*

"I know this is irregular, but there are changes coming which will make for irregular times," Joanne said. "The king is dying and I have yet to produce an heir. I find I rather like my seat of power and desire not to lose it."

"Why are you telling me this?" Iphan asked.

"I need a personal guard to protect my interests."

The tension left his body, but his brow furrowed. "Protect them from who?"

"Prince Gallium and the rest of the lords," Joanne said, she set her wine glass down without taking a drink. The crushed powder she placed in it might take extra time to work on Iphan, since he was larger than her. He could break her in half if he chose to be violent. She poured him another glass as he watched her curiously, working out the words she spoke.

"My father is Lord Windridge," he said, then downed his wine, his face flush and sweating. "I would have to ask his permission and the permission of the Master of… the master…."

"Oh, that is taken care of," Joanne said, leading Iphan to sit in the chair. She took out her wolf-headed dagger, feeling her own self slip further back away from the scene, giving control to the Mistress of Shadows. "I'm your master now."

Joanne watched as the Mistress of Shadows crossed to the incapacitated soldier, grab his jaw, and pull out his tongue. The blade cut cleanly across it, severing it by the root. Blood poured out of his mouth, and Iphan squirmed, unable to move his limbs. She took a hot poker from the fire and cauterized the wound. Burning flesh and blood cut through the fugue and Joanne would have wretched if she controlled her body. Iphan began to convulse.

Is he going to die?

The Mistress of Shadows took the wolf helmet from its place beside the bed. She placed it on his head, a warm glow reflecting from her hands. The flesh melded to the metal. Iphan grunted, unable to cry out, and went still. The Mistress of Shadows stepped back, admiring her work.

"He won't die," she said. "Now he truly lives."

The dark goddess smiled and Joanne wondered in the moment what evil she had unleashed into the world. *Sometimes evil was needed to defeat evil.*

Fraum summoned her every other night to attempt seeding her with an heir. Some nights he could hardly breathe and Joanne had to do most of the work until he grunted and ejaculated the thin, stinking squirt into her. After each visit she would summon the Master Physic who would administer the tincture. During the day she heard whispers from the servants as they passed her. Young men had begun to go missing from the barracks. She was approached by Captain Hollister when she came to inspect the parade grounds like any normal day.

"My Queen," Captain Hollister said and bowed. "I believe we have a problem with missing soldiers."

"Desertion?" She widened her eyes and placed a hand to her mouth like it was a dirty word.

"Not exactly," he said, taking her by the arm. "Let's speak in private."

Joanne allowed him to take her aside to a separate room, his office space by the look of it. There was a desk with papers stacked, ink and quill. Everything was in order, not a sheet out of place. She noticed several names written out on the paper. Names of young men who were all serving a different purpose.

"What did you want to speak with me about?" Joanne asked.

"There's been talk among the men that you have paid rather special attention to a few of them," he said, trying not to sound insulting while at the same instance being frank. "They say the ones who disappeared visited you. Now, someone who deserts would take their personal items with them, but their bunks are still made and their clothes are still in their assigned trunks. That's suspicious to say the least, milady. I am hoping you have some information on the occurrence before I have to report this irregularity to the King."

"The King is feeling rather ill," Joanne said. "If you must know something to ease your thoughts, Captain, then I will tell you the secret. I regret not informing you, but I couldn't risk losing out on this timely need."

"If you required anything, my Queen, you only needed to ask," Captain Hollister said. "Twenty-three men is a sizeable loss, plus they have family and other lords to inform on any special assignment you may have had for them. There's paperwork to file and requisitions to get signed off from the King."

"They were selected as my personal guard," Joanne said.

"Personal guard? No queen has required a personal guard in the history of Seaptum, let alone two dozen."

"Not all queens were threatened by their husband's brother," Joanne said. "Since my husband is very ill, I know that Prince Gallium will come for the throne. I also know that you support Gallium over Fraum, not that I blame you, and will not intercede on either of our behalf."

"Where are my men?" Captain Hollister asked, becoming more agitated, and grabbed her arm.

Joanne glared at him, but he didn't release her.

"I advise you to let me go," she said and there was a shift in her eyes, a darkening of her pupils that she felt and saw the uncertainty cross the Captain's face, "before you find out what happened to them first hand."

Captain Hollister released her as though he had grabbed hot coals.

"Forgive me, my Queen," he said and bowed. "I... I am concerned."

"I promise you, Captain, no more will disappear due to my design," she said. "Command the rest and think of them as a small contribution of the lords to their Queen who greatly appreciates their generosity."

"As you command," he said. "What will I tell the King?"

"Nothing," Joanne said. "He is dying and I will soon take over the throne."

Captain Hollister straightened his uniform and marched from his office. Joanne smiled, though it slipped as the dark goddess faded into the background. Captain Hollister was a proud man and wouldn't take this affront easily. *He'll retaliate,* Joanne said. *He'll get the lords to recall their soldiers in support of Prince Gallium.*

Let him try. The Dark Goddess laughed. *I've defeated stronger men, more powerful entities. He is a worm before my beak and I will mash him up.*

Joanne left the office and returned to her rooms. The Master Physic approached her in the vestibule, a tired and worried expression on his wrinkled face. His pace picked up when he saw her. He gave a curt bow. "My Queen, I've been looking all over for you!"

"What is it?"

"Come, it isn't good to speak of these things in the open," he said, rubbing his hands together like a fly. They went into Fraum's office, which was the opposite of the Captain's office—ink spilled across papers, the chair askew and something red stained the wall. The Master Physic closed the door. "I need you to recall that when I mentioned prior that the tinctures were to treat your husband's symptoms, but the disease would eventually kill him." He paused, waiting for her to acknowledge the memory, which Joanne did, by waving for him to continue.

"It seems the time has come," the Master Physic said. "He is weakening and grows worse every day."

"Is there anything you can do?"

"He is in the Mother's hands and beyond my skill to heal."

"Keep this to yourself," Joanne said. "In fact, let me take over his care."

The Master Physic seemed surprised by her proposal.

"But—"

"You said so yourself that he is beyond your skill," Joanne said. "Please allow a wife to see to her dying husband's needs in his last days."

"As you command, My Queen, but if you require any assistance, please notify me immediately."

"Thank you so much for your brilliant assistance in keeping him in his best health to this point. I will never forget your service," Joanne said.

"But—"

She hustled him out of the office. Closing the door, she slid down the wall, a strange shudder of relief thrumming through her limbs. It was all coming together. She would be free from him and his abuse, but she needed to make sure. *Can't allow him to recover.*

Opening the door, she saw the Master Physic shambling through the hall.

"Oh, Master, Master," she said, sounding a little frantic.

He turned and smiled, "Yes, my Queen."

"There is one detail I still require," she said, holding out her hand.

The Master Physic sighed and took the keys from around his neck. "Would you like me to assist?"

"I have seen you do it enough; I think I can manage," Joanne took the keys and went to the kitchen. On her way, she was stopped by Lady Hamlet. *Three visits in one day! Dark Goddess what could it mean?*

Nothing good.

She wasn't wrong.

Lady Hamlet handed her a message. Again, it was her father's wax seal. She expected it to be some sort of signal for victory, but her hands trembled as she read it.

Dearest Daughter,

Thomas is dead. The rebels overwhelmed at Heartwood Pines and the river runs red with blood. Their forces march upon the Keep. Alfred and I will hold them off as long as I am able, but our armies are depleted. Without Seaptum help, the Keep will fall and this will be the last message I write. I had hoped that the marriage would bring Nemus an ally, but I feared we have been betrayed by the Princes. Live well, my daughter. I'm truly sorry to have sold you into falsehood.

Yours in Fatherly Love,
    Desmond

Thomas was dead! Her body went cold, numb fingers released the letter. Like sand sifting through a broken hour glass, she was losing everyone. Thomas may have been a despicable ass to her, despised her and sometimes loathsome. He was still her brother and she had failed. The *Mors Faunis* she had sent weren't enough.

"What is it, my Queen, you appear as though you have seen a ghost," Lady Hamlet said.

"I have to go," Joanne said and rushed through the vestibule. She stepped out into the pleasant sun. Her body trembling over the loss and froze at the sight of a carriage. Lady Beaty stepped out with her four children. *What's she doing here?* The answer had to wait. Lady Beaty raised a hand to beckon her, but Joanne kept moving. Heart aching, and on the verge of melting into a useless puddle of tears and snot, she had to do something. Find a way to preserve what family remained to her. She ran to the barrack, but stopped when she stepped onto the parade ground.

A familiar grin greeted her.

"Hello, my Queen," Prince Gallium said. "I see you have been active since we last met."

"What are you doing here?"

"You don't know. I'm here to collect my crown," he said, "and to see you comfortably situated."

Several large men stepped forward, swords drawn. This wasn't going at all the way Joanne had expected.

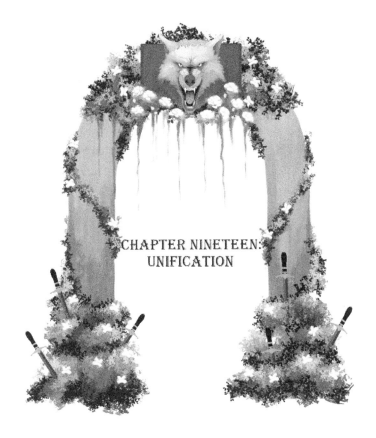

CHAPTER NINETEEN: UNIFICATION

The transfer of power must be peaceful.
One cannot wear the crown eternally
The dead cannot rule the living
And the living cannot rule if all are dead.
 —*King Bounty after the surrender of his brother at the "Battle of Ironwwod."*

"My brother isn't exactly dead, yet," Prince Gallium said. "Though I have seen corpses on the battlefield look better."

They were in her chambers. Prince Gallium was looking over her bookshelf, finger tracing the spines of several old histories. His uniform was a deep purple, the golden suns on his shoulders vibrant, reminding Joanne that every moment of delay would cost her father his life. She watched, without saying a word, and the one within her watched as well. *He thinks he has won.*

"I guess you have that effect on people," Prince Gallium said. "They stay around you long enough and end up dead. Good thing your dear, sweet cousin escaped your radiance of death. I cannot say the same for my brother, but I guess, I have you to thank for making what would have been a messy exchange easier."

"Are you accusing me of regicide?" Joanne asked.

Prince Gallium stopped by the box of tea, opened the lid, and stared inside.

He knows, the Dark Mistress said.

"Gods no!" Prince Gallium let the lid drop in a loud *thomp* and laughed. "Otherwise, you'd be in a different room, naked and bleeding, having your skin stripped until you confessed to killing your own mother, though she yet lives. She lives, still, right? I heard about Thomas's tragic defeat. Seems that he wasn't smart enough to handle a bunch of peasants. Beaty's grandmother and sister got out just in time, too. Last I heard, your father and last remaining brother were in some dire situation with the foxes sniffing around the henhouse."

"Why wouldn't you honor the treaty between my father and King Dryd?" Joanne asked. "You could have sent aide to Nemus, even a tenth of the troops here would have been enough."

"An agreement between dead men—well, one dead and other soon to be—is not something I would rely on to file a grievance with the King, who by the way, will also be dead, soon." Prince Gallium grinned. "We have a few choices on what to do with you, my Queen. I can marry you off to another lord, but none are brave enough to have you. You can be buried alongside your husband. Or, I can send you back to Nemus where the farmers and pig-fuckers will love to have another royal ass to poke."

"Before you decide my fate, can I at least be at the side of my husband while he dies?" Joanne asked.

Prince Gallium gave her a surprised look.

"Seems like the two of you got closer since he tossed your lover off the cliff to the sea wyrm," Prince Gallium said, he found the metal wolf mask and held it up like it was the thing speaking to Joanne. "You really shouldn't have sent her to Lady Freeman to plot against the same husband you profess to love dearly. Nor should you have confided in my wife your plans to move troops without my consent." *Selene! Gallium turned them over to Fraum? Why?* Anger and pain washed through Joanne. She bit back a snarl.

274

Don't let him know he hurt you. "Oh, by the way, where are the missing twenty something soldiers Captain Hollister is concerned over?"

"You'll discover that soon enough," Joanne said.

"Good, because I'm not one who enjoys a mystery." He placed the mask over his head. "This is of good quality. Did you craft this?"

Joanne stood from the chair, only no longer herself. Her pupils darkened and she gave a seductive grin. Joanne felt the power and satisfaction growing within as she surrendered control of her being to the Dark Goddess.

"No, I did," the Mistress of Shadows said.

"What—" Prince Gallium began to ask.

She moved like smoke, grabbing the snout of the metal mask before Gallium could raise his arms to ward her off. A quick yank and his head jerked forward, moving his body so she could kick him in the back of the knees. He dropped with a hollow grunt. The mask came off his head, angry eyes glaring at her. He didn't bother disarming her—a mistake, believing he could defeat her, but he wasn't fighting Joanne, and she laughed inside, knowing how helpless he must feel at her hands driven by the power of a goddess. She pulled the wolf head dagger from its sheath, gripped his jaw, squeezed until the tendons popped, and his mouth fell open. A wail rushed from his lungs and he tried to pry her hands away, but the Dark Mistress was in command and she was stronger than any mortal.

The blade's sharp edge sliced through Gallium's mouth. Blood ran down his broken jaw and pattered on the floor. Crawling, red gushing from his mouth and cut cheek, he reached for the door. The Mistress of Shadows lifted the poker from beside the hearth and smacked him across the head. He dropped face first onto the stone floor, laying in a pool of blood forming around mouth and cheek. A hot glow emitted from her hand and she placed it on the wounds, sealing them. Taking the metal wolf's helm, she placed it over his head, using the same glow to permanently fix it in place.

"Now you know everything," the Mistress of Darkness stroked the cool metal. "My pet."

Prince Gallium stood up, no longer a Prince and no longer Gallium. The permanent metallic snarl replaced his handsome grin. No more dalliances or getting bastards on other ladies, they would cower in fear. Fear of the *Mors Faunis.*

He was hers.

"Where's my husband?" Beaty asked, stopping her in the hallway. "I heard shouting. Is he alright?"

"I am glad you have such concern for me, cousin," Joanne said.

"I do, but I have no say in what happens regarding political matters," Beaty said.

"Political matters." Joanne laughed and shook her head. "All duty this, and duty that. Unless it is betraying Selene and myself."

"You were... are... overstepping your role," Beaty said. "You are the representation of your husband, but your willfulness would have destroyed the country. My husband—"

"Oh stop!" Joanne said. "The only reason you are here and have any sort of position is because I brought you. I brought you because I thought you would be of some use, but it appears the only thing you were good for is betraying me! Your cousin! Your blood and kin, but no more."

"Where is my husband?" Beaty asked again. "He will soon be your King and he will decide what happens, not you."

"Fine, you want to see him." Joanne whistled. "Here he is."

The *Mors Faunis* wearing the Prince's purple uniform stained with blotches of red, the golden sun on his shoulders disheveled and torn, stepped from her room. It wore the metallic snarl beautifully, a transformation beyond her dreams, though exactly like the creatures she had dreamt of in the woods, kneeling and offering themselves to her. The *Mors Faunis* made no sound, though his presence was loud enough, his stance no longer stately, proud, full of hubris and charm. It was a predator awaiting her command.

"Wha.... What is this... abomination?" Beaty's face went white as snow and her hands came together on her belly. "No, it can't be...."

"He is mine, now," Joanne said.

"What did you do?"

"What I was meant to do. What needed to be done for the unification our countries," Joanne said. "You see, cousin, that your husband and mine allowed my brother, Thomas, to die. Will allow Albert and my father to be slaughtered by the very peasants they protected."

"Protected," Beaty said, tears rolling down her cheeks. "The *peasants* aren't attacking anyone. Your father demands higher taxes on resources.

Thomas died because he brought an invading force into Heartwood Pines, to occupy the mines owned by Thramel."

Thramel! Again, that godsdamned name. *It couldn't be the one....*

"You're lying," Joanne said.

"He learned nothing from King Reuban's actions and the Ascension Wars," Beaty's knees weakened and she dropped to the floor. "You're worse. You ruin everything, Joanne. Everyone you touch, dies."

"How do you know this about my father?" She reached down and grabbed Beaty by the shoulders and shook her until her teeth clicked together. "How do you know?"

She stopped shaking Beaty, glaring down into her terrified eyes.

"Everyone knows. The King, my husband, even my sister and grandmother wrote me worrisome letters about the high taxes and the terrible demands Lord Desmond placed on the other lords," Beaty said. "You just didn't want to hear it! Complaining how you sacrificed yourself for your land. Really, your father traded you for more wealth, but the laugh was on him. They saw through his petty squabbles."

Doesn't matter, they still betrayed him. Betrayed me!

Joanne got to her feet and turned away from her cousin. Cousin! No, Beaty was another thorn in her heel. Painful and bloody, there was no more family for her. Joanne was alone, except for the Dark Goddess. Nothing remained for her to truly care about, except for the one promise. To unify both nations.

"What are you going to do to me?" Beaty asked.

"You were right about one thing. Everyone I touch dies," Joanne said. Tapping the *Mors Faunis* lightly on his shoulder, she spoke into the metal ears. "Toss her over the cliff and feed the sea wyrm. Toss her, her mother, her sister, and her children."

The *Mors Faunis* nodded.

"Please don't! I beg of you."

The *Mors Faunis* had no sympathy. It moved as Joanne directed, not caring that this used to be its wife.

"No, no, no, no!" Beaty's screams echoed behind Joanne, but she didn't look back. She had other important matters to attend.

Fraum was weak, lying in his bed, covered up to his chin. He couldn't talk, all his breath went into deep, rattling intake and a heavy squeal that was his exhale. He smelled of rot and decay, like his skin was a fleshy bag holding in rotting meat. Though she imagined his organs were slowly disintegrating from the low dosage of Dragon's Vein. The agony of it all was clear on his squinched face.

"Your brother came for a visit," Joanne said, and patted his hand. Fraum's eyes widened like he had seen a vision of death. "Oh, don't worry, he isn't here to take the throne." *Any more.* "In fact, he has pledged his services to us, or me, at least. When you pass, I'm going to be the first Queen Seaptum has ever had to rule without any male regent or guardian. I will be Queen in perpetuity."

Fraum didn't say anything to this, but she saw the frown on his face. He didn't particularly like the idea, not that he had any say on what happened any longer. He tried to move his hand, had only the strength to waggle one finger. Joanne grabbed it, and bent it back, enough to cause him pain, but not to the breaking point. He whimpered, a pitiful sound of some poor creature who deserved better, not one who had pinched, bruised, and struck her to the soul. No, he didn't deserve pity or any even this pain she gave him.

Let him rot from the inside. She released him.

"Seems his wife, my cousin, and her family had a great tumble off the cliff," Joanne said. "I'm sure the sea wyrm will stick around for more opportunities to feed. I do have some positive news. I did create my private guard. Although, it cost a few of them, trying to help out my brother, Thomas. He died at Heartwood pines, but you knew that, didn't you. You would love Heartwood. After I return there with my army and conquer it, I will name a town after you. Fraum's Farm. It has a nice, quaint sound to it. There the sheep and peasants can rut and remember your name."

His breathing quickened and he turned his head toward her, his eyes nearly crusted over with yellowish-guck. The hatred was clear. If he had any strength remaining in his frail form, she was certain he would use it to kill her.

"I have upset you, dear husband, and so I will leave you," Joanne said, kissing the palm of her hand and pressing it to his forehead. He was warm, nearly hot. "I will be back to visit soon."

She left him, his breathing hadn't settled any. She passed the Master Physic.

"He is in your care until I come back," Joanne said. "Let me know if his condition worsens."

"Aye, my Queen." The Master Physic bowed. "I'm grateful that you reconsidered."

"Make him as comfortable as you can," Joanne said. *I want him to suffer every day until his last breath.*

Joanne would sit with Fraum over the next three nights, watching his body slowly decay. He stank of urine and shit. She was glad she'd changed her mind about accepting the Master Physic's assistance—she was dealing with enough nasty mess without having to clean a grown man's defecations. The Master of Arms, Hollister left Argenti Lapisdom with half the army—possibly out of fear that they would disappear as well. A scout named Snout told her that he went to Lord Silversmith.

"I could smell the fear on his trail, My Queen," Snout said, his droopy eyes on her and he sniffed. "My nose never lies. Something spooked him good, like a horse feared for its life. Though, the rest of the soldiers refuse to abandon their post. Something about wild wolves stalking close."

That would be her remaining *Mors Faunis* returned from Nemus. The insurgents surrounded the tower and they returned rather than be apart of the sacrificial banquet. She required them more than her father and Albert. Especially with Lord Silversmith ready to make his move to put Argenti Lapisdom under siege and force her to surrender.

"Thank you, Snout," Joanne said, sipping from her wine glass.

He sniffed, "Sweet River wine?"

"I believe so," she said.

"I know it to be a very fine grape. It has a delicate bruised colored skin—"

"Yes, that will be all," Joanne said.

"As my Queen commands." Snout bowed and left her alone.

That one will come in handy, the Mistress of Shadows said. *Do not lose him. He will help greatly in bringing back what I need.*

What you need is a shape shifting child?

Yes, but I will continue to inform you of your duty when the time comes. For now, I have rather difficult tasks to attend. I must leave you.

Leave me! The wine slopped out of the goblet.

You will do fine without me. Staying inside you taxes my power. I need it to set events into motion that will shake the heavens! Besides, you are strong and wise enough to carry through on your own. I will keep a watchful eye and intercede should my presence be required.

With that, the shadowy form separated from her, leaving her empty like a piece of her soul parted. The dark goddess looked the same as when Joanne first saw her in the room. The same seductive curves, the dark cloak and trousers. Her smile was beautiful and Joanne wanted to kiss those lips, to be lost in her embrace.

"Serve me well," the Mistress of Shadows said and gave Joanne a soft kiss on the mouth.

Like smoke in a breeze, the goddess was gone.

All the loss gathered around her as she entered Fraum's chambers for the last time. She brought with her a flower in a vase. It had yellow and orange petals, a red streak down the center of each petal. She placed it on the side table beside the bed. Fraum's chest barely rose and fell. There was red spittle running down his chin and pink froth bubbled from his lips.

"Death is ugly," Joanne said. "You will soon be released of your pain."

Fraum's eyes remained closed, but she was certain that he heard her deep in the fugue of his pain. She smiled, no longer daring to touch him. He stank of rot and shit. She could almost feel the heat radiate from him. It was as though someone rang the life out of his body like a used wash rag.

"I brought you the very flower which killed your mother," Joanne said. "That was my fault as well, but not intentionally. It was meant for Lady Foxglow. The snarky bitch didn't drink the tea like she supposed to, instead gave it to your mother. That woman's only sin was birthing you monster princes. Spoiled, selfish bastards that I brought low."

Fraum's breathing quickened and his eyes fluttered, though they didn't open.

"I killed your mother like I killed you," Joanne said, taking a pillow from beside Farum's head and, placing it in her lap, she leaned over him, the stench nearly overwhelming. "Think of it as retribution for killing my brother, my love, and the rest of my family, you selfish son of a bitch. I would do it all again, twice as brutal if I could. For now, this will have to satisfy."

Joanne placed the pillow over his face. Fraum's hand shot up and gripped her right breast. He squeezed until tears came to her eyes and she couldn't pry his fingers off. Instead, she pressed the pillow harder over his face. His grip on her weakened and his hand fell away—a final, parting bruise for remembrance. She counted twenty rushed heartbeats before lifting the pillow. His lips were peeled back from his skull, yellow teeth revealing a death grin. Wide eyes stared at the canopy of his bed, as though he saw some horror in death. His chest no longer moved and his wheezing had ceased. Joanne stepped away.

He's dead?

She waited.

Tears blurred her vision.

I'm free of him?

She left the room and walked swiftly to the Master Physic's room. She knocked on the door. "Master Physic, I think something is wrong with the King."

The door flew open and a wrinkled face and wide brown eye stared at her. He had a bag in his hands. "What is it, my Queen?"

"Come quickly to his chambers."

He followed her to Fraum's room. She half-expected him to be sitting up in bed, the skeletal grin changed into a frown, an accusatory finger pointing at her. *She, that bitch, the one my father forced me to marry, killed me!*

His body was the same as when she had left it.

The Master Physic leaned over Fraum, placed a glass mirror under his nose, opened his mouth and placed an ear close. *How he could stand the smell without gagging?* She could smell him across the room. The Master Physic straightened, back popping, and shook his head. He closed Fraum's eyes.

"I'm sorry, my Queen," he said, patting her arm. "The king is dead."

She nodded, not trusting to speak since it might betray her joy. The Master Physic walked out, leaving her alone in the room with her husband's corpse. She stood at the side of the bed, smiling.

"Donn gag on your bitter heart and cast you into Arula," Joanne said. She smiled and giggled. "I would join you, but I'm going to be a god."

She changed into the outfit that Master Tailor Woolsie designed for her. Black trousers snug around her waist, belted with a pair of wolves-headed daggers—the one Alfred gave her and the other the Mistress of Shadows created and gifted to her—a black shirt with dark gold buttons and the rose wrapped dagger brooch attaching a purple cloak over her right shoulder. On her head she wore the Sun Crown. Two *Mors Faunis* shadowed her and she met the Master Physic on the parade ground A breeze blew and the air was crisp, clear. A new day of change.

Lining the dirt before the platform where Fraum had addressed the lords and ladies for the execution of two of their ilk, there stood three dozen servants, grooms men, cooks, and gardeners. Behind them was the remaining force of shield, pike, calvary, and archers. Armor shimmered in the sun. Joanne observed the concerned faces. How many will abandon her after the announcement? Will she maintain her hold as Queen? She shoved this doubt away.

A herald stepped forward and blew a horn to silence the already quiet crowd. "The Queen," he announced and stepped back.

Her stomach fluttered as she rose and moved to the front of the platform. The weight of expectant eyes was on her.

"As you may have heard, the king is in the arms of Donn," Joanne said, allowing a slight tremble in her voice. Whispers spread through the crowd, but she didn't wait until they quieted before pressing onward. "This leaves us with many questions, I know. Be assured that the King died from a weak heart, which the Master Physic who had attended him since he was a child when the conditions first arose, will attest. This leaves us without a king, especially since Prince Gallium is no longer an option and he has elected to serve a different role. Without a proper heir, another lord may move against us to claim the throne."

Fear flashed in the crowd of soldiers and servants.

"But, you are not without a leader. I remain Queen. I will resist any challenge to the throne. A new day has come to Seaptum, "Joanne said. "Soon, we will be one continent. One empire!" After a moment of silence, a smattering of claps resounded through the crowds. She waited for it to die down before continuing. "We must unify and stand as one!"

The claps grew louder.

Stand with me, or die.

"Let them come and we will take back my army!"

Dower faces full of fear and mistrust brightened. She had them, but not entirely. There was one last card to play. She clapped her hands and twenty *Mors Faunis* emerged at the edges of the crowd.

"Here are our new warriors. Blessed by the gods themselves for ferocity," Joanne said. "Only those who stand against us should fear their tooth and claw. Only those who betray me, will die on their blade. They are worth a hundred men! The gods are on our side!"

Although they moved in away from the *Mors Faunis*, the soldiers didn't try to draw a weapon. They seemed to admire these new warriors in the metal helms and purple cloaks. Some, she guessed, would figure this was the fate of Iphan and the rest who had disappeared. As long as they obeyed her, she didn't care what whispers they made in the dark.

Most important were those who thought they might desert, will think twice about it.

"First, I bury the king tomorrow," Joanne said. "Then we march to reclaim the kingdom!"

Joanne scanned the crowd. Fear, uncertainty, yet hope showed on their faces. They were hers, for now.

I will keep it that way.

After the talk on the parade grounds, Snout approached her.

"They smelled of fear and uncertainty," he said, "but that is normal when what they knew changed. I will keep an ear and nose out for those who might dissent."

"Do so, my loyal hound dog," Joanne said. "Then I may send the wolf after them."

Very few took a chance on defecting. Those who did were hunted down swiftly, left in chains and the stockades on the parade ground as an example of what happens to those who try to run like rabbits. The hound and the wolves would hunt them. A letter arrived from Lord Silversmith on the day of Fraum's funeral. It demanded that she step down and turn the seat of power over to him peacefully, especially since the bulk of the army went to him and his ally, Lord Foxglow. Joanne laughed at it as much as she did the proposals of marriage from lesser lords to sons and cousins with a promise of "protection" against the greedy lords. These all ended in the fire to warm her as she drank sweet wine after interring her husband in the family grave.

Lady Freeman arrived with her child who bore a striking resemblance to the former Prince Gallium. She sat beside Joanne as the priest droned on about Fraum's virtues, few though they may be, yet many when like sticky syrup stretched on a spoon. Lord and Lady Windridge came the next day to declare their support to Joanne. They brought a thousand extra fighters, many untrained, but a welcomed addition. Their eldest son didn't run away and was promoted to the new Master of Arms. Lady Willowcreek soon followed, though her husband desired to remain neutral, she came with a hundred house guard.

"Fool says he is too old to pick sides," Lady Willowcreek said. "I reminded him of who helped us gain our new fortunes and that Lord Silversmith wouldn't be very keen on allowing him to keep his holdings should he become king."

"A wise woman is always needed to guide foolish men," Joanne said.

That would be the end of her support. Joanne had hoped Lord and Lady Hawthorne would join with her, but a report came back that they supported Silversmith due to the sudden disappearance of Prince Gallium. *If they only knew he was always at my side.* Joanne laughed, though no one understood her jest. Not that she would reveal her secret.

They marched out the next morning, leaving the mountain path to strike the first of twenty lordling manors along the way. Minor skirmishes broke out between her army and the minor troops supporting their lord. In the end, the lord abdicated their position, swearing fealty to the Queen Joanne. Word must have spread to the other manors, since Joanne found them empty, all valuables gone and the granaries, barns, and fields, barren. She anticipated this, making certain to bring enough to feed her army for at least a year.

Lord Hawthorne's soldiers put up the greatest resistance. After two days of fighting to a standstill beside a river crossing, Joanne pulled back.

"To minimize our losses and to foster unity, we must not engage forces anymore," she told her Captain of Arms and his captains in the war tent. "Instead, we send in my creatures of the night."

They camped and Joanne unleashed her *Mors Faunis.* They did their duty and returned with the heads of Lord and Lady Freeman, staking their decapitated corpses and children out for the wild beasts to feast. Their remaining force surrendered the next day, nearly doubling Joanne's numbers.

The last place of resistance was Lord Silversmith's manor, which had been transformed into a stone fortification. Small watch towers were constructed where the main gate would be and an iron portcullis with murder holes from which arrows stung Joanne's forces. She had men that could overwhelm these defenses, but at significant costs.

"Seems he's been preparing for a long time," Snout said.

"Probably since my marriage to Fraum," Joanne replied. "We clear the area, damn up any waterways that reach his walls. Send supply wagons back for winter coats and blankets. We will wait him out."

Messages were traded back and forth. Offers of marriage to his eldest son, which Joanne ignored. A promise of complete annihilation, if Joanne didn't turn back. She disregarded these threats as a tantrum from a spoiled man-child. There were attempted raids on supplies and when the winter snows fell, one attempt of a night attack that her *Mors Faunis* thwarted. The winter was rather mild, which didn't favor Lord Silversmith. Joanne persisted out in snow and the cold, sitting at the fires with the men, listening to stories of the soldiers' families. Stories of love. Stories of conquests. Those nights she missed Selene the most. She dreamt of kissing her face and the soft touch tingling her body. If she had to choose again, she would have shoved Fraum over the edge.

May the worms eat his decayed flesh.

The Mistress of Shadows hadn't returned either, which didn't worry Joanne much, though she often wondered if she dreamed the dark goddess, that was until she looked into the shadows and saw the metal wolf heads, snarling as they kept watch.

Snout came to her on the day before her birthday.

"I've spotted a hole in the wall where people have been sneaking out," he said.

"How big is it?"

"Not much more than a wolf's den," Snout said and blinked his blood shot eyes. "Might be a way to send in a few unexpected guests."

"I will go," Joanne said. "It started with me, so it will end."

The captains tried to protest, but she pointed out that she wouldn't be going alone. Four *Mors Faunis* would escort her. It was a cold night, one where the crisp air crackled with every breath. She waited for the clouds to cover the moon. Then they ran to the wall, pressed against it and listened. No shouts came, no warnings. Joanne crouched down at the hole. It was big enough for her to easily fit. She slipped through, both knives drawn. There were two guards posted, but neither had been sharp at watching this hole. Long nights of tedious work dulled the wits. Her blade drew across the first one's throat and he fell without much sound. The second guard spotted her and began to cry out, but it was cut short by a gloved hand over his mouth and a sword in his back.

It pained her greatly to kill them, but some sacrifices had to be made.

Wood smoke rose from several buildings. The smaller ones she assumed were barracks for the soldiers and the larger one was the main manor. Finding Silversmith would be nearly impossible without some sort of map of the manor. She was there for him. Captain Hollister was her target. They moved to the first building and two *Mors Faunis* disarmed and incapacitated the guards out front while the other two took care of sentries around the back. These ones she didn't want killed—again, she would require as many men as she could maintain for her invasion of Nemus. Snout and the rest of the captains agreed that Hollister would be with the men, probably in a shed off set from the main building—he was always one to be prepared. Sure enough, a perimeter search turned up the building, a chimney giving off smoke. A light flickered in the window.

He'll be up checking his supplies and strategizing his attack should it come. Joanne touched the knob. It turned easily. The door opened inward and a rather annoyed face of Captain Hollister looked up from whatever paper he had been scrawling on, a quill in hand and a cup of tea close by, the steam rolling out in the cold.

"What is it—" His voice trailed off as the *Mors Faunis* entered the make-shift office.

"Good evening, Captain," Joanne said, closing the door behind her.

"How? Oh, I told them to close up the blasted hole," he said.

"It was a clever way of getting supplies in," Joanne said. "But, the problem with being clever is sometimes you out smart yourself."

"I suppose you have come to kill me," Captain Hollister said.

"No, I have another proposal instead," Joanne said. "Killing you won't end the siege and would only bolster the moral temporarily out of their need for revenge. More good men would die. For what? Half of Seaptum's lords stand with me outside these walls. Half hide away in here. Now, I know you are a good, loyal man. You didn't think I could hold this much power and control."

"You do so because you are god touched," Captain Hollister said. "That's how you created these creatures to serve your wicked commands. "

"Wicked?"

"Yes, you stole these men's lives."

"I gave them greater power for a greater purpose," Joanne said. "I could slaughter every single man and woman who sleep inside that manor with a single motion of my fingers. I could have all these soldiers put to the sword as well by opening the gates. But I won't."

Captain Hollister raised an eyebrow.

"No one else has to suffer if you perform one deed for me," Joanne said.

"What would that deed be, milady?"

"Surrender your army and join with mine. Then we can unite the continent, tying together three into one."

"If I don't," he said.

"Then you forfeit all these people's lives and I still lead my army into Nemus."

Captain Hollister stared at Joanne, a twitch in his eye. He finally dropped the quill.

"I will consider your offer," he said.

"No, you will choose now."

"So be it," Captain Hollister said. "I will give you back the army. The lords will not like it."

"They don't have to," Joanne said. "As sign of your good faith, I need you to commit to one last request."

Captain Hollister sighed and nodded. When Joanne explained the terms, he frowned. He didn't go back on his word, but scrubbed a hand through his thinning hair. Joanne wrote the terms out on a blank parchment and he signed, knowing she would send the paper to Silversmith if he backed away from his obligations.

"Thank you," she said. "Father bless you and your deeds."

Joanne took the parchment and the left Hollister to contemplate his choices. They moved unseen through the grounds and out of the hole. This was their one shot and she was trusting the lives of thousands to the act of one man. Back at the camp, the Captains and Snout greeted her.

"Do you think he will follow through?"

"We will find out tomorrow."

On the morning of her eighteenth birthday, Joanne was awakened by a messenger saying there was movement and noise from the manor. Joanne dressed, her daggers at her hips, and joined a contingent of soldiers, while surrounded by a dozen *Mors Faunis*. A great rattle of chains and the gate opened. A lone figure walked out. He had a bag in hand and a bloody sword in the other. Captain Hollister walked alone along the muddy path and approached Joanne. He cast the bag on the ground at her feet and stuck the tip of his blade in the ground, then knelt before her.

"The duty is done, my Queen," he said, eyes cast down. "The men are prepared to serve Seaptum and its Queen."

The bag was stained red and Joanne kicked it over to one of the soldiers. "Careful with that, it holds Lord Silversmith's head." The man held it out and carried it off. "I accept your pledge and your promise. You are forgiven, this time, but my forgiveness has limits. Abandon your post again and there will not be a next time."

"Understood, my Queen," Captain Hollister said.

"Go gather the remaining lords, and bring them before me. Those who wish to serve Seaptum will do so and those who do not will join Silversmith," Joanne said. "Gather the soldiers and bring them back into the fold."

"Yes, my Queen."

Joanne smiled.

Soon, Father, I will avenge your death.

CHAPTER TWENTY:
A NEW DAY

Blood purifies all.
— Queen Joanne upon unification
of Seaptum

"The gates are down, my Queen."

Foster's Manor was hers again. Only, it would be renamed to Shadow's Manor, in honor of her patron goddess. When her forces swept through Nemus it was like rolling up a rug. They met with very little resistance. The peasant forces scurried like mice to hide in their dark holes when the cat appeared. Joanne was rather disappointed that these cowards were what brought her father and brothers low. The men and women who defended Foster's Manor fought bravely. Here, Joanne had thought they would have a grand battle. One to warrant sending in her *Mors Faunis* to slaughter the captains, cripple them with a nightmare show of force. In a little over a day of fighting, even these soldiers were overwhelmed. No long siege, no grandiose battle. There were exchanges of arrows. For the most part, her calvary waited while the shield men marched up to the gate and battered it down.

"Where are all the fighters?" Joanne asked.

"These were all we found," Captain Hollister said.

A line of maybe two dozen boys—some not old enough to grow beards—stood shackled, heads down and staring at worn boots, and some bare feet. Joanne walked past them, examining their dirty faces and bloody uniforms. *At least they didn't surrender easily.*

"That one," Joanne said, pointing at a young man with dirty blonde hair.

Captain Hollister nodded and two soldiers lifted the young man to his feet. Joanne stepped close enough to him that she could smell the sweat and the blood on him. He has also urinated his pants. She couldn't blame him.

"Where are the other soldiers who were stationed here?" Joanne asked, keeping her voice calm and sweet. No need to frighten the young man more than he already was, fearing his life was over. Not that he was wrong.

The young man kept his head down. He could have been addle-brained for all she knew, but it wasn't the condition he was in, though the condition she wanted the other captives to contemplate regarding their own lives. Pluck a few feathers and one was about to squawk. She lifted the man's head by the jaw and she saw the far distant gaze. The one where he surrendered to his fate.

"Do you know who I am?" Joanne asked.

Recognition entered the pale blue eyes. A spark of light that quickly receded. *He knows.* Joanne drew her wolf-headed dagger. She slit the young man's throat, watching the blood cascade over his chest and soak his shirt. The soldiers holding him let the body drop. There were a few cries from the captives.

"Silence!" Captain Hollister shouted.

The captives went silent. She could hear a far off cry of a bird. Joanne waited, letting the quiet saturate the captives as they counted out their last heartbeats. Savoring their last breaths. Then she spoke, loud and clear.

"You are all going to die," she said. "All, but one. The individual who tells me the whereabouts of the soldiers who escaped the Manor will live. Not only will this Janus blessed person live, but I will personally see they are given a commissioned officer position here at what will be forever hence be known as Shadow Manor."

Again, silence.

"No one knows a single detail where these traitors who abandoned you to this fate, betrayed you and your family, and preserved their life over your own, may have gone?" Joanne paused, giving them a chance to consider her words. "All it takes is a single point of the finger. A little twitch, or even a singular eye roll in the direction. No one else will know until they are dangling from the tree, crows pecking out their eyes and maggots crawling across their tongues, and you are not there to join in their misery. Then they will realize their mistake and their regret will flavor their hearts a bitter seasoning for Donn."

Again, no one spoke.

Either they are brave or ignorant of where the others went. Either way, they are useless to me.

"Hang them all," she said to Captain Hollister.

Guess I will have to root them out. Right after I take the Keep.

A year had passed since she unified Seaptum under the golden sun and rose dagger. A year of teasing out conspirators and putting them to death. With the presence of her *Mors Faunis,* she was able to keep order with very few deserters. Standing in her childhood home, she knew this was just the start. Shadow Manor was one foothold into Nemus, the Keep would be next, followed by the South and Heartwood Pines. She would savor their destruction the most. As she admired the aftermath of the battle, a soldier approached her.

She was in the office, taking inventory of the supplies when a messenger approached

"My Queen, we have cornered some who tried to escape inside a tavern."

"How is this a concern for me?"

"He has asked for you by name," the messenger said.

"Take me to him."

The tavern was called the Leaky Bucket. A crude sketch of a bucket dripping water was drawn on a sign over the door. The inside smelled of stale ale and straw. In the far corner, sat a figure surrounded by six of her soldiers. He sat in the chair as though they were drinking buddies ready for a night of dirty conversation, ogling the barmaids, and getting piss drunk. She had to admire the boldness of such a man.

"Hello, Thramel," Joanne said.

291

"Hello, my Queen," Thramel said, taking a long pull from his mug. "Care for a game of cards?"

"I have a different game for you," Joanne said, sitting across from him. He had aged little since she last saw him. A few more wrinkles, perhaps a worry line here and there. He was the same calm gambler that she remembered, wobbling in his chair. *Was it all an act?* She was certain now that it was. "Let's call it the *Manus Poena*."

"When do I start?" He asked, like he invited her to a simple game of cards.

"You've already been playing it since the first time we met," Joanne said, and smiled. "Only now, you play for me."

ABOUT THE AUTHOR

Matthew Johnson is a graduate of the MFA Creative Writing program at University of Riverside Palm Desert. He has published short stories in various genres, a fantasy collection, a fantasy novel and a horror novel. Wooing the Dragon is his second play with Lazarus Rising, a zombie play, having completed a second successful run this past fall. He resides in Riverside California with his wife, director and actress Wendi Johnson, and his three lovable puppies. You can find more about his works at www.professorgrimdark.com

Horror

Plays

Fantasy

Gods War Series

Nightingale Saga

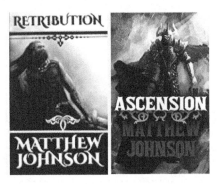

Made in the USA
Monee, IL
17 May 2024

58454581R00167